CROMM

CROMM

BY

KENNETH C. FLINT

A FOUNDATION BOOK

Doubleday

NEW YORK   LONDON   TORONTO   SYDNEY   AUCKLAND

A FOUNDATION BOOK

Published by Doubleday
a division of Bantam Doubleday Dell Publishing Group, Inc.
666 Fifth Avenue, New York, New York 10103

FOUNDATION, DOUBLEDAY, and the portrayal of the letter F
are trademarks of Doubleday, a division of Bantam Doubleday
Dell Publishing Group, Inc.

*All of the characters in this book are fictitious,
and any resemblance to actual persons, living or dead,
is purely coincidental.*

Library of Congress CIP Data applied for

to Nadine and Donald McCormick, my in-laws,
for their support, their interest, their acceptance . . .
oh, yeah, and for their daughter, Judith!

". . . these spirits do not believe in an eternal Hell, and like Blake they describe unhuman races, powers of the elements, and declare that the soul is no creature of the womb, having lived many times upon the earth."

W. B. Yeats, from his notes to
Visions and Beliefs in the West
of Ireland by Lady Gregory (1920)

PART ONE

AMERICA:
FIRST DREAMS

1

At first there was only blackness. And then the music began.

It was very faint—the rhythmic beat of drums entwined with the eerie piping of a wailing tune. He moved toward it, and as he did, its volume grew, drawing him out of the darkness into a red-gold light.

The light revealed him to be a young man, long hair rippling behind him, a heavy cloak about his shoulders. It glinted from the hilt and the silver-banded scabbard of a sword belted about his waist.

Before him towered massive statues of dark stone, spaced evenly to form a ring enclosing a vast space. The statues' forms were vaguely manlike, but also horribly not, each one somehow perverted, made grotesque. Their details were obscured by a thick, billowing fog that hung close above the ground, forming a canopy for the ring.

The swollen underbelly of the cloud was struck to crimson by the flames of bonfires lit within the circle of stones. Around these fires a vast crowd of dancers was milling.

There were hundreds of them, men and women, young and old, all naked in a night so chill that their breath puffed out in plumes of white that rose up to join the billowing cloud overhead. They danced with unrestrained energy—unbound hair flying wildly about them, the smooth, pale flesh of their flailing limbs burnished to a ruddy sheen by the firelight. They trilled out ecstatic cries that twined with the wailing tune.

CROMM

Around them, the circle of motionless statues looked down, titanic and alien beings aloofly watching these pitiful humans in the throes of their debauchery.

Like the statues, the young man also stood unmoving and untouched by the delirium that gripped the dancers. But as he watched the chaotic scene, his look of wonder changed to one of concern, and then of shock.

Within the ring of fires, the fervor was growing swiftly. The drums beat with an ever faster rhythm; the pipes wailed like creatures in some last, exquisite torment. Bodies moved sinuously, erotically together, twining until the crowd seemed one vast, writhing sea of limbs washed by the blood-hued flames. Soon the orgiastic frenzy reached its height.

And then, abruptly, the music stopped.

As the last notes died away, the dancing also ceased. The revelers stood suddenly still, suddenly quiet, turning to look about.

Another figure moved into view, a man clad in a long robe and an elaborate headdress, both made of feathers so brilliantly white that the bonfires created a glowing halo about his outline.

While he waited, the crowd before him parted, creating a wide avenue into their midst. Then he started forward with a slow and haughty stride.

From where the young watcher stood, the center of the area was visible for the first time. Another bonfire burned there, lighting a square, flat stone and another statue that squatted beyond it.

The man in the feather robe moved through the silent, intent crowd to the base of the statue. He stopped before it, lifting his head to look up at it.

The statue, glowing richly with red-gold ornaments, thrust up into the clouds above. Its hunch-shouldered body was a twisted parody of a man's. Its face, though mostly obscured by the shrouding fog, conveyed a sense of leering obscenity astonishing for a semblance crudely hacked from rough stone.

The feathered one lifted a sword before him as if in offering. The polished black metal of the blade took on a red gleam from the flames. Fat drops of a thick, red-black liquid suspended from its edge glinted in the light.

In response to his move, the statue seemed to come alive in the shifting fog and firelight. The distorted body seemed to stir slowly, the lips curling in a lewd and evil grin.

As the young watcher's face filled with revulsion, the crowd looked up to the grotesque being and cried out in jubilation.

The robed man turned, lowering the sword. He gestured sharply.

A group of women moved out into the young man's view, appearing from behind the statues at either side to enter the avenue opened through the crowd. All of them carried something. Before they turned away from him to walk toward the white-robed man, the watcher glimpsed what each one held.

Infants.

The women reached the waiting man, forming a line before him and the flat stone. The infants squirmed with discomfort at the cold. Some cried out. Piercing now in the silence, their wailing sounds lifting in a strident chorus that echoed away forlornly.

The young man stared intently, leaning forward slightly, body tensed.

The robed man gestured again. One woman came toward him. She lay the baby on the flat slab of stone and backed away. The white-robed one turned to stand over it.

The people around cheered in hoarse exhortation. A single drumbeat started—slowly, steadily—and with its rhythm a chant arose from the gathering, a single word shouted again and again, the volume quickly climbing toward a height of intensity as all of them now chanted together with the drum's beat, shooting clenched hands upward in repeated salute to the statue. The sound of the chant grew louder, faster, until each sounding of the word became a reverberating, throbbing thunderstroke:

"CROMM! CROMM! CROMM! CROMM! CROMM!"

The robed one put a hand firmly upon the infant's breast. It struggled feebly and whimpered, alarmed by the strangeness and the noise.

The young watcher's eyes widened in horror as he realized

what was to come. He started to run forward, only to be suddenly brought up short as he came between the stones.

Beyond them, the man in white slowly lifted the sword in his other hand.

The young man pressed forward, straining to move ahead. But it was as if an invisible wall closed the opening, cutting him off from the terrible scene beyond. He pounded desperately, savagely at the unseen barrier with his fists, as the blade rose.

The sword stopped. Light flared from its keen edge.

His struggles ceased as he saw it. Helpless, he stared in anguish.

The feathered one smiled. The sword began to fall.

The young man opened his mouth to cry out . . .

Mouth still open in a soundless cry, he jerked upright. His eyes snapped open to stare ahead. Around him was darkness.

He sat rigidly, gasping for breath, shuddering violently as if from extreme chill. His upper body was bare, his chest and face beaded with sweat.

He seemed to catch himself, his eyes shifting to look about him into the darkness.

He scanned a room that was lit by outside lights shining in through a floor-to-ceiling fan-topped window. It was night, but the lights faintly illuminated the room, revealing shadowy but identifiable features: dresser, chair, a table holding a small TV that stared back at him with its blank glass eye, and the double bed on which he sat so stiffly upright.

His gaze came around to a bedside digital clock. The glowing red numbers, proclaiming the time was 3:10 A.M., ticked off another minute of precious mortal time.

The sight of the clock seemed to reassure him. The tenseness of his body began to fade and his breathing slowed. He lay down again but stayed on his back, still rather stiff, arms at his sides, hands clenched. His face was drawn tight with concentration as if he were trying to will himself to relax. The unblinking eyes stared up at the ceiling with great anxiety.

Beside him, on the nightstand, the clock mechanically flickered away another minute of the night.

2

OCTOBER 28, 8:34 A.M.

The glowing red numbers flashed again: 8:35 A.M.

Rays of morning sunlight slanted down through the fan-topped window, casting a curved pattern of sharp-edged shadow across a bed now empty save for rumpled sheets and discarded pajama bottoms.

In the hard, white daylight, the room around the bed displayed a similarly rumpled and careless look. The few pieces of furniture were mismatched and battered; stray bits of clothing were scattered about and mingled in unsanitary chuminess with cracker boxes, empty glasses, and an open jar of Skippy with a sharp knife upended in it.

Next to the bed, an open door revealed the interior of a small bathroom beyond. There, busily at work on a morning's pre-shave lathering, was the young man.

The towel about his hips, his only garment, revealed a lean and athletically muscled torso beginning to go just the slightest bit soft about the middle. In looks he was pleasant enough, even bordering on the handsome, with wideset blue-grey eyes, a high forehead and strongly chiseled nose and chin, and a head of thickly curling red-brown hair.

As he finished the careful lathering of one cheek, he paused with shaving can in hand to meet his own gaze in the mirror. The view didn't seem to cheer him much.

His eyes did look somewhat the worse for his loss of sleep: bloodshot, lids drooping, a curve of shadows smudging the skin beneath. He closed them, held them closed for a moment, and then opened them abruptly, shaking his head.

Wow! he thought in revulsion. *They look worse from inside! I couldn't even get an organ bank to take 'em today!*

He shrugged resignedly, squirted a billow of foam into his hand, and finished his lathering.

Then, with immense and prudent care, he lifted a razor toward his defenseless chin.

His hand lowered the coffee mug onto the table top, settling it back into one of the countless interlacing rings created by previous cups that had rested there.

He sat at a fifties chrome-legged dinette table before another of the large windows, staring moodily out onto the scene beyond the glass.

The view was a third-floor one, up a street between mostly shorter buildings and a parking lot to a long stretch of green park. On the far side of this man-made scenery rose the taller buildings of the city's downtown.

Behind him was a living room, a loft space clearly converted from some more utilitarian use, with a rough wood floor and an outside wall of sandblasted red brick. A kitchen filled one corner. Some carelessly mismatched pieces of furniture dotted the rest of the expanse, like little islands littered with a washed-in flotsam of clothing, food, bottles, cans, and newspapers.

He sipped again at the steaming coffee, staring out toward the park but not seeing it. Instead his mind was recalling his dream's sights and sounds: the flaring torches, the shouts, the drums, and the sharp glint of that bloody sword.

He shook his head irritably, as if to cast the memory away, and looked around at a digital clock-radio battling for space on his dirty dish-filled counter. 9:05.

"Damn!" he cursed explosively and jumped up. He wore only a baggy turtleneck sweater and faded Levi's. He rummaged frantically through a jumbled heap of clothes on a chair just inside the front door, finally dragging out a very rumpled corduroy sport coat. Then he was out of the apartment, along a hallway, down three flights of stairs, and through a door into the outside world.

The ground floor of his street-corner building was occupied by the Casa Maitas Mexican Restaurant. He trotted past its large windows to the corner, braving the brisk morning traffic to sprint diagonally across the road.

He jogged on through a neighborhood clearly in transition, the old working places of the Victorian blue-collar classes giving way to the hunting and feeding grounds of the New Elites. Renovated warehouses had become apartments, offices, boutiques, art galleries, and restaurants.

Trees growing from brick planters set along the wide sidewalk were turning their autumn hues; leaves rustled in the chill gusts of a brisk fall wind, some shaking loose to skitter along the pavement.

The young man shivered in the gusts as he trotted along, pulling the jacket onto one arm as he crossed another street.

On its opposite corner sat a building of an era later than its Victorian neighbors, but into its own time of chic revival—a gleaming diner in the sensual chrome and neon curves of Art Deco.

Now in the process of shoving his other arm into the coat sleeve, he used his free hand to open the diner's door and enter its savory warmth.

It was a simple, clean-edged, bright and pleasant place, like something from a thirties movie, and the waitress behind the counter fit the setting—a large, handsome, busty woman with a go-to-hell manner and a big smile.

He moved past customers at the counter to the register, and she, setting down several plates heaped with eggs and hashbrowns, turned toward him.

"Colin!" she greeted him heartily. "Boy, you sure look like hell!"

He was still struggling with his sleeve. It seemed to be caught somehow, and he couldn't quite thrust his arm through. He paused to cast a rueful smile at her.

"Well hey, thanks, Thelma!" he said in mock gratitude. "You don't know how it just sets up my whole day to hear a compliment like that first thing. How about a quick Danish, huh? Apple?"

"Sure thing, lover," she said with a grin.

As he took up the struggle with his coat again, she turned around to the glass shelves lined with pastries, throwing back over her shoulder:

"Aren'tcha gonna sit down?"

"Nope. No time, Thelma. I'm late. Just toss it in a bag."

She picked a Danish from a shelf and turned back to him, clucking pityingly. "Late again." She shook her head. "Colin, you're not getting enough sleep. Up to no good?" She grinned leeringly and winked.

"No such luck, Thelma. Just bad dreams," he told her, ramming his fist into the sleeve with increasing violence in a vain attempt to force it through. There was a tearing sound.

"Oh yeah?" She pulled out a bag and dropped the Danish in. She held it out to him. "Eighty-five cents."

By this time, he was hopelessly tangled with both hands in the coat. He stopped, frustrated, looking imploringly to her.

She nodded in understanding.

"Just lean forward," she said.

He did.

"Here, take it."

She held out the bag, and he gripped it in his teeth.

"Pay me later," she told him. "And if you want *good* dreams next time, why don'tya give me a call." She winked again.

He smiled as best he could around the bag and was off, ducking out through the door past a man entering, and rushed on up the street still locked in fierce battle with the coat.

He jogged past the entrance to an alleyway beside the diner, barely glancing into it.

It was a narrow and smoke-blackened canyon dwindling away into a forlorn distance. A long passageway into a grey netherworld of litter and refuse, separate from the living outer world. Colin took little note of it, and no note at all of the other bit of life's discard—human this time—huddled just within the alley's mouth.

He was a haggard-faced man of straggling hair and beard, marked by a distinctive puffy scar of horseshoe shape that curved from his right temple around his eye and ended against his nose. A ragged green army overcoat was wrapped about him against the cold, and a bottle of cheap vodka lay empty at his side.

He stared blearily across the alleyway at a graffiti-covered wall, not noting Colin or the others of that world who passed by.

But then there was a sound as of rattling cans farther up the alley. It penetrated his booze-befogged brain, and the head on the scrawny neck turned toward it. Perhaps thinking of an early-morning trash dumping he might root through, the man levered himself up.

He stumbled along the alley, seeking the noise's source. An opening in the solid walls of the alley could be seen ahead. But as he approached, a grey-white cloud like heavy fog or steam began spilling out from it.

He paused, blurrily examining it, his expression puzzled. Then curiosity or need seemed to draw him on. He shuffled forward to the opening. He peered around its corner into a loading-dock area.

It was large enough to accommodate a good-sized truck, but its full dimensions were now obscured by a thick screen of billowing clouds. And as he stood staring in at this odd phenomenon, streamers of the grey-white clouds, like creeping vines, stole out to curl around him, envelop him, finally hide him from outside view.

Then, within the void the strange fog had created, other shapes became visible, drifting into view as if created by the sudden congealing of the swirling clouds. There were four of them. They moved at once toward the derelict, seeming to float forward over the invisible ground.

Their vague outlines at first seemed human; but they grew clearer to the man as they drew near to him, and then there was something about them not so human. Something unnatural. Something terrible.

Eyes opening wide in shock, the derelict started back, lifting his hands defensively.

A sleek blade of glinting metal shot forward, striking his chest, piercing through him like a knife rammed through a rotting fruit, slamming him back and pinning him to the black wall of the alleyway. He arched back stiffly against the brick for a quivering instant, then sagged forward, bright red drops of blood welling from his mouth and splashing to the filthy paving stones.

The four figures glided forward to close in about him. One of them knelt down, putting out a long and sinewy arm to lay a bony hand upon the body. A glowing light appeared from it, like a bright liquid flowing from its fingertips, like emerald-colored blood oozing out onto the old green coat. It spread quickly outward, trickling over the dead form, running down its sides, pooling beneath it, the glow slowly enveloping the man, swallowing him, creeping down at last over his face and hiding his curious scar and staring eyes.

Finally he was covered completely, his body only a dim shadow encased in the cocoon of the green glow. The light flared brighter then, running back up the arm of the one who knelt beside him. In moments that creature was encompassed as well, the two forms melting into a single ball of light.

Colin rounded a street corner into a pedestrian mall. Brick-surfaced, its central square was decorated with planters filled with once-bright flowers turned brown and sagging by the first autumn frosts.

It was busy here, with workers bustling to the storefront shops and to the offices of lawyers, architects, decorators, brokers, and the like that occupied the buildings' upper floors. On one corner a vendor was setting up a stall outside a lone produce warehouse that had survived from older days. Atop a pushcart, plump orange pumpkins were stacked in a pyramid, the top one carved into an evilly grinning jack-o'-lantern.

Colin made a last, desperate jab into his coat sleeve as he crossed the square, finally managing—with another, louder ripping sound—to thrust his arm through the sleeve. Taking the Danish in one hand, he opened one of a pair of tall glass doors and passed through.

What he entered was a combination of inside and outside: a passageway between two buildings that had been roofed over with glass, its walls opened up to create a three-level mall for shops and offices.

He went up two levels of stairs to where the shops gave way

completely to offices. He paused at one, peering warily through its front window.

Beyond was a large, open, high-ceilinged space, its white-washed old brick walls plain but for a few clean-lined, splashy posters, a wall clock, and a large sign in curving blue neon lights that read: *RIVER CITY GRAPHICS*.

A desk, easel, some small work tables, and some chairs in a simple high-tech style were the complete furnishings. A man sat at the desk, bent forward, apparently engrossed in work.

Colin sighed resignedly and went in.

The man at the desk lifted his head at once to glare across at Colin.

"Well, you look like hell today," he said bluntly.

"Gosh, that's really a great one, Harry," Colin tossed back sarcastically. "Do you and Thelma call each other in the morning to coordinate your dialogue?"

"Who's Thelma?"

"Never mind," he said, taking off the coat and tossing it and the bag down on the table by the easel, amidst a jumble of pencils, paints, pastels, rulers, and other artists' paraphernalia.

He filled a chipped and brown-stained cup from a sleek Braun coffeemaker on a nearby table, then plumped himself down on the stool before the empty easel. He pulled the Danish from the sack and contemplated it moodily.

Through all this, Harry stared at him with a look of growing irritation. He was close to Colin in age, but his dress-for-success attire, neatly cut hair, and dark-rimmed glasses made him appear older. He was more slender than Colin, though the swell of a developing paunch peeped out from behind the desk. His features were smaller, sharper, with a prim mouth just made to purse in disapproval, as it was doing.

"You know you have to have the drawing for the Olaffsen account ready today," he said at last.

Colin took a bite of the Danish, chewing it, speaking thoughtfully through it.

"Did you ever wonder just how good a pizza you'd expect to get from a guy named Olaffsen?"

"His pizza chain is becoming the hottest thing in the Middle

West, McMahon," the other shot back, "and he is coming in at three o'clock today!"

"Yeah, yeah," Colin said carelessly, taking another bite. "I know."

Harry waited another moment, glaring with increasing impatience as the apparently still indifferent Colin continued to eat his Danish and sip his coffee. Then Harry said in a slow, meaningful voice:

"Well? Don't you think you should get on it?"

Colin turned to look at him.

"Christ, Harry, if I'd wanted nagging, I would have stayed living with my mom and dad."

Harry leaned forward, face going tight, temper flaring in his words:

"Look, I'm not your parents. I'm your partner, and I stand to lose very big if we screw up this account! Three days and you haven't done one goddamn thing!"

Colin nodded, speaking now with a certain contriteness at the justice in this rebuke.

"Okay. Okay. I'll get on it." He drew an X on his chest. "Cross my heart!"

Holding the Danish in his teeth, he pulled a sheet of drawing paper from beneath the table and taped it onto the easel. He plucked a pencil from the jumble on the tabletop and proceeded to chew the Danish ruminatively as he stared into the vast emptiness before him.

Across the room, Harry watched him suspiciously for a while. Finally satisfied, he nodded and went back to his own work.

Colin stared at the paper, his brow furrowing. Then suddenly something seemed to come to him. He lifted the pencil and began sketching.

After a few minutes had passed, Harry glanced up to see Colin working busily and with apparent fervor. Harry watched for a moment, clearly surprised by the unusual activity. Then, surprise giving way to curiosity, he rose and crossed the room to his partner.

He came up behind Colin, stopped, and looked down over his shoulder.

Beneath the tip of the moving pencil, a shape had formed in the center of the sheet. But it was no logo for a pizza czar. Instead a small, humped shape had appeared, shaded quite realistically to represent the texture of stone, its surface decorated with deeply incised lines forming a curling, interweaving design.

Harry stared in shock for a moment, then exploded.

"What in the hell is that?"

Colin, who in his concentration had been oblivious to Harry's approach, now jumped like a schoolboy caught doodling obscenities in his textbook.

He looked around guiltily, speaking in confusion.

"Oh! This! Sorry. It . . . it's just . . . something. Something I . . ." his voice dropped to an all but unintelligible mumble, ". . . I dreamed about."

"You what?" Harry demanded sharply, leaning down closer.

"I dreamed about!" Colin blurted out this time.

Harry rolled his eyes in a "God-help-me" expression and sighed. Then he pulled a chair closer to the easel and sat down, leaning toward Colin.

Colin looked away, his shoulders hunching defensively. He stared sullenly at the paper.

"Colin," Harry began with firmness, "what is wrong with you?"

"I don't know," Colin said, shrugging. "Maybe I'm just tired. I haven't been sleeping too well lately."

"You haven't been doing too much of anything, lately! I've never seen you so distracted. And, boy, for you, that's saying a lot!"

"Gee, thanks."

Harry put a hand to Colin's shoulder in a fatherly gesture as he went on.

"I'm not kidding, Colin. I think it's this sublimely indifferent attitude you have toward life. I've warned you that it'd get to you sooner or later."

"You sure have," said Colin wearily. "And now you're going

to tell me I *need* something in my life. Just let me take a wild shot at this. A puppy? A turtle? A bed with a vibrator? Or, say, how about a nice wife and family like *you* have?"

Harry dropped his hand away.

"You don't have to get nasty about it," he said in irritation. "I mean it. Just take a look at yourself, Colin! You've got nothing. Your home is rented, your clothes are K-Mart, your furniture's Salvation Army. You don't own a car, you don't even have a faintly serious relationship with a woman."

Colin smiled at this, spreading his hands and answering in a carefree tone:

"I never do anything serious, Harry. That's my nature. It's my charm!"

"See what I mean?" the other said in exasperation. "You're the same way about everything. Never serious. No ambitions. No friends . . ."

"Hey, I do have friends," Colin said defensively.

"Those people you go out to party and get wasted with?" Harry said scornfully. "They're not close."

"Aw, Harry, I've got you," Colin replied, playfully mussing the other's neatly combed hair.

His friend jerked away angrily.

"Only because I've known you since college," he shot back. "Playing it all for laughs was okay then, but you can't keep it up forever. You're getting older . . ."

"For crissake, Harry, I'm only twenty-nine."

"Tick, tick, tick," Harry said ominously.

Colin lifted his hand in a gesture of defeat, speaking emphatically:

"Okay! Okay! I'm sorry I screwed up! I vow not to daydream anymore. I'll concentrate. You'll have your Swedish chef's pizza artwork by three!"

Harry seemed to accept this, but with misgivings. He gave his partner a long, hard stare, then nodded and rose.

"All right." He moved back toward his desk. "Now I've got to get going. I've got two clients and the printer to see before I pick up Olaffsen and bring him back here."

He took a suit jacket from a hanger on a clothes tree beside his desk and slipped it on. Colin nodded in obedient understanding.

"Yes, Dad!" he said in a dutiful-son voice. "I'll do all the chores while you're gone. Rake the leaves, wash the car, spay the goldfish and everything."

Tugging the jacket into neat lines, Harry shot Colin a sharp look. Then he picked up a portfolio from the desk and started for the door. But as he grasped the knob, he paused to fire back scathingly:

"It's *our* drawings, not just mine. And it's *our* money too! Just try to remember that!"

He yanked open the door and stormed out, letting it slam after him.

Colin watched him pass the windows as he stalked out of sight. Then the young artist's gaze dropped back to the odd drawing on the sheet in front of him. He sighed and shook his head in a weary way. His shoulders slumped as if from great fatigue and he leaned forward, putting elbows to easel, fingers massaging his temples hard, almost angrily, as if there were an immense headache raging inside.

He closed his eyes and sat motionless, staring into the darkness. The only sound was the soft, steady tock, tock, tock from the second hand of the wall clock.

But suddenly the sound began to change, swiftly growing and altering to something very odd: a rhythmic creaking and clopping. His body began to sway gently from side to side, as if the chair had been transferred to a boat riding the swells of a sea.

His eyes opened with surprise. The easel was before him. He stood up, his gaze rising over its edge to take in the scene beyond.

3

Beyond, the rounded hind ends and flouncing tails of two plodding horses were now visible. And beyond them lay an open countryside. It was over the curving rim of a wickerwork wall that he now peered.

He stood in a moving chariot.

It was a good-sized vehicle, with immense iron-rimmed wheels turning at either hand and basketweave bulwarks of wicker enclosing the front and sides of the cart in which he rode. At the open rear, where he stood, two brass handholds shaped like swans' heads curved outward from the wood rail that held the wickerwork in place. One of these he lightly gripped to hold his balance, swaying easily with the jolting of the cart.

The two horses—small but broad-chested and stocky animals with glowing chestnut coats—were harnessed at either side of a long pole and moved powerfully along, drawing the chariot. Their guiding reins rested in the hands of a short, dark, wiry-bodied man who stood just in front of Colin. He was simply clad in a baggy wool tunic and loose trousers, his long wiry hair knotted in a swinging braid at his back.

Colin was himself clad in a tunic, but trouserless, the gold-embroidered hem of the white linen garment hanging to just above his bare knees. It was fastened at his waist with a heavy belt, from which hung an ivory-hilted sword in a leather scabbard bound with silver bands.

About his shoulders the young man wore a long wool cloak of a bright green and blue check, fringed along the bottom edge. It was fastened at his throat with a large pin of silver, cunningly ornamented with an intricate curlicue design. A band of silver with a similar design caught back his long, wavy hair at the nape of his neck.

The iron-rimmed wheels rolled along a spongy, rutted lane, and the horses were splashed chest-high with the mud they were kicking up. On either side of the road, the vast, rolling countryside was soft and intensely green. Though mostly open, the land was dotted with groves of trees whose branches showed the thick furring of new spring growth, making bright patches of lighter green against the darker shirred garment of the fields. The air was sweet with the spring scent of renewed life; and the sun, shining through a scattered armada of sailing clouds, sent down broad shafts of light to make the land glow with that unique spring clarity.

He looked about with appreciation at the spectacular view of the bright countryside as they topped a rise.

"It surely is a fine place, this Connacht," he commented.

"And a large one too," the other said in a complaining tone. "We've been driving through it half the spring, it seems."

"Ah, it can't be much farther, Ailbe, since we've crossed the Sionnon. Dun Mauran can't be more than half a day now."

"Not soon enough for me," the other said, frowning. He was an older man, greying at the temples. His long, mobile, big-featured face—seeming too large for his small body—was leathery-skinned from years of weathering. "It's happy I'll be to have some good hot food and a dry place to lay myself again."

The younger man laughed, clapping a hand to his driver's shoulder.

"Ha! It's too soft you've become, Ailbe, lying about my father's dun and dreaming away your life."

"And who are you to talk, Colin MacMathghamhain? When it's the first time you've been out of your father's tuath yourself in your whole life?"

"But at least I'm looking forward to it!" Colin argued. "I've waited for it long enough! A chance to see something! A chance for some adventure!"

"A chance to ride nearly the entire length of Ireland," added the other grumpily. "My life was exciting enough at home, thank you."

The chariot rolled on, across another rise, high enough that it gave a good view down a long slope to the land ahead.

Colin stiffened suddenly, gripping Ailbe's shoulder.

"Pull up. Quickly!"

Surprised, Ailbe reined the team in hard, and the chariot slid to a stop.

"Look there!" Colin said excitedly, pointing down the slope.

Below, not far along the road and near the border of a fair-sized grove, a four-wheeled cart was pulled up, while a number of figures moved around it, apparently engaged in a wild melée.

The two could make out perhaps a dozen rather raggedly dressed men battling around the cart. One group of them moved about a warrior on the ground, whose skillful work with sword and shield was keeping them off. The others were trying to climb onto the cart where another figure stood, swinging about with a long staff to drive them back.

This figure was clad in a long, clinging gown that revealed the body's lithe curves as it moved so vigorously. Long, unbound hair of gold was flashing about the shoulders.

"That's a woman!" said Colin.

He turned and jumped from the cart, pulling out a large round shield of stiff leather stretched across a thick iron rim.

"What are you doing?" his driver asked in astonishment.

"Going to help," Colin answered briskly, slipping the shield on one arm. "Those two haven't a chance."

The driver leaned down and put a restraining hand to the young man's shoulder.

"Your father sent you here to buy him a bull, not to get into trouble," Ailbe said emphatically. "That there is nothing to do with you!"

"I'm a fighting man," Colin said with determination. "I'll surely not pass by! You stay here!"

He started off at a run.

"All right!" Ailbe called after him. "But I'll not go back to answer to your father if you get yourself killed!"

Below, the fight was continuing, but going badly for the beleaguered pair. The woman was still just managing to keep her assailants back. Below her, the warrior knocked one man away with his shield and sent another staggering off with a sword thrust through the shoulder. But a third came in and swept up a long lance, its point striking under the warrior's raised sword arm, sinking into his side.

He groaned and staggered back, pulling himself from the weapon, collapsing against the cart.

Up on the cart, the woman paused in her own battle as she saw him fall, casting a look of despair toward him. That momentary hesitation was enough.

A hand shot up from below her, grasping the end of her pole. It yanked forward. The sudden jerk pulled her off balance. She dropped to her knees before her adversary.

Close before her was his filthy, twisted face, a gap-toothed mouth smiling at her evilly. A sword was lifted in his other hand.

Then there was a shout behind him, and startled, he began to turn.

A sword swung across his forearm, taking it off. It fell, the hand still clasping its weapon. The man screamed and dropped back from the cart.

It was the blade of Colin that had saved the woman. Having just reached the group, he had fallen upon them and was now winnowing into them with both skill and power.

They turned, surprised, off guard and ducking away from his furious blows. The savageness and suddenness of his attack had thrown them into confusion. The ragged band of ruffians seemed to quickly lose courage, and he swept around the cart, driving them away.

Some of them, stunned, simply abandoned the attack and ran. A few tried to defend themselves, but he ripped through their defense and soon they too were abandoning the fight, rushing into the shelter of the grove, dragging along those too wounded to walk.

Colin moved on around the cart, and those remaining now scattered before his advance. But as he came around to the cart's far side, he saw that one attacker still persevered. A broad figure in ragged cloak and hood was still trying to clamber up the cart behind the woman, reaching out to grasp at her gown.

Colin moved up behind the hooded figure, swung out with his shield, and slammed the man around to face him.

It wasn't a human face that swung into view. Its features

were slothlike—chinless, browless, with a tapering muzzle—
and its enormous eyes were golden and slitted like a cat's.

He stared at the face in shock, but then reacted with a warrior's instinct as the creature dove at him. He thrust out with his
sword, driving the blade deep into the being's wide chest.

It gave a shrill, bestial cry of rage and pain, but to Colin's
astonishment it continued to come on.

A hand that was more like an animal's long-taloned paw
came swinging up toward him.

Before he could throw up his shield, the hand swept across
his throat. He jerked back, almost saving himself completely.
But not quite. The talons raked his throat and chest, barely
grazing him, but still knocking him backward as if the blow
had landed with tremendous power.

Colin staggered away, pulling his sword free, and then
crashed to the earth. Rather than follow up its advantage, however, the wounded being wheeled around and made off after its
fellows, loping on short, stiff, bandy legs.

Colin lay on his back in the muddy road, stunned, fighting
for consciousness, breathing heavily. His tunic was ripped open
at the throat, and across the flesh of his collarbone and neck
were the oozing red lines of four deep tears.

A shadow fell over him.

He shook his head, opening his eyes to peer up in a dazed
way.

A face came into view, at first dark against the light, then
coming clear as the person knelt beside him.

It was the face of a young woman, peering anxiously down
at him.

4

OCTOBER 28, 3:08 P.M.

The woman's face looked out from the white background of
the sheet on Colin's easel. Large, glowing eyes were fixed on his
with an intensity nearly matching that of a living person.

"Say, that's really quite good!" a voice said.

Colin started as if awakened from a trance, looking around from the easel.

A man now stood at his shoulder, bent forward to peer down at the drawing.

His long, big-featured face was that of a man perhaps fifty years of age, grooved deeply about the mouth and eyes in amiable wrinkles now drawn upward by a broad smile. A long jaw and emphatically hooked nose gave power to his looks, further enhanced by bright grey eyes that matched a striking, prematurely silver wealth of hair.

He was dressed in an oddly formal, somewhat dated manner, with a dark suit and vest of almost Victorian styling and a long grey overcoat. In one hand he gripped a walking stick of polished dark wood whose curved, silver handle was the sleekly stylized head of a crane-like bird.

Colin looked him over in a rather confounded way, clearly nonplussed by the man's apparently instant appearance from nowhere.

"I . . . I'm sorry," he said blankly. "What's good?"

"Why, the drawing, young man," the other answered, pointing down to it. "It's very good. Quite lifelike."

Colin looked back to the easel, to the image of the girl, staring as if he were seeing it for the first time. He looked down at the pencil in his hand and then up again, his expression still extremely puzzled.

The drawing was incredibly detailed for a pencil sketch: a young woman with light hair that washed about her shoulders in thick, curling waves, a pleasant but strongly featured face that might be called handsome rather than beautiful, and those large and luminous eyes that gazed out so boldly at him.

He shook his head as if to clear it; then his gaze scanned the room in a reorienting way, stopping short at the wall clock.

It read 3:10.

"Ohmygod!" exclaimed Colin. He looked back to the man, his face drawn in consternation. "I'm sorry. I . . . I didn't know what time it was. It . . ." He shook his head again sharply, still bewildered. "It just got away from me . . . somehow."

He looked again at the easel. Still so accusingly blank save for the two sketches, so empty of logos for impatient pizza magnates. In desperation he gazed again around the room. It was empty. No Harry. Where was Harry?

He looked back to the man again and spoke in an anguished voice.

"Look, I am really sorry! I know the sketches were supposed to be done. But . . ." He hesitated, excuseless, at a loss how to proceed.

Throughout this the man had remained quite at ease, watching Colin in a calm, bemused, but amiable way. He was very tall and broad of shoulder, and—with the formal clothes, rugged looks, and silver hair—a most imposing figure. However, he still managed to convey an air of affability and good humor rather than one of intimidation.

Now he responded in a voice that was firm, well modulated, and sophisticated, but with the softest hint of a lilting cadence that made it most agreeable.

"Think nothing of it, young man. It's quite all right." He moved around the easel to the chair beside it. "And you needn't be worrying about those sketches," he added with a casual, elegant little wave of dismissal as he sat down. "They're not crucial to me at the moment."

"Oh?" Colin said in puzzlement, turning to follow him around with his eyes.

"No," the man said, leaning forward to fix Colin with his own piercing grey eyes, speaking slowly and with great sincerity. "Actually, I'm more concerned with you."

Colin's look grew surprised.

"Me?"

"Yes. You seemed somewhat distracted as I came in." He gestured toward the girl's face. "Some kind of woman trouble, is it?"

Colin stared back, held by the gaze.

"No," he replied.

"I see." The man sat back in a more relaxed pose, laying the stick across his lap. "Then something in the past, perhaps."

Colin's stare grew curious. Clearly there should have been something disturbing in this—in being psychoanalyzed by this stranger. But though his reaction might ordinarily have been to balk at the personal question, that bright gaze still held him, and he seemed unable to refuse.

"No," he answered openly. "Not the past. A dream. Something in a dream."

"A dream. Ah!" the man said as if this was most significant. He nodded sagely. Then he sat forward again, speaking bluntly:

"You're Colin McMahon, aren't you?"

"Yeah," Colin replied, but with a trace of apprehension, clearly wondering why it was important.

The man only smiled again.

"It's a good Irish name."

"Yeah, well, I suppose," Colin said, relaxing. "My dad's parents came from Ireland."

"And what part?" the man inquired.

Colin shrugged.

"I don't know. I never got into that ancestor stuff."

The man shook his head.

"Too bad," he said regretfully. "I'm from there myself, you see, and I can feel the roots of it are strong in you."

"Ireland?" said Colin, examining the man more closely. "But I thought . . ." He stopped and shrugged again. "Never mind. Look, no offense, but I don't think of myself as anything but an American. I've never had any interest in roots. Sorry, it just doesn't mean anything to me."

The man raised a hand to point a long slender finger at him. His voice took on an admonishing tone:

"The blood has a stronger hold upon what you are than you may think. You know, it wouldn't do you any harm to consider the old land more. Visit her, even. Why," he added more emphatically, "it might be the very thing you need!"

"Visit?" Colin said, nonplussed by the sudden turn in conversation. "But . . ."

The other lifted a hand in a staying gesture.

CROMM

"Now, you needn't say anything about it yet. Just think about it." He rose, pulling something from an inside pocket. "Here. You might look through this while you do. It could give you some ideas."

The man tossed a small booklet down upon the work table beside Colin. With that, his manner turned abruptly brisk.

"Well, I have to be going. Nice to have met you."

He turned and moved toward the door, leaving Colin, caught by surprise, staring after him. He opened the door and paused, glancing back.

"Oh, and I would look out for myself, if I were you, Mr. McMahon," he said gravely. "It is that time of year, you know."

He smiled, but there was an odd, ominous tone to the words. Then he was out the door and moving away.

Colin watched him sweep past the window, out of sight. And it was barely a moment after his vanishing that Harry hove into view from the same spot, sailing smartly back past the window to the office door.

"Harry!" Colin said as his partner came through the door. "Where the hell were you? That guy, Ollafsen . . ."

"Yeah, yeah!" said Harry in a disgusted tone as he dropped a load of packages onto a table and began to take off his coat. "You can stop sweating it now, McMahon. You don't need anything today. When I got to his office I found out he'd been delayed somewhere. His secretary had to reschedule for Thursday!"

"Delayed?" Colin said in surprise. "But, that man . . ."

Harry turned to look at him oddly.

"What's wrong with you? What man?"

Colin pointed out the window.

"The guy in black. You must have gone by him on the gallery just now!"

"There wasn't anybody on the gallery," Harry said impatiently. "What in the world are you jabbering about?"

At a loss, Colin looked from Harry to the window, then back. He shrugged and shook his head.

"Never mind. It wasn't important."

Harry shook his own head in lack of comprehension for his partner's continued strangeness and stepped to his desk, removing his coat and hanging it neatly back upon its hanger. He shot the now brooding Colin a last, wondering glance before settling down in his chair.

Colin sat hunched in his own chair for a long moment, staring out the window to where the man had disappeared; then he turned to look at the empty seat in which the man had sat, as if wondering whether he had even existed.

Then his gaze dropped to the brochure.

He picked it up. It was labeled simply *TRAVEL IRELAND* and had a cover photo of a cliff overlooking the ocean, with a beaming tourist couple standing by a car.

Idly he leafed through the pages. Then his expression froze, his body stiffening, his eyes widening as their gaze fixed upon a photograph.

There, in the simple black-and-white picture, was an ancient stone, its rounded surface covered with a curious interlacing design. And as he lowered the pamphlet and lifted his eyes from the photo to the easel before him, his gaze centered on the object in his sketch.

They were all but identical.

Colin came out through the big doors of the mall passageway and onto the street.

The late afternoon sun slanted in sharply to cast a bright glow against the brick and windows on one side of the street, leaving the opposite buildings in deep shadow.

The many shops and offices were quickly emptying out. There were few cars parked along the street in that dead time between the ebbing away of daytime's retail trade and the new flood of the supper crowds and night people. The vendor on the corner was in the process of closing up his stand, carrying the pumpkins into the warehouse for the night.

Colin paused a moment to look down at the papers in his hand. Then he started away, expression thoughtful.

Inside the office, Harry still sat at his desk, working diligently over accounts, muttering to himself as he tussled with the numbers. So involved was he that he didn't even look up as the door opened.

"Forget something?" he asked.

"Colin McMahon," said a harsh rasping voice, like a stiff wire brush across a slate chalkboard.

"You just missed him," Harry said, finishing a last addition and lifting his head.

He looked at a squat, bow-legged figure in a much-worn quilted jacket, faded jeans, and battered cowboy boots. The broad, sallow face was shadowed with many days' growth, the long, greasy hair curled out over the upturned coat collar. Tiny eyes glinted from beneath shaggy brows.

"Where is Colin McMahon?" said the rasping voice. The mouth—wide, slack, and lipless—barely moved.

"Why do you want to know?" Harry demanded. "Who are you?"

The man took a step forward.

"I want Colin McMahon," he said, the voice becoming more insistent.

Harry glanced at the wall clock. It read 5:13.

"We close at five," he said, nodding pointedly toward the clock while still maintaining a polite tone. "Colin's gone. Why don't you come back tomorrow. Okay?"

The man moved forward again, stepping up close to the desk.

"Where is McMahon?" came the terse, grating question.

Harry rose.

"Look, would you just please leave?" he said with more force. "I'm going to close up now. I want to go home."

"Where is he?" the man demanded.

"I'm not going to tell you," Harry said, becoming angry now. "So, leave. Or . . ." His hand moved toward the phone on his desk.

A hand shot out, its thick fingers curling around Harry's tie below the knot, jerking him forward across the table. Thin lips pulled back to reveal ragged brown teeth. A foul breath puffed into Harry's face as the man spoke slowly, shooting out each word.

"Where . . . is . . . Colin . . . McMahon?"

"None of your damn business!" Harry fired back defiantly.

He tried to struggle, to jerk his tie from the man's grip. Suddenly the man shoved him back, letting go. Harry staggered backward, slamming up hard against the rear brick wall.

His breath exploded from him at the impact. He hung there, unable to move, panting, staring in astonishment as the man shoved the heavy desk out of the way with a single move of one arm and stalked toward him.

Before Harry could recover, the man had reached him and shoved a hand, palm open, against his chest, an easy pressure pinning the younger man helpless against the wall.

The intruder's other hand slowly lifted into Harry's view.

But it wasn't a hand. Instead the arm ended in a single claw: a knife-edged hook of polished black metal that was over a foot long.

It moved down again, out of Harry's sight, then swung in to press the keenly pointed tip against his groin.

"I'll rip you open from here to your throat!" the harsh voice promised. "Tell me!"

Harry's face was filled with horror now. His constricted chest heaved as he fought for air, managing to gasp out:

"Mister J's! The pub! Around the corner! He went for a drink!"

The hand on his chest eased up. The threatening claw swung back. The lax mouth smiled.

"Thank you. And you wouldn't warn him . . . would you?"

"No!" Harry assured him, shaking his head vigorously.

The tiny, glinting eyes stared deeply into his, probing them.

"No," the other rasped. The smile stretched higher in a brown-toothed grin. "Of course you wouldn't."

The clawed hand swung in again, but this time with an incredible swiftness and power. It tore upward.

There was a scream, abruptly cut off. Blood sprayed up to decorate the white brick wall in a broad, vivid fan.

The killer turned and let the split carcass that had been Harry slide limply down the wall. He started back toward the door, but pulled up short as his gaze fell on Colin's easel.

The little eyes fixed intently on the sketched face of the woman, cut away from the rest of the sheet and still taped there.

His mouth twisted in a snarl. The bloody claw shot out. Its knifelike edge sliced through the hard Formica of the easel's surface as it slid down across the sheet, raking a ragged, blood-soaked tear through the middle of the woman's face.

A finger stabbed down at the photo of the stone, and then at the sketch of the same object, now laying together on a small round table and surrounded by a triangle of three glasses.

"There, see?" said Colin emphatically. "Identical."

Two others seated at the small table—a shaggy-haired, bearded, square-built man about Colin's age and a younger, slim, fashionably dressed woman with a short-cropped bob of raven hair—leaned forward to look. Around them moved the other patrons in the elegant black-and-glass bar.

It was in another of the Victorian storefront renovations, and the three were seated at a table before a large window. The street of the old market area was visible beyond the glass, gone dusky in the swiftly fading light of a fall evening.

The packed crowd of patrons was a mixed one: a few after-work drinkers in uniform business togs, literally rubbing elbows with a wave of the consciously chic being seen in the right place and a gaggle of the consciously artsy trying not to seem consciously chic while in some ways looking even more so.

The tables were full, and other patrons stood three deep at the bar, all competing to be heard in loud, leading-edge, hope-fully impressive conversations about business, money, travel, art, film, food, and sex.

The bearded man beside Colin gave the two images of the graven stone a long perusal, then sat back with an air of indif-ference.

"They might be similar," he admitted.

"Similar?" Colin said disbelievingly. "Look at the damn things again, Tom. They're exactly alike!" He picked them up to shake before his companion. "I mean, look at them. Call that a coincidence?"

"Let me see them," said the woman across the table, plucking them from his hand.

They had been upside-down to her before. Now she looked at them carefully. The sketch of the stone had been cut from the full sheet, cut away from the sketch of the girl.

She sat with her back to the window, and the two men watched her as she studied the pictures. Neither took any notice of a figure visible through the window beyond her, standing in the shadows of a doorway across the street.

It was the figure of a thin man wrapped in a battered green army coat, his head only barely visible in the shadows. The dimly seen face was gaunt, bearded, the hair long and straggling. Around the right eye, from forehead to nose, curved the puffy white line of a distinctive horseshoe scar.

The eyes, sunken deeply in dark sockets, were fixed on the window of the pub across the street, a bright yellow square in the growing darkness, where the table with the three was like a stage setting, clearly visible.

The eyes stared at this scene, and they were not normal eyes. Far back in their black caverns a sharp light flared like a torch-flame.

And that light was of a brilliant ruby red.

The eyes watched intently as, across the street, the woman handed back the two pictures.

"Okay. You're right. They are identical." She shrugged. "But so what? You said you had Irish grandparents. You probably saw pictures of this thing before. In a scrapbook or something."

"I never saw anything like that," Colin said adamantly. "I've never cared about any of that stuff."

"That doesn't mean you didn't see it," Tom put in. "When you were too little to register it maybe. And it could stick in your mind without you remembering. You know how that works."

"Maybe," Colin said doubtfully. "But that doesn't explain that guy coming in and handing me a picture of the exact same rock." He shook his head. "I mean, the whole thing is weird. It's like he was reading my mind or something. And what was all that crap about 'the time of year'?"

Tom smiled with an attempt at sinisterness.

"Halloween's coming up in a couple of days. You know: *Do De Do Do! Do De Do Do!*" he sang in a poor rendition of the *Twilight Zone* theme.

The woman and Tom both laughed at this, but Colin looked irritated.

"You guys just think I'm being crazy, don't you? Well . . ." He looked at the pictures, then lost his anger, slumping back defeatedly and sighing. "Well, maybe I am. God," he said, rubbing his brow, "I've been so tired lately."

"Poor baby," said the young woman sympathetically, patting his hand. "Too much late-night wrestling?"

"Never enough for our Colin," said Tom, leering. "Cut out the trapeze stuff. That's my advice."

"Maybe you just need a good night's sleep," she said more feelingly, shooting Tom a disapproving glare.

Colin looked at her, then nodded, speaking with sudden decisiveness:

"You're right, Annie. I do. And I'm going to start getting it right now!"

He picked up his drink and downed the last of it in one gulp.

"What are you doing?" Tom asked in surprise.

"I'm going home," Colin answered, putting down the glass and rising.

"Now?" asked Tom. "But we were going over to the Twelfth Street Tavern. They have that new fusion group . . ."

"Not tonight, pal." Colin told him firmly. "I'm taking Annie's advice."

"What about dinner?" she asked. "Don't you at least want that first?"

"I'm not that hungry." He fished in his pants pocket and drew out some money. "I'll eat something at home."

"You actually have food there?" the girl asked in mock disbelief. "I mean, stuff that isn't fuzzy?"

"Very funny. Look, I'll pay my tab on the way out. See you guys later. Have fun."

The eyes of the man across the street followed Colin as he made his way from the table to the bar, handed money across to the bartender, then moved to the door. They stayed intently fixed on him as he came out into the growing chill of the autumn evening, stopped to pull his jacket tighter around him against the evening chill, shuddered as a sudden cold gust swept across him, then started briskly up the street.

The sidewalk was all but deserted. As Colin strode along, the watcher moved out of his sheltering doorway to follow, staying on the street's other side. The autumn night had fallen completely now, and the follower kept close to the buildings, within the partial cover of the denser shadows there. Only occasionally did light flicker across him brightly enough to illuminate the odd dark stains that marked both the front and back of the old coat.

Ahead, Colin moved on along the street. He seemed nervous, as if feeling the eyes fixed on him. He glanced back often, but saw nothing.

Until one glance picked out the figure behind him as it slipped by a lighted window from shadow to shadow.

Colin picked up his pace a little.

He reached the block's end and crossed the street to his apartment building. The follower came to a halt on the diagonal corner, looking across to him.

Colin passed by the windows of the Mexican café. Through them a good-sized crowd could be seen dining amidst a rainforest of potted and hanging plants. He reached the door to the upstairs apartments and opened it, pausing to again glance back.

The figure was more visible beneath the corner streetlight, identifiable now as one of the many vagrants who haunted the restored market area like wraiths, cadging drink money from the affluent evening crowd. A bearded, wasted stick of a man in a long and tattered coat, he looked both wretched and harmless.

But the sight didn't reassure Colin. He went in, climbing the three steep flights to his floor two stairs at a time.

He unlocked his door with a certain urgency and entered, slamming the door; he locked it and leaned back against it as his gaze scanned the room. It was unlit save for the streetlights shining in through the big window. He looked around him uneasily at the gathered host of shadows. Then he crossed to the window, and, standing at one side, peered out around the sash.

The street was empty, the opposite corner deserted.

He shook his head, his look one of disgust at his own paranoid feelings, then moved to a worn Barcalounger and dropped down onto it.

He sat there in the half-dark, his face lit faintly by the lights of the city beyond the window. He levered the chair out into its lounger configuration and lay his head back, giving a heavy sigh of weariness.

Colin stared up to the ceiling. A web of shadow floated there, cast by the various streetlights striking upward from different angles through the radiating ribs of the window's fan-topped sash.

A car cruised by slowly below, and the moving glow from its headlamps slid through the other lights, making the ceiling shadows seem almost to flicker as if from the shifting flames of a fire.

5

The tracery of curved shadows was now an interlace of slender poles, glowing a soft golden-brown in the shifting light.

He was looking at a ceiling of thatch, supported by the pole framework and curving up and inward in a rounded cone to a small hole on the top. A plume of yellow-tinted white smoke drifted up to vanish through this hole. The soot it carried had turned the grey thatch black around the opening; now, however, the smoke filled the air with a fragrance like burning autumn leaves, though more pleasing and soft, like a nostalgic dream of childhood.

Voices drifted toward him; they were not far away, but faint, as the two people spoke in hushed tones.

"Lucky he was," a man's voice said. "A bit closer and it would have torn out his whole chest. As it is, those scratches alone could have been enough. But the potion I've given him will counteract the poisons. I'm certain of that."

Colin tried to lift himself up, but it seemed too great an effort. The muscles of his neck tensed as he moved his head fractionally; then they relaxed as he gave up.

"I thank you, Healer," replied a woman's voice. "It's most kind of you to help."

"Think no more of that, girl," was the response. "That's what I'm for, isn't it? But I've no liking at all for what's happened to you. Is it certain you are that the time's not come for you to leave this place?"

"It's certain," came her firm reply. "There's no power can make our clan give up what they must do."

"Ah, you've courage, girl," the man told her. "But I'm afraid you don't really know what you face. Well, goodbye now. And take great care."

"I will, Healer. And Danu protect you."

"It's yourselves she should be looking after, my girl," was his grave reply.

There was suddenly a brighter, whiter light streaming into the room. Again Colin exerted an effort, neck muscles straining taut, this time managing to lift his head and turn it toward the voices. He saw the figures of a man and woman, dark silhouettes against the bright light beyond a low round-topped doorway. The man stooped and went out, the woman dropping a curtain of thick cowhide back across the opening.

The outside light was cut off, the only illumination once again the flames from a fire burning within a circle of stones not far from him. And with the bright light gone, that fire revealed the features of the room.

It was circular, some twenty-five feet across. Its walls were of clay daub over a wattling of woven sticks, and barely six feet high. But at its peak, the roof of thatch rose to a height of over a dozen feet. The framework of this roof was supported by half a dozen thick posts of wood set at equal distances around the central fire. The floor was beaten earth thickly strewn with rushes. The furnishings were simple: a plank table, shelves, a pair of iron-bound wooden trunks, and a few stools. Around the curved wall were arranged half a dozen pallets of piled rugs and furs, and it was on one that he now lay.

But Colin barely glanced at these surroundings. All his attention was on the woman's face, its smooth features softly glowing in the firelight, the long hair a shimmering flow of molten gold. She was the one from the fight at the cart.

She saw him watching her and moved quickly across to him, kneeling at his side.

"So, you are awake," she said, a tone of relief clear in her voice. "I wasn't sure. Are you all right?"

His lips moved, but no sound came out. He frowned in irritation at the weakness, then tried again.

"Your eyes . . ." he got out, hoarsely but clearly enough, ". . . they're green."

She looked somewhat bemused at this.

"They are," she said. "Why?"

"I knew they were light, glowing, brilliant like some jewels," he said with more strength, "but I couldn't remember their color."

"I'm surprised you remember anything at all, after that bashing about you had," she said matter-of-factly. "Can you move?"

"Of course I can," he announced with bravado.

The muscles of his arms and stomach now tensed as he put his effort into the attempt. He rose up to a sitting position, but his face went white and he swayed, nearly falling back.

Quickly she put an arm about his shoulders, steadying him. "Easy," she cautioned. "You're a bit weak yet."

He looked down at himself. He was clad only in the knee-length tunic now. His cloak was folded over a nearby bench. His sheathed sword was hanging by its harness on a peg in one of the roof pillars.

Feeling nearly recovered, he sat looking into the face so close to his. Their eyes met and he stared into the green depths of hers, held by them, momentarily distracted.

"Are you certain you're all right?" she asked, her concern brought back again by his odd stare. "Maybe you shouldn't be up so soon."

"No, no. I'm fine," he assured her, recalled to reality by the words. He looked around. "But where am I now?"

"You're in my clan's rath," she said. "Your charioteer helped me to bring you here."

"My charioteer? Ailbe? Where is he?"

"My clansmen are seeing to him very well. You just be thinking of yourself. Think of your wound . . ."

"Wound?" He seemed to have forgotten it. Now he craned his head farther down and around, glimpsing the pad of white linen that had been bound across his collarbone with strips tied over his shoulder and about his chest. The pad was streaked with wide stripes of dark red-brown. He lifted a hand to touch it gingerly, his look puzzled.

"Strange. I remember getting it now. But it's giving me no pain at all."

His fingers pulled gently at the pad.

"No!" the girl protested, putting out a hand to stop him. But too late.

He pulled the linen square clear of the wound. Only four white lines, like the marks of old scars, showed on his flesh.

"It's nearly healed!" he said in astonishment. Then he looked up to her. "But, how long have I been here?"

"A day and a night, only," she said, staring at the healed wound with her own amazement.

"Miraculous, this is," he exclaimed. "It should take a season to heal like this. A year!"

"The old man has greater sorcery than I thought," she said.

"Old man? The one who just left here?"

"Yes. A druid he calls himself. I thought he was only a wandering vagabond with a few healer's tricks. He has helped my clan before, but I wasn't certain he could deal with this." She touched the scars softly, her fingers running lightly over his throat. Then she looked up to see him intently watching her and flushed. She moved away, sitting back down beside him.

"You didn't have to stop," he told her with a grin.

"It's a bold one you are," she brusquely replied. But she gave him a little smile in return, and the flush deepened.

"Who was it that attacked you?" he asked.

"Just brigands," she said nonchalantly. "They roam the countryside about here."

"Just brigands?" he echoed in disbelief. "But that one . . . the one who did this," he said, touching the wounds, "he wasn't even a man. More like some beast he was. Didn't you see him?"

"That I did not. And neither did you," she said most positively. "Likely it was some dream you had from the wound."

"And what did this, then?" he asked, tapping the scars.

"Some rake or fork, maybe. Those scavengers use all kinds of things for weapons."

He looked at her, met her definite gaze, and shook his head.

"Maybe you're right."

"But," she added quickly, "don't be thinking they weren't still a most terrible, bloody lot, or that my brother and I wouldn't have been killed surely without your help." She smiled, adding earnestly, "You were most courageous to risk yourself."

"Your brother? He's alive too, then?"

"A clean spear thrust through the muscles of his chest won't keep Seadna down long," she assured him.

"I'm most glad to hear it," he said. Then, as before, he sat just gazing at her.

"Why is it you're doing that again?" she asked, clearly flustered by his intense stare. She raised a hand to her cheek. "Do you see something wrong in my face?"

"Nothing at all," he said most sincerely. "I was only wishing I could stay here to gaze a bit longer at it." Then he smiled regretfully and added, "But if I've been here a day and a night already, I must be getting on."

He began to rise. She stood too, first putting out her hands to help, then pulling back to watch instead, though ready in case he should seem about to fall.

He did sway a bit as he stood fully erect, but steadied himself at once.

"You're really certain you're well enough?" she asked.

"I'd like to say not, and use the excuse to stay here with your tending me." He reached out to take one of her hands. She didn't resist. He looked again into her eyes. "But I could never tell any lie to such a fine and honest woman as yourself."

"It's a brazen tongue you have in you, that's certain," she replied, but with good humor. "And how many girls has it gotten you into trouble with?"

"I'd hoped you'd be the first," he said, grinning.

This seemed to change her mood suddenly. Her own smile vanished and she pulled her hand from his, becoming abruptly distant.

"Well, if you must go, you'd best be going," she said. She turned away to take his sword and harness from the peg, and held them out to him.

"Oh," he said, momentarily nonplussed by the change in her and the blunt gesture of dismissal. "Yes, I suppose so."

He took the sword, buckling the belt about his waist. Then, while she fetched his cloak, he removed the bandage. His tunic was ripped at the throat, but when he put the cloak about him and fastened it with the brooch, the rip and the exposed scars were covered.

As he was completing the donning of his cloak, a boy slipped through the door-flap into the room.

"Seanan!" she exclaimed, moving forward as if to block the way. "I told you to stay out."

"But he's up!" the other protested, feinting in one direction and then ducking around her in the opposite.

He was a tall, lean boy with the gangly arms and legs of a yearling and the agility of a young hare, a bush of red-blond hair, and an eager pink face thickly dusted with bright freckles.

"Go away," she said angrily, swinging around to grab one of his elbows.

He struggled to pull free.

"No!" he cried. "He looks well enough now! You can't keep me away!"

"All right," she said in exasperation, giving up and releasing him. She looked toward Colin. "This is my little and most troublesome brother, Seanan," she said in a terse introduction.

"I'm not so little," he said indignantly, drawing up to his full height, which was nearly that of his sister. "I'm twelve . . .

almost." His critical gaze swept up and down the young warrior. "So it was you who saved my sister?"

"I helped," Colin said, clearly amused by the youth's brashness. "She was doing very well herself."

"*She* says you are the finest warrior she's ever seen," he frankly disclosed, much to his sister's obvious mortification.

"I'm just a simple fighting man," Colin said modestly.

"Have you seen far lands?" the boy asked eagerly, eyes bright.

"Just the far end of this one. Sorry, but I've no tales of adventuring for you."

"I'll wager you have," the boy said, unconvinced. "Why . . ."

"Enough now," said his sister impatiently. She grabbed one of Seanan's slender shoulders and pulled him back. "He must be leaving. You're only delaying him." She looked apologetically to Colin. "I'm sorry."

"It's all right," he assured her, clapping a hand to the boy's other shoulder. "I'm glad to know him. Maybe some time we can meet again and talk."

"I hope so," the boy said with great intensity.

His sister went to the door and pointedly pulled back the flap.

"You should be going now," she said to Colin. "Your time is flying on."

"Yes, I suppose so," he agreed reluctantly.

He went out and she followed, purposely dropping the door flap on her brother as he followed, leaving him to struggle through.

They came out into a circular, flat yard of hard-packed earth some one hundred feet across, enclosed by a ring of earth and stones topped by a palisade of spiked logs.

In addition to the building they had just left, there were six other, similar round houses and a slightly larger one of oval shape, all linked by graveled paths across the muddy yard. Against the outer wall were several square lean-to buildings. One seemed to be a storehouse, before which a stocky man in a blood-stained leather apron was butchering a side of beef on a great slab of wood. Another was a stable, where a boy of about Seanan's age was rubbing down a horse under the supervision of a tall man in warrior's dress.

"A fair-sized rath your clan has," Colin remarked, glancing around. "Where's my driver?"

"In the *teac*," she said, nodding toward the oval house. "But I think my father'll be wanting to talk with you first."

The boy grooming the horse noted Colin then, and pointed him out to the tall warrior. The man looked around and then spoke to the boy, who dropped his brushes at once and trotted off toward the oval house. As he did, the warrior started across the yard toward Colin, the butcher leaving his own work to follow but holding onto his long, blood-stained knife.

"This is my father," the girl announced as the warrior came up before them. "Flann O'Mulconrys, chieftan of our clan."

He was an imposing man—powerfully built as well as tall—perhaps forty years old though the only hint of his age showed in the weathering of his rugged face and a slight greying of the brown hair pulled back in a loose braid. He wore a simple warrior's garb, like Colin's, but the knob-ended torc of twisted gold strands about his neck suggested that here was a chieftan of some esteemed rank.

His eyes, a slate blue-grey like a winter's sea, swept Colin scrutinizingly.

"It's surprised I am to see you about so quickly, stranger," he said in a deep, brusque voice.

"A fact I believe I owe to yourselves, Chieftain, and to the skill of your healer," Colin graciously replied.

"It's little enough repayment to you, warrior, for saving my oldest son . . . and my only daughter, too." He added this last as an afterthought.

"Thank you, dear father," she put in sarcastically.

"For all the pain of it, I'd not hesitate to do the same again," Colin said, smiling at her, "especially since meeting your fine daughter."

"Ah, wouldn't you, now?" the chieftain said meaningfully, noting Colin's look with a raised eyebrow.

People were now coming out of the oval house and from

other parts of the rath as well. There were some hundred of them, including at least two score other men in warrior's dress, women of varied ages—one in an advanced stage of pregnancy —and a gaggle of excited children ranging from toddler to ten. And last of all, Colin's driver emerged from the oval house, gnawing on a half-eaten joint of mutton.

The people formed up behind their chieftain, staring curiously—the children somewhat fearfully—at the visitor. Ailbe, finally lowering the joint, approached his master with a look of great relief.

"I am glad to see you well," he said. "You don't know how I've been worrying over your wounding."

"It didn't interfere with your appetite, I see," Colin remarked.

"Don't be making fun of me now," the other protested. "Your father would have had the hide off my living body if I'd let you come to harm. The food's been my only comfort. And these people have been most generous."

"They have been that," Colin agreed.

"But we mustn't be holding our visitors any longer, Father," the girl said pointedly. "They must be going on."

"Must they be?" Flann said with some surprise. "But . . ."

He caught his daughter's eye then. A sharp light glinted there, and her mouth was sternly set. At once he nodded.

"Of course they must," he emphatically agreed. He looked to the stable boy. "Eanna, get off now and harness our warrior's car. Seanan, you go as well."

"I'll help them," Ailbe said hastily and followed off after the boys. In moments they were bringing Colin's chariot and horses from the stable shed.

"Your daughter says it's bandits that attacked her," Colin remarked to the chief as they watched his team being harnessed to the car. "Does your clan have much trouble with them?"

Flann hesitated. He looked uncertain of an answer. His gaze went to his daughter. Her head shook infinitesimally.

"No," he said tersely. "Nothing we can't deal with."

But Colin had noted the chieftain's hesitation, and he looked at Flann searchingly.

"Is that so? Well, if there's a danger of meeting such a lot again, I'd like to know."

"They'll not bother you, stranger," Flann said. "I'm certain of that. It's only ourselves that . . ."

"Father!" the girl said sharply, cutting him off. "Don't be going into one of your stories now. Just tell the man that it's only wealth or women that they're seeking, and that a traveling warrior will be safe."

He looked at her with obvious irritation, but then obeyed her, though speaking through tensed jaws.

"My daughter is right. I would say that you can travel safely on, especially after that bloodying you gave them. But still . . ."

"Your chariot's ready now," the girl said, cutting her father off again. "I know what a great rush you must be in."

She all but hustled the somewhat surprised Colin to his chariot, her clanfolk following. One of the women brought forward a large leather sack, stuffed to bulging.

"Here are provisions for your traveling," the girl said, taking it and handing it to him. "May good Danu watch over you."

He took the bag, putting a hand upon hers as he did so, trying once again to meet her gaze.

"Wait now," he said, "I don't even know your name."

"Aislinn is my name," she told him, pulling her hand away. "Now, you'd best be getting on."

"I hope to see you again," said Colin. "When my task is done—"

"Then I hope to see you on your way back to your home quickly," she said curtly, finishing his sentence.

"But, I thought to stop here on my journey home."

At that she fixed him with a cold stare and her voice was ice.

"Believe me now: there is no reason at all for your doing that," she said. "So be wasting no more time. The daylight's fleeting. You don't want to waste another night here."

"But . . ." he began, looking from her to the group of others who stood silently watching. His welcome here seemed definitely concluded. He shrugged defeatedly.

"All right, then. Ailbe and I thank you for your hospitality."

He tossed the sack of victuals into the car and climbed in behind the little driver.

Flann now moved up beside his daughter.

"Stranger," he said, "your name is unknown to us as well. Tell us, before you go, just who my clan owes for this help."

"Colin of Clan Mathghamhain I am, from Dun Garvan in Munster."

"From so far!" Flann said, surprised. "And what are you doing journeying here?"

"The traveling Ollafs have brought us amazing tales of cattle being raised here like no others in Ireland." Colin explained. "My father sent me to buy a breeding bull for our herds. I'm bound for Dun Mauran."

"Dun Mauran is it?" said Flann. His eyes went to those of his daughter, this time flashing a look of concern. Colin saw his look, and saw similar glances exchanged by others in the group.

"Is there something wrong?" he asked.

"Nothing at all," the girl said, her tone still brisk. "May the good Dagda make your journey a successful one."

"Aislinn," her father protested, "this is no fair way to treat . . ."

"Quiet, Father!" she said, firing at him a look so sharp that he jerked back as if jabbed. "I'll see to this!"

Colin leaned down toward her, his gaze searching hers.

"What is it that's really going on?" he asked her bluntly.

A flicker of emotion—blended of anguish, fear, and longing —showed in her bright eyes. But her face remained icy, her voice unwavering.

"Nothing to do with you, Colin MacMathghamhain. And unless you're more fool than you seem, you'll not seek to know. Buy your bull if you must, but then be out of this land and back to your own far home."

Clearly unsatisfied, but seeing no hope for more answers in that stubbornly set face, the young warrior rose upright and signaled Ailbe. The driver urged the team ahead. As they rolled across the yard, two of the men ran ahead to unlock wide timber doors in the outer wall and pull them open.

Colin looked back once as they rode out, seeing the girl and her clan watching after him. Then his chariot was rolling down a slope from the hilltop rath, the spokes of its great wheels turning within their iron rims.

6

OCTOBER 28, 8:03 P.M.

The glow of headlights played through the fan-shaped top of the window frame, casting a moving shadow of its radiating spokes across the ceiling.

Colin, staring upward at it, blinked, started in surprise, and then sat up, looking toward the window as another set of lights swept up through it. His expression was one of bewilderment.

"Are you all right?" asked a voice.

His head jerked around toward the lump of an ancient camel-backed couch squatting in the shadow of a corner. Another form was just visible sitting there, the play of light from the street faintly illuminating neatly creased black trousers and polished boots.

Colin jumped up. His hand swept out to a small table beside him, and gripped the object that sat upon it.

"Easy," said the voice. The figure on the sofa moved slightly and a goosenecked floor lamp beside the sofa clicked on. The cone of light from within the dusty, fringed shade fell upon the face and glowing silver hair of the man who sat there.

He sat quite calmly, completely at ease, long legs elegantly crossed, a silver-headed cane across his lap. He smiled at Colin in a pleasant, reassuring way.

"What the hell are you doing here?" Colin demanded, sounding both angry and a bit alarmed.

"Just stopped by to see how you were," the man said in a casual manner, as if they were old chums. "You seemed to be dreaming when I came in. I didn't want to disturb you."

Colin dropped into a slightly crouched, more defensive posture. His look was still apprehensive.

"How did you get in?" he asked.

"Oh, your door was open," the man said, gesturing toward it.

"Open?" said Colin. He looked toward the door he had most carefully bolted on coming in. It stood slightly ajar now, the chain dangling.

"I knocked, of course," the man went on, "but you didn't answer."

"So you just strolled on in?" Colin asked with irritation. He took a step toward the man. "Look, who are you anyway, pal? You sure as hell aren't the Swedish Pizza King."

"I don't recall ever implying that I was," the unflappable man replied.

"Then who are you? What do you want?" Colin demanded, taking another step forward. "Come on, Beau Brummel. Quick! Before I start dialing 911 on this."

The man remained totally unperturbed by this threat.

"I assure you, Mr. McMahon, I only came to help you. You can put down that rather grotesque . . . whatever it is."

Colin glanced down at the object he still held by his side. He looked embarrassed.

"It . . . was a gift," he said defensively, lifting it into view.

It was the heavy glass container of a lava lamp, snatched from the base that still sat upon the table, the red ooze within it now shaken into uncountable drifting globules.

Pointedly, he did not put it down. He stayed in his defensive posture, although there was more curiosity than hostility in his voice as he now asked:

"What do you mean, 'help'? Help with what?"

"With your dreams, Mr. McMahon."

This simple reply caused a new wave of confusion and alarm to sweep across the young man's face. He took another step forward, shaking the lamp before him violently as he spoke.

"Just what do you know about my dreams? How do you know about me at all? And what was all that crap back at the office?"

"It was meant as a gentle push," the man told him in a calming way. "A hint of the road that you must take. I had planned to let you follow it yourself in your own time, but now I sense that the time is rather shorter than I thought, and you perhaps more reluctant." He spread his long hands in a "here I am" gesture. "So, I came back."

Looking only the more bewildered by this cryptic response, Colin moved back to the lounger. He hauled it into its upright position and sat down again. He plunked the glass lamp back into its holder and stared across at the man contemplatively for a time. Then he shook his head.

"This is too much," he said with exasperation in his tone. "I mean, I just don't get it. You say you know about my dreams? All right. What do you know?"

"I know you must delve into them," was the still cryptic reply. "For me to tell you more than that would only drive you away from belief. You are likely already considering me a madman. What I could say to you would surely convince you, and could certainly cause great damage. No. You have to find out for yourself, with no greater manipulating. Then, perhaps, we can talk. But it must be soon."

"You say I have to find out for myself," Colin replied. "Okay. How? How do I find out about my dreams?"

"One of your libraries is not very far from here, I believe," was the response. "I'm certain you can find the answers there— or at least the start of them. But I must go now. My very presence near you may make things go too quickly."

He rose.

"Now, wait a minute," said Colin. "Tell me more. What do I look for?"

"You are an intelligent man," the other told him with a little smile. "I rather think you know that already."

He started toward the door.

"Wait. Don't go yet," said Colin, getting up to move after him. "You've got to tell me more."

"I've already said . . ."

"Yeah, I know. But you said you know about my dreams. Then do you know if it's normal to dream in sequence?"

This stopped the man. He paused before the door and looked

back, his face losing its assured equanimity for the first time and taking on a worried frown.

"Sequence? And just when did this happen?"

"Just now. I mean, now and this afternoon. It's like scenes in a TV show. With commercials for my real life!"

"My," the visitor said to himself, clearly concerned, "things are moving even more rapidly than I had feared." He looked to Colin, speaking with a sudden decisiveness: "Mr. McMahon, you must act quickly. The time is coming, and coming very soon. And be careful, careful of everything from now on." He lifted the cane, pointing toward him with its silver-shod tip in emphasis. "It could mean your life!"

"My life?" said Colin in consternation. "Wait a minute. What are you . . ."

"I believe that grotesque object of yours is about to fall off the table, Mr. McMahon," the other observed.

Colin turned. The lava lamp was sitting crooked in its base, but it was secure. He turned back.

The man was gone.

"Damn!" exclaimed Colin. "He's like the goddamn Cheshire Cat!" He shook his head. "My life!" he said in wonder. And then, "The library?"

He pulled the drawing and the brochure from his jacket pocket, looking from the sketched stone to the smiling couple on the Irish coast. Then his face hardened with resolution.

"Not much other choice!" he murmured.

He went to the clothing-heaped chair by the door, rummaged through it and dragged out a rumpled trenchcoat. He slipped it on and went out the door.

In moments he was emerging from his building, locking its street door and hurrying up the sidewalk, past the windows of Casa Maitas, around the corner and out of sight.

As he vanished from view, another figure appeared, gliding out of the dense shadows of a doorway across the street. The gaunt figure with the stained army topcoat and horseshoe-scarred face strode across the street. Its coat whisking through a switching cat-tail of steam that rose from a manhole and blasted it away in tatters.

The man moved up to the door. A bony hand reached out to the knob. It turned. He pulled the door open and slipped into the building, climbing the stairs to the second floor, stopping before the door of the first apartment there.

The hand lifted and knocked, the sound echoing hollowly in the corridor. The door opened. A scent of cooking food welled out as a slim middle-aged woman, in the grey skirt and jacket of office fashion, peered out.

"Colin McMahon," the dry whisper came from the barely moving lips.

"What is it?" said a booming voice. A hefty man appeared, wearing an apron with "I *heart* cooking" across the chest, clutching a spatula in one hand and looking past her at the caller suspiciously.

"He wants Colin," she told him.

"He's on three. Three-ten," the big man answered.

With no further word, the gaunt figure turned and stalked away.

"You're welcome," the woman called after him and shut the door.

"I don't like the look of him," the man said. "And what the hell is he doing in the building?"

She turned to him, leaning back against the door.

"Colin has some strange friends."

"Not that strange," he said with certainty. "And there's no way that guy should be in the building without Colin knowing. I think we should call the super."

"And if he's not home?"

"Then the police."

There was a crash. The woman jerked stiffly upright, head thrown back, mouth open in astonishment. Then she toppled forward, a crimson stain spreading on the center of her back.

Behind her, the long, sleek, glinting point of a spear was thrust through a splintered hole in the thick wood of the door. It seemed to glow, almost to pulsate with silver light as if electricity coursed through it.

The man stared, his eyes darting from the fallen woman to

the point and back; he was immobilized by shock. The spear was drawn back through the hole.

The door swung open.

The man watched, face drawn in horror, still motionless, as the gaunt figure in the long coat moved forward into the room. The glittering weapon shot out, jabbing toward the red heart on the broad chest of his apron.

There was a sharp grunt of pain. A heavy crashing sound.

The door of the apartment swung closed.

The five books were lifted from the shelf in a group, leaving a wide hole in the neat line.

Colin cradled them in one arm and moved back along the avenue of shelves, out into the open.

Scores of other shelves were ranked around him on four sides, surrounding a reading area and a central atrium where a broad stairwell ran to lower and higher floors. The library was a paean to modern minimalism: all simple lines in white concrete, glass, and chrome; all sharp-edged, clean, and brightly, whitely lit.

He moved along to an alcove with a single table, giving him a bit more privacy. Before the table was a window, and Colin paused for a moment to gaze out.

It was a second-story view of the city lights and of the park that began just across the street from the library's base. The strip of greenspace stretched away to the white square of another building which anchored the park's far end. Now, in the darkness, it was a swatch of black velvet against which the amber lights along its pathways showed like a string of pearls.

Colin turned from the window and dropped his books down on the table beside a stack of others. The titles were revealing: *The History of Ireland, An Introduction to the Celts, Irish Sagas, Ireland and Her People, The Story of the Irish Race.*

He sat down. Then, suddenly feeling as if he was being watched, he looked searchingly around.

The room was silent, the vast floor and many reading tables deserted save for an elderly, balding man with a fringe of white hair, a threadbare topcoat and an old fedora beside him on the table. He was looking through a magazine and nodding as if drowsing off.

Colin laughed to himself and shook his head.

"God. I really *am* paranoid," he muttered to himself, turning his gaze back to his table.

He glanced over the titles of his new gleaning of books, pulling out one called *The Life of the Ancient Irish*. It was a green-jacketed book, small and thin and apparently unpromising. But as he leafed through, he found its pages crowded with photos and drawings.

He came upon a chapter on appearance and dress, and stopped there suddenly. An artist's renderings of the period's clothing and grooming styles were most striking. He examined with fascination a man who appeared much as he himself had in the dreams: a shift-like tunic belted at the waist, a long cloak about the shoulders, clean-shaven face, long hair caught up in a mane behind his neck.

Colin looked most closely at a diagram showing a number of brooch styles popular at the time—heavy iron pins, mostly, but some ornamented with brightly enameled discs or intricate filigrees of gold and silver. He touched a fingertip to one very similar to that which had fastened his own dream cloak.

He began turning the pages with more intent, perusing more diagrams. His leather shoes, his sword, his shield, even the trousers worn by his driver were all represented here, just as he had dreamed them.

He moved on more rapidly, skimming each page until, in a section on housing, he paused again.

There before him was an archeologist's floor plan of a typical Celtic house: wheel-shaped, with single door and central firepit. Even more telling was an artist's perspective rendering of the interior. He stared in amazement at the thatched roof with its supporting frame of poles, the simple furniture, the fire in its ring of stones. His mind's eye superimposed upon this drawing the room in his dream, nearly identical to it. But his memory also supplied the smells, the sounds, the people, the detailed bits of reality that could never come from such drawings and descriptions.

He looked at the caption beneath the drawing. It read, "circa fourth century A.D."

He slammed the book closed suddenly, his face gone white, and jerked his head up as if something had been jabbed into him. His gaze scanned rapidly around the bright, modern reality of the room, across the man who was reading, the shelves of books; he stared out the window over the city lights, then down at himself as if to assure himself that he was still actually there. His breath was coming in short, quick pants.

Then he steeled himself. His look grew determined again. He slowly opened the book, at first just peeping in as if something unpleasant could leap out, and finally resuming his scanning, but turning the pages a bit more reluctantly.

Then, under a heading of "Fortifications," there was something else. The word *Dun* caught his eye and he read:

"*Dun*—the hill on which fortifications were built. These were much a feature of the everyday life of Irish Celts. Often extensive, covering many acres, they included a *faitcha* or yard, a main hall called a *teac mi-cuarta,* and satellite structures, all surrounded by a defensive rampart having a parapet walk and a stockade."

He read on, turning the page. And there before him was a skillfully drawn, two-page perspective view of what such a fortress might have looked like upon its hill.

As he stared, enthralled, the clarity of its details seemed to increase, its colors become more intense, its size expand until it filled his field of vision, drawing him into it, swallowing him.

7

The encircling timber palisade of the fortress formed a grey crown upon the bright green brow of the hilltop.

As the chariot carrying Colin and Ailbe rolled up the roadway toward the hill, the young warrior looked the place over evaluatingly.

"A good-sized fortress, Dun Mauran," he commented to his driver.

"It is that," Ailbe agreed. "Twice the size of our own. And look at these herds. I thought the tales we'd heard of them were from some bard's drunken fancy!"

There did indeed seem to be an uncountable number of cows grazing in the lush grass of the surrounding hills, more like crows upon a harvest field in their vast swarming.

But as the chariot drew closer to the *dun,* something else caught the warrior's searching eye—a row of objects set upon long poles stuck up above the spike-topped wall of timbers. They were spaced at intervals of about a man's height, so many that they appeared to encircle the full quarter-mile circumference of the palisade.

"Look there," he said to Ailbe, pointing. "See the heads!"

"By the Bloody Crow!" the other exclaimed. "Two hundred at least!" He looked to his young companion in alarm. "Is it such a fierce people we're going among?"

Colin shook his head. "I don't know, Ailbe. I've heard nothing about them to say that. Still, there was some . . ." He hesitated, considering. ". . . some feeling I got from Aislinn's people when they learned we were coming here. As if . . . well, as if it troubled them. What about you? Did they say anything to you about this place?"

"They didn't say much to me at all," the driver replied. "I mean, they were friendly enough. They fed me well. But they were quiet. More like dumb cows, to say the whole truth of it. When they did try to talk, that girl was about shushing them with a sharp look, or telling them not to be disturbing me. All but ran the place, she did."

"She did that," Colin agreed, smiling. "She even had that bull of a father gentled to a calf." He looked up toward the gruesomely decorated wall again, and the smile faded. "But I wish she'd talked to me just a little more."

"We could go home," said Ailbe hopefully. "Your father'd not put any shame on you for it."

"No," the warrior agreed. "That he would not. But I surely would myself. He set me on a task, and I'll see it through. We've come here as friends, not enemies, so these people have no reason to harm us. We'll go on."

"Of course," Ailbe said, but in a disappointed tone.

They were now just below the dun, moving up the slope toward the main gates. These stood open, apparently unguarded. No lookouts were visible on the wall. No armed men could be seen about the opening.

As they drew nearer to the wall, it became clear that the scores of heads upon it were far from fresh ones. Even those which seemed most recent were badly shriveled, their eyes gone to picking birds. Most had been reduced to nothing more than skulls covered by a stretched parchment of dry skin, the lank remains of their long hair streaming about them in the brisk spring breeze.

"Well, if they are warlike," Ailbe commented with definite relief, "then at least they haven't been taking heads this last few seasons."

They reached the top of the slope, their chariot rattling over a plank causeway that bridged the deep foss, and then rolling through the gateway.

Beyond they entered a *faitcha* that, in contrast to the grim atmosphere created by the heads, was one of bustling life.

Scores of people were about in the yard. A few warriors were at training, throwing spears against a row of thick, much-splintered posts. A lean but wiry-muscled smith hammered at the curved iron of a wheel rim, while a youth bellowed the hearth beside him to raging white heat. A dozen boys played a fast and brutal game of hurley, furiously knocking the ball around a marked-off field of muddy earth with their short, curved sticks. And close beside one section of the wall, sheltered from the brisk gusts of the spring winds, a group of women basked in the rare sunshine while they knitted.

The entrance of the chariot had an immediate effect upon all these inhabitants of the dun. The smith noted the arrivals first; he froze, maul raised for a blow, then slowly lowered the tool to stare. The warriors' practice and the boys' hurley game ceased abruptly and their participants also stood and stared. The women saw the chariot last, and their conversations died; they ceased their knitting, some rising up, all their gazes intense and their faces grimly set.

"A cheery lot they are here," said Ailbe sourly, looking around at them. "What do we do now?"

Colin too was scanning the interior of the *dun*. There was a large central hall, several satellite buildings of smaller size, and a row of stall-like shelters along the curve of outer wall. Those shelters nearest the gate were obviously stables, where several men in servants' plain wool tunics and trousers tended horses or labored at the cleaning of massive chariots-of-war.

"Stop over there," Colin ordered his driver.

Ailbe turned the horses and pulled the car up before the stable sheds. As the men here saw them, they too ceased their work to stand and stare, their gazes searching, expressions closed.

"I could still turn around and drive right out again," Ailbe told his master.

"Quiet, Ailbe," Colin said. "We're here as friends. Just climb down. But do it slowly."

As he and his servant climbed from the car, a man left the others in the stables and moved out toward them.

He was a thick, squat individual of indeterminable age. His block of a head sat on the massive, rounded cliffs of his shoulders. The features of his face were extraordinarily flat—the nose mashed down, the lips broad, the chin squared off—as if they had been driven against something with great force. Tiny eyes peered out over the high ridges of his cheeks.

He wore a leather tunic and carried in his thick hands a short knob-ended stick of polished black wood. Though not so tall as Colin, he was much more massive. And as he stopped before the warrior, he set himself in a clearly challenging way.

"Greetings to you," Colin said in a most amiable tone.

There was no answer. Only a stare from the tiny, glinting eyes.

Colin glanced questioningly around at Ailbe. The little driver shrugged, his expression one of growing uneasiness. His master looked back to the unresponsive mountain before him and tried again.

"It's a very fine *dun* you have," he said appreciatively. "Very fine."

"Just what is it you're wantin' here?" The words issued in a low rumble from the cavernous mouth of the man.

"Ah!" said Colin, clearly relieved that he had finally elicited some response. "Well, I've come to see your chieftain. Where is it I should go?"

"You won't have to be going nowheres," the man growled. "He's coming to you."

Colin turned to see three men striding toward them from the main hall. All were garbed as warriors, all tall, lean, and long-featured men. The one at their head was clearly their leader. The rank showed in his stride, his gold brocaded tunic and rich cloak, and the magnificent torc of gold pipe about his neck.

He was somewhat older than the other two, his features a bit more sharply honed by age, grey streaks showing in the dark brown hair braided at his back. Long, neatly plaited mustaches drooped at either side of his narrow mouth.

Colin watched this imperious figure striding toward him, then glanced again to Ailbe. Worry now displayed itself openly in the driver's large, mobile face. Colin pulled himself up straighter, setting his legs apart. His hand lifted to rest upon his sword's hilt.

The three reached the visitors, pulling up before them. Their leader glanced over the young warrior with a bright, probing, ice-blue eye. Then he lifted his open right hand, palm out, in a gesture of greeting, his sternly set mouth stretching up into a warm smile.

"I welcome you to Dun Mauran," he said in a most friendly way. "I am Laimainech, chieftain of the Clan of the Comains."

The effect of this was like that of a warm sun on a night's frost, instantly thawing the frozen inhabitants of Dun Mauran. They smiled as well, some raising their voices to call out their own greetings to the strangers. Then they were back about their activities, Colin and Ailbe apparently now accepted and dismissed.

Colin smiled in response, lifting his hand from the sword hilt, holding it up palm out as the chieftain had done.

"I am glad to see you so agreeable," he said, his voice revealing his relief. "I thought . . ." He glanced meaningfully toward the heads.

"Ah," the other said, nodding in understanding. "Well, we have had our clashes in the past. Our enemies and rivals no longer bother us. We've kept the heads only as a reminder to them. But no man who comes in peace to Dun Mauran has anything to fear."

"Well, it's surely in peace I've come," Colin told him emphatically. "I mean to barter with you for the use of a bull from your herd."

"Then you are even more welcome," the man said with delight. "For it's our greatest pleasure to help others share our wealth. Come into the *teac* with me now, and accept my hospitality." He looked to the stocky man from the stables. "Garbhan, will you see to his chariot?"

"I will," came the grumbled reply, and the man stepped toward the chariot, lifting a broad hand toward one horse's bridle.

"If it's all the same, I'll just see to it myself," said Ailbe. He slipped past Garbhan, standing before the team, lifting a hand to block the huge man's reach.

"You heard my Chieftain," growled the steward.

"And you hear me as well, my lad. This is my chariot, and no one sees to it but myself! So back away!"

The one called Garbhan stopped, glared down at Ailbe, his massive form dwarfing the little driver. But Ailbe stood his ground with a defiant return stare.

"Of course," the chieftain said easily. "Garbhan, let the driver care for his chariot. And see to any of his needs."

The thickly built steward, although still glaring, nodded and stepped back. With a nod to his own master, Ailbe led the team away toward the stable sheds. The chieftain turned his attention again to Colin.

"And as for you, young warrior, please come with me."

He turned to lead the way, and Colin, with a last glance back at Ailbe, fell in beside him. The two younger warriors followed behind.

"Tell me, now, who you are and where you come from," the chieftain inquired as they moved toward the main hall.

"Colin MacMathghamhain I am, son of the chieftain of our clan," he replied. "I've come from Dun Garvan in Munster."

"Have you?" the chieftain said, sounding much impressed. "Well, then it's a very long way you've come. You must be weary of the traveling. I'll find a place for you in my own house. Wash, rest, then join us at our evening meal. There'll be time for our talk there."

They reached the hall, the two accompanying warriors moving around chieftain and visitor to pull open its large plank doors. Laimainech lifted an arm to usher Colin ahead of him as they passed inside.

Across the yard the smith continued his work, now seemingly uninterested in the newcomers. His face and bare arms, blackened by soot, were streaked with sweat. His muscles strained with his rhythmic hammer-blows. But he glanced up once as Colin disappeared into the hall, and his eyes in the black face flared with a sharp crimson light, like the fine sparks flying up from his glowing fire.

Sparks drifted upward in the column of smoke, most only to flicker out high above. Some few survived to be wafted out the hole in the high-peaked roof of shingles and die in the night sky.

The interior of the hall of Dun Mauran was a most impressive place. The floor area encompassed by the outer wall was over three times that of the modest house of Aislinn's clan in which Colin had recovered from his wound.

The central portion was open, as in that other house, but an outer ring of it was divided by walls of wickerwork, running in to the open hub of the center like wheel spokes, forming separate wedge-shaped compartments.

In its decoration, the hall was far more elaborate, with woven tapestries hung upon the walls and burnished bronze sheathing the thick roof pillars that rose about the central firepit. The hearty fire in the pit warmed the air, and savored it with the rich smells of the beef and lamb cooking on the spits and of the simmering pots of broth and stews hung over the pit on chains. The room's golden light was provided by the flames and by scores of beeswax candles in wall sconces, on tables, and hung in candelabras from above.

The long, low dining tables that surrounded the firepit were laden with platters and bowls of food, goblets of glinting silver and glass, immense flagons of glowing copper. There a hundred or more warriors of the *dun* dined with enthusiasm, swapping tales, jokes, and boasts as they ate and drank. A score of busy servants tended them, cooks in linen aprons and flat white caps serving up the food to boys who rushed it to the seemingly insatiable men.

Colin sat at a table with the chieftain and a dozen of his men, older warriors mostly, their faces weathered and creased by wear, their hard bodies marked by the scars of many past combats.

Colin himself listened intently to the conclusion of a story Laimainech was relating.

". . . and when he pulled the spear out," the chieftain was saying, "the champion looked down at the deadly wound in him and said, 'Ah! So I see those broader points are coming into fashion now!' And then he dropped his length upon the sod!"

All the warriors at the table roared in laughter at this, but none so heartily as Colin.

"A fine tale that is," the young warrior pronounced with enthusiasm. He lifted a flagon with an elegantly stylized lion as its handle and poured a rich golden liquid into his goblet. "And a very fine honey mead," he added, drinking deeply.

"We are very proud of it," Laimainech replied.

"A most beautiful goblet, too," Colin said, examining its delicate glass bowl. He looked around at the matching goblets of the others at his table. "To have so many of something so rare," he remarked, "yours must indeed be as wealthy a dun as the bards have said. Why, even the hidden palaces of the Sidhe couldn't rival all this." He waved about him at the riches, at the bright and glowing textures of the room.

"It may be that even *They* haven't our own fortune," the chieftain said with a knowing grin, his mood grown expansive and exuberant with the drink. "And it's a fortune you might share."

"What do you mean?" asked Colin.

"You say you came to barter for the use of one bull. You might have much more. It's many others who have come to us over the years, as you have. We've shown them how they might share in our prosperity."

"How? By magic?" Colin asked, half humorously.

Laimainech suddenly became quite serious and intent, gripping Colin's arm, leaning close to meet his eyes.

"By faith, young warrior. Faith. Have that, and your prosperity will come."

"I did hear it said that some miracle happens here," Colin admitted. "That you have the powers of the gods aiding you . . ."

"Ah, but not the gods you're thinking of!" the chieftain put in, sitting back and waving an arm dismissingly. "No. Not your Dagdas and Morrigans and Bodb Deargs who care nothing of mortals. Someone more ancient, and much more powerful."

"And who would that be?" asked Colin, clearly most interested now.

"A god over the others," Laimainech told him. "A god of mists who can call up the earth's bounty with a . . ."

"My chieftain," said an interrupting voice, "may I help you?"

Laimainech looked up and Colin turned to see a new man now standing at the table. He was clad in a long, simple robe of snowy white, revealing a slender, narrow-shouldered form. His thin, receding hair was drawn back tightly, emphasizing a broad forehead. Small, bright grey eyes were set closely on either side of an emphatic hook of nose that made the thin-lipped mouth and sharply pointed chin seem very small.

"Dubhdaleithe, you're coming late to our feast," the chieftain observed in a reproving tone.

"I had my duties," was the man's reply, delivered in a

smooth, soft, but succinct voice that held no faintest note of concern for what Laimainech thought.

The warriors at once made a place for him, and he sat down across the table from the chieftain. His gaze traveled over Colin in an aloof but scrutinizing way.

"Just who is our young visitor?"

"My name is Colin MacMathghamhain," that warrior put in. "And who are you?"

"This is my druid," the chieftain explained. "It should be for him to tell you of our gods." He looked to Dubhdaleithe. "But, in your absence, I was taking on your task myself."

"Indeed?" the other responded, lips pursed and an eyebrow arched in obvious disapproval. "And just what have you told him?"

"Only that your faith brings your great prosperity," Colin replied, clearly irritated by the druid's pointedly avoiding speaking directly to him. "Although I must say truly, it's hard for me to believe. In my *dun* we observe all the festival days, of course, and our own druid keeps the proper rituals and reads the signs and keeps us on good terms with the Others. But it seems to me that in most things it's our labor and skills and the worth of our land that helps us."

"And can your skills and labors change the weather?" the chieftain asked in a drink-amplified, boasting voice. "Can it double your breeding, bring defeat on your enemies? Can it keep your people always in good health?"

"Our chieftain exaggerates," the druid quickly put in, shrugging dismissively, his smooth voice like a stream flowing over and submerging these claims. He shot a pointed look at Laimainech. "Especially when he is enjoying too much ale."

"I like this boy," the chieftain said defiantly, obviously roused by this humoring attitude. "He is interested in what we do. We . . ."

"Of course we will be glad to help him," the druid interrupted, "*if* he would benefit."

"I know he would," the chieftain said stubbornly, "and I mean to show him."

"Of course," the druid said soothingly, apparently realizing there was no point in arguing further with the drink-emboldened man. "But tomorrow will be more than time enough. Now it is growing late. Our warriors are retiring . . ." He glanced around the room. The glance seemed like a galvanizing sign. Immediately warriors began to rise and make their way from the hall.

The chieftain glared about, obviously displeased with the abrupt end to the evening. Then his gaze came back to meet the druid's. They locked for a moment, as if in contest, but this time it was Laimainech who surrendered, nodding in agreement and levering himself to his feet.

Though Colin was clearly puzzled by the behavior of his hosts, he hastened to accept the situation.

"Well, I *am* still weary from my long traveling," he told them, rising too.

As he did, his cloak fell back from his shoulder, exposing the torn tunic and the white stripes of the scars for an instant before Colin tugged the garment back into place.

But it was long enough for the healed wounds to be noted by the druid, whose eyes widened in surprise, and then quickly returned to their impassive gaze as Colin glanced up to notice him watching.

"Was there anything else, oh druid?" he asked.

"Only to wish good rest to you, young warrior," the man replied as he, last of all in the room, arose to leave.

A faint rattling from somewhere in the darkness woke Colin.

He sat up on his pallet, looking around. The wedge-shaped compartment in which he sat was cut off from the main room by a light partition of woven wicker. Through it the glow of the burned-down fire beyond could be seen as faint reddish streaks.

He sat listening intently. There were some faint popping sounds from the fire, but otherwise it was silent. And then he heard the soft fluttering of whispering voices.

They were so soft as to be little more than meaningless sounds, but there seemed to be at least two speakers, and occasionally a word could be distinguished drifting by in the flow. His eyes widened as one of those words reached him.

It was the name "Colin."

He threw off his cloak and rose up, peering around the edge of the partition wall. The fire's glow only faintly revealed the floor of the great hall. Above, a dome of deep shadow pressed down upon the fading ruddy cone of the embers' light. Still, the light was enough to illuminate two dark figures carefully pulling back another partition across the room and entering the black space beyond.

His jaw tightened and his eyes narrowed in suspicion. He drew himself up with resolution, then carefully, noiselessly shifted his own partition back and slipped out into the hall.

He approached the opposite compartment stealthily, skirting the firepit widely to stay out of its light. The central area was deserted, the only sign of other life an occasional snort or snore from behind the other compartment walls he passed.

At last he reached the far side of the room. He knelt at a corner of the half-opened partition, listening intently. The voices, though still faint, were mostly intelligible now.

"I knew I was right to be cautious," said the prim, disapproving voice of the druid. "And you, my fine chieftain, blurting out our secrets to that boy . . ."

"We used to welcome such as new disciples," came Laimainech's voice defensively.

"We cannot do that anymore. Things have changed. Don't you understand? We have new enemies now."

"And when have we feared any enemies? Our swords will do for them. You are too cautious."

"I understand what you do not," the druid shot back. "Swords are not enough with people like those. They have peculiar powers I don't fully comprehend. Many thousands all through Ireland have already succumbed."

"But this boy seems all right."

"Does he? What about those scars? They were given him on the road. He is the one who helped them."

"You don't know that," the chieftain argued stubbornly.

"I know the look of those scars. As does the Ladhrach. I

brought him here tonight to prove it to you. Ladhrach, is he the one?"

A new voice spoke, its sound harsh, rasping, sonorous.

"He is."

"You hear?" the druid said with finality. "He did help them. And somehow they healed him. That should not have happened. This is all very dangerous. We must be most wary. He might be one of these new ones, even sent by them to give aid to the others."

"I still say that he is just as he seems," the chieftain said stubbornly. "You worry too much."

"And *you* will listen to me!" came the druid's reply, his smooth tones now sharpening to a sword's edge. "Say no more to him. Sell him his bull, but let him discover nothing. Do it quickly and get him away. Do you understand?"

"Yes," came the sullen but obedient reply.

"And whatever you do," the druid added, "make no more mention of Cromm!"

There was a sound of movement. Colin crouched back into the shadows as the partition was shifted. Two men moved out past it, starting across the room. The druid's white robe was a shimmering rose hue in the firelight. The other figure was nearly invisible in a dark, hooded cloak.

They passed around the fire. As they neared the doors, the dark-cloaked one glanced back. From within the depths of the hood, large eyes glowed.

But it was not human eyes that Colin saw, reflecting the embers' soft red glow. It was the twin flares of bright golden eyes, and they were slitted, like the eyes of a great cat.

8

OCTOBER 28, 8:39 P.M.

The bright gold faded from the glowing points of light, leaving them fainter spots of yellow-orange.

Colin McMahon was staring through a library window at a pair of lighted jack-o'-lanterns in a window of the building at the park's far end.

He shook his head in a groggy way, like a boxer rising from the canvas after a near-knockout blow. His gaze scanned over the park, then around to the room where he sat. His eyes registered the library's stark white interior and the books, so solid, so bright, so modern. He gazed out across the reading space, still as it was before, except that the old man had sunk down with his head forward, dozing over the magazine.

Colin looked down at the book still open before him. His eyes fixing once more on the picture of the fortress, he stared intently at it for a moment, as if challenging it to take on life again. But it remained just a picture in a book.

He sighed and closed the book, pushing it aside to peruse the stack of others before him.

The title of one caught his attention. He pulled it out. It was a large, thick, red-jacketed book that looked quite old. The gold letters on its spine read *THE RELIGION OF THE ANCIENT CELTS.*

He opened it, flipping through to the index at the back. He seemed to be looking for something specific now, seized by a particular interest. He reached the index, turned its pages slowly, then stopped to run his finger down the column of subjects on one page, passing over the *C*'s. Exotic names flowed by beneath his fingertip: Cosmogony, Craniology, Creation, Creiddylad, Creirwy, Cromm Cruaich . . .

He stopped, his fingertip beneath the words, gaze fixed on the name, on those first five letters that seemed to pulse before his eyes, the word echoing in his mind, pounding out as that frenzied crowd in his dream had chanted it in the misty night—Cromm! Cromm! Cromm! Cromm! Cromm!

"Cromm!" he murmured.

A sudden disturbance of the air, like a chill gust keening through the branches of a winter-bared tree, whisked across him. The pages of the book riffled.

He looked up, looked around, as if expecting to see that a window had been opened somewhere.

There was nothing. The library was silent and completely deserted now. Even the old man was gone, having left his open magazine on the table.

Shaking his head, Colin looked back to the book. Finding the entry again, he checked the page numbers listed beside it.

"79, 236" he murmured, leafing back through the book's pages. "79, 236. 79, 236."

He thumbed swiftly and impatiently as he muttered. With his attention focused on the book, he was unaware of something moving through the stacks far across the room.

It was the figure of the old man, moving most cautiously, gliding silently along the aisles on worn sneakers, the hem of his overcoat whispering around his thin legs.

Colin reached page 79. His eyes scanned down the page, stopping as that name all but leaped out at him.

"Cromm Cruaich," it said in italics. He began to read.

"One ancient fertility god was known as *Cenn* or *Cromm Cruaich*," it said. " 'Head or Crooked One of the Mound,' or 'Bloody Head or Crescent.' "

As Colin read on, the figure across the room slipped closer, moving about the periphery within the shelter of the stacks. It paused at intervals to peer out through the rows toward him as if to make certain it was still on course.

"Vallancey, citing a text now lost," the book went on, "says that *Crom-eocha* was a name of Dagda and that a motto at the sacrificial place at Tara read, 'Let the altar ever blaze to Dagda.' "

There was nothing else referring to it on the page. He skimmed farther down, then shook his head.

"236," he murmured, and began flipping pages again.

The figure was only three aisles of books away from him now. It paused once more. The balding white-fringed head capped by its drooping fedora craned around the end of a stack to peek cautiously at Colin's back as he sat bent forward, intent on his search.

Colin reached page 236. This time the reference filled nearly the whole page.

"An ornamented stone statue of *Cromm Cruaich,* the god of

fertility, once stood with the statues of his twelve disciples on the plain of Magh Slecht, in County Cavan. Long since supressed, some of the only remaining fragments of the cult of Cromm are preserved in these verses:

> *He was their god,*
> *The withered CROMM with many mists . . .*
> *To him without glory*
> *They would kill their piteous wretched offspring,*
> *With much wailing and peril,*
> *To pour their blood around Cromm Cruaich.*

As he read the words, images flickered, like the lit windows of a passing train, through Colin's mind. A speeding montage of sharp, terrible images of fog-wreathed monstrosities looming over frenzied, dancing crowds; of a helpless baby struggling and a glinting, blood-sheathed sword starting its swift, terrible descent . . .

There was a faint but audible sound of movement. No more than a whisk, but, in the silent room, enough to bring the sensitized Colin around. Did he glimpse a shadow flitting in the gap between two rows of books?

He got up.

Colin stared intently at the open spaces between the stacks of books. There was no other sign of movement. Still, after a moment's hesitation, he moved forward, drawn by a curiosity that did away with prudence. He reached the first stack, peering through the shelf closest to his eye level. Still nothing more was visible.

He began to edge along parallel to the shelf. As he did, the figure stole along two rows away, moving in the opposite direction.

Colin rounded the end of his stack, moving cautiously. The figure slipped around the opposite end of its own row, coming into the one just beyond Colin's stack. It paused there, then crept slowly, noiselessly forward.

Colin neared the center of his row and stopped. He stood silent for a moment, listening, head cocked back.

The figure stopped also, holding still, waiting.

Colin began to turn slowly, carefully scanning the shelves of books, the openings at each end, and then the shelves behind.

The figure moved forward again, crouching now, shoulders hunched beneath the old coat. It stopped again. The white-haired, behatted head lifted up. Black, liquid eyes peered through the gap between shelves. Just beyond, Colin continued his slow scan of the shelves, visible to the watcher.

An age-spotted hand, skinny fingers knobbed and bent by arthritis, slipped inside the old coat. It grasped something, began to draw it forth. There was a sharp gleam as the object came into the bright fluorescent light.

Colin caught just a sliver of the light in the corner of his eye as it reflected from the white Formica of the shelves. He turned sharply toward the spot, trying to look through the narrow gaps between the ranks of books. Was there the dark shape of a form beyond?

In a swift move, both his hands lifted up a section of books just before his eyes.

A face thrust into the opening from the other side, grown in an instant's metamorphosis from the narrow shoulders of the old man.

It was a creature's face, its long streamlined skull shiny with a covering of slimy yellow flesh, its tiny round mouth pulsing open to show a circle of sharp yellow teeth, its enormous black eyes popping forward on sinewy stalks. And atop the massive dome of the head, an old fedora was perched absurdly.

Colin recoiled in surprise and horror. But as he fell back from the face, a sleek length of gleaming blade crashed through the row of books he held before him at chest height, driving for his heart.

There was an impact. Its violence slammed him back into the shelf behind him.

He gasped, then looked down to see the keen point imbedded in the books he still held up before him; it had stopped just inches from his chest. The black metal blade seemed to sizzle there, as if it was possessed of a great heat. Whiskers of smoke rose from the skewered books.

He released the books and slipped away, turning to run down the row. There was a low snarl of anger from beyond the stack. The blade withdrew at once, pushing the books off as it slipped back through the shelf. Then the monstrous figure was moving after him.

Colin reached the end of the aisle, charging out across the central open space. He glanced back to see a grotesque hunched form beginning to emerge from between two stacks, and the glinting of the long blade.

He didn't look back again as he dodged through the maze of reading tables at his best speed, finally reaching the stairway, vaulting down the wide stairs three at a time.

The female librarian behind the main floor desk looked up in surprise as he clattered down, coat flying, and rushed up to her.

"Please!" she said indignantly. "This is a library. There is no need for such . . ."

"Something's up there!" he gasped out. "Something . . . some monster! It tried to kill me!"

She looked at this panting wild-eyed man before her with that stony, skeptical gaze of one who has learned to deal with many peculiar types in a downtown library late at night.

"A monster, in the stacks?" she said calmly. "And it tried to kill you."

"It's after me now!" he said insistently. "Please! Call the police or . . ."

"Is that your monster?" she asked, nodding toward the stairs.

He turned to look.

The old man in the fedora—a frail, bent figure who moved with the slow stiffness of the acutely arthritic—was working his way down the stairs.

Colin looked to the librarian. The librarian looked at him, lips pursed, one eyebrow lifted.

He looked back to the old man who, noting his gaze, paused on the stairs, doffed his hat, and smiled.

The teeth in that smile were small and yellow, and very finely pointed.

Colin turned and rushed away across the library's open foyer, slamming through one of the turnstiles and out the door, leaving the librarian looking after him, shaking her head, and the old man still smiling.

He came out of the library, jay-running across the street to reach the park. He took a concrete flight of stairs that led downward to end at the bank of a narrow stream, which meandered away along the center of the long greenspace.

Here a bricked path began, following closely along the stone-lined bank of the stream, brightly illuminated by streetlights on high poles.

He slowed a bit, striding briskly along the path. It led through a landscaped area of smooth grass and bushes and occasional trees that sloped up from the stream bank on his left. The nearly bared trees had become elaborate traceries, their interlacing branches lit in golden outline by the lights above, showing starkly, sharply against a deep black sky.

Beyond them, the city buildings loomed higher, some only massive rectangles of shadow blocking out the stars, some banded by the single floors lit for cleaning crews or speckled with the occasional lighted window of a late worker.

There seemed to be no one else abroad in the park. Colin checked his watch. It showed 8:58. Early yet, but dark enough and chill enough at this time of year to discourage casual strollers.

He pulled his coat closer around him and walked along the lapping water.

The path gave way suddenly to a boardwalk, a docklike structure of planks and pilings. A sign proclaimed that paddle boats were for rent there, but the boats, like the strollers, had vanished with the summer.

His footsteps now echoed hollowly as he strode along.

He was nearly across the boardwalk when, abruptly, the sound of other echoing steps began behind him, moving closer rapidly.

His instant reaction was to stretch into a run himself, taking a few strides forward before glancing back.

A woman jogger in fluorescent purple sweats bounded past, earphones on her head, oblivious to him; she went on to disappear around a bend, long pony-tail bobbing.

He exhaled deeply in a relieved way and slowed to a brisk walk again, coming off the boardwalk and back onto the brick path. He passed a stone-lined alcove cut back into the slope, containing water fountains and a few benches. It was deeply shadowed there, and as he swept past he didn't notice a lean, bearded figure clad in a dark coat and stocking hat, huddled on one of the benches.

But as he passed, the figure rose to follow, moving with amazing noiselessness on heavily booted feet, almost gliding along. It stayed well behind him. One hand pulled out from the pocket of the coat to hang swinging at its side. A long, broad hand, with broken, dirty fingernails.

But it was so for only a moment.

The hand began to change, stretching out like something made of soft rubber, grotesquely shifting as if the bones within it rearranged themselves, grew, altered their shape. And it became in those few seconds something not of animal nor of man, but something bony-fingered and clawed, its yellow-green scales glistening in the light.

Then, as if triggered by Colin's passing, faint grey-white wisps began to lift from the surface of the stream. Though at first they were like splayed feathers of steam curling up from a boiling pot, rapidly they thickened, rising and joining, forming with incredible speed into a single cloud that billowed upward.

He continued, unaware of its rising, until the cock's comb of its peak fluttered into the glow of a light right overhead.

The flicker of shadow above drew his gaze up. He saw the curved plume of white arching over him and moving speedily forward. He looked around to see the great body of the suddenly risen fog, like a giant bird with outspread wings, sweeping toward him off the surface of the stream.

"What the hell?" he said, stopping in astonishment as the massive cloud engulfed him.

In a moment the area around him was shrouded by the fog, so thick that even the powerful streetlights were reduced to nothing more than glowing spheres of blue-white high above. The park had suddenly become a shadowland, its trees and bushes ominous forms of a deeper black. The stream so close beside him was nearly invisible through the billowing grey-white. The path had become only a faint ribbon vanishing a few yards away in either direction.

He heard footsteps again and peered back the way he had come, into the fog. A figure moved into view from the folds of thick cloud. It could barely be seen, a black outline with no details or features. But still there was something most definitely odd about the head, the body. And the eyes. A faint but definite light glowed there, as of reflected light, except for the fact that it was yellow-green.

Colin turned and trotted on. He heard the faint slapping of footsteps behind him now as the follower took up a matching pace.

Ahead, the faintly seen pathway turned sharply, twisting around and up toward the end of a footbridge: a slender framework of green-painted iron beams arching across the stream to vanish into the fog.

He started up the path toward it, then stopped.

Another form loomed there, waiting at the bridge's end. Though it was only a featureless shadow in the fog, he could see it moving as he stopped and leaned over the bridge rail to peer down. And another pair of eyes, gleaming silver sparks in the coiling white, fixed right on him.

He turned away from the path and ducked beneath the bridge, crossing the grass and hopping across the boulders at the water's edge, coming out beyond and back onto the pathway again. This time when he set out it was at a full run.

He sped ahead through the fog, not looking back, straining for greater speed with his legs flashing out and his coat flying behind. He stayed on the path, precarious though it was in this low visibility.

The ribbon of red brick seemed to stretch out interminably into the void of white. He began to get winded, his breathing coming loudly within the silent canopy of fog. Still he plunged on.

The stream began to widen, becoming a lagoon at its lower end. The pathway continued to follow the bank, turning in a wide curve to the right. He stayed on it, keeping up his speed, glancing back once to see nothing behind him. He smiled with satisfaction through strain-gritted teeth.

He ran on, now like a tightrope-walker treading the narrow path between the rock-lined bank and a bush-covered slope that rose steeply on his left. Ahead, the vast white square of a building showed faintly beyond the obscuring scrim of fog. This building marked the end of the park, a way out of the fog-filled valley and back up to the city streets.

And he was nearly there.

Something launched itself from the bushes above to dive fully upon him, and he crashed down, rolling sideways with it.

He got a quick impression of the thing he struggled with. It was massive, Great Dane-like, but the muscled body seemed more sleek, more sinewy; the face pressing down toward him as he gripped its throat seemed longer, more streamlined than that of a Great Dane, and the gaping, slavering jaws stretching for his throat seemed much, much larger.

The creature tried to snap at him, its clawed feet tearing at his chest and stomach as he fought to hold it away. Colin rolled over again, trying to smash its body down hard against the ground. It yowled shrilly but kept at him, forcing him back onto his back. Locked together in their struggle, they rolled over again, onto the rocks at the stream's edge. Here the retaining wall dropped away five feet to the water.

He pulled one of his legs up and managed to wedge it under the struggling thing's hard belly. In a great heave he shoved outward, grunting with the effort, while at the same moment releasing the creature's neck. His force was enough to launch it outward over the edge of the retaining wall, and it crashed down into the water.

Gasping for breath, Colin clambered to his feet. The thing was thrashing madly in water that seemed to boil furiously around it, creating a froth that all but hid it.

He stood for a moment, staring in amazement; then he caught a movement from behind and swung around. Two shadowy figures were coming into view there, moving toward him. The fight had taken only seconds, but the delay had allowed his followers to close in on him.

He was off again. His breath came in ragged gasps now, but he kept running at full tilt around the lagoon.

Beyond it, at the base of the white building, was a large playground with slides and swings, set in a massive sandbox bounded by concrete walls. A vast canopy of yellow canvas propped on steel tent poles sheltered it. In the fog this canopy was like an immense, ghostly bird hovering above the playground.

Colin slogged through the sandbox to its far side. There stairs led upward from the lagoon to the level of one of the streets bounding the park.

He used the stair-rail to haul himself up at his best speed, tearing free of the clinging fabric of the fog as he reached the top.

He stopped there, hanging onto the stone wall that rimmed the park, panting for breath as he looked around him in surprise.

For from here he could see that the strange fog filled only the low ground right along the stream, as if the weight of its dense clouds kept it from rising higher. Here, above the valley, the street and the city buildings beyond it were completely clear.

After only a few relieving breaths, he forced himself on again, charging directly across the nearly trafficless street and up the first sidestreet, heading back toward the renovated old market area.

There were few cars on the street he traveled, no pedestrians out, the few shops closed. He pressed on, moving into the heart of the commercial section.

He passed the shiny curves of the diner and ran on past other shops, finally rounding a corner to one of the area's main streets. There were more cars here, teenagers and a few older patrons braving the crisp night air to cruise afoot. A small band of girls hung out before a pizza place, smoking and trying to look at least eighteen. Other restaurants' glowing windows showcased dining patrons. The spicy smell of spaghetti and the thumping backbeat of music filled the night.

Reassured by these signs of normal life, Colin slowed down somewhat, but still walked briskly and looked behind him often. The sound of the music grew louder, a saxophone's distinctive wail clear now above the drums and wanging electrical instruments. He neared the middle of the block and stopped there, looking up.

He stood before a narrow three-story building of age-darkened brick. Unlike the other structures in the rehabilitated area, it had been left—seemingly as a deliberate show of independence—just as the wear of years had marked it. Above a large window made opaque by grime, a flamboyantly hand-lettered sign read TWELFTH STREET TAVERN. Above that, a weathered banner proclaimed "It's All in the Music!"

He pulled open a windowless steel door and passed into a tiny vestibule where a couple was jammed into a corner between cigarette machine and pay-phone, necking with an exhibitionistic flair.

He got past them with a bit of squeezing, opening an inner door. A wave of the music surged out upon him as if to drive him back, but he braved the assault, pressing forward into the dark room beyond.

As he did, four men rounded the corner onto the street outside.

The two officers in a cruising patrol car at the intersection took note of them. The four formed an oddly mixed bag of derelicts: one tall and rail-thin; another broad and barrel-chested; a third squat and hunch-shouldered; a fourth frail, old, and stiff. The officers watched them as they stopped on the corner, huddled together a moment in talk, and then split up, each heading in a different direction from the intersection.

"Choosing their territories for the nightly panhandling rounds," commented the older policeman behind the wheel.

"Shall we roust them, sergeant?" his younger partner asked with a touch of eagerness.

"What for? A little begging?" the other said derisively. "Naw. Let the poor bastards alone. I've seen them around here before. They're harmless."

CROMM

9

The interior of the saloon Colin entered was as unabashedly free of renovations as its outside. Yet it had maintained a kind of gritty chic of its very own.

A bar ran two thirds of the way down one wall of the long, narrow, and high-ceilinged room. At the back a tiny platform barely held the five musicians of the group, now animatedly involved in wailing out a hot fusion number.

The space left was jammed with a motley collection of tables and chairs, every one now occupied by enthusiastically drinking and smoking patrons. The atmosphere—in a modern, anti-smoking age—was another relic of earlier days; an acridly reeking blue-white haze rivaled the fog that Colin had just escaped.

Most of the light spilled out from a few spotlights on the band and a string of once-white Christmas bulbs draped around the bar's back mirror. This illumination was rather dubiously enhanced by some decorations of the season: a trio of glowing plastic jack-o'-lanterns on the shelves behind the bar, a fluorescent green skeleton suspended by the door, and a row of luminous grinning skulls around the little stage.

Combined with the haze of smoke, the weak lighting made visibility very poor. The individual characteristics of the patrons were made largely indistinguishable, beyond the fact that they were mostly young adults, casually dressed, and of at least two sexes.

Colin stood for a moment just within the door, peering through the smokescreen, trying to scan the faces of those at the nearby tables. Then he began to edge, force, maneuver, and squeak his way through the densely packed company toward the back, looking intently about him as he went.

Finally he managed to reach the rear section of the room. Here, beyond the end of the bar, there was a bit more floor room right before the tiny stage. But as elsewhere in the tavern, every possible inch of this space was taken up with tables encircled by seated patrons, while yet more people stood, lining the walls.

In this area, the real music-lovers had gathered more to listen than to drink, and the noise of the crowd was much reduced. The light close to the stage was better too, and the faces of the patrons more easily discernible. It took Colin only one sweep of the tables to spot Tom and Annie, his companions of earlier that evening. They were packed in at a table near the wall with a third person, Tom listening raptly to the music, Annie looking about somewhat distractedly.

He clambered through the other tables, finding his way toward them. As he approached he was spotted by the girl, who smiled with delight.

"Colin!" she cried as he reached the table. She slugged Tom on the arm to get his attention, shouting in his ear, "Tom! Colin's here!"

This was enough to break the music's spell, and Tom, also smiling, looked around toward his friend.

"So, you came after . . ." he began heartily; then his look grew astonished. "What the hell happened to you?"

Colin was somewhat the worse for his recent wear, still panting from exertion, clothes askew and dirty, coat ripped, and hair disheveled.

"I . . . I need help," he gasped out.

"Poor boy," Annie said sympathetically. "And TLC too, it looks like."

She leaned toward the man who sat at her other hand: a very large, very square, very jocky type with no neck and tightly curled blond hair. He sat twisted around in his chair to watch the band and hadn't taken note of Colin's arrival. Annie put a hand out to stroke his. His bulldozer-jawed head swiveled around to her at once, and she smiled a most provocative smile.

"Lester, would you please get me some more beer?" she asked.

The man looked at the smile, then nodded enthusiastically, leaped to his feet, and was off into the crowd, battling through toward the bar as if shouldering his way through a weak defensive line.

"Sit down," Annie told Colin, waving to the empty chair.

He plopped down into it, sagging back, exhaling a great breath of relief.

"God, I didn't know I was in such lousy shape," he said.

"What's wrong?" Tom asked, speaking loudly to be heard over the music.

"I got jumped down at the park," Colin answered, nearly shouting too. "And somebody's chasing me, I think." He glanced through the crowd in the direction of the front door, but it was completely blocked from his view.

"Jumped?" said the girl. "By who?"

"By these . . . guys, I think."

"Guys?" said Tom.

"Winos," Colin amplified. "At least, they looked like winos. Old derelicts. And . . . and a . . . a dog, or something . . . something hairless."

"Jesus, Colin, are you drunk or dreaming?" Tom said, clearly skeptical. "Winos and a hairless dog? Give me a break!"

"Does it look like I'm dreaming it?" the other countered. "Check my coat!"

He hauled one side of it up into view. The heavy canvas of the trenchcoat was badly torn, two of its buttons ripped away.

"Just relax," Tom said, passing his half-filled mug across. "Here, drink my beer. So, maybe it *was* a dog. There are always stray mutts wandering around the park."

"No! You've got to listen!" Colin said with intensity, pushing the mug back and leaning forward. Tom and Annie exchanged questioning looks, then shrugged and leaned forward too.

"I was at the library," Colin began.

"Library?" the girl interrupted. "I thought you went home. Why'd you go there?"

"Research. Never mind. Its not important now. I was there, and there was this old man . . ."

As he related his tale, their three heads remaining bent close together over the table, the door of the tavern opened and a figure came through.

It was a tall, lean man in black pea coat and stocking cap, his long face largely masked by a bushy grey beard and bristling mustaches. He moved through the crowd slowly, his eyes glistening sharply in the darkness as they scanned the faces intently.

Some of the patrons gave him odd looks in return, or—catching the scent of him—tried to move away. One young woman met the bright gaze directly at close range; she gasped and sat back sharply in her chair as if an electric charge had jolted her.

The eyes she'd met were a speckled yellow-green. And they were slitted like the eyes of a reptile.

The man kept moving on, along the bar. He brushed past the beefy form of Lester who stood waiting there. The young hulk glanced around irritably, then turned back to bang on the bar with a sledge-hammer fist.

"Come on! Where's my beer?" he demanded.

The bartender slammed two full pitchers down before him.

At the rear of the tavern, Colin was reaching the end of his tale.

". . . so I came up from the playground into the street, and there was none of that damn fog anywhere else," he was saying. "I took off running, and didn't stop till I got here." He reached over the table, grasping Tom's mug. "And that is it!" he finished, lifting the mug and taking a long drink.

The other two exchanged glances again. Their looks now held more disbelief then they had before.

"This hairless dog and the thing in the library are just too goddamn weird, Colin," Tom said at last. "Even this bit with the winos. I mean, I know there are a lot of them hanging around the market and the mall, but they're not violent guys. Hell, they can barely walk most of the time."

"I don't know," put in the girl. "I heard that somebody found one of them dead today. Stabbed right through the heart, all his clothes gone, stuffed up into an old ventilator. Maybe these guys did it."

Colin looked at her searchingly.

"I can't tell if you're serious or making fun."

The figure in the pea coat was still moving toward the back, forcing its way through the crowd. One man resented the pushing and pushed back, but a snarl and a flash of bared teeth and a piercing glare from the strange eyes was enough to send him retreating in alarm. The figure went on.

"It is nearly Halloween," Annie pointed out to Colin. "This stuff sounds like some kind of gag, you know? Costumes and spooky masks . . ."

"That thing was no mask, Annie," Colin said with certainty. "Steven Spielberg couldn't do anything this real. And that dog-thing wasn't playing any trick."

"Look, Colin," Tom said, "are you really sure this wasn't another dream? You said you were going home to sleep. Maybe you did. Maybe this didn't happen."

"Gee thanks, Tom," Colin said sourly. "Now you think I can't tell dream from real? No!" He banged the mug emphatically on the table. "I know this was real. And I'm sure it's all connected somehow. The dreams. That white-haired guy. These winos. Ireland . . ."

"Ireland?" Tom said in exasperation. "White-haired guy? Colin, are you listening to yourself? It sounds like gibberish. Now I know we'd better get you home."

The figure reached the rear section of the bar. It stopped there, its gaze panning slowly over the crowd.

"Don't treat me like I'm crazy," Colin said angrily. "I'm not. And I'm not going to let you . . ."

Across Tom's shoulder, his gaze fell upon the tall, standing figure. He stared in dismay.

"I think that's one of them!" he said in a tight voice.

"What?" said Tom, craning around to follow his friend's gaze.

The figure's head turned toward him. The slitted eyes met Colin's. They held there.

"He sees me!" said Colin in rising alarm, getting to his feet.

"Colin?" Annie said in confusion, looking up to him.

The being's mouth lifted in a triumphant smile. A hand began to pull out of the pocket of the coat. The hand was not a human one.

A massive form collided with the lean figure, tried to push by. But the one in the pea coat didn't budge. Its glinting gaze swiveled around toward the source of interference.

"Hey, could you move it, buddy?" said the big one called Lester. He grasped a full, slopping pitcher in each hand. "I've gotta get through."

The other still didn't move.

Lester drew himself up, his hulking form looking all the more massive beside the lean figure.

"Hey, toothpick," the young man contemptuously barked, "I said move it before I snap you in half!"

He started forward to shoulder the other aside.

With a guttural roar the lean one wheeled about. And in that move, its figure was no longer a man's.

In an instant it had swelled outward, upward, bursting from the body of the derelict. The clothes and the human form seemed to shred away as the thing transformed into something sleek, scaled, and muscular, thrusting forward a reptilian face with long, gaping jaws, and balancing a lithe body with a whipping tail.

A hand that was now long, knobbed, and taloned shot forward into the astonished Lester's chest. He was knocked back as if a charging lineman had hurtled into him. The beer in his two pitchers sprayed up and out as he slammed down onto a table surrounded by patrons, bringing it and them crashing to the floor in a tangle of splintered furniture, broken glass, and flailing limbs.

In seconds the other patrons close around the creature were on their feet, their cries of terror sounding through the room. Colin's friends rose too, craning to see the cause of the commotion, but their view was blocked by the wall of people scrambling to move away from the monstrous thing that had appeared from nowhere in their midst.

"What the hell is going on?" cried Tom.

But Colin, who had witnessed the transformation, stood speechless, frozen with his shock.

Ripples of panic were now racing outward in all directions through the crowd, infecting those who could not see the cause of the alarm. Complete pandemonium was rapidly setting in.

Two of the tavern's bouncers, burly and serious men with heavy truncheons, moved through the chaos toward its source. One pushed into the now cleared space around the creature to confront it.

"Look here, you . . ." he began authoritatively. Then his gaze registered what he was facing, and his eyes widened in terror.

The thing charged upon him. He tried to raise the truncheon in defense, but moved too late to block the swipe of a muscled arm that sent him flying sideways into the crowd. The second bouncer, who had been moving up purposefully behind, abruptly changed his mind, retreating into the mass of fear-crazed patrons pushing, clambering, clawing their way back from the creature.

But it had no interest in any of them. It wheeled toward the rear of the tavern again, massive tail whipping the air, yellow-green eyes searching out the one it hunted.

Across the milling heads Colin glimpsed the scaled peak of the thing's skull as it began moving toward him.

"It's coming this way!" he cried, brought back to life by the realization.

"What's coming?" said Tom. He and Annie, totally bewildered by this sudden panic, were still trying to peer through the crowd surging around them.

"That!" Colin shouted, pointing.

As the thing stalked toward them, the patrons between made haste to scramble out of its way. The intervening crowd grew rapidly thin. And suddenly both of Colin's friends could see what approached. Now *they* froze, staring.

"It wants *me*!" Colin shouted at them. "Get away from me!" He shoved at both of them. "Quick, go toward the front! I'll lead it the other way!"

And with that he turned from them, heading for the back wall of the tavern.

The patrons at the front of the tavern, having realized that the creature was moving rearward, were now making for the door. Those trapped at the back stood plastered against the walls, huddled in groups, or cowered beneath the tables.

It strode through them without regard, moving single-mindedly toward where it had last seen Colin. But with the way now cleared, it stopped, realizing he was no longer there. Its gaze swung around over the terror-stricken patrons, finally falling upon the back of the young man as he made his way through the obstacle course of emptied tables and chairs toward the stage.

With a roar of triumph that shook the room, it leapt forward in pursuit, shoving aside furniture as it moved, its tail sweeping over tables and smashing chairs as it passed.

But its momentary delay had given Colin time to reach the little stage. The hapless musicians, having no chance to escape, were jammed together back in a corner, holding up guitars, saxophone, and drumsticks in useless defense. He climbed onto the stage, rolled across and jumped down behind it. There was a narrow doorway here, and he went through, slamming its wooden door behind him as his pursuer reached the stage.

Colin found himself in a back storage room, boxes and kegs stacked high on either side. He moved ahead, reaching a rear service door of steel. It was locked. He fumbled for the knob of its dead-bolt.

In the room behind, the creature roared again, this time in rage. It grasped the end of the obstructing stage and heaved upward. The whole platform lifted, flying up and back, dumping musicians and instruments in a heap behind it as it rose to smash into the wall, burying them in its wreckage.

At the front of the tavern, those patrons not trampled on the ground or already outside were battling to push through the single door. The sound of the tremendous crash behind them produced increased cries of terror, and they looked back as if expecting to find the thing upon them.

Annie and Tom, at the rear of the crowd, glanced back across the wasteland of tables to see the creature stepping up to the door where Colin had disappeared.

"He did it!" Annie cried. "He led it away from us."

"Never mind!" Tom said, pushing her forward. "Just worry about getting out!"

"But it will kill him!" she protested.

"We'll tell the police when we can!" he said, his voice shrill with fear. "Let's just get out!"

In the storeroom, Colin still struggled desperately with the lock. Another crash sounded behind him. He looked around to see the storeroom's door torn away, the creature standing in the light from the room beyond, blocking out most of it.

He twisted at the lock with greater force, face glistening with sweat.

The thing's slitted eyes, shining intensely with a yellow-green light, fixed on him. It stalked slowly forward on muscled legs that shook the old plank floor each time a massive, taloned foot thudded down. The bony-fingered hands flexed, ready to grasp. The long jaws, lined with spike-like teeth, came open, spreading wide, preparing to snap. Saliva trickled from them, dripping out in strands between the lower teeth.

Colin glanced back once again to see it closing. He could smell the foul breath, see the gleaming talons on the long hand that reached out toward him.

The knob turned, the dead-bolt clicking free.

He yanked the door open and dived through, letting its spring pull it closed as the thing leaped forward.

He stumbled into the alley behind the bar as there came the explosive sound of the thing colliding with the door. He started off at a run, not looking back as the booming sound of rhythmic hammering started behind him and the thick metal door began to bow outward.

He was in a narrow, dark, and refuse-littered alley. He ran along it at a breakneck pace, clearly intent only on putting distance between himself and the tavern. Turning at the first crossing, he ran up the street for a block and plunged into another alley, out of sight of any possible pursuers.

The second long alleyway brought him to another street. He came out into it cautiously, looking around.

He had left the renovated area. What he had entered was obviously in the process of a redevelopment of its own. Five-

story warehouses rose up around him, black and abandoned
hulks, some already in the process of being demolished. The
street was dimly lit by a single working streetlight, blocked by
barricades and equipment, cluttered with debris, empty of life
—except for him. The only sounds were his own rasping breath
and the distant wail of a siren, growing swiftly louder.

He moved along, picking his way through piles of brick and
wood and twisted plumbing. He passed a building half fallen,
one wall a crumbled slope of rubble. An intersection was visible
beyond the equipment parked ahead, and there were more
lights. He started toward them at a quicker pace.

Then he stopped, staring ahead.

From behind the equipment, a thick grey-white cloud billowed up and rolled forward in a wave over the machines,
blocking out his view of them, filling the street before him like
a solid wall.

Two figures moved out from it. One was a stranger: a barrel-
chested, lank-haired man in a quilted jacket. The other was his
arthritic old man from the library. But there was no hint of
stiffness about his movements now. He and his companion
strode purposely forward. And as they did, their forms began to
change.

The transformations were swift but grotesque, the bodies
turning elastic, stretching, distorting, their humanness fading
away. The result was something even more horrible than their
changing had been.

The bigger man stayed the most manlike, retaining the
wino's clothes. But he was now a being with a massive head
like a boar, yellow tusks curling up to points beneath each tiny
eye. The old man had become a creature with a head more
sluglike than human, its liquid black eyes protruding on stalks
at either side of its smooth, slimy head, its pulsing mouth
rimmed with teeth. It arms—grown long and flexible—protruded from the sleeves of the worn old coat; and through the
gap in the coat's front, burst open by the thing's expansion, a
strange, rounded chest showed, smooth and glowing like black
metal armor.

Colin was for a moment held in awful thrall by the transformation. Then his sense of jeopardy galvanized him once again. He turned to run.

Another cloud of the sinister fog was pouring out from the alleyway he had just left, flowing across the street, filling it to form a blockade there too.

Another figure moved from it into view. It was his reptile acquaintance from the tavern.

He cast desperately around him for a place to run. The half-ruined building offered his only avenue.

He started to clamber up the steep slope of fallen bricks. But something leaped down from above, landing just before him.

He faced the creature that had attacked him in the park, now clearly recognizable as other than a dog. In shape it was more bull-like, with immense shoulders and chest. Its stocky, powerful legs did bow like a bulldog's, and the head and feet were vaguely canine; but its hide was hairless, wrinkled like an elephant's, and short thick horns curled back from its forehead. Its wide mouth drew upward in what seemed a ghastly smile, baring a carnivore's tearing fangs.

He backed away, turned and ran. But there was nowhere to go. With the creatures on three sides, his only avenue of flight was across the street. But here rose the wall of a warehouse that was still intact, its first-floor windows six feet above his head, its smooth block exterior offering no way to climb.

He turned, at bay, to see the creatures moving in on him. The doglike beast and reptile were unarmed, their teeth and claws the only weapons they would need. The thing that had been an old man grasped in froglike hands the gleaming silver sword that had nearly impaled Colin in the library. The boar-headed one held a double-bladed axe in one broad hand. Colin saw that his other arm was handless, but fitted with a single curving talon of black metal.

As the collection of nightmares drew near, he moved backward, eyes searching for an opening. His foot kicked something that clanged hollowly and he looked down to see a four-foot length of pipe. He snatched it up as he continued to move back, finally colliding with the wall.

A pile of rubble and twisted metal was close beside him.

Atop it lay the wrought-iron grating that had once shielded a window. He yanked it free of the tangle.

With pipe in right hand and grating held up in left, he crouched, striking a defensive stance. The beings closed in about him.

The slug-faced one drove in, thrusting at him with its sword. He parried the weapon with his pipe, knocking it away. The boar-head struck out with the metal claw. Colin lifted the grate, catching the hook, twisting it away, then kicking out into the being's groin. It grunted and staggered back. The dog dove in, trying to get under the grating and snap at his calf. It was knocked sideways by a blow of the pipe against its jaw.

Colin fought valiantly as they came against him, fending them off with the grate, parrying with the pipe, even striking back, moving with great speed and skill to keep them all at bay. After a first foray, the beings all pulled back, more leery now, looking for openings.

He glared around at them defiantly. Then an expression of surprise came into his face and he looked at the pipe and grate in his hands.

"How the hell am I doing this?" he muttered.

But he had no more time to consider it. They came in again. Again he battled, vigorously and successfully at first, but soon with more effort as the exertion began to wear him down.

Finally slug-face was able to lunge in, knocking his pipe aside with its sword. Boar-head butted against his grate-shield, smashing him back. Colin slammed into the wall, breath knocked from him in a gasp, and hung there, arms dropping to his sides.

The doglike creature crouched to spring at his now defense-less throat.

CROMM

10

A ball of blue-white light burst against the animal, the explosion sending crackling tendrils of lightning across it, enwrapping it in a sizzling net of energy.

The creature howled, held rigid in the web, eyes and teeth flaring with the blue glow, muscles twitching. Then the light flickered out. The creature, its hide scorched from the singeing power, turned on its heels and ran from the street, baying out its pain.

The slug-headed creature that had once been the old man watched it run yelping away, the protruding eyes wide in surprise. Then the slug-head gurgled in rage and turned back to Colin, lifting its sword to cut at him.

A second ball of light flared suddenly at the sword's tip, running down the blade in rivulets of light, twining about the arm, encoiling it in the intense brightness.

The being shrieked in pain as it was jerked violently around by the power of the stroke. It dropped the sword and fell to one knee. The other two creatures stepped back, shielding their eyes.

Colin, at first staring in amazement, now acted. Seizing the chance, he leapt forward with a renewed energy. He struck out at the lizardlike creature, swinging the length of pipe against its scaled head with all his power. The pipe struck with a force that should have shattered the skull, though it only slammed the head over at a right angle on the long neck.

Colin swung back again, the pipe knocking the head over the other way. But the thing only snarled at the massive blows, recovering to lunge at him, its slavering jaws opening wide.

A third ball of energy exploded within the yawning mouth, enwrapping the head with sizzling light. The creature screeched in pain, lifting its clawed hands toward its stricken eyes. Then, as the light crackled out, it turned and ran, clearly having had enough. The boar-headed one turned also and followed it away.

But now the slug-faced creature, seemingly the most persistent of the lot, took up its sword and rose to challenge Colin again.

Colin gave it no chance to attack, charging upon it as it came upright. He thrust the pipe forward at its chest. The pipe struck squarely, the end ramming into the round, armor-like surface. It cracked through with a sound like that of an immense beetle being crushed underfoot. It sank deep into a soft matter within the protecting shell.

The creature staggered back, its movement jerking the pipe from Colin's hands. It stood there a moment, head hanging, body bent forward. The pipe rose and fell with its labored breathing. A green, viscous liquid pulsed out around the puncture, smoking as it touched the air.

Then the creature raised its head and looked at Colin. The awful sucking mouth opened and closed. The bulbous black eyes fixed on him with a gleam of hate. As Colin watched in amazement, a long, knobbed hand lifted. Its thin, spatulate fingers wrapped about the pipe and, in a single yank, pulled it free.

The being rose upright suddenly, heaving the length of pipe at Colin. He managed to duck aside as it flew by, raising the iron grate to ward off a new attack.

But the slug-faced thing had apparently also had enough of this fight. After heaving the pipe, it turned and scuttled away, disappearing into the curtain of fog at one end of the street.

Colin looked after it, then glanced around at the pipe lying nearby. Its end smoked as if the green ooze coating it was an acid dissolving the thick metal.

He looked back to the wall of fog where the thing had vanished. The grey-white billows were shredding, drifting away, dissipating as quickly as they'd formed.

"That was very close," said a voice behind him.

Startled, he turned, crouching defensively, bringing up the twisted grate again.

The fog there had all but vanished too. Beneath the single streetlight, the figure of a man was visible. The light glowed in his distinctive mane of silver hair.

"Very unsporting of them," the cultured, amazingly unruffled voice went on. "Four against one."

"Was that you doing that?" Colin asked, gesturing around him. "That . . . that . . ."

"That little lightning thing?" the man supplied, moving forward, gesturing with a swirl of his silver-headed cane. "Yes, it was."

"How?"

The man smiled in amusement.

"I believe now the expression is, 'It's done with mirrors.' " He shrugged in a dismissing way. "Actually, it's most spectacular, but not very deadly. It was surprise mostly that frightened them away. That, along with your own skill." He pointed the tip of the cane at the metal grate. "You were very good."

Colin looked at the grate, and then drew upright, lowering it. An expression of wonder came into his face again.

"I can't believe it myself. I mean, how did I do that? I've never even been in a fistfight before. And those things . . ."

"Amazing what skills one remembers. Once learned, they're never forgotten."

"I never knew them! I mean, I've seen all the swashbuckler movies, but I'm no Errol Flynn!"

"You might be surprised," the man said, reaching the younger one's side. "But we've no time to discuss it here. When they recover, they will certainly be back. We must move quickly."

He led the way off the street, back into the alley.

"They've lost their chance of surprise," the man went on as they made their way along, "and, thanks to me, they believe you have the power to defend yourself. Still, they'd be more than a match for us both, if they would stand and fight together. It's our good fortune that their power is limited here, so far from the source, *and* that most of them are such cowards, as you know."

"I know?"

"Well, you will," the man said, then frowned in irritation. "I'm sorry. I shouldn't have said that."

They reached the alley's other end. Here they stopped, peering cautiously from its mouth. Though they had left the abandoned area, this section of street was just as deserted. It was quiet except for the sound of several sirens some blocks away.

"That'll be your . . . *'police'* is it? . . . seeing to the trouble at that drinking place," the man told Colin. "All this activity you've stirred up will make those creatures cautious too. That's also to our favor. But you'll still have precious little time to act."

"Act how?" Colin asked. "Go to the police?"

"No!" the man said with sudden intensity, turning to him. "That's really the most foolish thing that you could do. They'll never believe you, first of all. It could be they'd just lock you up somewhere, and that *would* mean the end. Even if they *did* believe you, they couldn't protect you from these things. You'd only get a great number of people killed, as you possibly did some of those poor devils in that tavern."

"I did?" Colin said in consternation.

"Never mind that," the man said soothingly. "It wasn't your fault. You didn't know then. But," he added more forcefully, "now you *do* know. And you must think carefully about your every move. You can't hang about here any longer. You have to go!"

"Go?"

The man moved closer. His voice was very deliberate. "Now listen to me, my young friend: you are in very great danger. I didn't know they'd find you here so easily. At least my warnings have saved you this far, but only just."

"They? Who the hell are *they*?"

"I . . ." the man began, then hesitated, his expression one of frustration. ". . . I'm sorry. I simply can't tell you." He shook his head. "It really is too bad. I had hoped the awakening process might go a bit more slowly, more naturally. Now . . . well, there's nothing else you can do but to go back."

"Back?"

"To Ireland."

"Ireland? I've never been there!"

"Sorry," the man said brusquely. "I only meant that you must go now. You've no other choice. Look, you've had the dreams, you've seen the books, and you've seen those dreadful things. You must find the answer, and I'm afraid that nothing short of going there can recall it for you in time. It's risky, and it'll be quite a shock—but there it is."

"There *what* is?"

"Sorry again. I can't tell you that either. It should be enough to know that those things out there will eventually and without a doubt hunt you down and kill you, and quite likely many others as well, and that there's not a power on earth that can stop them, except possibly for you."

"Me? How?"

The man shook his head. "I've already told you more than I should have," he said firmly.

"I just don't see how going to Ireland's going to help me."

"Because its source is there," the man said impatiently. "The awful, twisted soul of it all is there. Don't be so bloody dense, man. You must at least know *that* by now!"

Colin considered, and an awful image, seen faintly in a red-lit fog, flashed in his mind.

"Cromm!" he breathed.

"By the gods, man," the other said in alarm, looking around. "Don't say it aloud. It's like a beacon to them. Quick. We have to move again."

They moved into the street, rushing along to the next intersection, turning, coming back at last into the renovated area.

"But if the source of these . . . whatever is in Ireland," Colin asked as they strode rapidly along, "won't it be even easier for them to get me there?"

"No," the man briskly replied. "Look, they aren't ready to reveal themselves yet. They daren't act so close to their own home. You should be safe there, maybe safer than anywhere else . . . at least for a time. But that time is swiftly running out, for everyone."

"Everyone?" said Colin. "But . . ."

"We're here," the man announced, pulling up so abruptly that Colin nearly collided with him.

They had reached another intersection, and the man moved in close to the nearest building, peering around its corner.

Colin joined him, peeking past his shoulder. Across the street was his own building. Late patrons still crowded the Mexican restaurant downstairs. The streets were quiet, although the sound of sirens still echoed between the buildings from somewhere not far away.

The silver-haired man pulled Colin back into the shadows of a doorway.

"There you are," he said softly. "It doesn't look as if they're about here yet. You have a chance now. Go quickly. Get what you need."

"What I need?" Colin repeated blankly.

The man looked at Colin as if he were an imbecile; a pronounced irritation came into his voice.

"Haven't you been listening to me? I know you're confused, boy, but try to get it straight. You must go, and go tonight! Those creatures will have to recoup their energies after such a battle as they've just had. You should be free of them for a short while. So, if you mean to save yourself, there can be no delay. Every moment gives them another chance and endangers more innocent lives. Go, gather what you can for traveling. And don't forget your passport."

"Passport?" Colin echoed. "I don't even know if it's valid anymore."

"It is," the man said with assurance. "Go now. Fetch it."

Colin nodded. He took a step out of the doorway and realized the other man was not moving. He looked back to him.

"What about you?"

"They don't know I'm here yet. Hidden, I might still help you survive. But for the rest, you've got to learn it by yourself. My interference might destroy it. I may already have done damage. They're so fragile."

"Why the hell do you keep making me repeat everything you say?" Colin said in exasperation. "What's fragile?"

"Your dreams, my friend. They may be the only weapon left to us. If it's not already too late."

"Goddamn it!" Colin swore in anger. "You're talking more riddles again. How can . . ."

"No more time," the other interrupted. "They could return

at any moment. Hurry! I'll stay here, keep watch for them, protect you if I can. Just hurry, man. For great Danu's sake!"

Colin looked across at his building with clear uneasiness. Then he pulled himself up determinedly and strode into the street.

Halfway across he paused to look back.

"Great Danu?" he murmured in puzzlement. Then he shook his head and went on.

He reached the door to the apartments, quickly unlocked it and ducked inside. He rushed up the stairs to his floor.

Once through his apartment door, he switched on every light and looked around. All was as he'd left it.

He went through into the bedroom. Again, all was the same normal mess he'd left. He glanced out the window. Nothing was moving in the street. His new "friend" was not in sight.

He rummaged in a drawer, pulled out some cash and stuffed it away in a coat pocket. He found the passport and opened it to check the date.

"Valid," he muttered. "That son-of-a-bitch was right!"

He pulled a big, battered suitcase from under the bed, tossed it on top and opened it. He began to yank open dresser drawers and toss their contents hodgepodge into the case.

With the case heaped high, he paused, looking around him at the room.

"Tom was right," he said aloud. "This *is* crazy. I mean, really crazy! This can't be happening. It has to be another dream!"

The sound of a siren arose suddenly from close outside. He went to the big fan-topped window and looked down in time to see an ambulance flash by below, its spinning red and blue lights reflecting from the windows of the storefronts.

From this, his gaze was drawn lower, to the buttonless, torn front of his trenchcoat.

He stared thoughtfully at this evidence of the reality for a moment, then shook his head.

"Okay. So maybe it's not a dream."

With renewed motivation, he went to the bed to finish stuffing the pile of clothes into the case's confines. When the mass was mostly contained, he straightened up to look around.

"What else?" he muttered. Then, "Razor!"

He turned to the bathroom door and pulled it open.

A cadaverous figure in a green army coat leaped forward, thrusting out at him with a long javelin.

Colin threw himself sideways, out of the path of the glinting point, falling onto the bed. The spear point shot past. The thing wielding it moved out into the bedroom, then turned toward him.

Colin had a quick impression of it as it loomed above him. It was a man, but like one a long time dead. The arms thrusting from the coat were fleshless, wasted to bone and tendon. The head was a mummy's, its eyes black sockets glowing with a red light.

It raised the spear and drove it down toward Colin. He rolled out from beneath it and the point thudded into the mattress, driving deep. Colin rolled back, kicking up with his foot at the being's long bony jaw. The foot connected, rocking the creature back. It released the spear.

Colin tried to yank the weapon from the bed, but the creature leaped upon him. He grappled with it, and the two rolled back and forth on the bed.

The thing got atop him, pressing him back. Despite its wasted look, it possessed enormous power, forcing him down and moving its sinewy hands to grip his throat. The tendons of its arms grew taut like steel cables.

He struggled with it, trying to break the hold, kicking out with his feet. He succeeded only in knocking his suitcase from the bed. The being's grip grew tighter.

Colin looked up into the face so close above him. Its skin was a parchment, cracked open across the high cheekbones. Its dried lips were drawn back in a permanent grimace, exposing yellowed teeth. Its ears were gone, its nose twin caverns into the head's awful depths. Only the hollow eyes showed life in the ruby flames that now flared higher as Colin's struggle grew feebler.

But as Colin stared into the burning eyes, a light of dawning notion came into his face. He lifted a fist, sticking two fingers out of it to form a V.

"Try this, pal!" he rasped, and drove the fingers into the thing's eye sockets with savage force.

It shrieked in pain and released him, sitting up. Colin shoved it aside and rolled off the bed.

"Thank you, Larry, Curly, and Mo," he gasped out as he got to his feet.

But the thing was already recovering, rising up on the bed's other side, reaching out a wasted hand to the javelin.

"Look, are you really sure we couldn't talk?" Colin asked. "We could go downstairs for Mex. You look like you could use a good meal."

The bony hand closed around the javelin. A single yank and it came free. The bony jaw opened, the dried leather strip that was a tongue rattled as it hissed out its rage.

"That's what I figured," Colin said. He took a deep breath and launched himself across the bed onto the thing. They both fell back, slamming into the wall and then toppling to the floor, entangled again. They rolled back and forth, knocking over the nightstand, bringing empty bottles, glasses, crackers, peanut butter jar, lamp, and digital clock smashing down atop them. The light-bulb shattered, and they were suddenly struggling in the glow from the lights outside.

Colin saw the light glinting on something in the peanut butter jar. He reached out and grasped the handle of a dinner knife. The creature tried to throw him off. He knocked it back, grabbing the hand that gripped the spear and holding tight. He thrust the knife through the thing's wrist.

The blade tore through the leathery skin, slipping between the two bones of the lower arm. Colin pressed its serrated edge against the tightly drawn strings of the thing's tendons, sawing with great vigor. With a dull 'twang' a tendon suddenly snapped. The skeletal hand dropped back limply, the spear falling to the floor.

Colin released the arm and grabbed desperately for the spear. But the creature, seemingly given new power by this outrage, rose up and heaved him away with a lift of its other arm.

Colin hit the foot of the bed and bounced across the floor, crashing into the base of his bureau. Groaning with pain, he levered himself up to a sitting position, glancing toward the thing. It was climbing to its feet before the big window, reaching out for the spear with its undamaged hand.

Colin used the bureau's drawer pulls to haul himself up. He leaned against it, panting, white-faced, sagging.

"God," he rasped out, "this is turning into a long night!"

The thing had drawn upright now, its skeletal form a ghastly silhouette against the light framed by the floor-to-ceiling window. Colin could see the bright glow of the crimson eyes.

His hand went out. He grasped the handle of the portable television set that sat atop the bureau.

"You know, I am really getting tired of you guys!" he told the thing.

It gave a low growl and started forward, the spear rising for a throw.

In a single move Colin swung the TV up and around.

"Catch, sucker!" he said as he let it go.

It slammed into the center of the thing's chest, sending it flying backward, off its feet. It took out the big window, making it explode outward as the being toppled through, dropping down amidst a tangle of sash and flickering shards of glass.

The people in Casa Maitas saw the mass crash onto the concrete only a few feet outside the restaurant window. There were screams as they rose up from their meals in alarm.

Colin went to the hole that had been his window, peering out past the jagged remains of glass to the scene below. The thing lay on its back, spreadeagled within the glinting debris, the shattered TV resting on its chest.

"Well, that's the most entertainment *I've* ever gotten from the tube," he said aloud.

He left the window, quickly searching out the spilled suitcase amidst the wreckage of his room. He stuffed what he could back in, forced it closed, and rushed from the apartment with it.

Below, the being in the street began to glow. A white-green aura arose about it, enveloping it until it was completely hidden within the chrysalis of emerald light. And then that light burst, blossoming like an exploding rocket in a Fourth of July night sky, sending thousands of sparks shooting upward and spreading into the darkness above the buildings.

Colin reached the street, coming out to find people pouring from the Mexican place, staring up at the glowing mass. He paused too, watching in surprise as the lights winked out. He looked back to the street. There was nothing of the creature left, only the scattered remains of broken glass and sash.

The sound of another siren lifted in the distance and grew swiftly louder. He left the crowd and ran across the street. The doorway around the corner was empty.

He looked around him. There was no sign of the silver-haired man.

"Damn!" he growled. "No evidence and no witness!"

His gaze fell on a yellow cab rolling up the cross street, slowing as it came through the intersection, driver gawking out at the crowd curiously. Colin ran up to it, pulled open the door and jumped in while it was still moving.

"Hey!" said the surprised driver. "That's dangerous, buddy!"

The sound of the siren was getting louder.

"I'm in a hurry," Colin puffed out, still more than a little out of breath. "Late for my plane. Airport." He leaned over the seat to thrust a twenty-dollar bill out to the man. "Hurry!"

"Yeah. Okay. Sure," the driver said, taking the bill. He nodded out the window toward the restaurant. "Quite a crowd back there."

"Sure looked like it," Colin said brusquely. "I don't know why."

As the cab picked up speed, he glanced back. The red lights of a patrol car were just coming into view as it rounded a corner into the street before his building.

"So, you're looking for a Colin McMahon."

The ticket person, a tall, prim, bespectacled woman in the neat uniform of Northwest Airlines, looked across the counter at the two men. They were in plain clothes and holding police badges in their hands. The badges seemed to make no impression on the stone-faced woman.

The three were at the Northwestern ticket counter. The large digital clock above the woman read 2:45 A.M. Even at this hour, there was a good deal of activity in the airport terminal that spread out behind the men.

"He'd have been in sometime between nine-thirty and now," the older of the two plainclothesmen said.

"I don't know," she said bluntly. "That's quite a long time. I've seen a great many people."

"It's important," the man said patiently.

"Is it?" One of her neat eyebrows lifted fractionally. "Why. What did he do?"

"Geez, it was a riot," the younger man now put in with relish, moving up beside his partner. He was clearly amazed by that night's events himself. "Half that old market area downtown got trashed. A couple of places were ripped apart! All kinds of crazy stuff. And the bodies are still turning up!"

The older man turned and gave him a hard look. Abashed, he retreated. The woman's face now registered astonishment.

"My Lord! And this man did all that?"

"No ma'am, we don't mean that," the older man said gruffly, shooting his partner another look. "He's only wanted for questioning. Now, can you help us?"

"Well, I can certainly look at our records and see if he checked in."

She punched some keys on her computer console, scanned through the lists of green-colored names that flowed up across the screen, then shook her head.

"I'm sorry. There's no one by that name."

"He probably would have used another," the young policeman put in helpfully.

"Thank you, Bunger. That's brilliant," the older one said witheringly, then looked to her. "But if he charged the ticket, his real name'd turn up someplace. Can you check that?"

"Just one moment," she said, punching more keys.

Several moments actually ticked by on the big clock as she scanned lists, and the men watched impatiently.

Finally she shook her head again.

"No. No record of his name. And nobody has used cash tonight."

"Damn it!" the older man cursed. "Look, lady: a cab driver brought him here. He had a suitcase. He even said that he was going to take a plane. If he bought a ticket, there must be some record!"

"Not here, officer," she said curtly, "unless you think someone erased it."

He met her challenging eye for a moment. Then he slammed a fist on the counter and stalked away, the other following.

Farther up the counter, a man in Northwestern uniform glanced up from the work he had been bent over. He looked around at the departing men and smiled in a self-satisfied way.

He looked rather old among the other, much younger counter-people; his hair was a thick, waving mass of silver-grey.

The plane winged through the night sky. In one seat a much worn and somewhat tattered-looking young man settled back and let out a great sigh of weariness.

The female flight attendant, making her way down the aisle, paused to give him a closer look.

"Do you . . . need anything, sir?"

"Just some sleep," he assured her. "And a big Scotch later, if you've got one."

"Let me know," she said, and moved on.

Beside him, at a window seat, an elderly woman listened and eyed him curiously. He noted this and smiled, pointing past her out the window.

"If you see anything out there," he told her, "please, don't tell me."

He dropped his head back, letting his eyes close. The woman continued to stare at him, frowning, for a moment. Then she looked out the window into the blackness beyond. She gave a shudder as from a sudden chill and lifted a hand to pull down the little shade.

Beside her, Colin McMahon was already breathing in the slow, deep rhythm of sleep.

The plane flew on, sailing above the clouds, the bright and nearly full harvest moon glowing on its white hull and spreading wings.

II

The sleek, glowing silver form soared overhead on outstretched wings, gliding on the currents in a clear sky.

"That is a strange bird," Colin commented, watching it wheel to pass over him again.

Once more the young warrior rode in his chariot, behind his driver Ailbe. Beside them rolled the chariot of the chieftain of Dun Mauran, Laimainech.

They were traveling across the broad meadows of the chieftain's domains, the circular wall of his fortress showing on the hilltop behind them.

Laimainech glanced up at the bird, then shook his head dismissingly.

"Only a crane, I think. A rare good luck sign, but far from strange."

Colin too dismissed it, turning his gaze to the countryside around him.

"And how was your rest, last night?" the chieftain politely inquired. "Comfortable, I hope?"

"For me, I'm afraid the night was a very long one," Colin answered. "Much troubled it was by dreams of wild combats with monstrous creatures in a strange land all of stone."

"It was the drink," Laimainech quickly assured him. "Too much of our rich mead has given many a warrior nightmares of the *sheoguey* places and their beasts."

"Well, I was glad enough to see the day come, that I'll tell you truly," Colin said. He looked out across the broad meadows where a bright sun sparked emerald fire from the lush spring grass. "And I've surely seen few finer days than this."

"Yes. It's going to be a good spring," the chieftain replied with satisfaction. "Very fertile."

"It will be that," Colin agreed. He turned a searching gaze on Laimainech. "And do you thank your god for it?"

This the chieftain seemed not to hear. He looked away instead, pointing toward a low hill just ahead.

"Ah now, see there. One of our best bulls and his herd."

Upon the rounded brow of the hill a fine animal stood, tall, powerful, majestic, his cows grazing around him on the slopes.

The two chariots drew up below the hill, and Colin examined the bull appreciatively.

"And what great price would you be needing to ask for such an animal?" he asked.

"Ah, we're not so greedy as that," the chieftain assured him with a smile. "For this one bull, we have a dozen others just as fine. But what were you thinking to offer?"

"Well, we're not so rich as yourselves. But, if you were to let us have the use of your bull for one year only, to strengthen our herd's blood, why then you'd have him back after, and two dozen heifers with him, as payment for the loan."

"A very fair price that is," Laimainech said. "So, if that's agreed, let's go back to the *dun* now, and we'll be after closing our bond on it."

The chariots turned toward the fortress hill. But as they traveled back across the meadows, something to the north of the *dun* caught Colin's eye. He peered off toward it, lifting a hand to shield his eyes from the sun's glare.

"What is that place I see to the north of Dun Mauran, chieftain?" he asked, and lifted a hand to point. "There, do you see? Past that line of oaks there seems a broad plain with fine grass upon it. But I see no cattle."

"It's a deceptive sight that is," Laimainech brusquely assured him. "A bog lies through there. Very treacherous."

"Is it?" Colin said, peering more intently toward the spot. "But for a moment, through the trees, I thought I glimpsed tall stones upon it. Like great oghams they looked. Or part of a high wall?"

"Likely it was the grey stumps of rotted trees you saw," was the firm reply. He fixed Colin with a meaningful gaze. "Understand, young warrior: there's no man or beast would go there without risking its life."

"Indeed?" said Colin. Then he smiled most affably. "Well then I thank you for your kind warning, Chieftain."

Laimainech's only reply was to nod curtly, and they rode on in silence until they had drawn near to the base of the *dun.*

Just as they were to start up its slope a chariot appeared from the main gate, rolling down toward them. Behind its driver rode one of Dun Mauran's warriors, and as they approached the chieftain, he called out urgently:

"My chieftain, we've been waiting for you to return. You must come and check the herds to the south at once. There is some quarrel there amongst the clans as to whose cows should be grazing the *magh."*

"Again?" the chieftain said in exasperation. He sighed. "Every year is the same." He turned to Colin, his voice taking on an apologetic tone. "Sorry. It seems I must play the arbitor today. Even in a land of so much bounty as this, the clans still have to argue over their bits of land."

"I understand, Chieftain," Colin said graciously. "And why should your warriors be different from any others in Ireland?"

"Why don't you go on up to the hall yourself," Laimainech told him. "Have whatever food or drink you wish. I'll be returning soon, and we can conclude our bargain."

"I will do that," Colin assured him.

The chieftain nodded and looked toward his warrior.

"All right then," he said. "Let's go and remind these foolish men once more just who directs their lives."

He tapped his driver, and his chariot started off beside the other. But as they rolled away, he called back over his shoulder to Colin:

"Oh, but stay away from too much of the mead this time!"

"Have no fear about it," Colin called back, smiling with great camaraderie.

He watched the chieftain's chariot until it had rounded the fortress hill to the south and was out of sight. Then the young warrior's smile vanished, and he tapped his own driver's shoulder, pointing away to the north.

"All right, Ailbe," he said briskly, "now take us up that way."

The little driver looked around to see the pointing hand.

"What?" he said with surprise. He looked up the slope to the *dun*'s gate, close above. "But you said we'd go on up there!"

"And we will," Colin told him, "but I didn't say when. Good fortune has given us some time to ourselves, and I mean to use it to do a bit of looking around. Now, go that way."

Ailbe peered off in the direction Colin had indicated. His expressive face registered bewilderment.

"But that's toward the bog he warned you of."

"It is," Colin agreed. "I want to see it."

"Why?"

"Curiosity," Colin said bluntly. "Now drive on!"

The driver did as commanded, turning away from the *dun* and guiding the chariot out over the meadows toward the north, but he muttered darkly under his breath all the way. When they came into the fringe of the oak wood masking the plain, Colin ordered him to stop, and then climbed down.

"Pull the chariot into the trees far enough to conceal it, Ailbe," he ordered as he took his shield and a thrusting spear from the vehicle. "Tether the horses, then come with me. We go afoot from here."

"Colin, what is it you're thinking of?" the driver asked him in dismay.

"I don't want the chieftain's people seeing that we're here. I've a feeling they'd not like our poking about."

"Then, for Dagda's sake, why are we doing it?"

"It's that plain I had a glimpse of," he answered, looking into the trees. "There's something . . . something about it." He shook his head. "I don't know myself exactly, Ailbe. I only know I've got to see what it is."

So, giving a great sigh of resignation, the driver ran the chariot far enough into the fringe of the wood to screen it, tied up the horses, then followed his master into the trees.

The oaks here were massive, ancient trees, rising up from the ground like thick columns. Their outsweeping limbs entwined high above, forming a complex network roofing over the wood. Although that made it shadowy beneath, the half-developed spring leaves still allowed some of the bright sun to shine through and speckle the ground, lighting the way with a green-gold glow. Soon, when the broad leaves had reached full size, their solid canopy would plunge the area below into a deep gloom.

Colin moved forward slowly, constantly searching the way ahead. Behind him, Ailbe all but slunk along—crouching low, his gaze jerking about from shadow to shadow apprehensively, starting at every sound.

Colin glanced back and saw his driver lagging behind.

"Stay closer, Ailbe," he hissed. "I don't want to lose you."

"Nor I yourself," the other agreed, hastening to close the gap. "I've no good feelings at all about this place. There are things here. I can feel them watching me."

"Don't be foolish," Colin said, putting bravado into his voice. "This is a narrow band of woods. No great forest. There's nothing dangerous here."

Something whispered through the trees behind them.

Both men wheeled about in time to glimpse a long, low form sweeping across the dark space between two oak trunks.

"And what was that?" Ailbe demanded tremulously. "Two big for a hedgehog, wouldn't you say?"

"I think it was a hound," said Colin, peering toward the spot.

"Or a wolf, maybe?"

There was no further sight or sound of it. Colin shrugged.

"Let's just go on," he said stoutly. "It can't be much further now."

But for all his fearless talk, he moved more cautiously, with the spear up ready for use and the shield before his chest. And his little driver stayed so close he nearly trod upon the young warrior's heels.

Ailbe was looking behind him when Colin stopped abruptly, and the driver moved on past the warrior before noticing.

"I don't know," Ailbe was saying. "I've still a feeling I'm being watch . . ."

Then he too stopped, seeing his master staring past his shoulder, his face aghast.

The driver swiveled his head to find himself staring into the eyeless sockets of a rotting head only inches before his face.

He recoiled in horror, nearly losing his balance. Colin moved up to grip his shoulder.

"Steady, old friend," he said. "It's ugly but harmless."

It was a severed head, hanging gape-mouthed by its own long hair tied over a low branch of an oak. The eyes had been pecked away, as well as most of the soft tongue in the open jaws.

But, unlike the near-skulls atop the fortress walls, the flesh of this head had not yet withered and dried.

"This head is very fresh," Colin observed, examining the gruesome object. "A few days at most."

"So," Ailbe managed, swallowing hard to force his gorge back down, "they have been taking heads recently. Your chieftain lied."

"About much more than that, I'm afraid," Colin added.

He looked around. Other heads were visible, suspended at intervals in a curving line through the trees in either direction.

"Do you think they could be meant as a warning to keep out?" the driver asked.

"Maybe," said Colin. "Look at that one!" He moved toward a head suspended to the left of the first one, and peered into the decomposing face. "Why, this one's no more than a boy. Can't be more than ten or twelve."

"I think this one's a woman!" declared Ailbe, whose own morbid curiosity had drawn him toward the next head on the right side.

Colin joined him. He gingerly brushed back some of the straggling grey hair that half veiled the face. The features revealed that this was certainly the age-lined, beardless face of an elderly woman.

"What is happening?" Colin said in shock, looking up and down the ghastly line. "These are no warriors' heads. No honest trophies taken in combat. Old women and children? Only savages do such butchering."

"And I say we have nothing more to do with such butchers," Ailbe recommended with great feeling. He grabbed Colin's arm, tugging him back from the line of heads. "My warrior,

let's be out of this wood and away from this *dun* now, while we
still can be."

"No," Colin said, shaking off the grip and stepping forward.
"I must see what's beyond."

He pushed past the line. Ailbe sighed again, then reluctantly
followed.

Only a thin screen of trees lay beyond the heads. The two
men moved through it, coming out into the open.

Now the plain that the trees had masked lay revealed before
them, and the two men stopped again to gaze out across it
wonderingly.

The plain was quite broad and very level. It seemed from
their viewpoint to be formed in a near-perfect circle, bound all
around by the curved margin of the oak wood. Just inside the
trees, a ring of low, rounded stones spaced at wide but even
intervals seemed to mark the outer rim of the plain. And, clustered more tightly at the center of the circle, another ring of
taller, massive stones rose up starkly and with dramatic abrupt-
ness from the smooth earth.

"By all the gods my father's prayed to!" Ailbe proclaimed in
awed tones.

"Let's go closer," said Colin, starting ahead.

The driver gave a low, fretful whimper, but still followed,
though very reluctantly.

Colin moved past one of the outer stones, glancing down at
it as he did. It was thick and nearly knee-high, its smoothly
rounded top and sides deeply incised with a complex design of
curliquing lines and spirals.

"An odd thing," he murmured. "Have I seen stones like this
before?"

He went on, striding up boldly toward the inner ring of
larger stones.

As he drew nearer, their enormous size became more clearly
evident. Each was three or four paces in breadth and over three
times his height. The sides that faced out into the plain were
featureless, giving them the look of plain, roughly finished
stones.

"It's just one of those old stone rings," Ailbe said, trying to sound careless. "I've seen the like in other parts of Ireland. Come away now."

"No," said Colin. "It's something else. Come on."

They moved between two of the stones, into the circle they enclosed. The men stopped there abruptly, staring around them with eyes wide in surprise.

For the inner sides of the stones were sculpted, and the images they presented were of monstrous forms.

Though the carving of the sculptures was very rough, often seeming to follow the natural shape of the stone, this crudeness only added a strange power, an eerie vitality to the work.

Ailbe stood frozen at the sight, but Colin stepped further on, looking around at each.

One seemed a lizardlike being, crouched down as if to spring, its jaws wide and its whiplike tail coiled about powerful legs. Beside it sat a creature that seemed at first a wolf, but with a sleek horned head and a muscled body more like a bull's. Another was shaped as a man, but with a face like a wax sculpture half melted by the sun.

On around the circle there were other forms: an enormous ravenlike creature with great wings furled about it; another creature like something brought up from the sea depths, with bulging eyes and crablike body. And there was one that Colin examined most particularly: a being with a sloth's long head and pointed snout, its short arms equipped with long talons, its eyes slanted and slit-pupiled like a cat's.

He stared at it, and his hand rose to touch the scarred place at his neck. Then his gaze moved on, scanning over the rest of the ring of forms. Though they were powerfully sculpted and monstrous, still they were only things of stone, a harmless company.

"Twelve," he pronounced, as his eyes finished the circle.

"Twelve," came the querulous voice of Ailbe. "And that one!"

Colin looked around. Ailbe still stood where they had entered the ring. His body was rigid with his fear, his gaze fixed on another form of stone that rose directly before them, at the center of the ring.

Colin turned back, his gaze falling on the thirteenth stone.

"Yes," he said. "That one."

They looked at its rounded shape. From where Colin stood, it seemed like a figure hunched down, its shoulders up, head forward, back to him—a broad and featureless back. But even this had something malignant about it.

He started toward it, moving around it in a wide circle to stay at a distance. He reached the side of it, the front of it beginning to come into view. There he stopped, as if not really wanting to see what lay hidden behind the last sheltering curve.

Then his eye caught a glinting of gold. Though the other sculptures were plain stone, without ornament, this one was decorated. The fact pulled him on, curiosity overcoming any remaining fear or prudence.

An arm came into view, banded by many wide bracelets of gold. Then the rest of it became visible.

The body was like that of a thing wasted, its tiny, spindly limbs drawn up tightly to a small body with a bloated belly. The hunched shoulders were narrow but from them protruded a head of massive size, vaguely human, but with bulging skull and enormous wide-set eyes. Beneath them was a small, tapering face, like an infant's in the delicacy of its features, but imparting in the strange, bowed smile of the tiny mouth a malevolence, a mocking, careless evil that made Colin recoil in disgust.

But his first expression of loathing for the thing was quickly replaced by a renewed look of curiosity. He drew closer. What kind of thing was this, this withered being adorned with an untold wealth of gold?

He boldly moved up right before it. At its base was a vast slab of stone slightly uptilted. He examined it. There was a groove cut all around its outer edge, a channel, running to a spout set in the lower edge. The stone of this channel was stained a deep red-brown.

He looked at it. Then he looked up at the statue looming over him. From here he could see that the figure was naked, save for the ornaments. It was a male, this part of its anatomy most pronounced and rendered with a startling reality.

And one other feature was sculpted with great detail. From

the center of the bloated belly that thrust out toward him, there ran a line like a thick, twisted cable. It coiled around the figure, then ran down its side to the ground, plunging into a funnel of stone set in the earth against the statue's base.

Colin's gaze followed the strange cable down, but then he looked up again, drawn to the bracelets crowding the skinny arms.

"Is that all really gold?" he said softly.

He moved even closer, lifting a hand. It touched the statue's surface, then quickly withdrew.

"Warm!" he exclaimed in surprise. He looked up at the being smiling down at him.

"Cromm?" he said softly.

There was a peculiar vibration. As if the ground breathed, shuddered, sighed. A sharp breeze flicked across him, ruffling his cloak, then dying away.

"What are you doing here?" a voice demanded.

Startled, he wheeled about to see Dubhdaleithe, the druid of Dun Mauran, striding into the circle of stones. Behind him and on either side were the massive-bodied steward and the lean blacksmith. Beyond them, just outside the circle, something else moved. A hooded figure showed, then vanished into the shelter of a stone.

From the corners of his eyes, Colin caught other movements, other figures flitting in and out of sight. He glanced around him as the three men approached, but saw nothing except the silent, motionless statues.

"Can you explain why you are violating our sacred precincts?" the haughty druid asked him as they drew near.

"I'm sorry," Colin answered in a most innocent and apologetic tone. "I didn't know. Your chieftain told me this was all a bog."

"Most odd then that you should wish to come here, isn't it?" Dubhdaleithe replied suspiciously.

"I thought I saw something here," Colin explained. "I wondered what it was. I was only curious. That's all."

"Laimainech meant to keep you from violating this place."

"Then why didn't he simply tell me what it was?" the young warrior countered.

"It is our most sacred site," the druid shot back. "Nothing to do with you."

"Again, I'm sorry," Colin said. "I didn't realize it was so secret. Last night your chieftain seemed ready to tell me all about it."

"He was rash. You are an outsider. It's unlikely you would be found worthy of acceptance into our circle. Your faithfulness to your own beliefs would . . ."

"I have no real belief," Colin said. "The gods of the Others hold no power over me."

"And this new god the invaders have brought into Ireland?"

"New god?" Colin repeated, frowning in puzzlement. "I'm not sure what you mean."

"Do you not?" This seemed to deflate the druid's swelling hostility somewhat. "Well, maybe that is true. Still, you've made a great mistake in coming here. You've angered our god."

"Cromm?" Colin said.

"Quiet!" the druid commanded, roused to indignation by this single word. "No one but those who have accepted our way may speak the sacred name in this holy place!"

"I meant no harm," Colin tried to explain. "I . . ."

The druid cut him short. "No more. Our chieftain sees you as a friend, so I will not seek to punish you for this one mistake." He pointed the way out of the ring. "But be away from this place. Now!"

With no further delay, Colin did that, leading a much relieved Ailbe out from the circle, through the oak wood and its ring of heads, back to their chariot.

Ailbe untied the team. The two climbed in and the little driver guided the chariot out onto the open meadows once again.

Colin looked back, seeing the shadows of several figures within the fringe of woods, and the glint of eyes intently watching them.

"And now what, Colin?" Ailbe asked. "Back to the *dun*?"

"No, Ailbe. There's another place I mean to go to now."

"Another place? But what about the bargain for your father's bull?"

"Never mind that, Ailbe. Just head us back toward the rath of that girl's clan."

"Not back there!" Ailbe wailed. "Please, Colin, if there's something wrong here, let's just go home."

"Not yet, my friend," the young warrior said determinedly. "Not until I understand just what it is that is happening."

"Well, at least we'll be away from that awful place," the driver declared turning the chariot away from Dun Mauran, urging the team off at a trot toward the south and east.

But as they left the fortress and the grisly adornment of heads, neither man noticed a strange, sleek birdlike form rise up from the sacred plain and sail after them.

It glided behind and far above them, broad wings outspread on the currents of a spring breeze. The bright sun glowed softly against the smooth, silver-grey skin of its body.

PART
TWO

IRELAND:

DESPERATE
SEARCHES

12

The Aer Lingus plane glided down out of the clouds.

It slipped smoothly in toward the broad runway, touching down lightly, turning and taxiing up to its gate.

The stairway was brought up, and the passengers climbed down, walking in toward the gate. Near the end of the stream of people came Colin McMahon, trenchcoat slung over one arm.

He stopped at the foot of the ladder and let the last of the other passengers move by him as he stared around him through eyes squinted against the outside glare, looking thoroughly nonplussed.

Before him was a long, low, modern building with SHANNON INTERNATIONAL AIRPORT emblazoned on its tower. Around it, beyond the expanses of concrete, low green hills and the glinting waters of a wide river were visible, all bright in the sharp dawn light of a clear autumn day.

"So I'm really in Ireland," he muttered to himself as if comprehending it for the first time. "So now what?"

Then he sighed and shrugged and followed the others in.

The bulging suitcase plumped down on the low counter.

The man in the neat uniform of Irish customs looked from the suitcase to Colin as he presented his passport.

"Business or pleasure, sir?" the man asked, taking the little book. He was looking the young American up and down most carefully.

"Ah . . . I don't know," Colin said vaguely. "How about both? Or, neither?"

These were clearly not pleasing responses for the man. He frowned.

"A bit late season for the usual tourist things," he said pointedly, running his gaze over Colin again in an openly questioning way.

Colin looked down at himself, his rumpled pants, the stained and snagged sweater, the battered topcoat. He rubbed a hand over the stubble on his chin. His manner grew self-conscious.

"It was sudden," he said lamely. "I've got to do some . . . research. See, I work for a design company. I'm an artist."

"Ah, I see," said the man, as if this explained a great deal. He looked at the passport, opening it. Its cover was wrinkled, the pages badly dog-eared. "Your passport is rather worn."

"It went through the wash once," Colin explained, trying to smile at the humor of it.

There was no responding smile. The man looked at the passport, then at him, then at the bulging suitcase. Apparently deciding that no one illegal would make himself so conspicuous, he shook his head, stamped the passport, and handed it back.

"Very well, sir," he said briskly. "Enjoy yourself."

"I'll certainly try," Colin said with relief, taking up his case and moving past the counters into the main room of the terminal.

He stopped there, looking around him, eyes scanning the bustling throng of travelers. There were no signs of anyone watching him. His gaze stopped at the symbol for a men's room across the concourse. He rubbed his hand across his stubbled chin again, then set out through the crowd.

His hand yanked the handle of the dispensing machine. The compact grooming kit slipped out of the bottom slot and he grasped it, smiling with gratification.

In moments the open pack was on the back of one of the

sinks lining the men's room wall, and Colin was scraping away at his lathered face with the Bic razor.

He was stripped to the waist, his much abused sweater tossed over the case at his feet. As he shaved, he caught in the mirror the curious eye of a gentleman in an impeccable grey suit who was using a nearby sink. Colin grinned broadly. The man averted his eyes and hastily left.

With his shaving done, Colin opened his case, dug out another sweater—not much less rumpled but at least clean—and slipped into it. He tore open the little packet of cologne from the kit and slapped it on, then contemplated himself in the mirror. Shaved, washed, hair combed, and in a relatively fresh sweater he was still a little scruffy, but more or less presentable.

He put the remnants of the kit and the worn sweater into his case, closed it, then took his tired but trusty corduroy jacket from a nearby hook and slipped it back on. As he did, he noted something in the pocket crinkling. He reached in and pulled out two items: a wrinkled drawing of a stone and a bent Irish tourist brochure.

He gazed at them, and something seemed to strike him. He leafed through the brochure to the photo of the stone that matched the drawing. His eyes scanned the caption beneath: "Neolithic stone, one of many found in Ireland, this one in County Cavan."

An image of other words came into his mind, words in an old book in a now faraway library: "An ornamented stone statue of *Cromm Cruaich,* the god of fertility, once stood with the statues of his twelve disciples on the plain of Magh Slecht in County Cavan."

"Cavan," he muttered.

He stuffed the drawing and the brochure back into his pocket, took up his case and topcoat, and went out of the restroom.

Across the vast expanse of tile-floored concourse, before a row of high windows on the far side, the stalls of the car rental agencies were ranked. His eyes lit on the familiar Hertz International sign and he started toward it.

On an upper balcony, outside the duty-free shop, a figure in dark grey overcoat, tweed hat, and scarf stared down at him as he strode determinedly across to the stall.

There, a rosy-cheeked and dark-haired young lass looked up from her paperwork and smiled winningly as Colin arrived.

"Hello, sir. Welcome to Ireland. Will you be wanting to lease an automobile?"

"You bet."

"Very well then. All I need is a valid operator's license and any major credit card." She picked up a hefty stack of papers to pass to him. "And you'll just need to fill out these few forms."

He dug license and credit card from his wallet to trade her for the papers, then took up a pen from the counter to begin his work as she began her own.

"I'm going to Cavan," he commented as he filled in blanks.

"Cavan?" she said. "Yes, I know it. It's to the north. Not really very far."

"I'm looking for a place there. It's called . . . Maug Slecht?"

"I'm sorry?" she said, smiling blankly.

"It's spelled like this," he said, printing it out on the margin of a Hertz brochure. She looked at it and her face lit up.

"Ah. *Moy Slekt* is how it's pronounced." Then she shook her head. "But, no, sorry, I've never heard of it."

"**N**ever heard tell of the place, sir. No, I haven't," the man in the coveralls said.

He was bent over, head thrust in through the open window of the little Vauxhall. The young American was now behind the vehicle's wheel, holding up the brochure with the strange words written on it.

"I can give you directions to Cavan though, sir," he added more brightly. "Just wait a moment."

He straightened up and turned from the car to enter a glass-walled booth. They were at the gates of the car vending lot of the Hertz company. Scores of vehicles in neat rows filled the enclosure, the airport visible beyond them.

Colin waited as the man rummaged through a rack of folders within, then came out to him, unfolding a highway map.

He passed it in to Colin, then leaned down to give instructions.

"You see here, here's where you are now," he said, pointing out the airport with a thick finger. It traced the route as he went on: "You just go out to the main road, headed east. Take the first turning north. 'Gort Road' it'll be labeled. Head up that way, through here, going north and east, and you'll come upon Cavan."

"You're sure?" asked Colin.

The man straightened and smiled. "It's an entire county, sir. You can't get lost. Just follow the map."

"Well, okay," Colin said, putting the map on the seat beside him. He looked at the wheel in the left-handed car, and put his left hand down tentatively on the gearshift knob.

"You drive on the left side of the road here, right?" he said, without much enthusiasm. "I mean, correct?"

"Yes, sir," the man said as his smile widened. "Just keep a watch on the great chunk of machine that'll be sticking out on your left side. Don't be scraping it off on anything."

"Thanks for the tip," said Colin dryly. He started the car, carefully put it in gear, and gingerly started off.

On his first right turn onto the road outside the gates, he swung into the inside lane, then swerved violently to barely avoid a van that swept by with an angry blare of horns.

The watching lot attendant laughed and shook his head, then looked toward another watcher, a man in dark grey coat, scarf, and tweed hat, who stood outside the gate.

"An American," the attendant said, much amused. "Hope he survives."

The other only nodded in reply.

Colin, meanwhile, had turned onto the main road and was creeping along and looking at signs to the annoyance of others on the six-lane highway.

Soon he spotted the one he sought, announcing "Gort Road, North."

Braving the traffic, he switched lanes in time to turn, then settled himself resolutely behind the wheel.

CROMM

"Just follow the map," he muttered, glancing at the pleated sheet. "Follow the map and I can't get lost."

"I'm lost," he said.

The young man behind the counter looked up to him.

"I'm sorry?" he said.

"I'm lost," Colin repeated. "I thought I was on the road to Cavan, but suddenly I couldn't find any signs for it." He looked about him. "I don't even know where I am now."

Specifically, he was inside a neatly appointed little café, with tables along the windows in the front, and stools along the long counter at the back. It was an intimate, cozy place with the smell of coffee and warm baked goods in the air. But at the moment, save for Colin and the counterman, it was deserted.

"I thought I was going inland, and then I realized I was looking at the sea," Colin went on. "This is the first place I saw to stop."

"There isn't much along here," the young counterman agreed. "We're only here to serve the tourist buses and the lone travelers who come to use the beach. Not much this time of year."

"Well, could you help me?" Colin asked. He spread the now somewhat dog-eared map out on the counter, pointing to Cavan. "See, that's where I'm going."

The young man, clearly glad for some diversion, looked down at the map.

"I see where you went wrong. You're over here." He pointed to a sharp peninsula of land thrusting out from the Atlantic coast, some two inches west of Cavan on the map. "You must have turned in the wrong direction."

"No kidding?" Colin said with a touch of sarcasm. "So how do I get right?"

"Nothing simpler. Take this road back to the N16, then just keep on going east."

"East? How do you know for sure? With the way the roads twist around here, I can't tell what direction I'm going half the time."

The young man smiled. "I understand you. But just keep to

the primary road and look for the signs to Cavan. You'll not get lost then. It isn't very far."

"And just how far is that?"

"Oh, an hour's drive, maybe."

Colin glanced at his watch. It read 2:10 P.M.

"Great." he said. "Could you give me a coffee, a big one, to go?"

"I will."

He poured coffee from a percolator into a large Styrofoam cup while Colin folded the map.

"Thirty-five 'p'," he said.

Colin looked blank, then realized what he meant.

"God!" he exclaimed irritably. "I didn't exchange any money. Will you take American?"

"With pleasure I will. Would 75 cents be fair?"

"More than." Colin handed him a dollar. "Keep the change, and thanks again."

He took the coffee and map and went out.

In front of the café was a gravel carpark, and beyond, across the curve of road, was the sea. A brisk wind caught him as he came out, the cool air drawing steam off the hot coffee. He walked to his car but paused there, looking from the sea to his watch and back. Then he turned from the car and started across the gravel yard.

Beyond it a broad ramp led out to a stone platform. It was a good vantage point above the sea, and he stopped there, leaning on an iron rail, sipping the coffee and just gazing out.

Wide stairs led from the platform down to a beach below. The clean sands swept far north in a lazy curve to end in a craggy profile of cliffs. A beautiful beach, but too cold on a brisk autumn day even for strollers. So he stood alone, contemplating the sea for some time.

And then the girl appeared.

He hadn't seen her come. She might have walked down from the café or swept down on the sea breeze like the drifting gulls and he wouldn't have known. She was just suddenly there, alone, leaning against the platform railing a dozen yards away, the light wind tugging at her mackintosh and teasing her thick flow of hair.

Having taken note of her, he watched her curiously for a time. She was completely absorbed with the view, her face uplifted to catch the fresh sea breeze.

He opened his mouth once, clearly meaning to speak to her, but then seemed to think better of it, as if reluctant to violate her solitary appreciation of the scene.

Instead he turned his own attention back to the sea.

The Atlantic that day was a flat slab of green-grey slate, smooth and well polished. And, like the stone, it seemed unyielding and eternally calm.

"It's forever changing, isn't it?" a voice said from beside him.

He turned his head and found that she now stood at the rail right next to him, quite at ease, as if they had been together from the first. It did not seem to surprise him. It was as if this were quite natural, as if in that first moment they were already friends, had in some way been friends for a long, long time.

She still looked out to sea, and he could see little of her profile with the long hair fluttering about it. He looked back to the water. His reply came easily, with that total lack of self-consciousness that only close friends share.

"That's funny. I was just thinking the opposite. I've been trying to imagine waves crashing in, shattering to pieces on the rocks. But I don't think a ripple's rippled since I got here. It's like something frozen in time to me. You know . . . the Eternal Sea bit?"

"It's not so strange," she said. "In Ireland, such opposites are a part of the way of things. There's much here that seems changeless on the surface, but there's none of it the same one moment to the next, underneath. Nothing's really eternal."

"Nothing?" he asked, smiling and looking around at her. "Not hope? Not beauty? Not even love?"

This seemed to affect her. She turned her head away, and her reply came tentatively, faltering.

"Love . . . perhaps."

At that, the fragile spell of closeness that had fallen about them was dispelled. Suddenly they became a man and a woman, and all the terrible implications of that single fact rose up between them.

Colin made a face of irritation, mouthing a silent damnation of himself for his careless words. Quickly he shifted subjects as if hoping this might recast the spell:

"Do you like it here?"

There was a long, terrible moment when she stood unmoving and it seemed she would not answer. Then her face turned back toward the sea, and, when she spoke, the ease had returned to her voice.

"I love the sea. I wish I could be near it all the time."

"Don't you live around here?" he asked.

"Close by, but inland some way, at Ballymauran. My work brings me nearby sometimes, and then I can take moments, like this one, to come here. Strange though," she added in a bemused way, "I really hadn't planned to come here today. But suddenly I realized that here I was." She looked to him. "And what about you? What brought you to this place?"

He shook his head, eyes still on the ocean.

"I sure didn't plan it either. I don't know why I'm here, or where I'm going, or . . ." He shook his head. "Well, I don't even know how I could tell you. But it's the first time in, God, *days* it seems like, that I've had a chance to just stand still."

"Never mind," she said in a soothing, understanding tone, as if she sensed the turmoil in him. "We can still have our moments, anyway. They're not to be wasted on futures and pasts. Right now it's peaceful, and the sea belongs only to us."

"You're right, you know?" he said with enthusiasm, his mood brightening. "Right now nothing else does seem very important." He turned to her. "There's just the sea and sky, and we can . . ."

He stopped abruptly, looking fully into her face for the first time.

He found his eyes being met by a pair of bright grey ones. He gazed at a face boldly drawn in clean, strong lines, and deep-red hair that flickered with lights in the stirring breeze as if shot through with golden strands.

Except for the hair and eye color, it was the face of his

dreams. The face that had stared out this same way at him from the drawing on his easel.

"But . . . I know you!" he said in astonishment.

Her smile slipped away. Her smooth brow furrowed in puzzlement.

"That you do not. I'm certain."

"I do," he said, excited. "I can't explain how. But . . . but I want to explain. In fact, I *have* to explain."

His sudden intensity was clearly making her wary and confused.

"Now, look here," she said, "I only came down here to look at the sea. I saw you. You seemed lonely. Some impulse brought me to talk to you. I don't know why. But it was no more than that."

"Nothing else?" he said, leaning forward, his eyes meeting hers searchingly. "Look at me. Are you sure you don't know me?"

She stepped back in alarm.

"I've never seen you before. Now I'm sorry, but I must leave."

She started to turn away, but he moved to block her.

"No. You can't! I have to talk to you. Please, let me buy you lunch or dinner or something. Let me explain."

"I'm in a great rush," she said, trying to sidestep, but he moved into her way again.

"Then let me meet you later!" he said more insistently. "I can come and visit you. Just tell me where you live."

"That I will not." She sidestepped successfully this time, starting away at a quick walk. He went after her, grabbing an elbow.

"Please! It's important!" he told her urgently. "You've got to listen!"

She yanked her arm free and headed at a run for the ramp leading off the platform.

He started to run after her, but he had taken only a few steps when a tall figure came into his path. It was a man muffled in a heavy coat, tweed hat, and scarf, and he collided with Colin, swinging them both around in the impact.

Colin caught a quick impression of bright eyes glowing beneath the brim of the hat. Then the man was moving away along the platform, and Colin was after the girl once more.

He came off the platform into the parking lot. But he was too late. The square green hulk of a Land Rover was pulling away onto the road, the girl behind its wheel.

He stared after her. A look of utter defeat washed over his face. Then his expression lit with the dawning of a new thought.

"Ballymauran!" he said, and ran for his car.

"This is really stupid," he muttered irritably.

He told himself this as he piloted the Vauxhall along a winding, rabbit-track road, steering with one hand, tracing his course on the map across his knees with the other.

The way was not easy. The road was edged by many overhanging trees, closing him in. It twisted as if it had a life of its own. And there was a certain casualness in the placing of roadsigns that made following directions very difficult. This all conspired to cast a sort of Irish enchantment over his journey that took away any sense of real location.

But somehow, as if the map were a charm warding off the confusing spell, he still managed to draw nearer to the tiny point marked Ballymauran.

When the trees allowed, he caught glimpses of the passing countryside. Man's hand rested very lightly upon it here; and where it did rest, it left gentle marks.

The few buildings he passed were mostly cottages of whitewashed stone, roofed with slate or thatch. They were settled into the land easily, snugly, as if they had been there forever. At times he passed ruins of ancient tower houses, once-massive structures that had been largely reclaimed by the land, their half-crumbled walls now the trellises for climbing vines. In general the countryside had an easy, comfortable feel to it, like that of an old and familiar sweater slipped on against the chill of a fall day.

He passed a crossroads suddenly, its sign whisking by. He slowed the car, backed up, and stopped to examine the sign.

"Ballymauran" it read. He looked at the map, finger tracing along to the same name at a crossing of lines. It was only a short way ahead. He nodded in satisfaction, gunning the car forward.

Around a bend, a meadow opened up. As he saw it, his foot slammed onto the brake and the car slid to a halt.

"What the hell?" he said, staring.

Some way out in the meadow was a cluster of trees. They seemed to be growing around and within a circular mound of earth that rose too abruptly from the smooth swell of meadow to be natural.

Still staring, he got out of the car. He strode out into the meadow as if some irresistible force was drawing him there. As he approached the trees, he could see that the mound they half hid was really a ring of earth some fifty feet across, surrounding an indented place where more trees clustered.

But as he moved closer, gaze riveted on the site, the masking trees began fading away . . .

13

The ringfort ahead showed clearly now as the chariot carrying the warrior Colin and his driver Ailbe rolled swiftly toward it.

"Are you certain about this?" the little charioteer asked his young master.

"For the last time, Ailbe," Colin said with thinning patience, "I have to talk to her . . . to them . . . about this. Just drive on."

As they drew near the circling bank and palisade of the rath's outer defenses, a face appeared atop the wall, peering over the spiked timbers at them. Soon other faces appeared on either side of it. There was a glint of sunlight on the polished iron of weapons.

Ailbe pulled up below the wall, before the little causeway that bridged the outer foss. One of the faces on the wall above opened its mouth to call a challenge.

"Who is it who rides up so boldly to the rath of Clan Mulconrys?"

"A warrior come in peace," Colin called back.

"We've no reason to trust any man," came the curt reply. The figure raised itself up, revealing a long casting spear already cocked to throw. "Be away with you now, or have barbed iron through your heart for your trouble."

"But it's the chieftain of your clan I'm wishing to see. He'll know the truth of my words."

"It's his own son you're speaking to now, Seadna."

"Am I? Well, then, it's glad I am to see you so well, Seadna, for it's my own sword that helped you keep your life."

"Yours?" the other said, surprised.

"He is the one," put in one of the other warriors on the wall. "I know him now. Him and his little driver."

"Risking my life isn't enough," grumbled Ailbe. "Now I have insults, too."

"So, you're Colin MacMathghamhain," said Seadna, lowering the spear. "Well then, I do owe my life to you. You're most welcome in my clan's *dun.*"

He turned and disappeared behind the wall. In moments the double gates creaked open, and Ailbe drove the chariot over the foss and into the yard.

It was clear that word of their arrival had already spread to the rest of the fortress. The five score inhabitants were gathering, creating a scene resembling that of his leavetaking only the day before.

Seadna came up to Colin as he climbed from the chariot. He was younger than Colin, and seemed somewhat abashed. However, he held himself proudly erect, with a palm out in greeting.

"It's glad I am to be able to meet you," he told the visitor in a formal tone. "I am most ashamed for threatening you."

"You have no shame in defending your family's home," Colin assured him. "And you owe me no thanks. You fought well against high odds."

"I thank you," he said with clear relief, smiling. "It's great praise to come from so great a warrior as yourself."

Now it was Colin's turn to look abashed.

"I'm not such . . ." he began, but he was interrupted.

"Colin!" called a voice, and he turned to see the girl Aislinn rushing up to him.

She gripped his arms as she reached him, her bright gaze fixed on him anxiously, her voice filled with great concern.

"Colin, what is it you're doing here! I hoped never to see you again."

"Did you?" he asked earnestly. "Really?"

This flustered her. She pulled back, releasing his arms.

"I . . . I mean I'd hoped you'd be going back to your own home!"

"Colin!" said her little brother Seanan, rushing up behind her. He was openly delighted at the young warrior's return. "I knew that you'd come back!"

Behind him towered the imposing form of his father, Flann O'Mulconrys, gazing at the visitor in a guarded way.

"Why did you come back to us, son of Mathghamhain?" he asked bluntly.

"I want some answers from you," came Colin's equally blunt reply. "I think I've earned them," he added, his determined gaze going from father to daughter, "and I'll not even think of leaving here again until I've had them."

Flann and Aislinn exchanged their own looks at this. His expression was one of acceptance, hers one of anguish and indecision.

"Daughter, we must," he urged. "He's given us no other way."

"Very well," she said reluctantly. She looked to the young warrior again. "You may have the answers you wish. But any fate that may fall upon you from hearing them will be of your own choosing!"

"Tell me then, warrior," said Flann, "just what is it that you wish to know?"

He and much of his clan were now gathered in the rath's large oval hut. Warriors sat crosslegged upon the rush mats, forming a ring around the central hearth and its peat fire. The women and children stood or sat behind them. Flann sat upon a stool on one side of the ring, his elder son at one hand and Colin at the other. His younger son and his daughter stood behind.

The glow of the fire lit the faces of the assembled clan, revealing expressions of solemn expectation. It glinted in the scores of eyes fixed intently upon Colin as he asked his first question.

"Who is Cromm?"

There was a sigh that swept through the room at this, but it was not a disturbance of the wind. It was the collective release of tension in the gathering as that name was finally spoken aloud by the young man.

Flann took a deep breath. He looked toward Aislinn. She nodded.

"All right then," the chieftain said with finality. "He is a god. A very ancient one. So old he is that no one knows how long men have worshiped him. But some say he was in Ireland before even the first of the Others."

"It's said that once all mortals worshiped only Cromm," put in his elder son. "That he was more powerful than any other god."

"My son is right," agreed Flann. "Even in the days of my own father, men from all Ireland and far beyond came to give worship to Cromm and to win rewards."

"He had such power?"

"There is a tale that one high king of Ireland defied Cromm," said Flann, "over two thousand years ago. Tighernmas he was. A most honorable and civilized king, he first smelted gold and created the law that distinguishes the learned classes by the colors of their dress. It was his artisans who worked the gold that ornaments Black Cromm's withered limbs. But this king was proud, and thought himself second to no one—man or god. So on that greatest ritual day of Samhain, when he and all the tribes of faithful were gathered on Magh Slecht to give their worship, the god destroyed Tighernmas and two thirds of his people—slaughtered them there, upon the plain, to soak all its earth black with their blood. And those few who remained gave no more challenge."

CROMM

"And you were followers of Cromm?"

"We were, to our shame," said Flann. "We practiced the sacred rites as all the others did. And we had strength, peace, perfect health, and great riches."

"But what happened? Something brought you to challenge this Cromm's power."

From beneath his tunic Flann pulled a chain. Hanging from it was a simply wrought figure of bronze, a single length of wire looped to form the stylized likeness of a fish, the crossed ends making its tail.

"This is what happened. This is the symbol of another power. One more vast, but with none of the cruelty of Bloody Cromm."

"What is that?" asked Colin, examining it curiously.

"It is the symbol of a man who is also a god. It is the symbol of his new faith that has come into Ireland from the East."

"Tell him the story, Father," Aislinn urged. "Then maybe he can understand."

"Yes, tell him," said Seadna, joined by other coaxing voices in the group saying: "Tell him, Chieftain!"

"Daughter, it's for you to tell it," Flann said to Aislinn. "You have more skill in the words."

"But it was you who saw him first. You must tell Colin of that. So he knows of the magic."

He considered, then nodded.

"Very well," he agreed.

He fixed his eyes upon the glowing peat as if looking away into another time, focusing, staring intently to draw the images to greatest clarity. The red glow burnished his broad face as if it were a sculpture of bronze, its strong features thrown into sharp relief.

"Two years ago it was now that we traveled to the great Tailteen Fair held on the hill near to Tara of the Kings.

"It was the night before the fair that I first saw the man who would change our lives. The sacred night of the preparation for the festival's opening ritual. Like all other visiting chieftains, I was invited to Tara, to the great fortress of Ireland's High-King Laoghaire."

He looked around to Colin, adding in a more personal tone: "He's a great king, you know. Hard, tall, hawk-eyed, most proud in his bearing. A fierce but fair man. I'm most honored to have met him. Why, I even sat right by him. No further than you are from . . ."

"Father," said Aislinn, gently interrupting. "The story?"

"Oh. Oh yes," he said, recalled. "Well, we sat about the fire in high Tara's hall, and we listened to the bardic tales and the sounds of the harps and the *tiompan* and pipes, and we ate and we drank. Mostly we drank. But then the *ard*-druids of the king came suddenly amongst us. Very excited they were. They had found that visitors—strangers from some foreign land—had come and pitched a camp on the hill opposite. On Slaine Hill! Boldly within sight of Tara's *dun*. And . . ." he said, pausing for emphasis, ". . . they had built a fire!"

There were sounds of shock and amazement at this in the gathering and Colin looked around. It was clear that this tale, though Flann's clansfolk had likely heard it many times before, still held them fascinated.

Flann, obviously bolstered by this support, went on, his tone growing ever more dramatic as he plunged further into his tale.

"Well, as you know, it is the worst sacrilege for any fire to be lit on that night before the druids light their own sacred fire upon the hill of Tara.

" 'Who's dared to do this outrage!' Laoghaire stormed. Ah, he's a man of great wrath when aroused. Like a fierce wolf!

"The druids answered that a prophecy had warned of such a man coming to overthrow their power and the king's own rule." Flann's gaze was fixed on the fire, his voice very intense. "I remember their words as if they were being spoken now: 'If that fire on yonder hill is not extinguished this very night,' they warned, 'it shall never more be extinguished in all Ireland!' "

He shook his head and looked again to Colin.

"Well, of course Laoghaire couldn't sit idle for that! He ordered this offender dragged before him with all his company.

"It took the rest of that night for his warriors to raid their camp and march the captives back to Tara. We waited, drinking on, expecting what we thought would be good sport when these foolish strangers faced the king."

Flann's gaze went back to the fire. His voice took on a softer, more reminiscent quality as he recalled the next events.

"We heard them coming first, heard the chanting of a hymn. The *Faed Fiada* they called it—the Deer's Cry—that was to protect them from harm. 'God's hand for my cover,' I heard them sing, 'God's path to pass over, God's buckler to guard me, God's army to ward me against snares of the devil.'

"And then they came into the hall, marching in procession, in a long line, erect, unafraid, following The One who I saw then for the first time.

"He was no young man. His lean face was drawn and etched with lines. His hair was grey. He was spare as if from long hardship, sinewy as if from hard labor. But there was a great strength about him, a great power that was nothing to do with his form or age, but with a . . . a heat that seemed to waft out from him so strongly it was as if I could see the glow about him, like the glow of this peat fire, warming, comforting, wrapping about me . . ."

He seemed to be drifting away on the flood of this soothing reverie.

"The Challenge, Father," said Seanan eagerly, putting a hand on his father's shoulder. "Tell him about The Challenge."

"Ah, yes," said Flann, shaking off the spell recast by the memory. "Well, we chieftains and warriors all sat in our circle about him and his followers. Over the iron rims of our war-shields we glared fiercely upon the strangers. But that old man only looked about him, his gaze bold and fearless. Then he looked up to where Laoghaire himself sat at his high table, meeting the hawk's fierce eye.

" 'Let them that will trust in chariots and horses, but we walk in the name of the Lord!' he said in a voice clear and echoing in that great hall like the clanging of a bell.

" 'Defiler!' shouted the chief *ard*-druid. 'Desecrator! You dare to blaspheme within the very walls of our most sacred place? The power of the Others fall upon you for your crime!'

" 'I have no fear of the power of your gods,' the old man told him. 'We have the protection of a power much greater.'

" 'You have the look of a foreigner,' said Laoghaire, gazing at him with great curiosity. 'Yet you speak as one of us.'

" 'Your own father it was who may take credit for that,' the man replied. 'For it was his raiders brought me to Ireland as a slave, and sold me to the Antrim chieftain Miliue. For seven years, then, did I tend his sheep in the valley of the Braid and up the slopes of Slieve Mis. And there, alone for those many days and nights, I found the truth. I went far away for many years to learn more of this truth. But now I come among you again, this time to save you all.'

"The High-King laughed. 'Save us?' he said. 'And how can you do that?'

" 'By bringing a great, new light into your darkness.'

" 'Destroy him now,' the chief *ard*-druid urged the king. 'Quickly. For each moment he lives makes him a greater danger to our rule.'

"But Laoghaire was a fair man, as I've said. He looked at that slender, aged man, and he shook his head.

" 'I see no great danger in this one man,' he pronounced. 'If he claims to have such powers, we will test him. You, my own *ard*-druids, will match your own against his.'

"Well," Flann said with a little smile, "it was clear to us that his druids were far from happy about that. But they had little choice. They agreed to a trial.

" 'He has kindled this new fire on Slaine Hill,' they said. 'He claims to bring a new light to us. Very well, then we will snuff it out!' "

At this point, Colin glanced around the fire again. Warriors, women, children all were rapt, caught up fully in this tale that their chieftain was now rolling out with the full powers of his rich, booming voice.

"So a score of his greatest druids gathered together," Flann went on. "The stranger watched them, calmly, gravely, as they worked about the central fire in Tara's hall, combining their loathsome ingredients in boiling cauldrons, casting their powders upon the flames, sending up flares of colored light and streams of smoke to fill the hall with stench.

"But then The Darkness came. It flowed in through the roof hole, pouring down on us like molten pitch. It flooded in from all sides of the room, rising, filling the hall with a thick black, worse than any night, denser than the worst fog—a suffocating, stinking sea of darkness swallowing us all.

"I was blind, near choking. I could hear others around me wheezing, coughing in their own distress. I couldn't speak for it clogging my throat. But then a voice spoke up from the black, clear and ringing as before. The stranger's voice.

" 'Druids, I ask you now to dispel this dark,' it said.

" 'It is for you to do so,' came the gasping voice of the chief *ard*-druid.

" 'I ask you to try first,' the stranger challenged. 'If you succeed, then I will submit to your greater power.'

"There were mutterings, voices of disagreement as the druids argued. But then a chant arose from them, muffled by the blanket of dark. There were some low rumblings, a faint flash like distant lightning in the clouds, then nothing more. The smothering black was as heavy as before.

" 'We cannot raise the darkness,' came the chief *ard*-druid's voice, shrill in its despair.

" 'Then,' " the stranger said, " 'I will try.'

"And almost instantly there was the rising of a wind within the hall. It swirled around us, catching the dark as if it were a cloak of blackest wool, tugging it, sweeping it into a rising whirlwind. It swept faster and faster around us, pulling into an always tighter spiral, drawing the darkness into a dense, switching coil of black in the center of the room. Then it lifted up, drawing its writhing length out the smoke hole like a monstrous serpent. Light had been returned to the great hall.

"And there, revealed in the midst of the room, arms lifted, stood the stranger, a golden glow about his face.

"He dropped his arms. He looked around at us. A smile of triumph and beneficence and peace like I have never seen beamed out from him.

" 'Your druids can bring you only darkness,' he said in a calm way. 'I bring you the light!'

"The druids said nothing, cowering back in a group like a flock of frightened birds. But Laoghaire was much impressed.

" 'It is surely a great power that you have, stranger,' he said.

" 'I have no power at all, High-King,' the man replied humbly. 'It is all that of my Lord. I am only his servant.'

" 'I have no wish to see your lord's power invade my Ireland,' said Laoghaire. 'But you have passed your trial. Though you may be a danger to me, still I will give you life. And because you are a brave man, I'll give you something more. From this day you may travel as you wish in Ireland under my protection. Preach your new faith wherever you will. I ask only that you waste none of your words in trying to change me.'

" 'If you change,' was the old man's reply, 'it will not be by my will, but the will of God.'

" 'Then you may go, stranger,' the High-King declared. 'But, first, what is your name?'

" 'Patricius I was born,' came the answer, 'but the people of Ireland have called me Patrick.' "

Flann stopped there, staring into the fire, recalling the moment. There was a complete silence in the room, all the listeners still caught up in the drama of the tale. Then Aislinn spoke.

"Thank you, Father. You tell the tale most beautifully, as always."

"Patrick," said Colin musingly. "I don't know that name. But I think I have heard rumors of this new faith coming into Ireland. What is it called?"

"Christianity," Flann told him. "But it was not that first seeing of this man that turned us to it. That came the next day." He looked to his daughter. "Aislinn, it's you who must tell him of that."

She nodded and moved out past him, into the open space nearer the fire, turning to face Colin. The light from the burning peat made her white linen shift and pale skin glow with a rosy hue, and struck flickering fiery lights in her red-gold hair.

Colin stared at her, rapt by her before she even began to speak.

CROMM

"It was that next day, the day of the Tailteen Fair, that Patrick's work began," said the girl. She lifted her arms to take in all those around her. "We, all of our clan, were blessed to see it."

"It was a most grand fair," Seanan put in with enthusiasm. "The greatest I've ever seen. So many thousands come from all Ireland."

"It was surely that," his sister agreed. "And it was many wonderful and curious things we all expected to see that day. But none was so strange a sight as that band of men in their foreign clothes coming so boldly through the crowd, nor that one man of them, Patrick, who climbed to the very brow of the hill.

"We gathered about him, out of curiosity at first. But then he spoke, and the force in his words held us."

The firelight now seemed to strike a shining light in her bright eyes, and a great warmth came into her voice as she continued.

"He told us he had come to us as ambassador from the King of the World's kings. Patrick described His kingdom to us, and His infinite love for us, and His great wish to have all of us know Him.

" 'He sent His own son as a messenger to mankind,' Patrick said. 'A son of beauty, goodness, meekness, and love.' And then Patrick told us the tale of the son's torture and death to save us and bring us into His Father's kingdom.

"Those of us gathered about him on that hill were moved. The women, the herdsmen, the children were moved. Even the warriors—stern, hardened men and wild, eager ones—seemed tamed by the words. I tell you . . ." she said, putting a clenched hand to her breast, her voice coming with intensity, "I could *feel* the power of it sweeping through me. Something I had never felt."

She was taken by the recollected emotion now, carried again by it, raising her arms high, lifting her gaze upward, a glowing figure in the throes of this passion.

"It was a love. A peace. It swept through us all, and we were humbled, soothed, sweetened, moved more deeply than I can speak of, all in one great welling of emotion like a surging wave! One great sea of heads bowing as he gave us his blessing!"

Around Colin, eyes glistened and chests heaved and there were sobs of joy as all her clansmen relived with her this spiritual catharsis. Even in the eyes of the stolid Flann the glint of tears showed. The young warrior, also enwrapped by the spell of her tale, stared in fascination.

But with this final climax, the power filling her seemed to wane. She dropped her arms, looking around her as if recalled to reality, panting as if drained by the emotional outpouring.

Her gaze came back to Colin. When she spoke again, there was an anguish in her voice.

"It was then the horror came. Not for all those gathered on that hill, but for us, the followers of Black Cromm. The others felt only the new spirit that had come to them, drawing them to Patrick and his new light. But for us, my clansmen and I, it was like awakening from the most terrible nightmare to find the truth! Patrick's words washed away the hold of Cromm, like an enchantment broken. Suddenly, clearly, we knew the truth, and we understood what evil we have done."

"What *we* have done," said her father, "and what our people have done for generations past. The years of waste, all out of fear and greed. Cromm had taken control, and we had cared for nothing else, believed in nothing else. But we were freed of it —and we knew we must come back here, to fight."

"Fight?" Colin echoed.

"We had to fight Cromm," Flann's elder son Seadna explained. "It wasn't enough that we had escaped. We had to turn others from him. We needed to free them all from his power. To stop them."

"Stop them from what?"

"Sacrifice," Aislinn said, a great sadness in her voice. "So much sacrifice. So many, many thousands over the years."

"What? You mean thousands of people sacrificed? Killed?"

"To the good of Cromm," Flann said grimly, nodding his head. "You see, the monster lives on human blood."

14

The word "blood" echoed in his mind, fading away.

The light above him grew suddenly brighter and he lifted his head—to see, not the thatched roof above him, but the interlacing branches of trees.

He looked around. He stood inside the ancient ring of earth, in the shadows of the grove that had grown up within its shelter. Beyond, through the screen of other trees around the ring, he could see the sun glinting on the polished hood of his Vauxhall.

There was a gap in one side of the ring, and he made his way out through it, pushing through the trees and underbrush into the open fields again. He strode across to the car and turned there, looking back at the overgrown site.

He stared, envisioning this same place, bared of trees, superimposed upon the ringfort of his dream. It was possible that the two were the same place.

He shook his head, muttering:

"But how could I have been here before?"

There was no one to answer him. After a moment's meditation, he shrugged and climbed back into the car, heading on along the road to Ballymauran.

He reached the village quite suddenly.

From the tree-lined road he emerged without transition into an open area surrounded by a few shops and houses. Here three roads met to encircle a central monument: a massive stone high-cross. From there a single road ran down a shallow incline through the balance of the town.

He drove slowly down it, gazing searchingly about him. The village had the same settled aura as the countryside, the look of a stone wall that age had worked down into the earth until it seemed more natural than manmade.

Everything was softened by the years, by the rains that had

worn down all sharpness, all newness. There were no harsh colors here, just gentle ones: the natural greys of weathered thatch and wood, the quiet watercolor washes on the walls of stucco shops and cottages.

The air was soft, too, with the pungent, enveloping perfume of burning peat, the same scent Colin had already breathed in his dream life.

He sniffed the air, his face lighting up with the recognition of this one more bit of evidence. Then, realizing he was nearing the bottom of the hill and the end of the town, he pulled in to the curb and sat considering.

There was no clear sign of what he should do next. Not even anyone to question. The streets were empty. Though there were several cottages close by, a shop labeled "victauller," and a shed with a sign reading "peat yard," there were no people. It was as still and timeless as if a glass bell jar had been dropped over it.

He got out of the car, looking back the way he'd come. There were no signs for hotels or tourist information. Not even one indicating a bed-and-breakfast. His gaze scanned up one side of the street and down the other, stopping at a whitewashed building where two large windows flanked a door painted a glossy red. Above the door the name "O'Connor" was neatly painted and framed in the same red. At either side of it hung a metal sign depicting a tapering glass of dark liquid above the word "Guinness."

Giving a little shrug, Colin walked up the street to the building. He paused for a moment before its door, looking it over uncertainly. Then he drew himself up in a determined way and entered.

The day outside was fresh, clear, and cool. But inside the pub, the air was heavy, stagnant. It might have hung uncleaned in the room for a hundred years.

He wrinkled his nose, stopping inside the door to look about him at the dimly lit scene.

Softness and long, gentle wear marked the pub's appearance as it did the rest of the town. The often-polished bar, the age-scarred tables, even the patrons carried an air of settled age. Men of varying ages and types were somehow all the same in their cloth caps and working jackets.

There were a dozen of them scattered at the tables in twos and threes. Some talked in rolling sounds that seemed to blur together into a single, soft voice; others dreamed over mugs of rich brown drink. Smoke from their pipes and cigarettes rose up straight into the sluggish air and eddied in slow, lazy curves barely stirred by the faint currents.

But the breeze of Colin's entrance whipped through the haze, and the forest of thin smoke columns flung themselves away from him like some midnight gathering of wraiths alarmed by his intrusion.

Men looked up from their talk to note him, then held the looks on finding him a stranger.

Glancing around him as he walked, he moved through them to the bar. Behind it was a round-faced man, narrow-shouldered, broadening toward the stomach in a soft-looking way. The static occupation and the constant handiness of his own wares had left him red-faced, permanently flushed.

He stood behind the bar as if planted there. His only movement was the slow, monotonous wiping out of glasses.

He noted Colin and turned as he approached, fixing him with appraising eyes set in a stolid face.

"Hi. How're ya doing?" Colin offered brightly, smiling.

There was no return smile.

"And what can I do for you, sir?" the man asked coolly, his look flicking over the young newcomer. "Is it lost you are from the main roads?"

"Nope," Colin assured him. "Not this time."

"You're an American, are you?" The barman looked Colin over again, more carefully, from belt to hairline. Only his eyes moved. The rest of him was stone. "It's few enough of those who come through here. Can I be getting something for you?"

"How about a beer?"

"Ale?" the bartender countered. "Harp's maybe?"

"Sure. Fine. A Harp," Colin said agreeably.

"Right away," the man said and turned to take a mug from the shelves behind him. "Where is it you're heading?"

"Here, at the moment, I guess," Colin answered.

The man hesitated very slightly in his movement, turning his head to look back at Colin quizzically.

"Oh, really? There's little enough around here to interest a tourist."

Colin answered still affably, as if trying to build a friendly relationship:

"Well, actually, I heard about this place from someone I met this morning. Maybe you know her? A red-haired girl, grey eyes, middle twenties? I met her on the coast just west of here. She told me this is where she lived."

The barman turned back toward him in a quick move and brought the heavy mug down on the bar with a loud thud.

"We've not much use for tourists here," he said coldly, "and we've little liking of their disturbing us."

Colin's eyes widened in surprise, this sudden hostility having taken him off guard.

"Disturbing you?" he asked, rather blankly.

"There's nothing here to interest a young fellow like yourself," the man went on. He filled the mug from a tap with sharp, angry movements and slammed it back unceremoniously on the bar in front of Colin. "You'd best be going on to someplace where they've comforts for you."

Now Colin's look grew irritated.

"Hey, buddy, I think I can decide if a place interests me. It *is* my choice, isn't it?"

If Colin had hoped his return would make some impression on the barman, he was wrong. It had as much effect on the granite expression as would chipping at Mount Rushmore with a wooden mallet.

"We've no place for visitors here," the man said firmly. "We've no wish to have them hanging about and upsetting the quiet ways we have. Now there's your ale. You may have it from me without pay. But there's nothing else we can give to you."

He seemed to consider the conversation finished, and turned away. Colin was aware that a silence had fallen on the room, and he glanced about him. A number of eyes were quickly averted.

Colin's look of irritation darkened to one of anger.

"Now, wait a minute, pal," he said sharply, leaning over the bar toward the man, "I only asked a simple question, and I don't want any free drinks." He pulled out some change and laid it on the counter. "But I'll stay here as long as I want!"

The man looked around again. His gaze traveled from the change to Colin's face. His own had grown quite hard.

"Look here, young man. I don't know this girl you're speaking of. Now, best drink that ale and be getting on. It's a long drive back to the main highways."

"Matthew!" said a shocked voice from behind Colin.

The barman turned to look past his shoulder and saw a man in a long black cassock standing by the door. The dark garment made a startling contrast with a shock of white-gold hair and the pinkness of a lean face, now drawn in severe lines.

"Matthew," he said, "what way is that to treat a stranger here?"

Colin glanced at the barman. The mild reproof of the newcomer had a powerful effect on him. The flush in his face deepened to a hot red, and his head seemed to sink down into his shoulders protectively.

"I've told him nothing but the truth," he said with sullen stubbornness, but with all the granite strength now gone from it. It was clear that the figure in the doorway wielded some real authority here.

"You could do it with a bit more Christian fellowship," the other countered sternly. He came forward and extended a hand to Colin, smiling warmly. "Hello. My name is Father Bonaventure."

"Colin McMahon," the American replied, taking the hand.

The father was a small man, the hand he put out long and fine-boned, but he gripped Colin's hand with surprising strength.

Even close up it was hard to truly estimate the man's age. He was slender, trim and neat of figure. His features were emphatic and elastic, mouth wide, nose long, bright green eyes broad-spaced below a high span of forehead. There were no lines, no marks of aging on the smooth pink flesh. His bearing and manner were easy, youthful. He was over thirty, probably less than fifty.

"You must excuse Matthew," he said, shooting the barman another reproving glance. "He sees too few new faces here to treat one properly. Please, have an ale with me."

His show of friendship seemed genuine, but Colin shook his head.

"No. Thanks anyway, Father. I think I've worn out my welcome here. I'd better just get going. It was nice meeting you, at least."

He started toward the door, but the priest moved after him.
"Wait. Do you mind if I walk out with you?"

Colin shrugged. "Not much I can do to stop you." Together they walked out of the bar, leaving the money and the untouched ale. Colin didn't look back.

Outside the priest stopped him.

"I came out to apologize again for what happened in there," he said. "I assure you, Ballymauran is really a pleasant village."

He was so anxious about it that Colin relaxed enough to reassure him. "It's okay," he said, but still a bit grudgingly. "I guess I can understand why they might be a little unfriendly to outsiders."

"But they really aren't that," the priest said emphatically. "Though they are quite isolated here, I admit. I've been about here for nearly five years, and they're still a bit uncertain about me."

Colin smiled at that, and Bonaventure seemed relieved to see it.

"I didn't hear what began that little row of yours," he said. "May I ask what it was?"

Colin hesitated, looking into the bright, inquisitive eyes.

"Well, I said I was planning to stay here," he said finally, providing only part of the truth. "He didn't like the idea."

Bonaventure now eyed him even more quizzically.

"Much as I find this area intriguing, I must say that I wonder myself why you'd be interested in it."

He spoke in a nudging sort of way, and it was obvious that he was certain Colin must have some further motivation. But he was so amiable and open in manner that Colin stared thoughtfully at him for a moment, clearly tempted to blurt out his incredible tale to the man. Then he shook his head and smiled regretfully.

"Father, I can't even begin to explain my reasons for being here. I don't understand them myself. But there is one thing you could help me with," he said, and hesitated again, adding, "though I feel a little weird asking a priest."

"There's little of the 'weird' I've not heard in my life," Bonaventure assured him. "Ask me."

"You might be surprised, at that," Colin said with feeling. "But, okay. It's a girl, Father. See, the real reason I'm here is that I met a girl this morning. She said she came from here. I . . . I wanted to meet her again."

If Colin thought this might shock the priest, he was mistaken. Bonaventure's look of puzzlement was swept away by a broad smile.

"Ah, now I understand. A much more practical reason for a young man to go visiting somewhere than to see some crumbling ruin or bit of scenery."

"Not to your buddy Matthew. His dander really hit the fan when I asked him about her."

"I see. But that would explain his suspicions of you, don't you think? A handsome young stranger, an American to boot, comes in asking after a local girl. You can be certain he believed you were up to no good at all."

"I don't know about the handsome part, but, yeah, I guess there was a lot of the shotgun-toting daddy in his reaction. So why don't you act the same?"

"Oh, I've seen a bit more of the world. I think young people make their own mistakes and are welcome to them. Besides, you seem trustworthy enough to me. This girl, now, don't you know her name?"

"Ah . . . well . . . no," Colin admitted lamely. "See, I just talked to her for a minute, and she had to go off in a hurry. A big hurry."

The priest didn't catch the irony in his voice.

"A pity. But maybe I can help you then. What was it she looked like?"

"Red hair with gold in it. A pleasant, honest sort of face and bright grey eyes. She talked like she had to travel around a lot."

"Why, that must be Megan Conroy!" Bonaventure announced with certainty. "She travels to nurse those in the country about. On a sunny day her hair is like a flame." He gave Colin a knowing smile that drew a deeper pink into his cheeks. "You describe her very well . . . for a brief meeting."

"I have a good memory," Colin said quickly, looking a little abashed. "Do you know much about her?"

"Very little. She's been here only since the summer, and too busy for social things, though she seems a fine girl. Her home is not far from my abbey. I could direct you easily."

"Could you do it now?" Colin asked eagerly, then drew back, clearly aware that he was pressing. "I'm sorry. I suppose you must be busy."

"Not at all! I've only been out for my daily walk. I was on my way back when something drew me to stop in here for a small sip of ale. But I'll not get it now." He winked at Colin. "Let Matthew believe he's really angered me. It'll make him think the more on it. You have an automobile, I assume?"

"Right there," Colin said, gesturing toward the Vauxhall.

"Then give me a ride back to my abbey, and I'll show you where she lives. But . . ." he said, as he raised a qualifying finger, "only if you'll promise to stop at the abbey for a bit to tell me more about yourself and your trip here. It's little enough news we get about the wider world."

"That's a deal, Father."

Together they walked across the road to his car. As they got in, Colin noted that the barman had come to the tavern door and was watching them.

From his expression it was clear that he disapproved of this sudden friendship between the priest and the young man.

"Well, the hell with you," Colin said under his breath.

CROMM

The entrance to Bonaventure's abbey was half a mile from town, along another narrow winding road.

The lane they turned into was yet more narrow, leading them uphill through pastures dotted with trees and shrubs already half bared of their russet leaves by the autumn winds. The area had the appearance of a park that had once been well tended, but had been left to go back to a wilder state of nature.

The road passed into a dense grove of trees. Then, above the highest branches ahead of them, a tower came abruptly into view. Colin's first glimpse of it was sudden, through a gap in the foliage, and he gave a little grunt of surprise.

"What is it?" the priest asked.

"Just a sort of shock," Colin said. "Like . . . I was just dropped into another time. That tower is something from a fairy tale. Without this car, there's nothing to connect me to the real world." He gripped the wheel tighter and glanced at the black-robed priest. "Not even you."

Bonaventure seemed amused by the reaction.

"I've heard visitors to Ireland say that before. Especially Americans. But it's just the feeling of age, my young man. You've come from a country with two hundred years of history to one with five thousand. The years gather around you, I think, like a heavy mist, and the view of 'now' gets blurred into the 'then.'"

They came out of the trees into a graveled yard, and the abbey was now wholly visible, filling up the way ahead in a squat, brooding manner, like some archaic monster that had crawled from a medieval forest to stubbornly block the road.

They pulled up before it and got out. Colin stared at the building in awe.

"It's not really a castle, of course," said the priest. "Like much in Ireland, the truth is hidden by what seems to be. It's neo-Gothic, built in the 1820s—though it does have all the grotesque, romantic fascination its kind was meant to invoke."

"You really live there?" Colin asked.

"Oh yes. Though we use very little of it now. It was a school some years ago, with a large monastic population." His voice took on a regretful note. "But the children have gone with the changing of the times. And the brothers have dwindled away. It's only myself and two others now, since Brother Coleman's passing. Yes, a great, lonely pile it often seems. It's why I'm grateful for the visit of one such as yourself."

"Look, Father," Colin began, "about this Megan Conroy . . ."

"Megan. Oh yes," he said, recalled to the business at hand. "Well, you've not far to go to reach her house from here." He turned and pointed. "It's just off there, across the fields."

Colin looked in the direction to which he pointed. From the high ground where the abbey sat, the hills and pastures rolled away.

"It's actually closer across the meadows than by the road," Bonaventure went on. "Why don't you leave your car and stroll across? For a late October day, the weather is quite fine."

"Thanks, Father. That's a great idea. And can I tell her I know you?"

"You can," he said, "so long as when you come back, we have some tea and a bit of talk. And you can bring Megan if you wish." He gave Colin a speculative look. "I don't know why, but I've the strongest feeling you two should be close friends."

"Father, I hope you're right," Colin told him.

He waved goodbye and started off across the graveled yard. Beyond a small area of mowed grass and trimmed shrubs that made a formal garden area for the old manor house, the landscape became more wild, a rolling pastureland with scattered clumps of shrubbery and trees.

As Bonaventure had commented, it was an amazingly pleasant afternoon for fall, clear and still and with a warming sun. The meadow grasses were still green, but touched now with a golden glow. The leaves remaining on the trees were cast in warm shades from yellow to deep red, making bright spots like flames rising from the smooth land. Again he felt there was a timelessness, an eternal quality about it all, as if it were the landscape of a Constable painting.

To his left, down a gentle slope to a flat meadow of grass, he noted a prominent feature of some kind. It could have been a large natural hill, but it seemed too smooth.

He stopped to look at it in curiosity, then angled away from his path to pass by it.

He lost sight of it for a moment as his route took him behind the swell of a smaller hill. When he came around this, he stopped, staring ahead with a look of confusion.

The larger hill wasn't there anymore.

He pivoted around, but only the gentler swells of empty pasture surrounded him. No points of reference. The road, the abbey, and the large mound were nowhere to be seen. Nothing but the endless, indistinguishable fields stretching away in all directions.

He scrambled up the little hill he had just come around and scanned the countryside. He spotted the high tower of the abbey above the distant trees. From this landmark he scanned around, identifying the line of trees that marked the road, and then the peculiar hump of earth.

"Boy, that was stupid," he said aloud. "How'd I get so far off course?"

He moved across the meadow until he could once more see the abbey tower behind him, the big hill ahead, and the road down to his right. He headed directly toward the hill, this time keeping his eyes fixed on it.

He had covered half the distance to it when he looked around to see if the abbey was still in sight. When he looked back, the hill was gone again.

He stopped, swaying as if he'd been suddenly spun around and left off balance. He looked about him wildly. The abbey tower was also gone again, and so was the line of trees marking the road. Both had vanished in the same moment of time.

His gaze swept the bright, still meadows, a hint of fear in his eyes now. He was suddenly a tiny figure, alone, lost in the timeless countryside under the changeless sky.

He looked around again, pivoting slowly, then faster and faster like a marionette being spun on its strings until he realized his panic and stopped abruptly.

"No. No," he breathed. "That's making it worse. Logical. Be logical. Find a landmark."

He ran his gaze around him once more, searching carefully.

"West," he said, looking toward a lowering sun. "That's west. The road must be over there."

He moved ahead, finally topping a soft fold of hill. Not far below was the line of trees that marked the road. He sighed with relief, then looked around again.

Far away to the south of him now he saw that odd mound. It meant that somehow he had gone hundreds of yards off course in a heartbeat of time.

"I really am losing my mind!" he said softly.

Then his look of bewilderment and alarm changed to one of obstinancy.

"God damn it," he said loudly, as if speaking to the country-side, "I was an Eagle Scout! I've tackled *real* wilderness. Wilderness with teeth! No hunk of tame cow pasture is going to get *me* lost!"

This time he turned away from the mound, instead making for the line of trees that crossed the fields below from side to side.

"I can't miss that!" he declared. Still, to be sure, he kept his gaze on it without a break, giving himself no chance to wander off his course.

The rounded hill dropped from sight behind him. He drew nearer to the line of trees. This time they stayed put. Finally he reached them. He passed through.

There was no road beyond them.

15

OCTOBER 29, 4:24 P.M.

He stopped to stare, dumbfounded. He seemed momentarily paralyzed, like someone who has walked into a house he thinks is his, only to find it's his neighbor's.

All that lay before him now was another field, rolling and green and open and empty, like the rest. No road.

"Where in the goddamn hell is the road!" he shouted, his wrath breaking his stunned paralysis. "There has *got* to be a road!"

He wheeled around. There was now only more meadow behind him, sweeping away to a distant line of trees, with hills rising beyond. But then his gaze fixed upon something else there—upon a tiny figure standing by the trees.

Relief came into his face and he started toward the figure, focusing on it with some intent, as if fearful he might otherwise lose sight of it too. But it remained there, waiting.

As he drew nearer, his expression changed to one of surprise. For this waiting figure was the red-haired girl, Megan Conroy. She wore no coat this time, her slim figure clad in a simple skirt and sweater. She stood with hands on hips, foot tapping, like one awaiting a very late bus. Her face was drawn into a frown.

Still his own face lit with a smile as he saw for certain that it was her, and he waved, moving ahead faster.

"Hello!" he said with exuberance as he came up to her. "You don't know how glad I am to see you!"

Her own response lacked a matching enthusiasm.

"So, it is you then," she said flatly.

"Hey, I'm sorry," he said, taking a step back and lifting his hands palm out in a gesture of peace. "I didn't mean to come on so strong. I'd have been happy to see even a hairy old guy just now. I was lost."

"Lost?" she said, clearly skeptical.

"Yeah, lost!" he said defensively. "You know? Like getting separated from your folks at Disneyland on July Fourth, or being dumped drunk in the woods by your fraternity brothers at midnight? That kind of lost. I was trying to walk down from that old abbey, and I got completely screwed around."

"Really," she said. She turned her head and looked up toward the hills. The tower of the abbey was clearly visible thrusting above the trees.

He stared at it, then shook his head.

"Cheez, I don't get it." He looked around to meet her doubting gaze. "Okay, I know it looks impossible, getting lost in open country in broad daylight. I don't know how it happened. I was trying to get to the road. It just wasn't there!"

"The road?" she said, skepticism even more apparent in her tone. "This road?"

She waved a hand toward the line of trees fifty yards behind her. He looked more closely. Through the screen of trunks and bushes a road was now clearly visible.

"But I just came through those trees," he said in astonishment. "Didn't I?"

He looked around him in complete bewilderment once more. Then he realized she was still watching him narrowly, still tapping her foot with distinct impatience.

"Look, this isn't just an excuse to meet you again," he told her. "I mean, I would never have thought of anything this dumb! Really! I was just walking down here . . ."

"Why did you follow me here?" she asked abruptly.

"I didn't follow you. Well, not exactly. You told me the name of the town. I found it myself."

"Why?" she asked with more vexation.

"It's kind of hard to explain. I . . . I don't want you to think I'm crazy . . ."

"You don't think you've given me that idea already?"

"Yeah, yeah," he admitted. "I suppose so. But believe me, I'm not dangerous. It's just that some strange things have happened to me, and somehow you might be part of it."

"Me?"

"I said it would be hard to explain. Please," he implored, "I only want to talk!"

She stared into his earnest face for a long moment. What she saw there appeared to pierce through her wall of hostility. She unbent, but only very slightly.

"It wasn't some fear of you that drove me off," she explained. "I simply had no time then. And I have little more now. Excuse me?"

She turned on her heel and started off. This time he was quicker off the mark. He caught up to her and walked alongside.

"Look, I really didn't come here to chase you, I mean, not in a . . . a girl-boy way. That's not what I'm interested in."

"Well, thank you for that!" she shot back. "Now I don't even have to feel flattered."

"No, that's not what I meant! Sure I would have been interested, without this other thing. I know I would have. I mean, I was before. Or, at least, *he* was before. And I guess I'm him, sort of, maybe, or . . ."

Abruptly she stopped walking and he turned to her, meeting her probing gaze.

"Are you certain you're all right, Mr. . . . ?"

"McMahon. Colin McMahon."

"Mr. McMahon. You seem to constantly lapse into nonsense. A head injury perhaps? You look as though you may have been in an accident."

"I always look that way," he said, trying for a winning smile.

It lost. She only nodded curtly and started off again.

"See, it's just that I know you," he said, moving after her. "I think. I mean, I've seen someone who looks like you, sounds like you." His gaze scanned from her long legs up to her swaying hips as she strode through the grass. "She even has your walk."

"You never mind my walk," she fired over her shoulder as she passed through the trees to the road.

He followed her to a small, neat cottage across the road, its stucco sides painted yellow, its roof of clean black slate. Except for the power line running to the cottage, and her Land Rover parked nearby, it might have been part of a scene from two hundred years before.

She crossed to it, and he was close behind her.

"Look, when we first met I thought we had hit it off," he told her reasonably.

"I won't say I didn't find it pleasant," she agreed.

"So why couldn't we continue it? Just talk? I really want to talk to you. And I really am safe. I even know Father Bonaventure from that abbey. He thinks I'm okay."

She stopped at her car and turned.

"Mr. McMahon, whether you know the Father or not means little to me. You may be a very fine man for all I know, but I still have no time for you. I came home from my afternoon rounds to have a bite of food and now I must be off again. My work keeps me quite busy day and night. The only reason I've delayed leaving is that I saw you wandering the meadow. I am now, thanks to you, late. Good day to you, and I hope you can find your way *back* to the abbey."

She put a hand to the door handle. He put a restraining one atop it.

"Please," he said urgently, "I really need help. Something is going on that I have to understand. I'm in a nightmare and I just want out. I think you can help me. I think you feel that too, or you wouldn't be running away from me."

She looked around to him. Their faces were now only inches apart, their gazes locked.

"I am *not* running away," she told him with certainty, but the shadow of a doubt flickered in the bright eyes.

"Aren't you? And are you still sure you don't know me? Not even from a dream?"

"Dream?" she said, clearly taken aback by that.

"Just let me talk to you," he pressed. "Let me try to explain. Anytime . . ."

She stared into his face, into his intense gaze. Then, against her better judgment, she sighed in resignation and nodded.

"All right, Mr. McMahon. If it's the only way I'll get my peace again. But I've no time free for it. If you mean to talk, you'll have to ride with me on my rounds."

"Fair enough," he eagerly agreed. "Now?"

"Not now. I'm far too busy on the evening rounds and far too tired at the end of them. But tomorrow you can come with me, if you must."

"I must."

"Then be here at 7 A.M.," she said, opening the car door. "I leave then, promptly. I won't wait."

"I'll be here," he assured her, stepping back as she climbed in. "This is your house?"

"It is."

"Cute little place. How'd you find it?"

"Find it?" she echoed, starting up the engine. "I was born in it. Goodbye."

She ground into gear and the car leaped forward, sweeping around in a tight turn onto the road and roaring away.

Smiling in satisfaction, he watched the car vanish around a curve. Then he lifted his gaze up toward the hillside where the abbey tower showed. His smile was replaced by a frown.

"Hope I really *can* get back," he murmured, and started resolutely off.

"Mr. McMahon. And did you find your lady home?" asked Father Bonaventure.

The priest moved from the main door of the abbey to meet the American as he came into the graveled yard. He had obviously been awaiting Colin's return, and made little attempt to hide his interest in the young man's quest.

"I did, thanks," Colin told him. "Though calling her 'my lady' is overstating it a lot."

The priest looked distressed at that.

"Ah. Did something go wrong then?"

"No. At least, I don't think so." He shrugged. "Let's just say things have been generally confusing lately. But," he added more brightly, "she did promise to let me go with her tomorrow."

"That's something, then," Bonaventure said, smiling. "She seems a very fine girl, but lonely. At the best, there's not much social life in a small village. So it may be you'll give her some company."

"You said you didn't know much about her?"

"No. I don't go into the village as much as I used to, so I've only met her on occasion. And she came here to treat Brother Coleman. Quite marvelous she was in helping him, though she couldn't save him in the end."

"She said she's busy all the time."

"That she is, being nurse to half the county of isolated little towns and separate farms. I do know that she came here from Dublin."

"Really?" Colin said in surprise. "She said she was born in the place where she's living now."

"Maybe. I've heard nothing about that."

"Well, it's no big deal. My problem at the moment is that I've got to find someplace to spend the night."

"But that's no problem at all!" Bonaventure said with delight. "I'd been thinking to offer you a place here at the abbey, though we've few comforts now what with only the three of us left. But great fortune has smiled on us both. Brigadier Robert Dudley called me while you were gone. He has a fine home just south of the town. I told him of your visiting, and he said that he'd be most pleased to take you in."

"Are you sure?"

"I am. He's a retired British officer. I know him well, and we've had many a rousing debate on society and politics and God. But he misses having those of the wider world to talk to, as I do. When I mentioned I had a young American, he was most eager to give you a room. And the only pay he'll ask is that you'll sit an evening and have a talk with him, and myself as well."

"That's just fine with me," Colin assured him. "I could use some friendly company too, right now. I've been kind of feeling . . . well, I guess you could say lonely."

"Marvelous," the priest declared delightedly. "We've just had vespers. It'll be getting dark soon. We should go over right now. Why don't you follow me in my car? But stay close."

"Right on your bumper. I'm not getting lost again."

Colin turned his car off the main road behind the battered old Morris Minor driven by the priest. They followed another, narrower lane up a low hill and into a paved drive before a house.

Though much smaller than the abbey, it was an imposing home of pleasing appearance. Georgian in style, it was simply and precisely proportioned in the elegant symmetry of its type, with a three-story central section balanced by lower wings on either side, and a front portico lined by clean, slim columns of white stone. But even its sharp, rationalist proportions were compromised to fit this country's atmosphere, softened by the close crowding trees and vines that masked all but the windows, as if trying to swallow it into the landscape.

The two men parked their cars and got out.

"That left side is the main family rooms," the priest pointed out as they walked toward the building. "Sleeping quarters in the center."

"What's on the right?" asked Colin.

"Servants' quarters, garages, and a stable." Then, noting Colin's odd look, he added, "Oh, the animals don't enter the family life. That's all separate. It's simply built to look as if it's part of the house. The Brigadier only keeps a pair of fine riding horses there."

A narrow-shouldered man with a long, dour face was at work raking leaves from the bushes along the home's front. He paused a moment to tip a hat as he saw them, but his expression never changed.

"That's Seamus," the priest explained. "He tends the grounds and does other work about the manor."

They stepped through the row of columns to the front door, and Bonaventure used its heavy brass knocker with great vigor. The noise of it boomed back in a hollow echo from inside, and Colin looked at the priest in some surprise.

"I'm not being too loud," Bonaventure assured him. "Jenny's often in back, and Robert becomes so immersed in his work he'd not hear doom crackin' about him."

"Who's Jenny?"

"The woman who cleans and cooks for him. Seamus is her husband. With them, there's only the three living here."

The door swung open, and they faced a broad, short man of late middle age, clad in loose trousers and a heavy sweater of Aran knit. He was bull-necked, round-shouldered, built like a barrel through his chest and belly. He faced them solidly on short legs spread wide as if to meet any situation, like a fighter awaiting an opponent's charge. But his square, battle-hard features lit with a real joy when he saw the priest, robbing them of their harshness.

"Father! It's good to see you," he exclaimed in a hearty voice. "Come in. And this must be your Colin McMahon!"

He ushered them into a hall that went up the full three stories in a corkscrew of broad, open staircase with a banister of light wood.

"He's badly in need of a place to stay, Robert," said the priest, his voice echoing in the space.

"So you told me. And an American, too!"

He took Colin's hand in a fist that engulfed it, but applied only a friendly pressure. "I'm happy to meet you, and you're most welcome in my home. Please, follow me."

He led the two visitors through a broad doorway on the hall's left, into a front study lined with bookshelves and dominated by an immense desk of a black and much scarred wood, its top littered with papers.

Beyond, another open doorway revealed a long, beamed living room of quite modern decor, well furnished, with an immense stone fireplace at its far end.

At the desk, Dudley paused to punch the button on an intercom. A woman's voice came from its speaker at once.

"Yes, Brigadier?"

"Our visitors are here, Jenny. When will supper be ready for them?"

"It's ready now, sir."

"Fine. Serve in the dining room. We'll be right through."

"Supper?" said Colin.

"The Father said he was sure you hadn't eaten," Dudley replied. "I told him I'd feed you both."

"Thanks," said Colin. "But, I should pay you, or . . ."

The Brigadier held up a restraining hand.

"Think no more of that. You're my guest now, and to say the truth, I'd pay *you* to have someone new to talk to in this place. So eat. You look as if you could use it. Afterwards we'll have a talk."

The cut facets of the whiskey glass caught the ruby firelight and broke it into shifting, kaleidoscopic fragments as Colin lifted it to drink. Across its rim he could see the Brigadier setting down his own glass, lifting a Waterford decanter to pour more for himself and the priest sitting beside him.

The three men now sat ensconced in easy chairs about the living room hearth. A fire of peat bricks burned in the grate, scenting the room and tinging it with a soft ruddy glow.

Through opened doors at one side of the room, a woman could be seen clearing dishes from a long dining table. She was a slim and sharp-featured woman with raven-black hair that set off a pale white skin and bright green eyes. She seemed to pay no attention to the three men talking in the next room as she worked diligently.

"So when I retired just over a year ago," Dudley was saying as he poured, "I determined to settle down someplace and write my memoirs. Seems a popular enough thing to do nowadays, and I've been about the world and seen more than most. Besides, I wanted a chance to say what I thought."

"The Brigadier is of a mind that civilization is nearing its collapse," Bonaventure put in from his other side.

"Well, how can you think otherwise?" Dudley asked. "I've seen it everywhere. Systems breaking down. Institutions crumbling. No values, no honor, no courage. Why, look at the state of Christianity!"

"I can't agree with you in that," Bonaventure responded. "Religion is not crumbling. It's . . ."

"It's already crumbled!" Dudley finished. "Look at your own Ulster! Christians killing Christians, cities divided into fortified camps, fighting men everywhere, war chieftains ruling their clans, everything plunged into bloody chaos. Why, it's like the Dark Ages come again."

Bonaventure opened his mouth to argue further, but Dudley lifted a staying hand.

"No, Father. We shouldn't go on with this right now with our guest here." He smiled at Colin. "Enough to say that I believe I have enough tales of things I've seen to make a lively story."

"I have to admit I must agree to that," the priest grudgingly put in. "I've heard tales from this man that would truly curdle the blood."

"I'd like to hear them," said Colin with a smile. He was feeling relaxed for the first time in days. He finished his drink and set the glass down.

"More?" asked Dudley.

"Sure. A little. It's great stuff."

"None finer than the Irish, I've found," the Brigadier said, winking broadly. "And I can assure you, I have tried them all and often."

He leaned forward to pour for Colin. As he did, he asked in a casual way:

"Now tell us what it was that really brought you all the way from America. It surely wasn't this girl that Bonaventure told me about."

Though it was casual, there was a definite probing nature to the question, and some of Colin's sense of relaxation faded. A wariness came into his eyes.

"No, no," he answered, managing to keep his tone easy and amiable. "She was just somebody I happened to run into. My real reason for coming was to do research."

"Research?" said Dudley. "Are you a writer?"

"That's right," said Colin, not hesitating to seize upon the offered explanation. "I'm doing a book about Ireland. About the old days."

"Old days?" asked Bonaventure.

"The real early Irish. Maybe a thousand years ago. The Celtic period, it's called." He pronounced it "Seltic."

"Ah, I see," said Dudley, exchanging a look with the priest. "Well, then Bonny here might help you. He's some interest in that area."

"My main discipline is in the old tongue," the priest said. "But I've a fair knowledge of the ancient tales. My interest runs more to gods than heroes, though."

"Really?" said Colin with interest. "Then maybe you *can* give me some help. There are some things I'd like to find out more about."

"I'd be most happy to help," the priest said with delight. "What kinds of things?"

"Well, there's some bunch called 'the others.' And it sounded like it had a capital O."

"Sounded?" asked Dudley.

"I heard somebody mention it," Colin supplied vaguely.

"Ah," said the priest. "You must mean the *Tuatha de Danann.* They're the old gods. Took their name from the mighty goddess Danu who gave them their magic skills. They once were powerful in Ireland, the tales say. But when mortal men came and took control, they withdrew into hidden places underground. Still they continued to have some influence in the world. That's why mortals called them 'the Others,' fearing that using their real names might invoke their wrath. There are still some who believe in them."

"And what about 'the Dagda'?"

"He was one of the greatest of the old gods. The 'Good God' he was. Huge, hearty, and good-natured, and a most formidable warrior as well."

"Okay!" said Colin, clearly fascinated by these decipherings of some more cryptic fragments of his dreams. "Then, how about a god called Cromm?"

There was a sharp explosion.

Colin jerked up as if shot. All heads turned to look toward the source.

Jenny stood over a pile of plates she had dropped, shattering them to wide-sprayed fragments on the floor. Aghast, she looked from them up to the staring men.

"Sorry!" she said in a piping, pitiful voice. "They just slipped!"

"Never mind," said the Brigadier, the old soldier not having batted an eye at the explosion. He waved dismissingly. "It's all right, Jenny. Nothing valuable."

She nodded and quickly knelt down to begin picking up pieces. He looked back to Colin.

"Now, it was Cromm, you said?" He shook his head. "Well, I've heard of those others, but not that one." He looked to the priest. "What about you?"

"I don't think so," Bonaventure said, considering. "It's surely not one of the gods of the *Tuatha de Danann.* Sorry."

"What else?" Dudley asked his young guest.

But Colin was still looking a bit flustered, his face drawn and rather pale. He glanced again toward Jenny, busily picking up, and then back to the two men, and shook his head.

"I don't know. That's all I can think of now. Maybe I'm getting tired."

"Of course you must be!" said the priest with sudden commiseration. "You've had a very long day, and we're being most cruel keeping you up for our own selfish pleasure." He got to his feet. "Brigadier," he announced firmly, "you must put this young man to bed. And I must leave."

"Of course," Dudley agreed readily. He and Colin rose too, and they followed Bonaventure out into the hall.

"Well, good night, Colin," the priest said at the front door. "Get a very good rest, and," he added, smiling, "I hope your outing goes well tomorrow."

"Thank you, Father," Colin said, shaking his hand. "Thanks for everything."

"I hope that I can see you again. I very much enjoyed our chat."

"I'll do my best," Colin replied. "I'm not sure of exactly what I need to do just yet."

"Well, you can stay here as long as you need," Dudley told him.

"Thanks for that, Robert," the priest told him warmly. "You're a good man." He shook the Brigadier's hand. "Well, I'm going then." He opened the door. "Good night to you both. And God bless you."

He went out and Dudley closed the door, turning to Colin.

"Well, come on then," he said briskly. "You really do look done in. I'll show you to a room."

They crossed the hall to the foot of the stairs, where Colin's battered suitcase now sat, his trenchcoat draped across it. He took them and followed the Brigadier up the wide, curving staircase.

At the second floor they turned, taking the landing around to a door.

"Here you are," Dudley said, opening it. "It's always kept ready for a guest."

He ushered Colin through into a large, high-ceilinged room with bright decor and clean, modern furnishings.

"You should be comfortable here. Jenny goes home now, so I'm afraid you'll have to fend for yourself if you need anything."

"That's fine," said Colin. "It's all great!"

"Good," said Dudley, going back out the door. "Well, a good night's sleep to you then."

"Thanks," said Colin, starting toward the big bed with his suitcase. "That's all I want right now."

The Brigadier began to swing the door closed, then paused.

"Oh, there is one thing," he said.

Colin looked around to him. "Oh?"

"That word is pronounced 'Keltic,' not 'Seltic.' The C is always hard in Gaelic. If you were any kind of researcher, you'd know that. Well, good night once again."

And, with that, he pulled the door closed.

"What the hell am I getting into?" Colin asked aloud.

Colin lay asleep in the Brigadier's big guest bed.

The light coming from the nearly full moon through the long bedroom windows lit his face, relaxed in sleep. But it also showed his eyelids flicking nervously as the eyes behind them moved in a dream.

He was walking the broad meadows again, alone. This time, however, they stretched away flat in all directions; featureless, empty, brown wastes under a flat ceiling of grey sky.

"Goddamn, I'm lost again," he said in despair.

"No, you're not," said a voice beside him, and he turned to see Megan walking at his side, quite naturally, smiling at him in an assuring way. "I'm here."

He smiled in return, then realized that there was something wrong. The countryside behind her was changing, growing hazy, and her red hair seemed to be glowing with a golden light . . .

16

It was the girl Aislinn who walked easily beside him, her golden hair glowing in the sun.

He stopped suddenly, gazing about him. The countryside was rolling, soft, lush with the brilliant greens of the new spring growth. Not far away across the meadowlands, the ringfort and palisade of the girl's rath were visible upon their swell of ground. He looked down. He was clad in his tunic and cloak, sword belted about his waist, his round shield upon one arm.

"What's wrong?" she asked him, noting his look of puzzlement.

"Odd," he said. "I had the most strange feeling—as if I were somewhere else."

"Somewhere else?" she repeated, still puzzled.

"I'm not certain what I mean," he said, shaking his head. He looked to her. "And you," he said, "your hair's like bright flax."

"Yes?"

"It seemed as if I was seeing you with red-gold hair."

"My mother had that," she said. "Great billows of it. What could have put that in your mind?"

"I don't know," he said in a musing way, looking about him again. "But like an icy hand run up my spine it was. I felt the hairs on my neck rising." He gave a little shrug. "Oh well. Some trick of the mind." He smiled at her. "Let's be on with our walk."

They moved across the meadows again, walking side by side.

"I have so many other questions to ask," he said. "I hope you don't mind me bringing you away from the others. It's easier to talk this way."

"I understand. And it's all right. I think my father is quite relieved to leave this in my hands. And . . . I've wanted a chance to talk with you alone as well."

He stopped to look at her searchingly. "Have you? I thought before that you wanted to avoid me. You ran away . . ."

"Ran away?" she said, confused.

He looked a little confused by this himself. "No. I don't know why I said that. I meant that you sent *me* away, as if you wished to be rid of me."

"I only meant to keep you out of this. It was a most painful thing for me to do. But I hoped that the less you knew, the less you'd become a part of it."

"It might have worked, too, if I'd not heard that chieftain Laimainech and his druid plotting in the night."

"Laimainech is not an evil man," she told him. "He's only under Cromm's spell as the rest are. He believes it's Cromm's power that keeps his people safe and well and rich. He thinks that what they do is for the best. The druid Dubhdaleithe is another matter. He's a willing servant for Cromm, drawing the blood, feeding the monster. He gloats over the innocents he slaughters."

They reached a little stream that cut across the meadows, forming a ravine. A spreading oak below cast a shade across the water and a jumble of boulders lining the bank.

"It's a warm day for strolling so far," he said. "Why don't we sit awhile?"

He held out a hand and she took it. They walked down the grassy slope to the bank and beneath the leaf canopy of the oak, out of the bright sun. He helped her sit upon a weather-smoothed boulder and then sat beside her, pulling off his shield.

"Tell me now," he said, "what was it exactly that your clan tried to do to stop Cromm when you returned from the Tailteen Fair?"

"We had hoped that bringing others the message of the new faith would be enough to break the spell on them, as it had on us. That others would see the truth, come to doubt Cromm's power, and join us in defying him." She shook her head sadly. "In that we've failed. Oh, we have managed to reach some few, and they have begun to question. But Cromm has realized we are a threat, and his power has tightened. His agents now sweep out from the ring, across the countryside, trying to reach all who have begun to doubt and frighten them into denying us."

"Agents?"

"Dreadful creatures who serve Cromm. Twelve of them there are, each more terrible than the rest. You saw one. The Ladhrach. It gave you that scar." She touched the spot on his throat lightly.

"That thing with a cat's face? I saw a statue of a thing like that, in the ring of stones by Dun Mauran."

"You've seen Magh Slecht?" she said in astonishment. "But it's a secret place, for Cromm's initiates only!" She drew back, her look growing alarmed. "You didn't . . ."

"I didn't join his company, if that's what you fear," he assured her with a smile. "I stole away and sneaked out there to see what their secret was." He neglected to add that he had been caught in the act.

"Then you've seen the rest of Cromm's disciples as well."

"Statues. I saw only twelve statues ringing another one with a great head and shrunken body."

"That withered one is Cromm himself," she said with revulsion in her voice. "Bloody Cromm. Black Cromm. The Drinker of Life. The others are his creatures."

"The statues? But they're only stone."

"Each one is like a shell, like a moth's chrysalis. It shows the true appearance of its own creature. Within, like the moth's larva, the awful beings live, waiting for the call. But only the power of Cromm can draw them forth and send them out to act for him."

"What are they supposed to be?"

She shook her head. "No one knows. One ancient tale says he gathered them from all the most terrible parts of our world and the worlds of the Others. He promised them eternal life and power if they would follow him. Now they are slaves to him, living only from his strength, as much imprisoned as the mortals under his spell."

"And just what kind of power are they supposed to have?"

"They seem only able to follow the will of Cromm, and to have little of their own. But each has its own skills and weapons, and all are most savage and cruel fighters. And one thing more: they have the power to shift shape."

"Shift shape?"

"They can take on any mortal's form they like. It is the form only, but it can still let them move in the mortal world unknown."

"Shape-shifters?" he said doubtfully. "Monsters called from the stones? I don't know, Aislinn. This tale of yours is growing almost too strange for me. It's many lifetimes that have passed since my own clansmen believed in any powers beyond the mortal ones. These creatures of yours are like something from old bardic tales, meant only for scaring small children in the dark."

"Believe me, they are real. You saw one."

"I saw some poor man with a misshapen face. And why should I believe he was more than that? It was yourself who told me before that it was only a dream I'd had!"

"Because I wanted to keep you from knowing of the trouble upon us," she told him earnestly. "So you would ride safely away."

"And perhaps you're telling me this now to frighten me into doing the same."

She looked indignant, turning away from him.

"It's little you think of me if you believe that I see you as a coward, or that I'd not tell you the truth after promising to do so."

He relented, taking her hands.

"I'm sorry," he said, pulling her gently back around to him. "I do believe that you think these things are real. But you could leave," Colin reasoned. "Why risk yourselves here?"

"We can't walk away from this," she said, amazed by his suggestion. "We're part of what Cromm's done. It's for us to redeem ourselves by stopping his evil. We still believe that someday we will grow strong enough to challenge Cromm."

"As High-King Tighernmas did, so long ago?"

"He challenged Cromm out of greed, seeking power for himself," she said in a righteous tone. "We seek only freedom. The power and right of Christ, our Lord, will prevail!"

"And in the meantime?" he asked.

Her righteous tone gave way to one of sorrow: "The sacrifices will continue. Even now they are probably gathering victims for Beltainne. They have only two more days."

"Sacrifices? Who will they be?"

"Firstborns of the winter season it is."

"Their babies?" he said in shock. "Their own children?"

"The hold of Cromm is strong and the spring Festival of Rebirth one of the most vital," she replied. "Yes, to keep Cromm's favor and to insure the safety and wealth of the clans, they will let their own babies die, just as they always have."

"By all the gods of Danu!" he breathed.

"So now you know the worst of it," she said. "You can still go. Go quickly. With luck they still believe you an outsider. The longer you stay . . ."

"But how can you think I'll go?" he asked, surprised. "What you've said only makes me more certain I must stay."

"I'll not let you risk yourself with us," she told him sternly. "It is our fight. You feel none of the pull of our new faith."

"No," he admitted. "I feel nothing about this Christianity. But I feel nothing of any belief: in the *Tuatha de Danann,* your Cromm, or this Patrick's god."

"Yet you feel something."

"I'm a warrior," he said simply. "I understand truth. I understand bravery. I know that you need help. I can't turn away. And there is more." His hands moved to her shoulders. He looked into her eyes. "I also know that I could never ride away and leave you."

"Colin . . ." she began.

But he pulled her to him. His lips met hers, and she responded willingly, her arms encircling him as his slid around her body. When the kiss ended, they remained in the embrace, she turning her head to lay it against his breast.

"Oh, Colin," she said, "it would be a pain in my heart also to see you ride away. But that's the very reason why you must go. What I feel for you makes me wish to see you safe."

"It's the same thing that I wish for you," he told her earnestly. "That's why I mean to stay. I can't believe in these creatures, or this power that Cromm has. It sounds to me a trick of magic, spun by druids like this Dubhdaleithe over the many years to make you fear and believe. I mean to prove that."

"How?"

"You said it is only two nights until Beltainne. I'll go and see this sacrifice myself."

She pulled back, her appalled gaze meeting his.

"No! That's madness. What if you're caught?"

"I'm still an outsider, remember?" he told her. "I can always tell them I was only curious about their god. Laimainech liked me. He'd believe. And I don't think it can be so dangerous as you say. I . . ."

A shadow flitted across them. It was like the shadow of a soaring bird. But it was much larger.

Aislinn was on her feet in an instant, as if something had stung her. Her head lifted, her gaze scanning the skies.

"What is it?" he said.

"Come. Quickly!" she told him, starting up the slope of the ravine.

He rose, but stood looking after her in puzzlement.

"What's happening? Why . . ."

She turned back, grabbing his arm and tugging, her voice urgent.

"Never mind! Please just come now!"

He grabbed up his shield and followed her, both of them climbing up the steep slope of the ravine at their best speed.

"Tell me what's happening!" he demanded as they struggled on the slippery grass.

"We may have come too far. We're in danger. Look out. Look up. Be ready!"

They reached the top of the slope, coming onto the level meadows.

"Ready?" he said. "For what?"

She threw herself suddenly against him, knocking him from his feet. They both went back over the edge of the ravine, sliding down the slope just as a large shape whisked through the place where they had stood.

Colin lifted his head to see it as it soared overhead and then swept upward. It was a silvery-skinned creature of human size, with long neck, pointed beak, and immense leathery wings like those of a bat.

"What in the Dagda's name is that?" he asked, staring.

"The Ialtag," Aislinn supplied. "Most cruel she is. She eats men's flesh. We must get to the rath."

"We'll never make it that far," he said. "You get back under that tree and stay there. I'll see to it."

"She's one of Cromm's champions," the girl told him. "She can't be killed. And she has teeth as well as a beak and claws."

"And *I* have a sword," he told her valiantly. "Now, get under that tree!"

He climbed to the top of the slope again as she moved back under the shelter of the oak. Drawing himself upright on the open ground, he settled the shield firmly on his arm and looked about. He spotted the creature wheeling high above but it dove downward at once as it spied him, wings back, long beak stretched out, giving a shrill caw of triumph.

He drew his sword and stood, unmoving, awaiting the attack. The creature shot toward him, a long blur of silver light, the pointed beak like a spear point.

Still he waited, letting it close.

Then, in a swift move, his arm swung back and he lifted the sword to strike. But the creature's own move was even swifter. Before Colin could swing, it wheeled suddenly, sweeping into a tight turn. Its jaws opened. He saw the rows of pointed teeth as they clamped down upon his sword, snapping shut, the head jerking around to wrench the weapon from his grasp and send it spinning away.

He stumbled and fell forward to his knees. The creature swept over him, the talons of its bony feet raking across his back, tearing away his cloak but missing his flesh. It banked sharply and then lifted again, wings flapping to pull it upward; then it released the cloak, which fluttered back to earth.

Colin jumped to his feet, looking around him for the sword. It had landed, its point sunk deep in the sod a dozen paces away.

He started toward it, but a "whoomping" sound behind him brought him pivoting around.

The thing was already coming in at him again, low to the

ground this time, wings stroking with great power, jaws open to strike.

It was nearly upon him, and he threw himself out of its path, lifting his shield in defense. It shot by him, the snapping jaws missing his head. But one of the great wings slammed into his shield.

The circle of iron was torn from his arm as he was thrown violently backward, somersaulting over the edge of the ravine, tumbling down the slope.

"Colin!" cried Aislinn in terror as he rolled to a stop at the edge of the stream, legs splashing into the water. She started out toward him.

"Stay back!" he cried, levering himself up, dragging himself from the water.

He shook his head, looking around groggily as he clambered to his feet. He was weaponless, sword and shield at the top of the slope. The creature was above him, climbing again, preparing for another strike. A final one.

His gaze fell on a water-rounded stone the size of his two fists. He lifted it, hefting it in one hand.

The Ialtag heeled over and began to dive. Its wings were back, its long beak thrust forward, ready to stab into its waiting prey.

Colin made no move to run, awaiting the creature as motionlessly as before, holding the rock down at his side.

The being shot directly in, like an arrow aiming at Colin's throat.

Colin's arm lifted, cocked back, and fired the stone upward toward the diving creature. The two rushed to their collision, the well-aimed rock slamming against the sleek dome of the thing's long skull.

Stunned, the creature rolled in the air and began helplessly to plummet, dropping from sight beyond the rim of the ravine.

Colin scrambled swiftly up the slope to the meadow. Not far away was the crashed Ialtag, a tangle of wings and neck and limbs, struggling to rise. The young warrior rushed to pick up his shield and then his sword. The creature saw him. Its struggles to untangle itself became more frantic.

Colin ran toward it, intent on finishing the fight. The thing managed to get onto its feet and began to run clumsily away. The warrior drew closer. The Ialtag managed to get both wings unfurled, and they flopped on either side as it worked desperately to get itself airborne.

Colin was nearly upon it. He raised a whooping war cry, lifting his sword to strike at the silver body. But the creature was suddenly up, the stroking wings lifting it clear of the ground, the legs folding up beneath it.

On the ground, it was no match for Colin's speed. Once it was airborne, however, he was quickly left behind. It skimmed away for some distance across the fields; then it lifted and soared up. He stopped, watching in frustration as it flapped upward, gained altitude to clear a grove of trees, and glided out of sight.

"Colin!" came Aislinn's voice behind him.

He turned and she threw herself upon him, hugging him tightly.

"I was certain you were dead," she said in relief. "Now do you believe me? Do you believe how dangerous they are?"

"I do. But I still mean to go to Magh Slecht."

She looked up at him, her face anguished.

"But you can't. Not now. The Ialtag has seen you here. They'll know you're one of us. If you're caught, they'll surely destroy you."

"Listen to me, now," he told her earnestly. "They can be hurt. They can be killed. This Cromm can be beaten, and I mean to find out how. The secret lies in that circle, and in that druid's rites, I'm certain."

"You are a fool," she said. But she lifted her face and he lowered his to meet her waiting lips.

CROMM

17

There was a sound, faint but unmistakable: a low gutteral sound.

Colin opened his eyes. His face was buried in something soft and he jerked back. He was hugging his pillow.

"Damn," he said, sitting up and throwing the pillow away angrily. "First one of those dreams I'd like to keep going and . . ."

Once more there came that faint rumble of sound, like a soft growl.

He was out of bed in an instant, his naked body a gleam of white in the flood of moonlight through the tall windows. He scanned the bedroom, anxious gaze searching the unfamiliar shadows. There was nothing moving there, no signs of grotesque shapes or glowing eyes.

But there was a sound of movement from beyond the bedroom door. A swishing sound, as if something had brushed across the outside of the door.

He padded across the room toward the door, taking up a heavy pitcher of Waterford glass from a table and holding it by the neck as a cudgel.

He reached the door. Crouching, holding his breath, he took the knob, turned softly, then jerked it open, lifting the pitcher to strike.

There was nothing on the landing. But a soft creaking came from the stairs below.

He stepped out to the landing, leaning over the rail, peering down into the darkness of the hall. Watery moonlight floating in through the windows that flanked the front door lit the hall floor to a lighter grey than its surroundings. Enough to show a barely darker patch for an instant as it whisked around the base of a banister and vanished into the deeper blackness under the stairs.

He stood, staring down, body taut, still holding his breath, head cocked to listen. No other sounds were heard in the house.

Suddenly light flooded down into the hall from above.

"Ah . . . Mr. McMahon?" came a voice.

He expelled his breath in a gasp of surprise and looked up. The Brigadier, in a long dressing gown, holding a large automatic in one hand, was peering down at him most curiously from the landing above as he stood there, naked and exposed in the light, leaning over the rail with the expensive pitcher upheld in one hand.

He stood back from the rail, lowering the pitcher, looking more than a little abashed.

"This . . . um . . . probably looks a little strange to you?" he said.

"I've seen sights with more obvious explanations," Dudley agreed, though he was seemingly quite unruffled. The handgun's muzzle was pointed rock-steady at Colin's bare chest.

"I thought I heard something. Outside my door."

"Really?" said Dudley. He lifted an eyebrow skeptically, but the gun was lowered.

"You don't have a dog, do you? A big dog?"

"No, Mr. McMahon. The nearest large dog is a wolfhound at the MacCulloch farm, a half-mile away."

"It couldn't get into your house, could it?"

"Mr. McMahon, I really don't think . . ."

"I know. I know. But I'm sure I saw a shadow moving at the bottom of the stairs."

"It may have been Jenny coming back to fetch something."

"Like a stick? I mean, does she walk on all fours when she does that?"

"Are you certain you weren't having some kind of dream, Mr. McMahon? From your . . . appearance, you seem to have risen in a great rush. Sleep-walking perhaps?"

Clearly realizing the awkwardness of his position, Colin decided to surrender.

"Yeah. Yeah, you're right," he conceded. "Never mind. It probably was just a dream. In fact, I'm sure it was." He backed away under the wondering stare of his host. "Sorry I woke you. I'm going right back to bed."

He collided with the door, the knob ramming into his bare backside.

"Ouch. Sorry." He felt behind him, got a grip on the knob and turned. "Well, good night then. See you in the morning." He pushed the door open, lifting the pitcher as he stepped backward into his room. "Oh, and I'll just put this back. Very carefully."

"Thank you," Dudley said as Colin pulled the door closed.

Inside the room, Colin leaned back against the door, shaking his head angrily.

"Crap!" he said in disgust. "There's *another* one who thinks I'm crazy now."

A fully dressed Colin McMahon came down the stairs into a hall now palely lit by early morning light from the front windows. At the bottom he glanced around, then went through the doors into the study. It was empty.

He moved on into the living room, but it was empty too.

"Brigadier?" he called in a tentative way.

"Mr. McMahon?" a voice responded from somewhere beyond the dining room. "We're in the kitchen. Come on back."

Colin made his way through the dining room and then through a swinging door that opened into a kitchen. It was large, very modern, and filled with light from the tall, wide bay windows.

Colin's host was at an electric stove, laboring over a skillet. Father Bonaventure sat at a table set in the bay alcove. The priest waved cheerily and smiled as Colin entered.

"Mr. McMahon," he said with delight, "I'm pleased to see you're looking so rested."

"I am?" Colin said, moving into the room. "There's a surprise."

He eyed the Brigadier's broad back with some trepidation, clearly nervous about his reception. But Dudley only glanced back and asked pleasantly:

"Rashers and eggs for you?"

Colin glanced at his watch. It was 6:19.

"I don't have a lot of time . . ." he began hesitantly.

"Nonsense," was the hearty response. "It's nearly ready. Have a seat."

"Well, I sure can't say I'm not hungry," Colin admitted.

He sat down at the table across from the priest. The windows gave a view of lawn and neatly trimmed yew hedges, still green amidst the browning autumn scene.

"The eggs smell good," he remarked.

"I hope so," Dudley said, smiling. "It's a terrible battle I've had with these innocent-looking things today. I thought I was quite good at this, but one should never trust an egg. That's a lesson to be taken to heart."

Colin watched him at the stove, smiling himself at the incongruous sight of the tough-visaged, muscular man, an apron about his broad-chested body, working delicately at the skillet with a spatula.

"Are you certain you won't stay to eat, Father?" the Brigadier asked.

"Ah, no," the priest assured him. "I won't be imposing on your hospitality any longer." He looked to Colin. "I only stopped by so early in hopes of seeing you before you went out with Miss Conroy. I wanted to give you this."

With a pleased smile and a theatrical little gesture he lifted a book from his lap and laid it on the table before Colin.

The young man examined it with interest. It was a small but thick book, its green cover greyed with the dust of ages. Its faded gold letters proclaimed its title: *Celtic Myth and Legend.*

"After our talk last night, I looked through the abbey library," Bonaventure explained as Colin took up the volume. "I found this one. It's quite old—1910 or some such, I believe. But it mentions your Cromm. I marked the pages."

Colin noted the slips of paper, opening the book to the first one. He scanned down the page, stopping as his eye caught the striking word.

"Yeah, here it is," he said, and read aloud:

" 'In *Cromm* we find faint evidence of the awful customs practiced in pagan Ireland. One of the only remaining sources for this information lies in the . . .' " He hesitated over the next word. "The *Dinnsenchus?*" he ventured then, looking up to Bonaventure.

"Dzijn-hen-kus," the priest pronounced. "They're ancient Gaelic tracts enumerating famous places in Ireland and the legends relating to them."

Colin read on:

" 'One of them describes the practice of sacrifice among the ancient Irish. The poem records the reason why a spot in County Cavan received the name of Magh Slecht, the "Plain of Adoration."

" 'According to the verse, one third of the healthy children were slaughtered, along with other human sacrifice, at ritual times in the year to wrest from the powers of nature the grain and grass upon which the tribes and their cattle subsisted.' "

"A grisly sort of chap, this Cromm of yours," Dudley commented. Then with more heat, "Ah! The devil take these eggs. I pronounce them well and truly done. Let's eat."

As he began to pull plates from a cupboard, Bonaventure rose.

"Well, if you're ready to eat, I must be going."

"Bonny, don't rush away because of that," said Dudley, scraping the eggs unceremoniously onto the plates. "Stay and have coffee at least."

"I've other duties now," the priest told him. "But I'll surely come back later, if you'll have me."

"You're welcome anytime, Father," the Brigadier assured him, taking bacon strips from another skillet to toss upon the brown shreds of egg.

"I'll be off then. And don't bother seeing me out. Eat your food hot." He looked to Colin. "Keep the book as long as you wish. There are several other references you might like to read. Oh, and have a fine morning with our young Megan." He gave a knowing wink and a wide grin and then went briskly out.

"He's sure a nice guy," Colin pronounced. "If you can call a priest that."

"He's certainly quite a character," said Dudley.

He brought the two plates over and set them on the table,

fetched silverware and a stack of buttered toast and two steaming mugs of coffee, then settled himself across from Colin.

Colin picked up a strip of the thick bacon and took a bite.

"The bacon's perfect," he pronounced.

"That's something, anyway," the Brigadier accepted, and they both began to eat.

"Doesn't Jenny cook the meals?" Colin asked.

"No. She's asleep, most likely. I enjoy being on my own early in the morning."

"Then why do you have such a big place? If you don't mind my asking."

"Not at all. It was ridiculously cheap and it was isolated," Dudley answered simply. "Just what I wanted. Beyond my visits with Bonny, I see very few human beings from day to day except for Jenny and her husband. I can live and work as I wish."

They ate in silence for some time, Colin eying the book speculatively and Dudley eying Colin the same way.

"You wouldn't know if this Magh Slecht it talks about is around here?" the young American finally asked.

"Haven't heard of it. Don't know that there are *any* plains about. But that would have been fifteen hundred years ago."

"It's so damn frustrating," Colin said irritably. "There's almost nothing written on Cromm."

"Not so hard to understand," said the Brigadier. "The Irish don't have a known history of human sacrifice. They took heads, of course, but supposedly only as battle trophies."

"I saw them," Colin said, unthinking. Then, noting Dudley's odd look, he quickly added, "In drawings. I meant, I know about them."

"Yes, well no doubt some patriotic sense caused it all to be hushed up. Like some scandal in the family. The tales lost, the place names changed, the whole thing forgotten over the years."

"Forgotten," Colin repeated in an ironic way. "I wish I could forget."

Dudley tapped the book. "You think you might find something in here of help for your . . . ah . . . research?"

The implication of the final word was clear. Colin returned his probing stare straight on.

"Look, I know you don't believe me . . ." he began.

"I didn't say that," Dudley interrupted. "But I do know the look of someone in trouble. Father Bonny is a very trusting man. I just wanted to be certain . . ."

"That I'm not some kind of criminal or lunatic?"

"I've already satisfied myself in that. I've never been mistaken in judging men. No, you're not dangerous or an outlaw. But you are a man under great stress, hunted by something, and fear is a part of it. I've seen enough soldiers in that state before."

"I wish I could explain," Colin said, sincerely. "I mean, I am *dying* to explain, to somebody, before I go nuts! But I don't know what you'll believe, or do. You see? So I can't say anything."

"And you don't need to," Dudley assured him. "I won't pry. You just seem . . . well . . . rather at loose ends. And I want you to know that, if you need help, you can talk to me."

Colin met the level, honest gaze of the old soldier's eyes, then nodded.

"Maybe I will," he said, "if I ever know what's real myself. But it just gets worse and worse!" He shook his head angrily. "God! It's too bad I can't call it delayed battle stress or shell shock."

"If that's the way you feel, are you certain you should be wandering about Ireland alone?" Dudley asked. "Perhaps you should be home, or seeking some kind of help."

"Hell," said Colin in a despondent way, "maybe you're right. I should just go home and check in with a shrink and get my brain roto-rootered. I should have listened to Harry." He stopped, struck by a realization. "God! Harry!"

"Who's that?" asked the Brigadier.

"One of my friends. Back home. And I'll bet he's wondering where I am. Tom too. Things have been moving so damn fast . . . Geez, I should call them." He looked to Dudley. "How do I do that? Can I use any phone? Or should I go into town, or . . ."

"There's no need for that," Dudley said. "You can use my telephone."

"To call America? But, the cost . . ."

"Is much less than you think," Dudley assured him. "We can settle that later, if you insist. But, please, make your call. If you'd like, I'll help you put it through."

A faint sound of static came from the telephone receiver. The Brigadier listened, his voice drawn in a frown.

He sat at the desk in his study. Colin sat in a chair nearby, watching expectantly. The doors to the living room and front hall were closed for privacy.

"What in the bloody hell is going on there!" Dudley barked into the mouthpiece. "I've been holding for ten minutes."

A faint voice came from the receiver, a woman's voice, the words a blur but the tone apologetic.

"All right then," he snapped. "But ring me at once when things clear."

He slammed the handset back into its cradle with a certain force, looking around to Colin.

"Sorry, lad," he growled irritably, "but the trans-Atlantic lines are 'out of use' at the moment. Some kind of weather interference the excuse is. But I know damn well its just the bloody inefficiency of the operation. You face it everywhere these days."

"Don't worry about it," Colin told him. "It can keep."

"Are you certain you wouldn't just as soon fly home?" the Brigadier suggested. "Shannon's not so far away as that, and there are flights every day. You could be back with your friends by tonight."

"You don't know how tempting an offer that is," Colin replied sincerely. He looked at his watch. "Hey, it's nearly quarter to seven. I've got to get going." He rose. "Got a date."

The Brigadier rose too, walking with him to the study door.

"Can I expect you back for dinner?" he asked.

"God, I don't know," Colin said with some despondency. "I'm not even sure anymore why I'm doing this."

"I still don't understand what it is you're after, lad," Dudley said frankly, "but you've a place here as long as you wish it. And a sympathetic ear if you've a need."

"Thanks," said Colin with warmth. "Meeting you and Father B's been a great help."

He put out a hand and Dudley took it in his big grip, shaking it heartily.

"I just hope you find whatever you're seeking," the Brigadier told him. Then he slid open the door to the front hall.

Jenny stood nearby outside, a broom in her hands. As the doors opened, she started as if surprised. Then, in a self-conscious way, she began busily to sweep.

The Land Rover sped along the narrow road, the big vehicle negotiating the tight turns easily under Megan Conroy's skillful hands.

"You're very quiet," she remarked to Colin.

He sat hunched in his seat, staring out the window at the passing countryside. His expression was downcast. He didn't answer. She tried again.

"We've made three stops, driven thirty miles, and you haven't said a word."

"Sorry," he at last responded gloomily. "I was thinking . . ."

"It's just that I thought you wanted to talk."

"I know. And I do. I guess. I mean . . . I don't know." His voice took on a musing tone. "I was just thinking of something the Brigadier said. About being driven by fear. And I don't know now if it's fear of those things that're after me, or of finding out that I'm really nuts after all."

"I'm sorry?" she said, clearly bewildered by this. "What do you mean?"

"That I'm starting to believe maybe all of it is just one big dream."

"You're rambling again, Mr. McMahon," she said impatiently. "Now, I've humored you this far. You have to either tell me what you want or leave me alone!"

"See? There you go," he said in frustration. "I *knew* you were going to say something like that. So why should I even try telling you anything else? I'll only be making sure one more person thinks I'm a fugitive from a Looney Tune. There's no reason for me to even waste my breath. I say, let's forget the whole thing."

"All right then," she returned sharply. "If you mean that, I've one final call to make, and then I'll take you back, and that'll be an end to it."

"Fine."

"Fine."

After that, Colin sat sullenly as she steered the Rover off the road and up a rutted path. She pulled into an overgrown yard before a cottage and stopped.

Colin peered out. The cottage was small, weather-battered, its thatched roof sagging. The roof on a small outbuilding beside it had completely fallen in.

"Somebody lives here?" he asked in surprise.

"An old woman named Slany O'Brien. I've been looking in on her. Her mind's been wandering a bit lately and she's been ranting and wailing and wandering the fields like a banshee, frightening the neighbors. She must be at it again. I found a note from someone when I got home last night, asking me to stop by here today. It's only the eccentricities of age and living alone, most likely, but around here they say the Fool of the Forth has gotten her."

"Fool of the Forth?" he repeated.

"An old superstition," she said, climbing from the car. "He's one of the Others who steals your reason when you intrude upon his hidden place." She moved around the Rover, opening its back. "Slany's had quite a reputation around here for, oh, a good fifty years. Some called her a healer and some a witch. See that shed?" She pointed to the ramshackle outbuilding. "They tell me she used to consult invisible friends there and make her cures. Anyway, no one will come near her now." She took out her bag, slamming the back of the car closed. "But don't you be worrying, Mr. McMahon. I won't take long."

She strode across the yard to the house and knocked on the warped boards of the little front door. Receiving no answer, she pushed the door open and vanished inside, leaving Colin to brood upon the scene.

It was not a spirit-raising sight. The countryside of browning meadows lay empty, stark, and lonely beneath a grey canopy of overcast sky. The drooping, forlorn cottage was overhung by a skeletal leaning oak with gnarled and nearly leafless branches.

He gave a little shudder, looked away, and pulled Bonaventure's book out of his overcoat pocket. He opened it to the second of the priest's paper slips and began to read.

"In a prose dinnsenchus preserved in the Rennes manuscript is found one variation of the legend," he read. " 'Tis there' (at Magh Slecht), it runs, 'was the king idol of Erin, namely the Crom Croich, and around him were twelve idols made of stones, but he was of gold. Until his destruction he was the god of every folk that colonized Ireland. To him they used to offer the firstlings of every issue and the chief scions of every clan.' The same authority tells us that these sacrifices were made on the heathen *Samhain*—Summer's End—when the sun's power waned and the strength of the gods of darkness, winter and the underworld grew great."

A wind began to rise, sweeping across the hill, making a shrill keening sound through the bare tree limbs. Somewhere the mournful baying of a dog lifted as if in answer to the howling wind.

The gusts quickly turned sharper, and Colin shuddered again from the chill. He put a hand to the window crank, began to turn it closed, but stopped. Megan had come out through the cottage door.

She had taken off her mackintosh. The wind blew her long skirt tight against her legs and sent her red hair streaming out at right angles. She pushed through the gusts as she crossed the yard to him, leaning down to the window to be heard above the sound.

"You have to come in!"

"What?" he said in surprise. "Why?"

"She said . . ." Megan hesitated. "Well, she said she needed to see the one who had come. The young man from far away."

"You told her I was here?"

She shook her head. "She already knew! Now just come in! She's very bad. You're all that can calm her."

He climbed from the Rover, slipping the book back into his overcoat pocket, and followed her into the cottage.

Coming from the grey outside into what was at first almost total blackness, he stood for a moment, letting his eyes adjust.

Most of the light came from the open door, through slits in the shuttered windows, and from the red glow of a peat fire in the stone fireplace. The pile of sod-like material smoked heavily, scenting the air with its pungent smell, mingling with the odors of decay and mustiness to create a nearly gagging atmosphere.

He coughed from it, standing in the open doorway and peering around him at the room. The furnishings were scant: a large plank table piled with dirty plates and bits of rotting food; battered wooden chairs, an iron-bound trunk. Some shelves held a few bottles and jars, and some odd, unidentifiable objects, all thickly matted with dust and festooned with cobwebs.

"Close the door!" came a rasping voice.

It came from the room's far corner and he squinted toward it. The low, long shape of a bed filled it. The flame of a candle stub on a bedside stand flickered feebly in the air currents from the door. Megan had crossed the room and now stood at the bed's foot.

He closed the door, shutting out the wind but making the room darker. Then the candle flame steadied in the stilled air, providing a brighter yellow glow.

"Now come closer," the voice demanded. "I can't see you."

He moved toward the shadowed bed with some reluctance. In the candleglow he could now faintly see a figure lying there, the face a white patch in the grey shadows.

He came up beside the bed, looking down. It was an ancient, sagging bed, its mattress filthy and its covers worn to tatters. He looked at the figure upon it, clearly visible now. His face revealed the revulsion that he felt. Megan, looking up to him, noted it and gave him an angry glare.

An old woman lay upon the bed, eyes closed, shallow breath rattling through open lips. Her face that might once have been round and flushed with life was shriveled and deathly white as if the vitality had been sucked from her. The limbs under the bundling rags of her clothes were withered; the hands upon the coverlets were knob-jointed, parchment-covered bone. She looked more like a mummy than a living being.

Then the eyes opened, revealing a flickering light of life. It steadied as the candle flame had, glowing with brighter energy as her gaze fell upon him.

"It is you!" she said, amazement and elation mixed in the harsh voice. "You've come back!"

"Come back?" said Colin, looking questioningly to Megan.

The young woman shrugged and shook her head, bending down to say soothingly: "Please, just lie easy, Mrs. O'Brien."

The woman ignored her, straining to lift her head toward Colin, speaking with intensity:

"You be careful now. Be careful. Don't let them be putting you Astray again. They'll kill you if they can. Oh yes, beware! Like they're killing me. I'm too strong for them. Oh yes, too strong. But still they're wearing at me. Wearing at my mind. My mind. They're trying to climb in."

This rambling speech seemed to exhaust her. Her head fell back, the eyes closing again. The wind outside rose higher, shrilling louder around the house. The thatch shivered.

Megan leaned close to him, speaking softly:

"She's raving again. She's been like this before lately. Mostly incoherent. Talks of spells, chants, spirits, monsters, and the like."

"Monsters?" he said, looking to her. "Like what . . ."

The old woman's eyes flicked open again.

"I'm sane," she said fiercely. "Sane as you. *They* want me dead! Oh yes. Since It's come alive. I know it. They wanted to stay hidden, but I knew. I felt."

The wind whipped up higher, booming across the chimney. It shot a sudden gust down, blasting at the fire, sending a grey cloud of acrid smoke puffing into the room, whirling out in eddies.

The woman started in alarm, lifting up to peer past Megan toward the hearth and the coiling smoke.

"It's them," she said, her creaking voice shrill in fear. "They're meaning to finish me now . . . now you're here." She looked to Colin, fixing him with her desperate gaze. "You have to listen while we still have time."

The wind was shrieking constantly around the cottage, beating at it as if in punishment. The little building groaned, thatched roof flapping, windows and doors rattling violently. More smoke billowed back into the room.

Slany leaned closer to Colin, her withered face only inches from his.

"I knew," she croaked, her voice fainter now and more husky, but still clear. "I knew, but they couldn't just kill me. Oh, they wanted to. To drain my blood for him, eat up my brain. But they were afraid. Afraid someone would find out before . . . before the time. They feared me . . . like they fear you."

She started to cough, a hacking, liquid sound from deep inside. She fell back on the bed.

"Can't we open a window?" Colin said irritably, looking at the shuttered one just above her bed. He lifted a hand to the latch.

The woman's hand shot up. The wizened arm demonstrated amazing strength as she gripped his arm, jerking it down.

"No! You'll let them in! Just listen! *You* must believe me. *You* know." She held his arm in a steel grip. "It's around. It's in the mist. The mist rises and *they* come. Into my house. Into my mind!"

A sudden immense gust of wind slammed like a giant fist against the house. Door and window shutters exploded open at once and wind roared into the house.

"By all my gods!" she shrieked, sitting suddenly bolt upright. "They're coming now! I can't stop them!"

A fog blew in on the blasts of wind, streamers of dense grey cloud geysering through the openings, filling the room. The old woman yanked him closer, gripping both his arms, her voice strained to breaking with her urgency.

"I've waited! I've held on! To tell you! It's only *you* now. You can still stop it!"

The jets of wind combined, forming a whirlpool that swept around the room drawing in the smoke. The fire now blazed up, making the rolling clouds glow a lurid red. The tiny candle flame was blasted from existence.

Slany ignored this rising chaos, pulling him even closer, forcing out her words as if against an enormous resistance:

"The power's strong now. Stronger each day it comes closer. There's still time. But once the power is full . . ."

She began to convulse, releasing him so that he fell back. Her body shuddered. Her head thrashed from side to side.

"Hold her," said Megan. "I have to sedate her."

Colin got a grip on her to hold her still. Megan began a search through her bag. The house shuddered around them.

"No. Don't!" the woman managed to get out as her body spasmed in his grip. "It's too late. Just listen!"

The spinning winds tore at them. Megan pulled out a bottle and hypodermic needle, managing to charge the syringe. The convulsing woman struggled to force out more words.

"I . . . must . . . tell you. I . . . know . . . where! I . . . can . . ."

The whirlpool contracted suddenly around the bed. The woman screamed in greater agony. Colin threw his arms around her, gripping the thin body so violently wrung by spasms that it seemed the thin, brittle limbs must snap.

Megan, holding the syringe, moved toward her, but the torrent of wind pushed her away.

"They . . . have me!" Slany gasped out. "No . . . more . . . strength! You must . . . find him. Destroy . . . him!"

The whirlwind raced higher. The woman convulsed with an even more terrible, wrenching force and screamed again.

Megan struggled to move forward, but the wind threw her back, pinning her helpless against the wall. The blast tried to tear Colin away but he hung on, hugging the woman tighter, hunching forward, his face close to her, trying to both shield her and keep her still.

"Who!" he cried to her through the battering, howling wind. "Destroy who?"

She went suddenly rigid, arching back, every muscle wringing taut. She seemed to concentrate all her energy, and her mouth opened. As the single word came out in a shriek of intolerable pain, it was caught by the winds:

"CROMMMMMM!"

The woman suddenly went limp.

The wind died instantly.

With it, the fog swiftly faded, the fire died to a faintly smoldering glow. In the sudden intense silence, Megan recovered. Staring in a dazed way, she moved up beside Colin, the unused syringe in her hand.

He released the woman, easing her body down gently onto the bed. She seemed even more wasted now, a loose pile of sticks. Megan put a hand to the woman's throat, then looked to him in shock.

"I know," he said grimly. "She's dead."

18

OCTOBER 30, 2:22 P.M.

The nondescript, three-story brick building filled half a block. It could have been any kind of institutional structure save for the large doors marked "Emergency" at one side and the large sign above the front door reading "CAVAN MEDICAL CENTER."

Megan Conroy came out the front doors and down the steps, crossing the street to where the Land Rover was parked against the curb. Colin sat in it, going through the book again, reading to himself:

"Who then was this bloodthirsty deity?" he read. "According to one source his name, *Cromm Cruaich,* means 'the Bowed One of the Mound,' and was applied to him only after his fall from Godhead. But from another source we glean that the word *cromm* was a kind of pun upon *cenn,* and that the real title of the 'king idol of Erin' was *Cenn Cruaich,* 'Head' or 'Lord of the Mound.' Professor Rhys, in his *Celtic Heathendom,* suggests that he was probably the god most feared and worshiped by the Gaels, surrounded by the twelve chief members of his Pantheon."

"Reading again?" Megan asked as she opened the Rover's door.

Colin looked up as she climbed in behind the wheel.

"This book Bonaventure gave me is interesting stuff," he explained. "Besides, it helped kill the time."

"Sorry. The formalities do take a while. There are a score of forms. And I had to explain the circumstances of her death."

"All of them?"

"Only her own physical ones. And even that got me some very odd looks. They'll certainly do a post-mortem. I'll see to the other arrangements later. She had no family."

"Did anyone even make a guess at what actually killed her?"

She shrugged. "They weren't certain. There were no signs of external causes. Likely something to do with her age is all they've ventured so far—stroke, heart, something like that."

"And what do *you* say?" he asked frankly.

She turned her head to meet his probing gaze with one of determination.

"I say that we had better talk now."

He nodded, smiling with a certain relief. "All right, then. Where?"

She consulted her watch.

"Look, it's well past two. I usually pack a lunch. I've brought a hamper with enough for us both. I know a place where we could eat and talk uninterrupted. What do you think?"

"No argument from me. I'm ready. And hungry."

She started the Rover and drove away from the hospital.

The avenue she followed took them through the main street of the town of Cavan. The way was narrow, edged closely on either side by a nearly solid wall of buildings. Here, as everywhere else in Ireland, past and present existed side by side in a hodgepodge of seventeen hundred years of architecture. Neat Georgian, ornate Victorian, and bland modern buildings rubbed shoulders with the coarser grey stone masses of Medieval structures.

The narrow way opened abruptly, the street dividing to pass around a central square—a small patch of green surrounded by a parking area for cars. There was a great deal of activity here, people putting up stalls and hanging festive decorations.

"What's this about?" Colin asked as Megan steered them around the square.

"It's a *fleadh*," she said. "A fair. They have it here every year at this time. People from all the county come to it."

"What's the occasion?"

"Halloween."

"You have that here too?" he said in surprise.

"Oh yes. In fact, we gave it to you. Children put on their costumes and go about begging treats. And there are games and the like. Lots of customs and superstitions. All very old. You even got your jack-o'-lantern from us, I believe. It replaced a real human head."

"A human head?"

She nodded. "It was the custom to collect *those* in the olden days. They put them on spikes and . . ."

"I know all about it, thanks," he said, grimacing. "Weren't there any more . . . ah . . . pleasant customs?"

"Well, there is one game I played as a girl," she said nostalgically, giving a little smile. "We put out four plates, with straws in one, earth in the second, water in the third, and a ring in the last. Each of the girls would go to them, blindfolded, and put a hand in one. It was the ring we all wanted to choose then. It meant marriage."

"What about the others?"

"The water meant a voyage across the sea. The straws meant we'd be rich."

"And the earth?"

She hesitated, the smile vanishing. "That meant we would be dying," she said at last, and then laughed. "But we always put it far out of the way."

"And did you ever get the ring?" he asked.

"If you're meaning to ask if I've been married, Mr. McMahon, I haven't," she answered curtly. "And I've no interest in such girl's fancies now. I've too much work."

They were well past the square by this time and had passed through the rest of Cavan. She turned the Rover onto a road that took them toward a rocky knoll rising just beyond the fringes of the town.

Colin peered up at the hill as they approached. It shot up abruptly, jaggedly from the smooth swell of the surrounding countryside. Atop it, the massive ruins of what appeared to be a church were visible, thrusting the castelated tops of walls, a spired steeple, and a minaret-like round tower toward the low, grey ceiling of the sky.

Megan turned the Land Rover off the roadway into a small parking lot, behind which a steep, rocky cliff of the knoll rose fifty feet.

"Here we are," she announced, pulling up close to the cliff.

"Where's here?" he asked as they climbed out.

"Dromlane it's called," she said, opening the rear gate. "A cathedral and monastery. I've come here often. It's a most spectacular place." She pulled out a large picnic hamper. "Fine view. Quite tourist-ridden in summer, but now we'll likely be alone."

"It's going to rain," he said pessimistically, looking to the overcast sky.

"Maybe," she said carelessly, "but we're used to that. And we can't expect much better this time of year. Come on," she said, thrusting the hamper out to him. "We'll find a sheltered place above."

He took the hamper and followed her without enthusiasm. They went along a pathway at the base of the cliff to reach the only visible avenue leading to the top. Here they hiked up stone stairs that led through a crumbling gatehouse, bringing them out onto a flat, open space. The walls of the cathedral now loomed ahead of them.

It was a ghostly-looking place in many ways: long abandoned, roofless, overgrown. It was like a wasted carcass, thrusting its bare ribs toward the heavy grey sky that seemed to hang so close above. A breeze keened through the ragged stones and ruffled the tall, dry grass of the graveyard spread around it.

Beyond a low stone wall a panorama of countryside was laid

out before them, its broad meadows patterned with the neat squares formed by stone walls and dotted with the white specks of cottages.

He followed her to the edge of the hilltop and peered over the wall. Cavan was visible below, its main street paralleling the cliff's base. And directly beneath he could see the parking lot and its lone occupant—Megan's Rover.

The view seemed to invigorate the girl. She lifted her head, her bright hair floating in the breeze, and took a deep breath of the fresh fall air. But the atmosphere seemed to have an opposite effect on Colin, and he turned to contemplate the towering grey pile of the cathedral with a melancholy gaze.

"Just how old is this place?" he asked.

"Thirteenth century mostly, though some parts are much older. That round tower, for instance," she pointed. "It dates back to the tenth."

The structure she indicated was the minaret-like tower. An elegant, tapering column eighty feet high and a dozen thick, it sat separated from the wall of the cathedral by some five yards. Its outside was smooth, featureless save for a door ten feet above the ground and a small window just below its conical cap. But its clean lines were now obscured by a complex network of steel pipes and wood planks encircling its full height.

"What're the tinkertoys for?" he asked.

"The scaffolding? Oh, they've been restoring the round towers all about the country. They're unique to Irish architecture, and there are few of them left now. It's a slow process, and they can work on it only in the warmer months."

"Yeah. I can see why they're not here today," he said, turning up his coat collar. The day itself wasn't uncomfortably cold, but the breeze across the exposed hilltop made the air chill.

"We'll find a sheltered spot inside," she promised, leading the way again.

Colin examined the massive headstones as they moved through the cemetery toward the cathedral. Some dated back as far as the 1500s, the grey stones weather-worn, spotted with circles of white mold. But then he came upon a new-looking one and stared at it in wonder.

"This is only five years old!"

"Ah yes. You'll find that often. Families have been using these grounds for centuries. And they'll continue to. No matter how old, how long deserted, you'll most likely find the church graveyards still active."

He looked at her, grimacing. "I'm not certain I like that word."

"Sorry," she told him with a little smile. "But look at this place," she added, sweeping her arms about her. "If you must be buried somewhere, this is it. Windswept ruins, a view of the country, and fine company . . . kings and bishops at least. And knights as well."

"No pawns and rooks?" he asked gloomily.

"I don't think you're enjoying my place," she accused.

"I've had picnics in cozier spots."

"You really are spoiled, aren't you?" she said, shaking her head pityingly. "Come on then."

She led him into the cathedral, through a wide jagged hole that had once been a door; it opened now into the vast, roofless space of the main nave.

As they entered it, a sudden flapping caused Colin to look up in surprise.

Huge ravens that had been occupying the countless nooks and crannies in the upper parts of the stone walls had all flown out in alarm at their intrusion. They now rose upward with a soft flapping.

"Like the souls of the black-robed monks who lived here, they always seem to me," Megan said, moving on into the nave.

"I'm just realizing what a morbid turn of mind you have," he observed.

"Not morbid," she corrected. "Just Irish. Life and death and God and fairies and joy and melancholy—they're all part of the one here."

She stopped below a great groin vault that upheld the spired steeple that rose above the center of the church. Sheltered beneath it lay a massive, flat-topped slab of plain stone, like an ancient altar.

"How about here?" she asked. "Well out of any wind and rain."

Colin looked at the stone, running a hand over it. The image of another stone—this with a groove about its outer edge—flashed in his mind. Then he shrugged and set the hamper down.

"Here you are," she announced, opening it and taking out a thermos, plates, vegetables, fruit, bread, and cold meats. "Have what you want."

He put together a sandwich and poured steaming coffee from the thermos. She made up a plate of food for herself and sat down on the slab, beginning to eat with gusto. Colin hesitated to begin, glancing around him nervously.

"What's wrong now?" she asked.

"There's just something about the feel of this place. It's like I'll see some ghost creeping past the corner of my eye, if I turn too quick."

"It's only a very old church," she said. "There's no reason to be having fear. Why do I sense such a great dread in you?"

"Maybe I have good reason for it," he said defensively. "If you really want to hear about it."

"Very well, let's see. Tell me your tale, Mr. McMahon."

He looked at her, took a bite, looked at her again, and then shook his head.

"You're going to say I'm nuts."

"I said I'd listen," she said, keeping a patient tone. "Please, let me decide."

He unscrewed the thermos, pouring more coffee as he considered.

"All right," he said. "Here goes." He took a swig of coffee and set himself determinedly. "The whole thing started with the dreams . . ."

He drained the last of the coffee from the thermos, lifted the cup and sipped, contemplating her over the rim. She was looking down into her own cup, her expression unreadable.

"So, what's your diagnosis, Doc?" he ventured. "Am I as crazy as you thought?"

She hesitated, taking a sip from her cup, not looking at him.

"I . . . I'm not certain what to say," she said at last. "You must admit, it sounds quite unbelievable."

"Oh yeah, yeah. I'll give you *that* free. Monsters, mayhem, and magic. The three *m*'s of any good fairy tale."

She looked to him. "Then why did you tell it all to me? You must have known how I'd react."

He looked uncertain, considering.

"Well," he said at last, "I did think about leaving out the Boogey Man bits. But . . . I don't know . . . once I started telling, it kind of just all spilled out. I've been keeping it in, itching to tell someone, and you were sort of my last shot at finding something real in this. I guess I was hoping that if anyone'd believe me, it'd be you."

"Why? Because of the girl in your dreams?"

"Maybe," he said musingly. He gave her a searching look, then nodded. "Yeah. I guess that *is* why. See, we . . . she and he . . . they kind of have a . . . well . . . they're sort of . . ."

"I am not that girl, Mr. McMahon," she interrupted to point out firmly.

"Too bad," he said with regret.

"But I'm not saying that you haven't had these dreams!" she went on in a reasonable tone. "And it would be quite natural for you to fix upon me as a solid point of reality—and perhaps a help. Still, that doesn't make any of the rest of it more real. And I certainly can't play any part in enforcing your . . . delusion."

"Delusion? And what about what happened to your Slany O'Brien? You sure seemed to think something was going on there. And something that had to do with me."

"I did. But that's before I heard this . . . this incredible tale. No. There can't be any connection except coincidence."

"Give me a break, lady!" he said with heat. "Coincidence?"

"Slany was an old woman," Megan staunchly expounded. "She was very sick. I'll admit that the way she died gave me a turn. But in the confusion . . . all that wind and smoke . . . well, I'm not really sure what happened, if anything."

"And what about the stuff she said to me?"

"Coincidence. In her delirium, she seized upon you as a place to fix her hallucinations. It was only her old 'invisible friends' come back to haunt her."

"Oh yeah? And what about that name she used?"

"Cromm?" she said. She said it clearly, loudly. It echoed from the walls of the cathedral.

"Jeez!" he exclaimed. "Don't say it so loud!" He hunched his shoulders and looked around him at the high enclosing walls. "It's like a beacon for them."

"Why? Because you believe that this white-haired stranger told you so? Or is it more likely that the first time you really heard that name was when Slany used it. You heard, and you fit it into your own dreams."

"So, you've got everything all covered with a nice, neat, one-step coat of logic," he said irritably. "I knew it! I just knew that was going to happen. Congratulations. You proved the old lady was crazy, and so am I. Or maybe *I'm* just a liar!"

"I don't think that," she said. "I think it's possible that you believe what happened to you was real. I just think that you're . . . confused. These dreams have caused it. You said yourself you weren't certain how much *was* a dream anymore. How can you know that *any* of it has happened?"

"I . . . ah, hell . . . I guess I don't know."

"And has anything happened since you came to Ireland? Anything to prove that your dream's linked to a reality?"

"Just you," he admitted reluctantly.

"No. Not me. Believe me, Mr. McMahon, I can't help you. But I do know people who can. Let me drive you to Dublin. I have friends . . ."

"Oh yeah? Doctors, I suppose? Guys with the white coats and straitjackets and nets and needles? Or police?"

"I don't mean . . ."

A shadow flitted across them.

His head jerked up toward it.

"What's the matter?" she said, looking up as well.

His gaze searched the sky above. "Something flew over. Something big."

There was no sign of it now.

"Another raven," she said.

"No," he said with certainty.

His gaze dropped from the sky to the top of the surrounding walls. Something was showing there: thick, curling white like foam in a pot, rising to boil over the edges and roll down the stone walls into the nave.

It was something that looked very much like fog.

"We've got to get out," he said, jumping down from the big stone. "Come on." He grabbed her hand, pulling the startled woman to her feet.

"Wait!" she protested. "My hamper!"

"Forget it! Come on!" He began to tug at her. She started to resist, but his urgency and strength changed her mind.

"I thought you weren't violent," she said, moving along with him.

"So humor me," he said. "Just move fast!"

The fog was now oozing down to form in puddles on the nave's stone floor. More was rising above the cathedral, arching over it, gliding in from all sides, joining to create a vault of clouds over the roofless space. A shape glided silently through the grey mass—a large, dark shape with immense outspread wings.

Colin and Megan neared the ragged doorway. Not far beyond it rose a wall of grey, a fog barrier encircling the cathedral, blocking out all view of the world beyond.

"Where did that come from?" she said in amazement.

"A gift from a friend. Keep going!"

They moved through the opening. The stones of the cemetery loomed up ahead as black shapes in the clouds. The two started through them toward the old gatehouse and the stairs down the hill.

But from behind one of the stones a ghastly figure loomed up to block their way.

It was an appropriate figure to encounter here, like one of the resting warriors risen from his ancient grave—a spear in his bony hands, a tattered cloak fluttering about him, his sunken eyes glowing with a ruby light.

Megan pulled up, staring in shock. Colin reacted more practically, turning around and pulling her back with him toward the doorway.

"Run!" he said with urgency.

It took no more to convince her. As the creature started in pursuit, they passed through the opening into the nave again, running across the vast floor, dodging debris. Colin scanned their surroundings. There seemed no other way out of the cathedral.

"This way!" he called to her then, heading for the corner where the main nave met the crossing transept. They stumbled toward it, managing to get around the corner and out of sight just as their pursuer came through the doorway.

It stopped there, skeletal head tipped back as if to listen with its fleshless ears, red eyes scanning the empty nave.

Colin peeked around the corner toward it. It was unquestionably the being who had attacked him in his apartment, but it showed no signs of their previous encounter. It seemed undamaged by its meeting with Colin's television set, and its fall to the street outside Casa Maitas. The tendon that Colin had severed with his dinner knife looked intact, the hand gripping the spear tightly. Colin pulled back, grimacing in disgust.

"Damn," he muttered. "I thought I'd finished *that* one at least!"

"What is it?" Megan breathed.

"The grim reaper," he whispered in return. "We've got to get out. Where?"

"That's the only open entrance," she said, more calmly now, clearly already recovering from her shock.

He peeked around the corner again. The thing was moving forward slowly, its gaze searching every shadow and rock that might give cover. Then it turned as a skittering sound came from the doorway. Another figure appeared there, trotting forward to join it. This one was the low, sleek doglike creature that Colin had met before.

"Not that one too," he murmured.

He watched as the mummylike being raised the spear to gesture sweepingly around the cathedral. The other beast at once moved away and, with head down and nose close to the floor, began slowly, methodically to investigate the vast space. Colin turned and looked around. The only other possible avenue of escape was a narrow, dark opening in the wall of the transept not far from them.

"Where does that go?" he whispered, pointing to it.

"Up into the central tower," she said.

"Come on."

Moving as silently as possible, they went through the doorway and up a tight, circular stairway. They came out into the open, finding themselves now atop the high walls of the roofless church. From here there were only two possible ways to go. One was the parapet walk, ringing the outer walls just within the upper battlements.

The other avenue was a walkway that led out to a doorway in the soaring central tower. Both walkway and tower were supported by the church's arching groin vault, and seemed to hang suspended above the floor five stories below. In addition, the narrow walk of crumbling stone had neither protecting walls nor guard rails.

Still, Colin chose that way to go, leading Megan across it and into the tower. They maneuvered around fallen stones in the inner darkness as they moved through the tower. They emerged upon another walkway, leading across to another doorway and another staircase that went right back down to the church floor.

Colin stared down the stairs in frustration.

"This doesn't *go* anywhere," he hissed.

"I know," she said.

"This is a great time to tell me!" he said irritably.

"You acted as if you knew what you were doing!" she shot back.

Colin and Megan peeked over the edge of the walkway. The beast was still sniffing around the upper part of the nave. But the bony one had now moved down directly beneath the tower. Here the being spotted Megan's picnic hamper, angrily thrusting the spear through the wicker top and smashing it to splinters against the stone. Then the thing began to pace back and forth under the vault, now able to watch both the transept and the nave while staying in sight of the only door.

"Jolly Roger's going to spot one of the stairways up here in a minute," he whispered.

He looked around him, his gaze falling on a large loose block of stone lying near the edge of the walkway. He went to it and peered over again. The thing's pacing took it right beneath them. Colin smiled with grim satisfaction.

"What are you doing?" she asked him.

He put a hand on the stone, made a sign of tipping it, then pointed to the thing below.

"If I hit it," he whispered, "the nice doggy will romp right up here. It goes up one way, we go down the other and get out of here. Simple."

"You're not meaning to just drop that stone on it?" she asked in some surprise.

"Why not? Hell, it looks dead already!"

"I . . . I don't know. It just doesn't seem . . . right somehow."

"Oh yeah? You want me to leap on the thing bare-handed? No thanks. I did that number once. This *rock* may not even hurt it. Now get ready to run."

"All right," she agreed reluctantly.

"And keep an eye on them while I shift this," he told her.

He crouched behind the stone, put his shoulder to it, managing to shift it forward slowly while making a minimum of noise. She kept her gaze on the two creatures moving below.

Neither she nor Colin noted the hand appear over the battlements behind them.

It was more a paw than a hand, long, slender, and tipped with curving black claws five inches long that caught like grappling hooks over the top of the wall. A second clawed hand appeared beside it. And then a face slowly rose up into view. It was slothlike, with a long muzzle and sloping forehead, and its eyes were slitted and golden like a cat's.

The eyes peered across at the pair who crouched on the walkway, their backs turned. The wide, drooping mouth lifted in a smile. The creature began to haul its body upward, using the sinewy muscles of its abnormally long arms. A long foot, taloned like the hands, gripped the edge. The lanky, muscled body, clad in a ragged robe, was pulled over the top.

Colin had worked the stone along to the walkway's edge. He then carefully, painstakingly inched it on out, farther, farther, until nearly half of it hung over empty space. Little more than a push could tip it now.

Behind, the slothlike being lowered itself down within the battlements. The long talons on its feet withdrew and it padded noiselessly around the wall toward the pair.

They were still fully absorbed, watching the mummylike one pacing below. Colin was tense, squatting and leaning forward to gaze down, a hand ready upon the stone. Megan crouched beside him, her body tensed as well.

The new arrival reached the connection of the battlement walk to the tower walkway. It turned out, now only yards from Megan and Colin, creeping more cautiously toward its unwary prey.

The bony creature that was stalking below Megan and Colin stopped under the vault and turned. It started slowly back, each stride bringing it closer to a point beneath the rock. But then it stopped again, looking around as if sensing some danger.

"Damn!" Colin murmured in frustration. "Come on. Come on, Bony Parts. Move!"

As if it heard him, it took a step, and then another. At last it was directly beneath the stone.

A faint sound of movement brought Megan's gaze whipping around to the slothlike creature.

"Colin!" she cried in warning.

It charged at once, sweeping out at her with a clawed hand. She threw herself backward and the claws whisked by.

Colin tried to stand as it struck out at him. He ducked, but he was off balance and he teetered, then went over the edge.

Megan gasped in horror. The cadaverous one below looked up. Directly above it, Colin hung on to the walkway edge with his fingertips, his body suspended over the stone nave floor forty feet below. The red eyes of the thing blazed bright in hatred.

On the walkway, Colin's attacker was moving in on him,

raising a clawed hand to strike again. Below, the other being raised the javelin in its bony hand, the glinting, barbed tip lifting to point at the dangling American.

Colin's helpless gaze moved from the javelin now cocked for hurling, to the talons prepared to tear off his head. Behind the slothlike thing Megan was climbing to her feet. The creature paid no notice, its attack focused on the young man. It leaned forward to swing down at Colin. As it did, she adroitly and boldly moved up close behind it, planted her foot squarely in its backside, and shoved hard.

It fell forward, screeching in surprise, arms windmilling in an attempt to save itself. But it tripped across the balanced stone and toppled over the edge with it, just missing Colin.

The wasted being below had no chance to move back as they plummeted down. Stone and creature slammed upon him, and they all crashed to the stone floor in a tangle.

Above, Megan immediately dropped flat onto her stomach on the walkway, sliding forward to grip both of Colin's wrists and take the strain from his slipping fingertips.

"Find a spot for your feet!" she told him. "Push up!"

The houndlike beast had now run from the upper end of the nave to its fellows. They were trying to heave themselves up, but the cadaverous one was trapped by one leg under the stone, and the sloth was wrenching at the javelin that had rammed through its side, impaling it. It shrieked loudly, the awful sound echoing in the nave, but the cry was more of rage than pain.

Colin found a foothold in the supporting stonework of the walkway. He levered himself upward, getting his arms over the edge. Coolly, dexterously, Megan slid forward, over his back, reaching down and gripping his belt to haul him upward.

Below, the cadaverous one stopped his struggling long enough to emphatically signal the houndlike creature toward the young couple above. The beast was off at once for a stairway. The sloth finally managed, with a quick jerk and a last high scream, to tear the spear loose from its side. Then it set to moving the stone from its companion's leg.

Overhead, with a final pull from Megan and a push of his own, Colin managed to heave his body up onto the walkway.

Megan released him and they got to their feet. She seemed unruffled. He was decidedly shaky.

"Thanks!" he said in a most heartfelt way.

"Now what?" she briskly replied.

They looked over the edge. The two beings right below them were on their feet again, moving toward a stairway. Both were limping a little, but seemed to have no serious damage.

"The other stairs!" he gasped out.

"That dog-thing was headed that way."

"Okay," he said defeatedly, "your turn."

"All right then," she said briskly. "Follow me."

She led him toward the side farthest from the hound. As they passed the doorway there, the two creatures below were just reaching the bottom of that set of stairs. At the same time, the houndlike creature was leaping from the opposite stairway into view, pausing to snarl as it spotted Colin and Megan rounding the corner onto the battlements.

The young couple ran out the battlement walk, turning onto the far end of the wall. Colin stopped there, looking out an embrasure at the long, sheer drop to the ground.

"There's no way down!" he shouted desperately.

"Yes, there is!" She pulled him on, toward the next corner of the battlements. Here they were at a point closest to the round tower that rose outside the cathedral walls. "There!" she said, pointing at the tower.

"What about it?" he said.

"Jump to it!" she said simply.

"What?" he gave her a disbelieving look. The tower itself was fifteen feet away. With the scaffolding, the gap was reduced, but was still a good two yards.

"It's not far," she told him.

"It's the goddam Grand Canyon!" he fired back.

Behind them, the hound-creature had reached the parapet walk and was racing around the battlements toward them.

"There's no other choice!" she said. "Jump for the scaffold!"

And with that she climbed into an embrasure, crouched, and leaped across the space.

She seemed to fly effortlessly across, gripping one of the

scaffold's vertical rods, swinging herself in to drop lightly onto the planks. It appeared quite a simple act for her. Colin shrugged and climbed into the embrasure. He looked down at the long drop. Then he glanced around to see the hound only yards away. He took a deep breath and jumped.

His stomach hit a rail and he doubled forward over it, head swinging in and down to slam on the planks, feet flying up. She grabbed his legs and pulled them over the rail. His body crashed onto the scaffolding. The whole construction shuddered.

"Is this going to be some kind of habit?" he asked as he pulled himself to his feet.

"Start climbing," she ordered. "Down!"

She knelt, grabbed the outer rail supporting the plank floor, and dropped over the side. He watched, amazed as she gracefully and fearlessly swung down to drop lightly onto the planks of the level below.

"I can't do that!" he called in desperation.

"Look out!" she cried, pointing up past him.

He turned to see the houndlike beast leap from the embrasure toward him. He rolled sideways as the creature flew past, struck the planking head first, tumbled forward, and thudded into the stone of the tower.

Hesitating no longer, Colin grabbed the lower rail and swung himself over the edge. Megan grabbed him around the waist to pull him in and he dropped beside her.

"How can you do this?" he asked.

"Gymnastics training," she answered simply. "Come on. There's a ladder!"

They moved around the tower to where a narrow ladder of pipe ran down the scaffolding to the ground. Above them the beast had regained its feet and was rushing back and forth, craning its neck over the side in an attempt to see them.

Megan climbed onto the ladder, starting down. Colin followed, looking up to see the beast's glowing eyes and slavering jaws a few feet above. It snarled in rage.

Thus motivated, Colin climbed downward with greater speed. But the beast had no way to follow, no means of moving downward without hands to grip the rails. It ran back and forth, growling in frustration. Then, defeated, it made the leap back to the cathedral wall.

Megan, meantime, was nearly to the ground, hands and legs clamped on the ladder's outer rails and sliding rather than climbing down.

Colin, more cautious, was descending rung by rung, and she was waiting impatiently when his feet touched earth again.

"Finally," she said.

"Sorry to hold you back!" he returned. "Now what?"

The wall of fog was still around the cathedral, shutting it off from the outside world.

"If we go over the east wall we can climb directly down to the parking lot," she said. "Can you make it?"

"Hey, what's another drop?" he said gamely.

They moved toward the edge of the hilltop, plunging into the wall of fog. For a few strides nothing but the billowing grey was visible. Then, suddenly, they were through it, the low wall and the countryside coming into view.

The girl looked around in surprise at the wall of fog now behind them.

"Never mind," said Colin. "It's just magic."

They glanced over the wall. The Rover still sat alone in the tiny lot.

Megan went over the wall, and Colin, this time without hesitation, followed. The cliff face was steep but rough, with ample handholds. Again Colin moved cautiously, creeping down the cliff. A glance down at Megan showed her clambering down with amazing speed and agility, reaching the bottom in moments.

Colin slid down the last few yards on to the gravel, and then stood panting there to examine his scraped hands and torn trouser knees. He looked to Megan who, save for some dust on her skirt, was unmussed and unwinded.

"How do you . . ." he began breathlessly.

"I did some mountain climbing as a girl," she supplied. "Come on."

They had just begun a run for the car when a telltale *woosh* sounded behind them.

"Get down!" he cried, grabbing her around the waist and pulling her to the ground as a form swooped low overhead.

"What in God's name . . . ?" she said, pulling away from him and looking up.

The huge, batlike creature of Colin's dream was lifting above them, stroking upward with its broad leathery wings.

"The Ialtag!" he said. "Damn! I forgot it!"

As they climbed to their feet Colin's gaze fell on a loose lump of rock the size of his two fists. He took hold of it, hefting it and looking upward.

The Ialtag had soared away and gained some altitude. It was now starting a swing back around toward them.

"Get in the car," he told her. "I can take care of this."

"But . . ." she said, looking from him to the creature.

"Hey, *you* trust *me* this time!" he announced with towering confidence. "Go!"

She ran for the Rover and Colin set himself into position, his arm down at his side, the rock concealed.

Megan's keys were in her hand as she reached the car. She wrenched open the door, climbed in, and jammed the Rover's key into the ignition slot. Then she looked back for Colin.

He was still standing where he'd been, motionless, seemingly without defense. The Ialtag was directly above him now and began its descent, wings back, needle-beak thrust forward, a speeding arrow aimed right at Colin's chest.

She caught her breath, eyes going wide in fear.

The creature was only a dozen yards above when Colin's arm shot up and forward, flinging the rock with all his power. Fired with an accuracy rivaling that of his dream counterpart, it flew upward to meet the creature's descending head. Colin gave a sharp, triumphant laugh.

But this time the Ialtag wheeled suddenly, pulling up. A clawed foot thrust out, grasping the rock and then dropping it back upon the young man.

Astonished by the move, Colin had no time to duck completely out of the way. The rock struck him a glancing blow on the rear of his skull, jerking his head back.

He staggered forward, dropping to his knees, swaying groggily. The creature wheeled again, swinging around to dive in at him.

Megan went into action as well. She slammed the Rover into gear, gunned the vehicle into a sharp, skidding turn, its spinning wheels spewing out a shower of gravel as it came around.

The Ialtag swooped in along the cliff base, skimming the ground, beak opened and talons forward to tear at the stunned Colin, now on his hands and knees with his head sagging downward.

The creature was nearly on him when the Rover shot into its path, sliding to a stop. With a shrill caw of anger it pulled itself upward, barely missing a collision with the vehicle's roof, soaring over it and banking away.

Megan slid across the seat and opened the passenger door. Colin lifted his head and stared dazedly, unable to move. She leaned out, grabbed one of his arms and hauled him bodily into the car. As he collapsed across the seat he looked up to her.

"Funny . . ." he said in a faint, bemused way, "it worked so well before."

Then his head dropped limply over the edge of the seat and a tide of black washed across him, engulfing his view of the girl, the car, and everything, leaving him in total darkness.

19

The darkness seemed nearly complete at first. But then tiny glimmers of light became visible.

They were stars thickly patterning the sweep of a night sky, providing a jeweled setting for the spectacular white-gold oval of a nearly full moon that coasted above the black tracery of tree tops.

Colin looked around him, the moonlight enabling him to see little Ailbe, his driver, standing beside him at the reins of their chariot.

"All right," Colin ordered softly, "stop here."

The chariot pulled up just within the fringe of the grove of trees. The ancient oaks loomed up before them like a massed host of giant, menacing creatures. The area beneath the canopy of their interlacing branches was a black void. Ailbe looked into its depths and sighed unhappily.

"Never thought to see this *sheoguey* place again," he muttered.

"This time you stay here with the chariot," his master told him. "Stay in it and stay alert. It may be we'll have to leave this place very quickly."

"Not quickly enough for me!" the driver replied.

Colin climbed down from the cart. He slipped his shield onto his arm and took a casting spear, pulling the loop of its tether over his wrist.

"I don't see how you'll find your way in there through that blackness," Ailbe said, shaking his head.

"I've only a narrow band of trees to pass. I'll go straight through."

"Will you? Well, may Danu go with you and guide you. And remember to watch for those dangling heads."

"Thank you for the reminder," Colin said dryly. "I'll be back soon."

"You had better be," Ailbe told him, "or you may find a driver gone gibbering mad with fear."

Colin waved a farewell and moved off, vanishing into the trees. Ailbe looked around him again, shuddered, and put a hand on one of the other spears racked within the cart.

Meantime, his young master was making his way boldly into the depths of the sinister wood. It was extremely dark here, with only widely scattered spots of moonlight flashing down through rare gaps in the tree branches to light the way.

He strode on purposefully for some distance, but then he slowed, his expression growing uncertain. He peered ahead, then to right and left. He stopped, gazing around him, his face drawing into a frown.

"I should be nearly through the trees by now," he muttered. "Shouldn't I?"

He looked searchingly around once more, but the black

woods seemed the same in every direction. He took a few more hesitant steps forward but then stopped again.

"The Bloody Raven take it," he softly swore, "I don't know *which* way now!"

Then something caught his attention. A faint sound. He cocked his head and held his breath, listening. It was a distant thumping sound, soft but steady, like the pounding of his own heartbeat. He turned toward the right where it seemed the loudest and started off that way, moving slowly, quietly, ear still cocked to catch the sound.

It grew louder, resolving into the sound of several drums throbbing out a slow, emphatic rhythm. So intent on following the sound was he that he walked into one of the suspended heads before seeing it. The eyeless, gap-mouthed horror was knocked backward by the impact, swinging away and then forward into the startled warrior's face.

With an exclamation of disgust he hurriedly pushed past. Now he could hear the sound of pipes too; a strange, high, eerie tune that followed and twined around the steady thudding of the drums like fantastic vines woven through a row of stakes.

Through the trees ahead a light became visible. He had come to the end of the band of woods at last, and he stopped, poking his head cautiously out through the final screen of trees.

Across the moonlit plain, the circle of statues loomed up, silhouetted as masses of black against an intense and ruddy light that filled the space within their ring. The glow poured through the gaps between the stones, radiating outward in spreading wedges from the blazing hub so that the entire plain became like a great wheel, the dark shadows of the stones its spokes.

An echo of this wheel of light showed also in the sky above the plain. For there a smooth, solid canopy of silver-grey mist hung, reflecting the fire below, so low above the circle of stones that it seemed to be upheld upon the statues' heads.

Colin stared out at this sight, his expression one of fascination, but of perplexity too.

"I've dreamed of this . . ." he murmured, ". . . haven't I?"

He shook his head, his expression hardening with determination as he crept forward out of the shelter of the trees. Taking care to stay within one of the spokes of black thrown by the stones, he approached the ring.

The sound of the music was quite loud now, and growing rapidly louder as he drew near the source. At least a score of pipers followed the pounding rhythm of as many drums. A movement within the circle of stones was now visible as well, a sea of shadow washing about the fire, ebbing and flooding with the movement of the tune.

At last he reached one of the stones, sliding cautiously around it to peer directly into the ring.

The interior was brilliantly aglow with twelve massive bonfires, one placed before each of the statues, casting the monstrous images in shifting crimson light. The tongues of flame licked up against the body of clouds suspended close above, turning the shiny grey-white to an incandescent red. The garish hue was reflected on the naked forms of a throng of several hundred men and women who danced wildly below, unbound hair flying, limbs flailing, bodies interweaving in a rising sensual frenzy to the increasing tempo of the music.

Suddenly the music stopped.

As the last notes faded away, the flushed, panting crowd stood motionless and silent, waiting expectantly. And then from somewhere the druid Dubhdaleithe appeared, now clad in a glowing robe of white feathers, a fantastic headdress of curling white plumes atop his head. He strode directly into the crowd and it parted before him as he made his way toward the center of the ring and the obscene statue that squatted there.

Colin's angle of view would allow him to see no more. He was too far around the ring to look up the opened avenue. Boldly he slipped across a space to the next stone, then the next, and the next. He moved unobserved by the gathering. All their attention was riveted on the druid.

Colin reached a better vantage point. Now he could see the center of the circle and the monstrous, hunched shape of Cromm's statue, glowing red in the bonfires' light. The strange, perverted infant's face seemed to shift with the moving flames, casting lewd and malevolent looks across its adoring throng.

The druid stopped before the altar at the statue's base. Then, at the signal of his lifted hand, a group moved out of the crowd into the avenue. A score of women formed the group, each carrying a squirming white object in her hands: an infant.

They moved up the avenue through the hushed throng, lining up before the altar. The druid looked their little burdens over with a glinting red, rapacious eye.

One baby began to wail, its cry sounding rail and piteous in the night. The woman who held it seemed oblivious to this, her look entranced, like the rest, and focused on the druid as if caught up in some dominating spell.

The druid signaled to another of the women. She started forward, her movements stiff and mechanical, stepping up to lay her baby down upon the hard stone of the altar. She stepped back.

The druid looked at the form so alone and so tiny on the massive slab, and then looked up to the statue glowering down at him. "Now we will feed you," the druid said loudly, his voice echoing within the ring. "The warm blood will rise up into your own belly and nourish you and give you strength, and you will smile upon those who serve you with their love and their firstborn."

From within the white robes he then drew out a sword. The honed edge of its long, slender blade glinted like a line of flame. The druid held it up toward Cromm in both hands as if in offering.

The stone face of the statue seemed to shift, the small mouth drawing into an awful leering smile. The bent and shrunken body seemed to writhe as if in arousal.

A look of revulsion filled the face of the young warrior at this, but those in the crowd voiced hoarse, ecstatic cries.

The druid turned back to the altar. From behind the stone he drew out a bowl of finely worked silver that flared a brilliant crimson in the firelight. He placed it at the lower end of the altar, below the spout leading from the channel carved about its top.

He moved back to stand over the infant. It was whimpering now, feebly thrashing its limbs in useless struggle.

The druid held his sword out above the infant. At this move

the drums began again with a slow throbbing, but one quickly increasing in pace. With their beat, a chant rose in the crowd, the hundreds of voices joining in a single shout, pounding out the name:

"Cromm! Cromm! Cromm!"

"They're actually going to do it!" Colin breathed.

He lifted his spear and shield.

"No!" he said fiercely. "Not *this* time!"

He stepped boldly out into the wedge of light between the stones, starting forward.

But then he was brought abruptly to a stop. Frowning, he pushed forward but made no headway. There seemed to be some kind of resistance, as if an invisible barrier closed the space between the stones. He pushed forward with more force.

Within the ring, the sword lifted higher. The chant grew louder.

"Cromm! Cromm! Cromm! Cromm! Cromm!"

"I will not be stopped!" Colin grated out, setting himself and driving forward. "This druid magic has no real power to keep me out!"

The sword reached the high point of its arc and stopped, hanging there, glinting with ruby light. The chant was now nearly deafening, each shout a thunderclap:

"CROMM! CROMM! CROMM! CROMM! CROMM!"

The resistance Colin had experienced seemed to break suddenly and he stumbled forward into the ring. He recovered and began to run boldly toward the center.

As he moved through the crowd, the people became aware of him. The sudden appearance of this intruder seemed a great shock. They started back, gasping in surprise, blinking in astonishment like people coming from darkness into sudden light. As the wave of their consternation swept about the circle, the chanting faltered and died. The druid, startled, lowered his weapon to look around.

"You! Blasphemer!" he called in anger on seeing Colin. "Go out from our circle or Cromm's wrath will surely fall upon you!"

"That I will not, murderer!" Colin called back, moving steadily closer. "I'll not let you kill those babes."

The people around him exchanged bewildered glances.

"Stop him!" the druid cried, a touch of desperation in his voice as Colin drew near.

But the reactions of the people were those of rudely awakened sleepers; moving sluggishly, their looks were confused, disoriented. Many gazed about them in dismay as if suddenly recognizing the bizarre nature of the surroundings and their own nakedness.

Thus Colin, unhindered, reached the altar before Cromm.

"I said stop him!" the druid shouted. "Someone stop him!"

This time a figure moved forward. It was the chieftain Laimainech, naked like the rest, his tall, muscled body gleaming with ruddy light. His face was set, holding no expression, but he moved with intent, charging unarmed at Colin.

"I'll kill no unarmed man," Colin said.

He swept his shield out as the man came in, stopping the charge. A swing of his spear slammed the pole against the chieftain's head, knocking him sideways, and the man fell stunned into the crowd.

There were gasps of shock, cries of fear. Those around the altar backed away. The line of women scattered as Colin moved up beside the stone. The one who had left the infant there swooped in and snatched it back again, clutching it to her as she vanished into the crowd.

The druid stepped toward Colin, bringing the sword around. With a snarl of rage he swung a savage cut at the young warrior's head.

Colin knocked the sword aside with his lifted shield, then drove in with his spear. It struck home in the center of the druid's chest, cracking through his breastbone, sinking into his heart. Colin hauled back on the thong, yanking his weapon from the man. The barbed head of the spear tore free in a spray of blood, jerking the druid forward to slam against the altar, then fall limply across it.

Screams of terror rose at this. Colin wheeled to face the crowd, his shield and spear up, expecting an attack. But those around him were in full panic now, moving away from him, pressing back toward the stones of the ring.

Colin turned, looking all about him. Everywhere the crowd was moving away. He turned back to the altar. The druid's own red blood was spreading down in a fan across the surface. Caught by the groove, the thick crimson liquid poured into the silver bowl.

Above, the lewd face of Black Cromm grimaced down. And then it seemed to shudder.

Colin stared up at it in wonder. The whole body of the statue actually seemed to be shaking as if from an ague. A peculiar, undulating growling noise began to rise from deep within the ground. With this rising sound the stone of Cromm began to glow, not with the reflected red light of the fire, but with a greenish light that appeared to come from within.

The warrior looked around him again. The crowd had gone mad with fear and confusion, stampeding headlong away in all directions, climbing on one another to pass between the encircling statues, rushing out into the surrounding night.

And those other statues were also beginning to glow.

From somewhere a figure was suddenly beside him. Unlike those of the stampeding crowd, this one was robed and cowled in a dark cloak. It grabbed his arm.

"Come, quickly!" it said in an urgent voice.

Colin was alarmed and jerked away, turning and raising his spear and shield defensively before the strange figure.

"Stand away, creature!" he told it threateningly.

"I'm your friend, you hot-headed young fool!" the other replied sharply. "Not one of Cromm's creatures." A hand lifted to pull back the hood. It revealed a large, strong-featured face topped by a bushy mass of silver-white hair. Colin stared in surprise.

"But, you're . . ."

"You have to leave here now!" the other interrupted. "You've started something which could destroy you too!"

The lights grew brighter, flaring now with a luminescent, white-green glow that was expanding quickly. The statues teetered, rocking violently as if to fall. In the center of the ring Cromm's twisted figure had become totally obscured by the light, forming a blazing emerald ball that swelled upward and outward. The oscillating growl from within the earth had become a near-deafening roar.

"Quickly," the man told Colin. "If those lights join about us, we'll be trapped!"

The circle was nearly empty by this time. The two followed the last of Cromm's fleeing subjects, running across the hard-packed earth toward the ring of stones. The swelling lights had engulfed each statue and were near to filling the spaces in between. Cromm itself was an immense globe of light, expanding outward like some blossoming flower of enormous energy, horrible and beautiful at once.

Colin and the silver-haired man leaped through a narrowing gap between two lights. In the garish green glow, the figures of some of the naked people could be seen streaming away across the plain in all directions. The two men made their way after them, running to the trees.

Behind them, the lights of the individual statues joined to form a solid wall. The light of Cromm within the circle swelled farther, touching the outer ring of light, filling all the central space, forming one green-white blaze. It began to lift higher, a dome that pushed up above the stones, forcing up the low canopy of clouds.

Colin glanced back once as they passed into the band of woods, but his new companion jerked him around by his cloak and tugged him forward.

"Don't look back," he urged. "Just run!"

They moved on through the trees, their going made easier by the eerie shafts of emerald light that now shot down through the branches from the rising dome. Around them they could hear the crashing of the others making their way through.

The silver-haired man led the way unerringly to Colin's chariot. Here the frightened but steadfast Ailbe still waited, holding the horses with a great effort. The steeds were rearing and whinnying, fear-stricken by the strange lights and sounds in the woods and by Cromm's subjects fleeing out of the woods around them. Ailbe himself was gazing around in wide-eyed wonder and alarm at the flood of naked people.

Colin grabbed a handhold of the chariot and leaped up behind Ailbe. The little man jumped and turned to him, white-faced, gasping out his relief as he recognized the young warrior.

"Colin! Thank Danu you're back! What in the Dagda's name is going on?"

"Just get us away from here," the silver-haired man demanded, climbing in beside Colin.

"And who's this?" the driver asked, looking at the stranger.

"Never mind who I am," the other said sharply. "I said get us away from here. Quickly."

"Do it, Ailbe," Colin put in. "We could be in danger."

"Could be?" the silver-haired man repeated as Ailbe urged the team forward.

They pulled out of the woods and onto the open meadows. As they rolled away, all three looked back, staring in awe.

Behind, the dome of light was rising up above the encircling band of trees, casting its glow across the surrounding countryside. It revealed the tiny figures of the fleeing people streaming away like insects from a ruptured nest. It cast the faces of Colin and his companions in an unearthly greenish hue and made the grassy fields seem to blaze with emerald fire. It lifted like a luminescent thunderhead rising before some alien setting sun, swelling outward above the trees, forming a vast mushroom of light covering the whole of Magh Slecht.

"By all the gods . . ." Colin said in amazement.

"Yes. You've certainly caused a bit of turmoil," was the silver-haired man's dryly understated comment.

"You," Colin said, looking to him. "Just tell me now, who are you?"

"Gilla Decair is the name I go by," he replied. "Aislinn's people call me the Healer."

"You're the one who saved me."

"Twice now, I believe."

"And have I seen you before?"

"No, lad, that you have not," the man assured him. "But

never mind me now. You've started something. You must go back and tell Aislinn's people about it."

"I've saved them," Colin said with a note of pride.

"You've done something," the other said. "There's no denying that. And they must know of it—now."

Colin looked back again. The emerald glow had risen higher to form a growing stalk atop which a still swelling bloom of light was a painfully glaring ball against the blackness of the night.

20

OCTOBER 30, 3:23 P.M.

The ball of light in the darkness filled his eyes.

He blinked and shifted, sighing softly.

The glare slipped sideways and was gone. The scene behind began to come into focus. A face became visible above him, faint and fuzzy, but undoubtedly a face. The face of the girl.

"Wh . . . When am I?" he said blurrily. "Now or then?"

The face came fully into focus. The torrent of bright hair about the shoulders could be clearly seen.

"Red hair," he said. "I'm now."

"Mr. McMahon, how do you feel?" Megan Conroy asked him anxiously.

They sat in the Rover, he lying across the seat, his head pillowed in her lap.

He snuggled it in, closing his eyes, sighing this time in contentment.

"Comfortable," he said dreamily. "I'm just . . ."

Suddenly his eyes flew wide again.

"My God! What happened!" he cried, sitting up. "Ow!" He grimaced in pain, putting a hand to his head.

"Easy! You've had a hard blow."

"No kidding!" he said with gritted teeth, squinting through

the pain to look around. They were parked on the edge of Cavan at the base of the road up to the cathedral.

"It's all right," she told him. "That flying thing turned back when I started down the hill. It's gone now."

He peered up toward the looming structure, stark against the grey sky. The heavy fog had vanished from about it. A streak of sun through a gap in the overcast ran across the grim stone like a beam from a spotlight, revealing only empty ruins.

"Pulled out again," he said musingly. "Back home to Daddy."

"What do you mean?" she asked.

"I'm not sure, but I guess they sort of run out of steam after an attack like that. Or they need to replace the batteries. Or something. Besides, they can't think for themselves. Cro . . . I mean, the head guy does it."

"And just how do you know that?"

He looked at her. "You . . . I mean *she* told me."

"Look here, are you certain you're all right? That rock only struck you a glancing blow, but it did put you out." She put a hand to the back of his head. "There's a lump there. It could be serious."

"It's just a headache," he said irritably, pulling away.

"Please listen," she said earnestly, "I don't see any signs of concussion, but I can't be sure. You should have it checked."

"Still trying to get me to have my head examined?" he accused.

"That I am not," she said indignantly. "I believe your story now."

"Then you know why I'm not checking into some hospital. Got any aspirin?"

She sighed and turned to hunt in the medical bag on the seat behind her, pulling out a bottle.

"Those things," she commented as she opened the bottle, "they're still incredible, even though I've seen them."

"So you really do believe me now?"

"Have I any other choice?" she said simply, shaking out two white tablets and handing them to him. "Unless it's to accept that I'm mad as well."

"Finally!" he said triumphantly, taking the aspirins. "Look, can I get some water for these things?"

"Sorry," she said. "I know a place."

"Let's try to make it a more crowded one this time, okay?" he suggested.

She drove the Land Rover back along Cavan's main street, into the busy central square, pulling up before a large pub. Here they left the car and walked inside.

It was a quite modern place, clean and open, with a scattering of patrons who looked to be largely middle-class. A television set behind the bar was broadcasting a fast-moving soccer game. A wall was lined with pinball and video games, one of which a young man was playing enthusiastically.

"It's good to see a place like this," he said, looking around. "I've had the weirdest feeling I wasn't even in the twentieth century anymore—awake *or* asleep."

They found a table in a corner, away from the noise of television and video games. A young waitress detached herself from an admirer at the bar and came over.

"Anything?"

"Scotch," he told her.

"I thought you wanted water," Megan said.

"Okay, Scotch with a water back. But a double Scotch."

"I can't advise that, after your head injury."

"Megan, I almost died," he told her. "For about the fifth time in three days, too. A lousy drink's not going to kill me now."

"All right. If you insist on being foolish, I'll have one too. But Irish, if you please. I'll be right back."

The waitress took the order to the bar and Megan made off for the ladies room. While Colin waited, he pulled Bonaventure's book from his overcoat pocket once more and turned to another of the marked references to Cromm.

He was reading intently when Megan returned.

"What's so fascinating?" she asked.

"It's part of a poem. About . . . You-Know-Who. I read a little of it once before. There's more of it here. Listen:

"Here used to be
A high idol with many fights,
Which was named the Cromm Cruaich;
It made every tribe to be without peace.

"Around it stood
Four times three stone idols;
To bitterly beguile the hosts,
The figure of Cromm was made of gold.

"T was a sad evil!
Brave Gaels used to worship it.
From it they would not without tribute ask
To be satisfied as to their portion of the hard world.

"To him without glory
They would kill their piteous, wretched offspring
With much wailing and peril,
To pour their blood around Cromm Cruaich."

The young waitress, setting down their drinks, stopped and looked at him on hearing this, made a face of revulsion, and then hurried away. Colin went on.

"Milk and Corn
They would ask from him speedily
In return for one third of their healthy issue:
Great was the horror and the scare of him.

"They did evil,
They beat their palms, they pounded their bodies,
Wailing to the demon who enslaved them,
They shed falling showers of tears.

"Around Cromm Cruaich
There the hosts would prostrate themselves;
Though he put them under deadly disgrace,
Their name clings to the noble plain."

He stopped and looked up to her.

"What name?" she asked.

"The Plain of Adoration," he said. "Magh Slecht. That's where Cromm is. And I've seen it. I told you about that. And I was just there again. Or he was."

"You had another dream?"

"When I was knocked out. Not a dream exactly," he said, clearly struggling with the concept. "God, I don't know what to call 'em. They're as real as this."

"And do you think that they *are* real? Are they something that happened?"

"What, some broadcast from the past I'm tuning in on?" He took a sip of Scotch, considering. "I don't know. It all jibes with the history books and with what little I've found out about . . . our boy." He nodded. "Yeah, I suppose it could be."

"What happened this time?"

"Well, I saw the ritual, the wailing, the idols, the whole bit."

"So, you went," she said with interest, "just as you promised her."

"You mean as *he* promised," he corrected. "But not just to watch. He went and dived right in! Jeez, he's a hot-dogging son-of-a bitch." He shook his head in disbelief.

"What did he do?"

"I'm not sure. They were sacrificing babies. Just like in the poem."

"My God!"

"I . . . he . . . that idiot ran in to try to stop it."

"He sounds very brave."

"Yeah? Well, he was very stupid, charging alone into a mob of a thousand people. Anyway he killed that druid. The one who ran the show. And then the whole place blew up."

"You mean he destroyed Cromm?"

"Shh!" he warned. "Watch the name. Yeah, it seemed like it." He considered, then added musingly, "You know, maybe that's what they're afraid of. Maybe they think he . . . I can do it again!"

"Can you?"

"How the hell should I know? That old woman sure seemed to think I could. And that silver-haired guy said something about the answer being in my dreams. He said they might be the only weapon left." Then he had a sudden realization. "God! That guy! He was in the dream too! He was back there! The same guy! Decair he called himself. Gilla Decair."

"So now you've met two of us in both places?" she asked.

"I guess so. Only it seems like *he* remembers being back there. God, I'd like to get my hands on him."

"But, now *I've* seen these things too. Couldn't we tell anyone together?"

He shook his head. "Hey, remember what *you* thought of my story? Don't you figure they'd just put us both away or maybe ship me back home in a padded crate?"

"Yes," she agreed. "You're very likely right. But what else can we do?"

"There's not much we can do until I figure out where Cr . . . old Whatsizname is hiding out before he finds me."

"You mean 'us,' " she corrected.

"Oh. Yeah," he said more soberly. "I guess we had better figure that they'll be after you too now. Sorry. I really didn't think about that angle when I got you into this."

"It's not your fault," she assured him. "Neither of us can turn away from it. There's a great deal more at stake than just ourselves."

"What do you mean?" he asked, clearly not following.

"Well, if what you've told me is true, if this . . . this ancient creature and his disciples are somehow loose again in the world, then many other people could very well be harmed, or even die as Slany did."

"Maybe," he conceded. "And that's too bad. But look, lady, I don't know about you, but *my* main interest here is to get out of this with most of my skin on and my blood still in my veins."

"You're not concerned with whether or not anyone else is hurt?" she asked in disbelief.

"I didn't ask for this," he told her bluntly. "Just because some guy a thousand years ago horned in on somebody else's fight, why should *I* be stuck?"

"I got the impression you thought that this 'guy' was you," she said.

"No way," he adamantly replied. "I'm an artist, lady. A simple-minded doodler who wants no complications and a good time. Not Mr. White Knight."

"I'd say *he* is a most courageous man," she said in a defensive way.

"Yeah, I'm sure you'd love him," he said sarcastically. "Now could we forget him? Let's stick to our troubles in the here and now, like trying to find the 'Big C.' He's got to be in the village."

"But you can't think that this evil is there," she said.

"Yeah, I do. It *has* to be. I mean, you're not the only clue. There's what Slany O'Brien said, and there's that ringfort outside town—just like the one in my dreams. And there's even the names."

"Names?"

"Sure. The place in the dreams is called Dun Mauran. I know a *dun*'s a fort. What does 'bally' mean anyway?"

"It's Irish for 'village.' "

"There, see? Ballymauran. Dun Mauran. Village or fortress, it's still the same Mauran. There're just too many things for coincidence."

"All right," she said. "Granting all those things, if Cr . . . if 'he' *is* there, why didn't the creatures just attack you when you first came?"

"Because I actually think they were afraid of me." He sat back, smiling a little smugly. "I mean, no bragging, but I have beaten the crap out of them a couple of times."

"Have you really?" she asked, fixing him with the intense gaze of her blue-grey eyes.

"Well," he said, clearly made uncomfortable by the look, "I guess I have had a little help. Okay . . . a lot of help."

"No need to make excuses," she said. "I thought you handled yourself well . . . for a simple-minded doodler."

"Thanks," he said. "Even if it was mostly luck. Anyway, I

don't think they've wanted a confrontation, especially so close to home. Too big a risk. I think they've just wanted to stay hidden and hope I don't find them."

"But then why the attack today?"

He sat forward, his voice becoming more intense. "Because I must be getting too close. They're getting desperate. And that's another reason I think they're in your village. Do you see? They still couldn't risk taking a shot at me there. But as soon as I was as far away from it as possible—wham!"

"I still cannot believe such a monstrous thing could exist in Ballymauran," she said. "In my village! I grew up there! I know every old tale. Every tree. Every inch of sod. I've never heard of any of these things before, and I've surely never seen a place like your Magh Slecht."

"Yeah, yeah," he said with some frustration. "That's what the Brigadier said. But it's got to be!"

"This isn't helping us," she said in a defeated way. "And I don't see how I can really be of help."

"Meg, don't give up on me already," he said, putting a hand on hers.

Her gaze went from his hand to his face, her expression one of musing. He drew back the hand.

"I mean, look," he said, "the thing keeps on coming back to you. You're the only solid link I've got. There's got to be a reason why you're here. Why did you come back to Ballymauran?"

She considered, shaking her head.

"I . . . I don't know. I suppose I just felt a need. As if something was calling me home."

"No dreams?"

"Nothing like that. Just a feeling that I needed to come back. That the people needed me."

"Because they were in trouble?"

"No. And I didn't see any signs of such when I returned. It was much as when I'd left. The people were a bit shyer of me, but I'd expected that. Fifteen years had made a Dubliner of me, you see. An outsider."

"There wasn't anything weird at all? How about deaths? Maybe a high infant mortality?"

"My God, Mr. McMahon!" she said in shock. "That's a horrible notion."

"Yeah, but it's also possible, if the Black Death is back in business."

"You're right," she agreed. She considered, then shook her head. "But there was nothing like that. Oh, well the mortality rate *may* have been a bit higher than normal before I came. But there'd been a hard winter, and it's a rural area, and those who died were mostly elderly. I've noticed nothing else since I came."

"Since you came. In the summer?"

"Yes. In July. Only four months, but I'm sure I'd know."

"Not if they were being careful. Think harder. Hasn't there been anything at all?"

"Other than Slany?" She considered. "Well . . . there was Brother Coleman."

"Coleman? Oh yeah, Bonaventure said something about your helping. He died, right? What about him?"

"He got some kind of fever. I was called in. I did what I could, but it was too late. They never identified it exactly. Just blood poisoning. He had some scratches."

"Scratches?"

"On his leg. Four scratches."

"Scratches," Colin repeated, putting a hand to his neck. "From what?"

She shook her head. "It could have been anything: branches, rocks, a tool . . ."

"How about a claw?"

"A claw? You don't think . . ."

"You're damn well right I do. You saw the nail job on that thing up on the hill. Where did Coleman get these scratches?"

"I don't know. He was already delirious when I saw him. It was Father Bonaventure who found him. He'd been able to talk to the Father for a brief time. He said that he'd been out taking a walk. I don't know the rest."

"Then Bonaventure's the one we have to ask," Colin said with certainty.

The library of Glendon Abbey was an impressive place.

The room was high-ceilinged, octagon-shaped, with a massive central stone pier that contained a fireplace. From the pier, stone ribs arched up and radiated out to form a high, groin-vaulted ceiling. Every other wall had inset cases of dark polished oak, filled with books. The walls between were hung with heavy tapestries, their once-bright hunting scenes now faded with age.

Before a wood fire that was dwarfed by the massive hearth, Bonaventure and his two young visitors sat about a small tea table. A slight, balding man in dark cassock was just setting down a tray of tea and biscuits on the table.

"Thank you, Brother O'Dea," said the Father. He poured out tea as the other left, taking up the conversation with Colin and Megan.

"Delighted you came by. It's nice to see the two of you together."

"Oh yes, we're going great guns," Colin told him enthusiastically. "Megan's been taking me all around. Right?" He patted her knee.

She gave him an odd look at that, but followed his lead, smiling with seeming warmth, speaking with apparent sincerity. "Oh, yes. Colin's really just enormous fun."

"Glad to hear it," Bonaventure said. "And is everyone in the countryside doing well?"

Megan grew sober. "Well, I am sorry to say that Slany O'Brien passed away this morning."

"Ah, is that so? Too bad," the Father said, clearly saddened by the news. "Well, I can't say I hadn't been expecting it, from what I've heard about her health lately. She was a strange woman, but a good one by accounts. Knew the old healing ways, it's said, though I'm not to believe in such things myself. And did she receive last rites?"

"There was no time, Father," said Megan. "She went very suddenly. They're seeing to her at Cavan Hospital now."

CROMM

"Still, I feel badly," he said. "I don't know if the woman was even Catholic, but I should have called on her. Was her end a peaceful one?"

"Well, she was . . ." Megan began.

"She just went peacefully off to sleep, Father," Colin interrupted, ignoring the sharp look she shot him. "But, you know, it got us to talking about somebody else who's died since Megan came. Your Brother Coleman."

"Ah, yes." Bonaventure shook his head regretfully. "A very fine man. Back just a year from Africa to rest here. And he badly needed it. The missionary work was very hard."

"Meg said he got scratched?"

"Yes. But we didn't ever know if that's what caused his death. Perhaps some strange illness he'd brought back, the doctor told me, though they tested and searched and found nothing certain in the end."

"He was supposed to have been on a walk when it happened?" prompted Colin.

"Brother Coleman often took long walks in the evenings. Then he came back with a curious tale of having gone Astray."

"Astray?"

"Its an old superstition," the priest explained. "Very peculiar. Here. I'll show you."

He went to one of the bookcases and searched along its shelves, finally drawing out a book. He carried it back to the fire and sat down, opening it. It was a thick blue volume, looking dusty and quite old.

"This is one of Lady Gregory's books," Bonaventure explained to Colin. "Do you know of her?"

"Sorry," he said, exchanging a glance with Megan.

"She helped to compile much of the old lore of Ireland in the 1920s, along with W. B. Yeats. This volume of her work is called *Visions and Beliefs in the West of Ireland*. It can explain things more easily than I can."

He leafed through the book, stopping and scanning down a page.

"Here," he announced. "Here it is. The chapter called

'Astray, and Treasure.' This story was told to Lady Gregory by an old army man."

He began to read aloud in his soft, rich, lilting Irish cadence that matched that of the man who'd first spoken these words so many years before.

" 'It's only yesterday I was talking to a man about *the Others,* and he told me that the castle of Ballinamantane is a great place for them, for it's there a great stand was made long ago in one of their last fights. And one night he was making his way home, and only a field between him and his house, when he found himself turned around and brought to another field, and then another—seven in all.' "

Bonaventure looked up to his guests. "And *that's* what's called 'going Astray.' "

"But that happened to me too," said Colin, clearly intrigued. "When I was going across to Megan's that first day."

"It did?" said Megan. "How?"

"I told you about it, remember? I got lost. I was kind of going off course, toward this funny-looking hill . . ."

"Hill?" she repeated.

"A round-looking thing."

"Oh, you mean the mound," she corrected.

"Mound?"

"Yes," put in the priest. "It's a common enough artifact in Ireland. Likely an old burial place from Neolithic times. Like Newgrange."

"A mound!" said Colin, excitement entering his tone.

"We used to play on it as children," Megan said. "The old people warned us off. Said the fairies would get us. You know, the *Others* that book spoke of. But no one got led Astray or anything like it."

"No. Listen," Colin said earnestly to her. "Cr . . . I mean Whatsizname . . . he was called Crooked One of the Mound *after* he was destroyed. Or supposedly destroyed. I just read it."

"Excuse me?" said the priest, obviously curious about their odd exchange.

"Sorry. It's nothing, Father," said Colin, quickly assuming a nonchalant air. "You know I'm doing some research. This thing's kind of interesting." He looked at Megan and smiled. "Hey, you remember we were looking for an excuse to take a walk." He put a hand on hers. "Here's a chance." He looked to the priest and winked. "You know?"

Bonaventure smiled. "Ah, I understand. But now?" He looked at an immense and elaborate old clock squatting on the mantel. "It's nearly half past five. This time of year the dusk will be coming soon."

"Too dangerous?" Colin asked.

"Well, you'll have little chance to see much. And the way will be most treacherous after dark."

"Yeah, right," Colin acceded. "We'll go . . . some other time."

"When you do, you may want to take the charm," said Bonaventure.

"Charm?" Colin repeated.

"Does it sound foolish? Still, Brother Coleman looked it up before he went out again. In this very book he found it. Here, listen to the rest of the passage on the man who went Astray:

" 'And he remembered the saying,' " the priest read, " 'that you should turn your coat and that they'd have no power over you, and he did so.' "

"Turn your coat?" said Colin in surprise.

"Yes. Reverse it. See, here's another account from a different man. He says, 'Once I was led Astray in that field and went round and round and could find no way out—till at last I thought of the old Irish fashion of turning my coat. And then I got out of the gate in one minute.' "

"Great, Father," Colin said, smiling. "Sounds like sure-fire to me." He looked to Megan. "Well, honey, shall we get going?" He stood up.

"What?" she said, taken rather off guard by his abrupt move.

"You know, our date! Time for some dinner. My treat." He put out his hand to her.

"Oh," she said, taking his hand and getting up. "Yes."

"Ah, good," the priest said, beaming in delight. "It's nice to see young people having fun. Megan works too hard."

"Well, she's having a great time now," said Colin, holding

on to her hand and pulling her close to him, while grinning back at the priest.

"I certainly am," she agreed with another seemingly genuine smile of her own.

Bonaventure saw them to the door and waved goodbye as they walked to her Rover, Colin still clasping her hand.

"Why didn't you tell him?" she asked as they reached the car, safely out of the priest's earshot.

"Why get him involved? I'll just be putting him on the list of people who're sure I'm crazy. By the way," he added, turning to her and speaking more earnestly, "did I thank you for believing that I'm not? I was getting a really empty feeling."

"I'm sorry I didn't believe you sooner," she replied in a regretful way. "It must have been a terrible thing for you, alone."

"Hey, forget it," he said, waving dismissingly. "You had good reasons. Heck, you almost had *me* convinced you were right. But I've got you now, and that's what counts."

He grinned at her, squeezing her hand more tightly. She smiled in return. Then he noted Bonaventure still at the abbey door, beaming happily too as he watched them.

"Say, do you thing maybe we should kiss?" Colin suggested. "Just for the Father's benefit, of course."

He started to pull her to him, but she pulled away and yanked her hand from his, flushing.

"None of that from you now, Colin McMahon," she told him firmly, climbing behind the Rover's wheel.

"Sorry. I forgot you don't have time for that," he said dryly. He waved goodbye to Bonaventure and climbed in beside her.

"Do you really mean to go up to that mound?" she asked him, businesslike once again.

"Its the best bet we've had so far," he answered. "And I remember now that Slany O'Brien said something about my not letting them lead me Astray again. This must have been what she meant."

"Don't you think it's very dangerous? If Coleman died . . ."

"Sure, I think it's dangerous," he said, climbing in beside her.

"But just sitting here is dangerous. If we're going to do anything about this mess, we have to know where Blacky's hiding. So I'm going there. Tonight."

"Tonight?"

"Hey, the sooner the better."

She nodded. "All right, then," she said emphatically. "I'm going with you."

"You?"

"I'm in this as much as you are now, if you'll recall," she pointed out. "Besides, you may need help."

"What kind?"

"I think I've established my ability to take care of myself," she said austerely, "and you as well. I'm going, and you can't stop me."

"Okay," he agreed. "And if you'd smile more often, like you did a minute ago, I might even be glad of the company. Remember, we *are* supposed to be dating."

He slipped an arm around her, leaned close and puckered up. She grimaced, shoved him away, and jammed the key into the ignition.

The Rover's engine roared to life.

21

OCTOBER 30, 5:39 P.M.

Megan Conroy pulled her Land Rover into the little yard of her cottage. The dusk was on them now. The countryside was falling under a greyness.

"We can leave the car here," she said as they climbed out of it. "This is the best place to go up from anyway."

"How do you know?"

"I told you, I played here as a girl. I know all this countryside like an old friend."

"An old friend," he said in an ironic tone, looking around him. "I hope it still is one."

"The mound is at its closest point from the road here, and easy to find." She pointed north. "The abbey is over there. You can just see the lights of it."

A few glinting points were visible above the trees.

She pointed south. "And over there, that faint twinkling is from the lights of the Brigadier's manor." She moved her arm to point directly up the slope. "The old mound should be just up there, almost midway between them."

"Okay," he said. "So now we wait till it gets dark."

"Fine. And while we wait, I'm going to change. This skirt is a bit awkward for climbing."

"Need any help?" he offered brightly.

"Just stay outside, if you please," was her brusque response.

"Never hurts to ask," he called after her as she went inside. He looked around the yard, poked about in a little gardening lean-to against the house, then went to his car and opened the trunk, rummaging inside.

In minutes she came back out of her house. She had traded her sweater and skirt for baggy khaki pants and a bulky green military sweater set at elbows and shoulders with leather patches. Military-style boots were on her feet. She carried a jacket bundled in her hands.

He ran an appraising eye up the slender figure now so well disguised in the voluminous garments.

"Fetching outfit," he commented. "I suppose you got it in an army surplus store."

"I served for four years, actually," she told him soberly, "after I'd completed my nurse's training."

"I thought I was just kidding," he said, impressed.

"What is it you're looking for?" she asked, peering over his shoulder into the trunk.

"Weapons," he said. "Ah. Here we go!" He pulled a crooked piece of heavy metal from the trunk. "Tire iron," he explained, slapping it into the palm of his hand in a meaningful way. "How about you? You know what our little buddies are like. If you're going with me . . ."

He stopped speaking as she pulled something from the bundled jacket, lifting it in one hand. It was a four-foot length of black metal, a large ring at one end, a point at the other.

"It's the spit from my own hearth," she told him. "Very effective. The old heroes like Cuculain and Finn McCool were always using them for swords in a pinch."

He glanced from the deadly-looking length of metal in her hand to the now ineffectual-seeming tire iron in his own.

"Ah . . . wanna trade?" he asked.

She laughed at that, then held it out. "Why not? I brought it for you anyway. You're the one who's had the warrior's training, from what you've said."

"You mean *he* has," he said, taking it.

"Why are you so determined? Maybe you *are* him."

"I can't be. I'm not that stupid." He handed her the tire iron.

"Do you mean that brave? That self-sacrificing?"

"Is that the same as stupid? Look, forget it. I know I'm not him."

"How do you know?" she argued. "Next time you're dreaming, why don't you try looking in a mirror?"

"Yeah, right," he replied with a touch of sarcasm. "I'll remember to do that."

He slipped the metal rod into his belt, then began to strip off his overcoat.

"Now what are you doing?" she asked.

"Guess," he said, pulling the sleeves inside out and reversing it.

"You're not doing what the Father said?"

"Why not?"

"That's just an old country superstition!"

"You said there were still a lot of those things around."

"That doesn't mean they're real."

"Oh yeah? Like Old Black Magic and his friends?" He slipped the coat back on, its plaid lining now showing. "Look, if there is an Astray—and I *know* there is—then it must work on the mind somehow. I don't know, maybe this bloodsucker has a way of affecting minds. Those people at his little ceremony were sure in some kind of trance. Anyway, if we *believe* we're safe, maybe the charm actually works—you know, makes

some kind of shield for your brains, or helps you concentrate
. . . whatever."

"All right," she grudgingly agreed. "I suppose there's no
harm in trying." She unfolded her jacket and reversed it as he
had, before slipping it on.

"Great," he pronounced, examining the effect. "It really does
wonders for your look. Might be a big new fashion for fall!"

"I still feel a little foolish," she said, looking down at herself.

"And you look it, too. But nobody's going to see you . . .
I hope."

He looked around. The night had fallen now, save for a fan
of greyness in the western sky.

"Dark enough," he said. "Want to lead the way?"

She started up the hill, Colin close at her heels. The faint
grey faded behind them. The night was cool, fresh, crisp with
that first sting of chill foreshadowing the coming winter. A soft
breeze rustled the dry grass and rattled the dried leaves still in
the trees. The sky was cloudless, the stars brilliant points against
the deep black, and the nearly full moon a glowing white oval
whose seas showed with startling clarity.

"I love this," Colin murmured, looking around at the effect
of bared treetops like skeletal fingers waving before the disk of
lustrous moon. "Like 'The Legend of Sleepy Hollow'—the Dis-
ney version. I keep waiting to hear the hoofbeats behind me."

"You wanted to go tonight," she reminded him.

"I know," he said. "Never mind me. Just keep concentrating
on where we're headed."

"I will," she said, "if you will too."

They worked their way uphill for some minutes. The ground
was uneven. The moon cast silver light across the high spots,
and deep shadows in the low ones. As they were making their
way through one of these dark areas, she stumbled.

"Ow. This ground is treacherous."

"Your 'old friend' trip you?" he asked, smiling.

A pencil-thin line of light flashed down to the ground.

"What's that?" he asked.

"A pocket torch. I thought we might need it."

"Well, don't use it. We can't advertise we're here."

"Sorry. You're right," she said contritely, and the light went out.

"I'm just hoping none of them can see in the . . . Oh, hell!"

"What?"

"I just remembered . . . the one who slashed me . . . *him.* The thing with the claws we saw today. It had eyes just like a cat's."

"Fine time to tell me."

"It doesn't matter. Let's just hope it's home doing its nails."

They moved on, picking their way farther up the hillside in the dark. Finally she stopped, pointing ahead.

"There. There it is," she said. Above them, the odd, evenly rounded slope showed as a darker object against the starry sky.

"Just keep staring at it and head on," he said.

They hiked up toward it, but as they grew closer they made their strides with greater effort, as if the slope was growing steeper.

"Do you feel anything strange?" she asked. "As if you're . . . moving through thicker air?"

"Yes," he said. "I think it's some kind of shield. Maybe what sends you Astray. But we're still getting closer. That old trick must be working."

"The sensation's fading," she said. And they began to move ahead without difficulty again.

They passed a grove of trees. The hill now loomed above, longer than a football field and swelling up to a height of some sixty feet. They stopped and examined it.

"Does anything look familiar?" she asked softly.

"After fifteen hundred years? In the dark?"

"How do you know it's been fifteen hundred years?"

"The Brigadier said so. Crap," he said in frustration, "it's all different. How could this be? I was thinking maybe they'd just buried it. But this. . . ."

He started toward the mound, but took only a few steps before suddenly pitching forward.

"Are you all right?" she asked, moving up to him.

"Some goddamn rock," he said, feeling around, peering at

the thing in the moonlight, a vague whiteish lump. He put a hand to its surface, then grunted in surprise.

"Give me that light," he demanded sharply.

"You said it was dangerous."

"Give!" He extended a hand.

She slapped the slender flashlight into his palm—a little harder than necessary. He shot her a look, then fumbled with the light, locating the switch, flicking it on. Cupping the narrow lightbeam, he directed it onto the lump.

Light fell on an object badly weathered, but still identifiable: a rounded stone cut with a curious pattern of interweaving curlicues.

"This is it!" he exclaimed.

"What?"

He slipped a hand into his inner jacket pocket and pulled out his rumpled sketch of the stone, directing the light onto it. "Look. It's the same thing I saw in my dreams about Magh Slecht. This has to be it."

She looked from the sketch to the stone, then up to the black swell of earth. "It's still only a mound. No sign of statues or anything else."

"Let's look closer," he suggested, snapping the light off again. "But be careful."

They moved slowly up to the mound, taking cautious step after step. It remained solidly before them. At last they safely reached its side.

He looked up at the curve of it, and pushed tentatively against its side with a foot. Nothing happened. They climbed a few feet up the grassy slope and he knelt, examining the surface.

"Grass and dirt," he said with a disappointed air.

"What did you expect?"

"Let's move on around it," he suggested. "You go at the bottom. I'll be up here."

"Looking for what?"

"Anything."

They moved slowly around the mound, he edging along above her, looking up and down the slope. But it was uniformly smooth, rounded, featureless.

CROMM

"Damn," he muttered after they had gone nearly halfway around, "there's nothing."

"Just an old mound after all," she said.

He took another step, peering ahead. Then, in a sudden move, he turned and leaped upon her, pulling her down.

"What are . . ." she began in surprise, struggling.

He put a hand over her mouth.

"Quiet!" he hissed. "Keep down!" And he pointed ahead.

Past the curve in the mound, only ten yards away, a head had popped suddenly into sight. It moved out from the mound, its body coming into view. It was quickly followed by another form, then several more.

The forms were of human beings. The moon shone on their faces, revealing their features. All stared ahead into the darkness in a fixed way. Their movements were unnatural, stiff, mechanical.

"I know them," she whispered to him as they moved away from the mound. "Keith McCormac, the peatman. Tim O'Donal, a farmer. Peter Delaney, the victauller."

The last figure came into view. But this one stopped suddenly as if sensing something. The head twisted slowly around toward Colin and Megan, who then ducked back into the cover of the hill. The figure stared fixedly for a moment; then the head swiveled back and the man went on. They peered out cautiously after him as he vanished into the dark.

"And I know that one," Colin whispered. "Matthew, the hostile bartender."

"My God," she said. "All people from town."

"Subjects of Cromm."

"We don't know that. What were they doing here?"

"Better yet, where did they come from? Come on. Let's see."

They edged around the mound.

"That first one seemed to be coming right out of the hill," he said, climbing up along the slope. "It must have been right about . . ."

He gasped and tumbled forward, falling into a heavy netting which he carried down with him, disappearing into a hole.

"Colin?" she said in shock, moving forward.

There was a furious upheaval that seemed to be crumbling the whole section of the slope into which he had fallen. Then he popped into view again, clambering up and out of the hole, back onto the solid hillside, sliding down to join her.

"Are you all right?" she asked him anxiously.

"Yeah. Hell, I should be getting used to it."

"What happened?" she asked.

"This is some kind of camouflage," he said, leaning down to grasp and lift a corner of a heavy netting fabric. "Help me."

Together they rolled back the large netting that had been pegged across that section of the hill. Behind it a square tunnel, six feet high and ten wide, was revealed.

They examined it by moonlight.

"It looks like this tunnel's been opened pretty recently," he said.

She looked at the heavy slabs of rock at either side of the opening and a thick lintel stone that lay across their tops. All were deeply inscribed with the same kind of elaborate, curlicue-ing design they had seen on the rock Colin found earlier.

"It is very like Newgrange," she said. "I've seen it. But it's just a tomb, as Father Bonaventure said. Thousands of years old. It can't have anything to do with . . . with them."

"We have to go inside," he said with certainty.

"Inside?"

"It's the only way to be sure. I mean, they dug this out for something. And why were all those guys in there? But maybe you should wait outside."

For the first time, her self-assured manner seemed shaken. She stood bent forward, gazing intently into the darkness of the tunnel, her expression one of uncertainty. Then she lifted her head, striking a determined stance, her expression hardening.

"No," she said with force. "I'll come."

He pulled the iron spit from his belt and led the way past the screen, snapping the flashlight on again. Beyond the entrance they were in a passage, the walls constructed of smooth stone slabs set upright at either hand with another laid across the top. Strange spirals and swirling designs were etched in them as well.

He swung the flashlight around as they moved. The ceiling was low, nearly brushing his scalp.

"Lots of traffic here," he said, flashing the light down at the floor. The earth of it was packed hard by the passage of many feet. He flashed the light ahead. It vanished into a dark void.

"My God," she said. "It's like being swallowed."

"You wanted to come."

The passage ended and they moved out into the void. He stumbled into something that rattled, and swept the light around to it.

It was a floodlight set high on a tripod.

"A light," he said. "Must be power somewhere. You didn't see a wall switch by the door?"

He swung the light again; the thin beam flashed up into the depths, faintly reflecting the paler stones high above. The beam swept around, coming suddenly onto a monstrous face, broad, sleek, doglike, but with curling horns. It grinned evilly down at them.

She recoiled, exclaiming in surprise.

"Easy," he said. "Just stone. One of the boys."

"The Tarbh-Faol," she said.

"Tarfol?" he said, trying to pronounce it.

"It's Gaelic for Bull-Wolf."

"How did you know its name?"

"I . . . I don't know," she said, nonplussed. "It just seemed right."

He swept the light around. Another statue loomed up at the right—one of a grotesque, almost shapeless creature with a dozen tentacles curling like a nest of snakes around its base. Then the light glinted from the metal fittings of an incongruous mass of modern machinery sitting just beyond.

He moved toward it. Megan close behind. The atmosphere was thick, musty, tinged with a cloying, sickly-sweet odor. He passed the tentacled form. Ahead, beyond the machinery, another statue of a spindly, multilegged creature—part spider, part praying mantis—could be faintly glimpsed. He shone the light up past curled, spiny forelegs to curving pincer jaws.

"It's like being in George Lucas's attic," he remarked.

"This is a generator," she said, looking over the machine.

"Oh, yeah?" he said, fiddling with a panel of levers and buttons. "How the hell's it start?"

She leaned past him, flicked a switch and pushed a button. There was a stuttering before the motor caught. The generator rumbled to life. All around them, white spots appeared as the filaments of large bulbs began to glow, gaining strength quickly to become incandescent spheres, flooding the space with light.

They could see now that they were at one side of a vast chamber. It was some two hundred feet across. Its ceiling was made of immense slabs of interlocking stone, forming a rough cone that sloped up to a dome fifty feet high in the center.

Within the vast space was a circle of massive stone sculptures, twenty-five feet high, spaced at intervals to form a circle nearly fifty yards across. And in the center of it, bathed in the light of a dozen floodlights, stood a hunched black form of immense grotesqueness.

"My God!" said Colin. "It's the whole damn circle! They buried the whole thing here."

She looked around in amazement at the monstrous forms. Then her eyes fell on the one on the center.

"Cr . . ."

He put his hand over her mouth.

"Quiet."

She nodded and he took the hand away.

"Sorry," she said. "It's just as you said you saw it. In your dreams."

"Yeah, and I wish it wasn't," he said, searching around. "But it's not quite the same." He moved to examine the base of the insectlike sculpture. "These statues have been reset. Look how the dirt's been piled in around the bases. That's fresh. And this place," he said as he looked around at the room, "it's got to have been cleaned out. I mean, my room's buried in spider-webs and dust after a week. These things have been under here for fifteen hundred years!" His gaze came around to Cromm. "And look at Our Boy . . ."

He slipped the spit into his belt and strode toward it, Megan following.

"He's really taken a beating," Colin said, stopping before it. The gold ornaments had all been stripped away from the wasted limbs. The black stone was battered, chipped, clearly pieced back together in spots.

He looked up at the stone visage still leering down as it had in his dreams.

"Well, he sure did get it," Colin said. "I guess that ruckus I started must have blown the whole place to kingdom come."

"It's still horrible," she said, looking up at Cromm with an expression of disgust. "It's like an immense, awful fetus. Something half developed. Look there," she said, pointing to the sculptured semblance of a twisted rope extending from its swollen belly, "it even has an umbilical cord."

"Yeah," he said. "They must have poured blood into that bowl at the base, and the kid sucked it in."

"That's a revolting notion," she said, moving closer to the statue. "It means that mankind becomes its mother, feeding it life-blood. The earth becomes its womb."

"Except this baby is never born," he added.

She was near the base now, peering down at the stone basin set against the foot of the statue.

"They must have just built this tomb over the remains and left it," said Colin, looking up at the stone vaulting overhead. "Damn, it's huge. The whole inside of the hill must be hollow."

"Colin!" she said, crouching by the stone basin. "These stains . . . I'm certain they're dried blood."

He stepped up beside her. "Like I said. They must have used it to . . ."

"I don't mean from hundreds of years ago," she interrupted. "This blood is recent!"

She leaned forward to examine the stained basin more closely, putting a hand against the black stone of the statue to steady herself. She recoiled instantly.

"The stone's warm!" she said in shock.

There came a faint rumbling, as from a truck's distant passage. She looked up at the statue looming over her. The lights shining upon it seemed to flicker infinitesimally. But their effect was to cause the stone features to leer at her.

"The thing is alive!" she cried, jumping up and moving back.
"So they really are doing it again," he said, shaking his head.
"God, I was really hoping that wasn't it."

"You expected to find this?" she asked.

"Sure. I knew it was possible," he said, looking curiously at
her. "Didn't you? You said you believed my story."

"Yes," she agreed. "But I guess . . . not really this!" She
looked around her, appalled. "Not something like this!" She
turned back to him, her voice urgent now. "Let's go! Let's get
away from here. Now!"

"Hold on a minute," he said. "Not so fast. I want to check
this out some more. Maybe there's a way I can finish this thing
now."

"You mean you really think you can destroy it? Destroy
this?"

He shrugged. "I did it once. Hell, maybe I can again."

"But how?"

That made him frown in uncertainty. "Well . . . I guess I
don't know for sure." He stared thoughtfully at Cromm. "The
druid was here then . . . and all those people . . . and
I . . ."

He broke off abruptly. She looked at him. He was standing
stiffly, staring ahead in a blank way.

"Colin?" she said.

His eyes shifted to her, staring fixedly.

"Colin?" she said again and started toward him . . .

22

Colin saw Aislinn rushing across the yard of the fortress toward him as his chariot rolled through the gates of her clan's
ringfort.

He jumped from the chariot before Ailbe could bring it to a
stop. She reached him, throwing her arms about him, pulling
herself tightly to him. He hugged her in return.

She wore a light shift, a blanket thrown about her against the night's coolness. The others of the fortress were coming out of the houses also in various states of hasty dress, clearly just awakened by the sentries who had admitted Colin's chariot. Warriors were hurriedly buckling on swords, slipping on shields, fastening cloaks.

"Colin . . . you are all right!" she said in relief, pulling back to look up at him.

"Aislinn," he said with excitement, "I've done it. I've saved you."

"Saved us?" she said in surprise. "How?"

"What's this?" demanded her father, Flann O'Mulconrys, as he strode up to them. He looked both puzzled and irritated, fumbling to fix the cloak about his shoulders. "Just why is it you've come back here like this?"

"Chieftain," Colin said, turning from her to face the man squarely. "I went to the Plain of Adoration."

"What?" Flann said in astonishment. "And escaped alive? That's not possible."

Exclamations of wonder and disbelief also arose from the others now gathering around the young warrior's chariot.

"The lad did do it," said the silver-haired healer, climbing down from the car.

Flann turned to him. "Gilla?" he said in even greater bewilderment. "And what is it that *you're* doing here?"

"I was at Magh Slecht as well," the man replied. "But I think you should let our young warrior tell what happened there."

Flann looked back to Colin, his disbelief now turned to shock.

"What kind of madness would bring you to go to that place?" he demanded. "You said you were leaving. We thought that you meant to go home."

"He did tell *me* what he really meant to do, Father," Aislinn boldly admitted.

"You knew? And you didn't tell me?"

"I vowed to keep his secret," she answered.

"And when is your loyalty to him greater than to your own father and your clan?" he said in outrage.

Colin moved up before her defensively.

"She was seeking only to keep her people safe," he told Flann.

"He said he wanted only to risk himself, not involve us at all," Aislinn explained.

"And I told her I meant only to see the ritual," Colin added.

"See it?" said Flann. "Why?"

"I hoped I could find its secret," Colin answered simply.

The sounds of laughter arose in the crowd. Dismayed, Colin looked around him, seeing derisive smiles on many in the circle of faces. Flann also looked around at his people, smiling too and shaking his head pityingly.

"Secret? The lad didn't know there is no secret. Only the power of Cromm."

"Father," said Aislinn, "Colin says he's saved us from Cromm."

Flann swung back toward Colin, his smile vanishing. A stunned silence fell on the gathering.

"Saved us?" Flann repeated. "How could you have done such a thing?"

"Listen to me, all of you," Colin said, raising his voice to address the entire crowd. "It was as I thought. No god or monsters, but only the trickery and enchantments of a clever druid. He cast a spell on you and frightened you and made you believe in his creations. But I killed him."

"Killed him?" Flann looked to Gilla. "Healer, is this true?"

"The lad marched into the midst of the throng and drove a spear into Dubhdaleithe's heart." Gilla replied. "The druid fell on his own altar, staining it with his own blood."

"And what part was it that you had in this?" the chieftain demanded.

The healer raised his hands in a defensive way. "I went as a watcher only. I've been keeping an eye on the boy since I healed him. I had a . . . a feeling about him. When I realized he was going there, I followed and watched. Just watched."

"Believe the truth of what I'm saying," Colin told them. "After the druid fell, the spell on the people was broken. They ran from the ring in panic. And it took no magic of this new god of yours to defeat the power. Just the will to face the druid, and a good spear!"

"Colin!" cheered Seanan, Flann's younger son. He ran in and clasped the warrior's hand. "I knew you could do it! You're a greater warrior than any other!"

"Are you telling us we might have defied Cromm at any time?" asked Aislinn. "Killed this druid? Stopped the sacrifices?"

"No!" cried Seadna, Flann's elder son. "I can't believe it could be done so easily. What else happened? How do you know you caused the end of Cromm and his twelve creatures?"

"Why, I saw their statues destroyed," Colin announced with a note of pride. "With the druid's magic gone, it was as if they were seized by some great fit. They shuddered and moaned and a blinding glow swallowed them."

"Glow?" Flann echoed. He leaned toward Colin, his voice becoming urgent. "What color was the glow? The hot red–gold of fire?"

"No," Colin replied. "It was a cool green light, as from a glowing emerald."

There were gasps of consternation, cries of fear from those gathered. Aislinn turned to face Colin, eyes widening in dread.

"Oh Colin, no," she said in a hushed voice.

"What?" he asked her, thrown aback by her reaction. He gazed around him at the ring of faces.

"I knew what danger he was in," said Gilla. "I brought him away while there was time. I knew that he must come back and tell you. So you might prepare."

"Prepare?" said Colin in growing bewilderment. "For what? What's happening?"

"Chieftain," came the urgent voice of one of the sentries upon the wall, "come here. Quickly."

Without delay Flann left Colin, moving through the ring of his people to the wall, mounting the ladder to the palisade walk. His son and other of the warriors followed.

"I think you'd better go as well," Gilla recommended to Colin.

The young warrior exchanged a puzzled look with an anxious Aislinn, and then went, climbing up the ladder to the walk.

As he came onto it, he glanced out beyond the pointed logs of the wall's top; then he stopped abruptly, staring around him in astonishment.

All about the fortress, bouncing spots of red-gold light were flaring in the night, moving closer. And as he watched, they resolved themselves into the flames of many scores of torches, their ruddy glow lighting the faces and glinting from the arms of the warriors who carried them.

Colin moved to the wall where the other warriors were lined up, gazing out upon the approaching host. He stepped into a space between the chieftain and his son.

Flann looked around to see him. He spoke, his tone harsh and his words scathing:

"That emerald light you saw was not the death of Cromm. It was the awakening of his full power!"

Now something else became visible in the night. The torches of the advancing warriors revealed the grotesque forms of many creatures moving forward with the host. The disciples of Cromm, called from their stony cells, now stalked toward the lone fortress of Aislinn's clan.

And at their head strode the druid, Dubhdaleithe.

23

OCTOBER 30, 8:15 P.M.

A hand gripped his shoulder, shaking him hard.

"Colin!" said a voice urgently. "Colin!"

He turned to see Megan Conroy beside him, looking at him in puzzlement. The circle of monstrous statues rose around them. The dome of the vast stone chamber arched overhead.

His expression of disorientation cleared.

"Megan!" he said. His gaze rose to the battered black statue looming above him. In the shock of realization, he gasped, "My God! Megan, I didn't destroy him!"

"What?"

He looked back to her.

"I didn't destroy him," he repeated emphatically. "I only made him mad!"

"What are you talking about?"

"We've got to get out of here," he said urgently, grabbing her hand to pull it. "Come on!"

"Now wait," she said, yanking her hand free. "Don't be doing *that* again. I'm not . . ."

There was a sudden surge of power. The bulbs grew brighter, the generator speeding to a high velocity, the sound of it rising to the level of a shriek, the floodlights flaring to a blinding intensity. Blue streams of energy crackled across the machine, popping like tiny lightning bolts.

The bulbs of the two score lights then blew at once, plunging Megan and Colin into absolute darkness. The generator cut out, its whine fading away.

Around them the dense blackness was almost palpable, without a faintest glint of light showing. But with the generator sound gone, it was evident that a soft, low, rhythmic sound now filled the vast space like the throb of a distant engine revving and slowing, revving and slowing.

"Colin!" she said in rising alarm.

"Here!" he called.

There was a shuffling sound and a soft thud of collision.

"Oof," he said. "Yeah, that's me."

"Oh, Colin," she said with relief.

"Hey, do you always hug like that on the first date?" he asked.

"Never mind," came the sharp reply. "Just use the flash. Get us out of here."

"You're afraid of the dark?" he asked in surprise.

"Are you afraid of heights?" she returned. "Please, turn on the light. Anything could be out there."

"If there is, do you want to show it where we are?"

"I don't care. Just turn on the bloody light!"

There was a click. Then there was another. No light appeared.

"Damn thing," Colin cursed, and there were several more clicks. "It won't go on."

"Wait," she said. "It's getting lighter."

"Your eyes are adjusting," he said.

"No," she said in an odd voice. "It's them."

He looked up. Cromm and the other statues were glowing faintly, not as they had been from the external lighting, but in a luminescent way, as if the source was inside them. And the glow was greenish-white.

"Oh, hell," he said. "I've seen *this* movie before!"

The light was growing stronger, the undulating hum growing louder at the same time.

"What's happening?" she asked.

"I think the boys are coming out of hibernation."

There was enough light for them to see about them now.

"Quick!" he said, leading the way across the floor.

They reached the two statues flanking the passageway. They were quite bright now, looking almost like translucent emerald glass, their sculpted outlines growing hazy from the glow.

And then, within those outlines, smaller forms, no more than vague shadows, began to stir.

"Geeez, there they are," he said. "Run!"

They moved into the passage. The intensifying lights were filling the room, beaming up through the tunnel of stone past the two people. They ran out of the mound into the night. From behind them the light streamed out the passage mouth like a searchlight, casting a widening beam across the meadow below the mound, revealing a line of figures moving up the hillside toward them.

Colin and Megan pulled up outside the tunnel mouth, peering down at the advancing figures.

"What's that?" he asked.

"It's the people from the village," she said. "They're coming back."

"Well, we know *they're* not immortal," he said, yanking the iron spit from his belt.

"No," she said, grabbing his arm. "I know them. We can't hurt them."

"But they're coming in from all around!"

"It's open to the south," she said. "This way!"

She led him around the curve of the mound, then away into the darkness.

"Is there anything this way?" he asked her while they moved as rapidly as possible over the shadowed ground.

"The Brigadier's manor."

"Great. At least we can get some help there."

"What can we do?" she asked. "You were so certain about destroying it . . ."

"Okay, okay!" he said sharply. "So my dreams were wrong. So there's nothing I can do about it anymore. At least we found the thing. We'll tell Dudley, call the police or somebody. I don't know. Let somebody else figure it out."

They picked their way through trees and across meadows, trying to keep to darker patches, rushing across open moonlit ground. He pulled her to a stop once and stood listening.

"What is it?"

"I can't hear anything." He peered back to the open hillside they had just crossed, showing clearly in the moonglow. There was no sign of movement. "I don't think they're following."

"Or maybe they couldn't find our trail in the darkness," she said. "Come on. The manor's just ahead."

They came through a last belt of trees onto the paved driveway of the house. Lights showed in the front study window.

They ran to the door and Colin used the knocker with great effect, the booming sound echoing away inside.

Soon they heard movement within and the door was opened by Jenny. The dark-haired woman seemed startled to see them, standing and staring at them, speechless.

"We want to see the Brigadier," said Colin.

"No!" she said, managing to speak. "He can't be bothered now. It's late. Go away from here."

She began to swing the door closed. Colin moved up to block it.

"Wait a minute!"

"Who is it, Jenny?" came the Brigadier's voice from inside.

She looked around, hesitating, then said, "It's the American, sir. And Miss Conroy."

"Well, bring them in!" was the hearty reply.

"You heard him," Colin told her. "Let us in."

She released the door and they moved past her into the hall. She closed the door and ushered them on into the study.

"Hello!" Dudley greeted them cheerfully, getting up from his desk. Then, as he got a first good look at them, his expression grew astounded.

"But, what's wrong with you? You're quite a sight!"

Colin glanced at Megan, her coat still inside out. She looked at him. That *he* was quite a sight was by now an understatement. His pants were ripped and filthy, his hair mussed, his face stubbled with beard, and his coat ludicrously inverted to its tartan plaid lining. He looked down at himself and shrugged.

"It's been kind of a busy day."

"And you look done in by it," said the Brigadier. "Come on through!"

He took them into the living room. A cheering fire burned brightly in the hearth.

"Have you eaten?" he asked. "It's well past seven."

"Like I said, we've been busy."

"Jenny," the Brigadier called out, "bring some food."

"Never mind," said Colin. "We might not have much time."

"Sit down. Some whiskey then at least. Jenny, bring it."

They went up to the fire. Megan laid her tire iron carefully on the hearth. Colin pulled the iron spit from his belt and put it down on the floor beside his chair before sitting. When they were all seated, Dudley looked at the two pieces of metal and then at them, even more clearly puzzled.

"You two, where have you been?"

"Brigadier, we found . . . I mean . . . crap, I don't know where to start."

Dudley looked to Megan. "Young lady? Would you care to make a try?"

"It *is* hard to explain," she said, and looked to Colin. "Especially without sounding like a lunatic."

"Now you know how I felt," said Colin. "Look, Brigadier, do you remember what I said I was looking for?"

"Do you mean this Cr . . ."

"Right!" he interrupted. "Sorry. But please don't say it. Anyway, I . . . we found it, tonight."

"You found your . . . ah . . . plain of whatever?"

"Plain of Adoration. Yeah. It's only half a mile from here."

"What? But there's no plain such as you described. Nothing like one."

"Not anymore. Now it's a mound. And what I'm after is inside."

Dudley looked from one to the other in bewilderment mixed with some concern. Jenny brought in the drink tray, putting it on the table before the chairs. She appeared sullen, flashing Colin a sharp look as she moved back.

"Jenny, please stay," said the Brigadier.

She obeyed, pulling up by the door, standing stiffly, looking away into a far corner of the room.

"Sounds most interesting," the Brigadier said carefully, pouring the whiskey, "but I'm not certain I understand what it means. If it's some kind of archeological thing, I'm sure that's exciting, but . . ."

"No, no," Colin assured him, sitting forward. "It's a lot more. Do you remember what I read this morning about that old god and the sacrifices? I think it's happening again. It's back."

"Back?"

"That . . . whatever it is . . . is alive. So are its twelve little buddies. They're out there. They live in that mound."

"Oh?" Dudley said with raised eyebrows. He looked to Megan. "And do you support this . . . this story?"

"I do," she said with force. "I've seen them. There are creatures, monstrous ones, and I think Colin is right. Their . . . home . . . their source is in that mound."

"I see," he said neutrally. Then he turned to his housekeeper. "Jenny," he said in a casual way, "would you please ask Seamus to step in here too?"

She nodded curtly and left. The Brigadier took a larger shot of whiskey, contemplating the pair thoughtfully.

"Is that for another witness or to help subdue the raving?" Megan asked.

Dudley gave a little smile. "Miss Conroy, you must admit this is rather a strange tale," he said, not answering her question. "I mean, a plain that's a mound? Living statues? Monsters?"

"Brigadier," she said, "I have great difficulty believing all of this too. But I believe what I saw, and something terrible is happening."

Seamus came in through the door from the dining room, Jenny behind him. The dour man looked unemotional. He and his wife stood within the door, silent and watching.

"Look," said Colin, "you said this morning that you didn't think I was crazy. Hunted is what you said. Well, it's these things that are hunting me. They need to keep themselves secret."

Dudley stared searchingly at him for a long moment. Then he shook his head.

"I don't know. Granted, you seem sane, and I'd judge Miss Conroy rational. Suppose this is true. What do you want me to do?"

"Just call for some help: law, army, whatever. Get somebody out here to see the thing, and fast."

"Why?"

"Brigadier," Megan said earnestly, "we don't know for certain what will happen. But we know it is dangerous and that it may cost human lives. We must have help."

"Very well, Miss Conroy. I understand your concern. It's just that I'm not certain whom to call. There's no evidence of any crime having been committed. I don't think the *Garda* will rush here on the strength of your story, unless it's to lock you away somewhere until you've sobered up. Haven't you anything more concrete?"

"Not here," Colin said, at a loss. "At least, nothing we can prove."

"Then, why is it so urgent?"

"Look, Brigadier, I've seen what these things can do. They

could be after us right now. They could be tearing down your walls any second."

The Brigadier remained unimpressed by this potential threat. "Even so, I'm afraid no one will come out here."

"Couldn't you try?" pleaded Colin. "You must know somebody who'll listen."

Dudley shook his head. "I'm sorry," he said regretfully. "I'm a stranger here too, remember. I really don't know anyone who would help."

"Damn," said Colin in frustration, getting to his feet. "Then let me call. I'll tell them I'm a homicidal nut or something. Anything to get somebody else out here."

"No, Colin," Megan protested.

"We've got to do something, Meg," he told her. "I'm going to call."

"Wait," she said, also getting up. "I'll call. I'm a nurse, and I know the *Garda* in Cavan. I don't know if it was human blood I found in that mound, but I think my fear that it might be is enough to bring them here."

She started for the study.

"I'm afraid you'll find the telephone isn't working," said the Brigadier, getting to his feet.

"What?" said Megan. She and Colin both turned back toward Dudley.

"You can't call anyone from here."

"Well, look, how about your car?" Colin said. "Let us use it. Or drive us to the next town."

"I don't think that would be a good idea either," Dudley said in a soothing way. "Look here, you two are overwrought. Sit down again. Rest. We'll discuss this logically."

Meg eyed him, frowning. "Why are you so anxious that we stay?" she bluntly asked.

"I just want you to calm down," he said. "Relax."

"How did you know about the statues coming to life?" she fired at him. "Colin said nothing about that."

"What?" he said, clearly taken aback. "Why, I . . ."

"And how did you know Magh Slecht existed fifteen hundred years ago?"

"What are you talking about?" said Colin, confused by her questioning.

"Colin," she said urgently, "I think we had better leave here —right now!"

Dudley's hand slipped into his jacket pocket and reappeared clutching an automatic pistol.

"I'm afraid you can't leave," he told them. "Now, sit back down, please."

Colin looked in surprise at the gun.

"Hey, I was just kidding! I'm not really dangerous."

"I think that's likely true," Dudley agreed.

"Then you don't need that," Colin reasoned. "Look, if you won't help us, just let us go. We'll walk."

"Sorry again. Although there's really nothing you can do to interfere now, still we do want you."

He looked to Seamus.

"Go out to the mound," he ordered. "Tell our friends that these two are here. Quickly now."

Seamus nodded and went out.

"To the mound?" Colin echoed, nonplussed. "Friends?"

"My God, Colin," said Megan in exasperation, "don't you understand?"

"Yes. Our friends," said Dudley. "You've met some of them already. Now sit down!"

Colin and Megan moved back to their seats. The Brigadier stood before them, legs set apart, the gun rock steady and pointed at a spot midway between the other two. His gaze was fixed on Colin.

"You should have listened to me when I warned you away from Magh Slecht, young Colin son of Mathghamhain," he said. The voice had lost the crisp, clipped tone of the old soldier, replaced now by one softer, smoother, and more finely honed.

"You? What?" Colin said in confusion. "That can't . . ."

Dudley nodded. "It is the same druid you speak to—Dubhdaleithe."

"No," Colin said emphatically. "I don't believe you."

"Then look." The Brigadier put a hand to his shirt, yanking

it open, popping off the buttons, baring a hard, hairy barrel chest. There, on the man's sternum, the flesh was marked with a ragged stain of livid purple.

"Remember?" asked Dudley. "You gave this mark to me. You drove a spear through here, into my heart."

Colin's gaze rose from the mark to the wide, hard-visaged face.

"That guy wasn't you," he argued. "He was thin, kind of wimp-faced, with this long, pointy nose . . ."

"No more insults," the man said warningly. "You don't believe because I don't look the same? As you do? And Miss Conroy? Well, genetics is a most peculiar thing. Sometimes the physical traits pass down as yours did. With me it was the memory, buried, but traveling with me from life to life. Sleeping, yes, but awakening at once when Cromm called. Yes, my memory of that time returned totally. But yours . . ." He shook his head pityingly. "You really don't have a clue, do you?"

"How do you mean?" asked Colin.

"When Cromm sensed that you were out there, he feared that you might recall; that his own stirrings would awaken your memories as they had mine.

"They all thought you were extremely dangerous, quite likely impossible to destroy. I thought that you were just very very lucky. I invited you here to stay so I might test my theory. And it appears that I was right." He gave a sneering smile. "Poor, foolish mortal. You have no powers, and you've no real memory. You've just admitted you don't know how to destroy Cromm. I sensed that was true this morning. I even argued that you should be left alone. But then you talked to the old woman."

"Slany," said Megan.

"Yes, Miss Conroy. A tough and skillful old witch. Her mind too strong to accept Cromm. Not like these others. Cromm couldn't be sure what you had learned from her. So when the chance came to kill you, it was taken. You'd told me that your friends at home still had no idea where you were. And you had gone far enough from the village with Miss Conroy that suspicions wouldn't fall here—not until too late, in any case."

"But the guys blew it again," Colin reminded him with satisfaction.

"Not for any skill of yours, I'm sure, McMahon," the other nastily replied, "but because they are cowards and fools. So you needn't be so smug about their failure. Why, if they had managed to surprise you properly, that first time, a great deal of wasted effort and carnage would have been avoided."

"Carnage?" Colin echoed.

"Oh, yes," Dudley said offhandedly. "Several street derelicts. A couple in your apartment building. A man at your office . . . your partner, was it?"

"Harry?"

"Yes. He met the one called the Torc. I suppose you know him as the one with the face of a boar, and a blade for one hand."

"Harry's . . . dead?" Colin asked in a strangled voice.

"I'm afraid so. Cromm's disciples are not very subtle. They weren't expecting the complexity of the modern world after the simple life of the fifth century. And then, they didn't expect to have so much difficulty in tracking you down."

"Harry," Colin repeated in a stunned way. "Dead."

"Of course, subtlety wasn't a consideration in sending them after you," the man went on calmly. "If they had caught you by surprise, as we intended, you would have been no bother. And no matter how bizarre the circumstances of your death might have been, so far away, and with no connection between you and ourselves, no attention would have been drawn here."

"Why you son-of-a-bitch!" Colin shouted suddenly and launched himself from his chair toward the Brigadier.

The stocky man moved quickly, stepping back, swinging out the gun in a hard blow into Colin's stomach that doubled him up. The young man fell back into his chair, the wind knocked from him.

"After what you did, please don't tempt me," Dudley said. "I keep you alive only because Cromm wants you himself."

CROMM

"What are you doing in that mound?" Megan asked while Colin recovered.

"Reviving Cromm," Dudley answered simply. "Two years ago I felt him stirring down in the deepest portions of my mind. The memories floated up from the depths. I knew who I was, what I was meant to do, what scores of my other selves had been waiting to do for fifteen centuries. Cromm called me here. I found this mound. The manor was handy. Its owner was elderly, sickly, ideal as one of the first of our victims."

"First?" Colin gasped out.

"There had to be a few, at the spring festival of Beltzinne of course. And then again at Lughnases, in midsummer. They began the revival. It was quite easy in the beginning, isolated out here, without anyone to really question how the people died. No one from outside to comment on their . . . loss of blood. Cromm's power grew, and he began to dominate the minds of the villagers. The simpler ones were first. But they brought others here, and *they* brought others, each new mind strengthening the mind of Cromm, making it simpler to control still more, until nearly all the villagers were within his domination. But then you came, Miss Conroy, and it grew more difficult. As with that fool priest and his monks, destroying you was too risky, and your mind couldn't be reached. We had to become more secretive, move more cautiously. But that time is nearly over."

"You restored the statues?" Megan asked.

"Opened the mound, cleared it, all of that, yes, with the help of your villagefolk. All that remains now is the final revival of Cromm's full power."

"And once he's revived?" she asked.

"Why, he'll take his place, Miss Conroy," Dudley said with anticipation. "It's time for that. Time for him to take his rightful place again."

"His place?"

"As great god of the world."

"What a crock!" Colin spat out, breathing more easily again and sitting upright. "Have people crawling to that hunk of stone again? Killing babies for it? No. That thing of yours can't have that kind of control. Not now. Not in this world."

"Can't he?" said Dudley, smiling in a smug way. "Look more closely at the world, McMahon. It has never been riper for the return of my master. Societies are collapsing. Systems are breaking down. Religions are bankrupt. Christians massacre Christians in the streets. We are entering an age when superstition, fear, greed, and self-survival are again as dominant as they were for prehistoric man."

He sat down at the edge of his chair, but kept the gun steadily on them. His tone became more conversational.

"As we have a few moments, let me explain to you. Five thousand years ago Cromm was man's ruler. The people believed in him. They believed their worship of him made them safe. But then there came new things. What you call civilization made them self-assured, and Christianity gave them a hope and a love for each other. That caused the people to draw away from Cromm, encroached upon his territories, his powers, drove him back to this last bastion, this isolated corner of an island where the civilizing hand lay most lightly.

"Here he hoped to continue undisturbed. But you interfered with that, Mr. McMahon—or, your brash self of that time did. And so Cromm was forced to slumber fitfully through the centuries, awaiting the time."

"How did he know it would come?" Meg asked.

"His mind is not like ours," Dudley replied. "It is infinitely more clever. He knew the animal spirit within man. He understood that these nobler aspirations for soul and society were only the faintest ripples upon a vast ocean of human emotions. Below, in the black depths, lie the passions, fears, longings, like vast and terrible creatures waiting to rise again. Hitler plumbed those depths. Cromm will do the same, but on a much vaster scale."

"What's he going to do, put on TV ads?" Colin said. "The politicians will have him beat on that."

"Your continued attempts at humor amaze me, McMahon," the man said caustically, "considering your position. Cromm may obtain a physical strength from blood, but his real power comes from minds, from minds that weakness and fear have made open, willing to accept him. The minds are already opening by the millions. I can feel the surge of them, like a sea of dark energy, flooding all about Cromm. When the moment comes, and the other worlds are fully open to this one, Cromm will reach out to them. And with each mind taken he will have the power to reach farther out, not as ripples but as a tidal wave, sweeping across the sea, stirring it to its deepest points."

The man was clearly caught up in his vision, eyes bright, body tense, chest heaving with the excitement.

"And then real chaos will come. Chaos from which he will gain even greater control. Think . . . a world so capable of destruction, fear, greed, and with so much warm, rich blood. Oh yes, Cromm was made for this world."

"And when will this happen?" Megan asked.

This recalled him from the throes of his arousal. His voice became matter-of-fact again.

"When the powers of light are weakest and the powers of dark and cold most strong. The fabric between this world and the others is thinnest then, and their forces can be drawn upon."

"Is that what they call *Samhain?*" asked Colin.

"Very good," the man said, nodding. "Your research has helped you."

"Colin," said Megan in dismay, "Samhain . . . that's what they call Halloween now. It's tomorrow night."

The Brigadier looked at his watch. "Little more than twenty hours from now. The ritual begins as the light of day fades. The last rays of the sun will glint along the passageway and strike Cromm, and the revival will commence."

"There's still time to stop him," said Colin. "Until then, your boy's still vulnerable."

"Hardly," Dudley said dismissingly. "There's no threat that Cromm can't be protected from now. Had you escaped, you'd still be harmless. No one would believe your tales, and if they did, any force that might be scraped together in so little time would only die or be turned to Cromm as well."

"Yeah? But what about me?" Colin said. "He was afraid of me."

"But we both know now there was never anything to fear," said Dudley. "We believed that you would be *him*—that bold but foolish warrior of so long ago." He laughed at the idea. "But you're not, are you? You're just a frightened little man too, like the rest. You're just another man of this new world . . . no values, no honor, no courage, just a need to protect yourself. Not a threat to Cromm at all. It's obvious the awakening did not happen. And now it will never have a chance to do so."

"What do you mean?"

"That you will be a part of Cromm's revival. You and Miss Conroy. There is little that would please him more."

The iron spit still lay beside Colin's chair. In a sudden, desperate move he grabbed it up, rising halfway from the seat.

Dudley lifted his gun.

"No!" cried Jenny, rushing forward.

Taken off guard by her move, Dudley swept the gun around toward her. Frightened, she staggered back. Colin leaped forward then, swinging the spit up. The Brigadier lifted his free hand and gripped it, holding it back. Colin grabbed his gun hand, forcing it away. The two stood straining forward against each other, feet shifting for a better point of leverage.

Megan slipped up beside them. Reaching around Colin, she shot a hard uppercut to the point of Dudley's chin. His head snapped back. Suddenly he went limp, crumpling to the ground. Colin stared, open-mouthed.

"I'm trained in unarmed combat," she explained briefly, pulling the gun from Dudley's hand.

"Sure you are," he said. "So, let's get out of here."

"Jenny, are you all right?" Megan asked the woman who sagged against a table, her face white.

"Yes. Yes," she sobbed. "I'm sorry. I'm so sorry. I'm not one of them. Please, please, believe me!"

"Better help her," Megan said to Colin. "It's shock. She may collapse on us."

He put an arm around the woman and helped her walk. The three of them moved into the study. Meg picked up the phone.

"Dead," she said, dropping it back. "Just as he said."

The front door opened. They turned to look out into the hall as a familiar slothlike creature lumbered through the doorway into view.

Without hesitation, Megan raised the gun and fired. The slug tore through the tip of the thing's long nose. It screamed and pulled back.

"Out the back!" said Colin.

They moved back through the family room into the dining room. Beyond its window other grotesque shapes could be glimpsed slipping by in the dark. They came into the kitchen, heading for the French doors that opened out the back.

The doors suddenly blew inward in a shower of glass as an immense insect creature smashed through, thrusting forward spiny forelegs, giving a shrill, rattling cry.

Megan shot directly into the mantislike head, the force of the impact knocking the spindly creature back.

"Don't tell me," Colin said to her. "You're a trained sharpshooter too."

But more monstrous forms were looming up beyond the smashed doors, and others were pushing through from the dining room.

"This way," Megan said, leading the way around the end of the kitchen counter and through a narrow door.

The room beyond was a pantry, eight feet square and windowless. A single bulb illuminated shelves, boxes, bins, and a table in the center stacked with mixing bowls.

"They can't get at us here," said Megan, swinging the door closed.

"And we can't get out," Colin said.

"No other choice," said Megan. "Put out the light! Get behind some cover!"

Jenny went to huddle in a corner behind a barrel. Megan turned the table onto its side, sending the crockery bowls crashing to the floor. Colin flicked off the light and crouched behind the table top beside her.

He hefted the spit, ready, looking down at it. Faint light through the crack of the door caused the dull iron to glow very faintly.

But as he stared at it, he was surprised to see the metal growing brighter; a red light was burnishing it, running along the length of the spit as if it were the sharp-honed cutting edge of a polished blade . . .

24

Colin MacMathghamhain stood looking at his sword, its tapered length of black iron gleaming with red light from the scores of torch fires circling the fortress of Aislinn's clan.

He looked up from the weapon and out over the foss to where the druid Dubhdaleithe stood glaring across, his face drawn into a mask of hate. His headdress was gone but he still wore the white feathered robe, vividly stained with a wide swath of crimson spreading downward from the point where Colin's spear had so recently pierced his heart.

"Cromm demands the life of the one called Colin son of Mathghamhain!" the druid shouted to those in the fortress.

The chieftain Flann who stood beside Colin on the wall called back:

"We'll not give in to any demands of the bloody Cromm."

"Take care, O'Mulconrys," the druid warned. "Cromm has tolerated your existence for this long. Don't bring down his full wrath on you now."

"It is ourselves that *Cromm* should be fearing," the chieftain fired back. "If he challenges us, we'll see who wins the fight. Don't think that you can defeat us so easily. Cromm has no power over us, and the might of God makes our arms strong!" He waved his sword high, and his warriors followed his move, shouting out an exultant battle cry.

"You provoke Cromm past the point of his control," said Dubhdaleithe. "You will all die."

"Then we will do so in our God's name and as people free of the slavery of Cromm," said Flann. "So come against us, Dubhdaleith. But it's yourselves who should be prepared to die!"

"Kill them . . ." the enraged druid ordered, turning to his chieftain.

"But . . ." the chieftain Laimainech began in protest.

"Do it. Cromm commands!"

The chieftain Laimainech looked around him at his warriors. They exchanged glances, hesitating.

"Cowards," the druid said scathingly "You are four times their strength."

"Don't put the name of cowards on us," Laimainech retorted. "That chieftain was once a friend. I know his warriors and what damage they will do. My men are *mortals!* Many will die and many more be wounded. If Cromm commands their destruction, then let his own immortal creatures lead the way."

"Are you daring to defy Cromm too?" the druid cried. "If you do not attack, you will find Cromm's wrath falling on you as well as on these traitors. Do you want to see your people devastated, the lands laid waste?"

The chieftain snarled angrily. But then he lifted a hand to signal up and around him into the night. The warriors moved forward.

Colin looked around him. The fifty warriors of the fortress were now upon the walls, armed and ready. Women, children, and old men were busy passing more spears up to them. In the yard other women and children worked to stoke up several fires to light the area. Gilla Decair and Aislinn, with the help of Ailbe and the boy Seanan, prepared a hospital, laying out pallets and wrappings, setting cauldrons of water to boil over the fires.

"All right," Flann called to his warriors, "stand ready then. And the blessing of God be on the heads of all."

The warriors of Cromm came into the ditch.

Spears rained upon them. Many did not make it across. For a time the defenders did well, making the ditch a most deadly place to enter. The attack faltered. Warriors began to withdraw.

The druid then lifted his arms and signaled the monstrous agents of Cromm forward. They moved into the ditch, taking the lead in the attack.

Some were struck by spears, but the weapons had little effect on them. The beings reached the wall quickly. Some—like the clawed Ladhrach and a boar-headed creature—started to climb at once, digging talons and iron hooks into the wood of the palisade. Others—including a skeletal warrior and a slug-faced being with protruding eyes and shell-encased body—waited for the warriors to advance behind them, bringing up ladders and grappling hooks. Meantime a massive reptilian creature, unable to climb, began batting violently at the timber gates of the fortress with its tail and powerful legs, ignoring the spears that skittered off its scaly hide. Beside it paced an animal that seemed half bull and half hound, snarling in frustration.

Colin moved back and forth along his section of wall, kicking a ladder away, slicing the rope of a grappling hook with a cut of his sword. Then a shout from across the fortress drew his attention around.

There, two of Cromm's disciples had gained the wall. Seadna and a half-dozen fighting men battled desperately against the skeletal warrior who seemed unstoppable, and a squat armored being, more like a bear than a man, who fought with two strange weapons. They were round blades that spun in each hand. Their barbed teeth ripped through anything they touched, splintering posts, tearing into flesh, cutting through the thick leather faces of the shields.

Not far away, others of the creatures now fought their way onto the palisade walk. The chieftain Flann moved in to challenge a tall being of weasel head and long, flexible body who fought with two broad, curving swords, slashing with great speed. Other warriors tried to hold back a toad-faced being of broad, drooling mouth and a hunched-shouldered form who swung a massive ax.

Colin started to help them when there was a scream behind him. He turned to see a warrior fall back, neck slashed open. The slothlike beast was climbing over the wall, blood dripping from one of its taloned hands.

Colin moved toward it, lifting his sword. It stepped back defensively. But behind it another figure was hauling its thick body over the spiked tops of the logs.

The young warrior looked around him. No one else remained on the wall near him. All were occupied elsewhere. He moved to the challenge alone.

He knocked away the sloth's talons with his shield, driving in a thrust with his sword that the agile creature sidestepped. The boar-faced creature behind the sloth swung its iron claw downward at Colin's head, but he pulled back. The claw slashed into the planks of the walkway, sinking deep. Colin swung his shield sideways, slamming its iron boss across the creature's face with all his power, jerking the head violently around. The claw tore loose from the planks as the being was knocked sideways by the blow, stumbling into the spike-topped wall, teetering there, and then toppling over.

Colin wheeled back toward the taloned one, his shield and sword up, holding it at bay. But something else charged in from his right and he turned his defense in time to meet the new attack.

It came from the creature of the sluglike head. The shining black shell that encased its rounded chest slammed into Colin's shield. Its long sword, glowing with a strange silver light, clanged against Colin's, crackling and sparking at the contact.

The two locked together. Colin looked at close quarters into the awful face of the being. Its popping black eyes peered at him over the rim of his shield. Its round mouth opened, stretching out as if to suck him into the circle of teeth. Colin looked down the pulsing throat.

A movement at his left flickered in the corner of his gaze. With a sudden move he wrenched his opponent around and into the slothlike creature that was creeping up to strike at his unprotected back with its poisoned claws. The two creatures slammed together and staggered. Colin managed to break away and move back, preparing for a new attack while his opponents recovered.

He gave the fortress a quick, desperate, sweeping glance, clearly seeking help. What he saw was far from encouraging. With the creatures now on the wall, the warriors of Cromm were also beginning to swarm up the palisade. The warriors of the fortress battled desperately to drive them back.

Then something swooped down suddenly from the night

sky, drawing Colin's gaze toward the yard. His eyes widened in dismay at what he saw.

While Gilla labored over a wounded man lying by one of the fires, Aislinn bravely fought off the diving attack of the leather-winged Ialtag. She used a flaming brand, while her little brother Seanan and the driver Ailbe were at either side, gamely helping her with their own torches.

The creature was sweeping in tight circles over the three, wings spread, jaws snapping out at them while they swung their torches up at it. As Colin watched, it shot in again, its sleek head darting forward, jaws grasping Aislinn's torch. The girl struggled fiercely to wrench it free. Seanan and Ailbe batted at the thing's grasping claws with their own brands as it flapped violently above them.

But Aislinn's peril served as a dangerous distraction for Colin. For as he stood staring down into the yard, a form dove upon him.

It was the boarlike being who, having regained the wall's top, now slammed into the young warrior. The creature knocked Colin from his feet and the two crashed together onto the planks, their impact shaking the walkway.

The stunned warrior's shield was wrenched away. His sword arm was pinned by a thick, muscled leg as the beast came astride of him, its full weight on his chest.

Colin looked up to see the boar-head over him, the tusked mouth smiling, the tiny eyes glinting with victory as it lifted the curved iron hook of its one hand above him and began to swing it down at his unprotected throat.

He tightened, awaiting the impact and the quick, blinding flash of the last pain.

25

OCTOBER 30, 9:40 P.M.

Instead, it was the pantry door in front of Colin that shook under the impact of a massive blow.

The explosive sound of the blow jarred Colin to awareness. He looked from the iron spit in his hand back to the door as another blow struck and the tip of a curving ax blade cut through, splintering the thick wood inward.

"Colin! What's wrong?" asked Megan, noting his dazed look.

He looked to her, face white and drawn in shock.

"Megan, I was just there again. I was there!"

"Now?" she said in disbelief. "A fine time for dreaming this is!"

"No, listen!" he said "Dudley was right. I never destroyed Cromm. I screwed up. I mean I really screwed up!"

"What? What are you saying?"

"I think I just got myself . . . him . . . you . . . her . . . all of them back then . . . I just got them killed!"

The door shivered again under another heavy blow. This time the wood gave way completely as the immense ax blade drove on through, opening a ragged gap.

The ax withdrew. Another blade appeared, this time the slender, tapering blade of a finely honed sword. It slashed at the opening, slicing into the hard wood as easily as if it were cutting balsa, hacking a wider hole. The tips of the splintered wood smoked as if the blade were blazing hot.

"Well, be ready," Megan told Colin grimly, bracing herself and lifting the gun. "Because the same fate is likely coming on us as well!"

PART THREE

MAGH SLECHT:

FINAL BATTLES

26

The sword crashed through the door again, the blade tearing the gap even wider. It pulled back and the head of the sluglike creature was thrust into the hole, its glowing black eyes moving forward on the stalks to peer into the darkened pantry.

Megan lifted herself up from behind the table. Coolly she leveled the gun and fired. The explosion was thunderous in the tiny space. The bullet blasted through one of the creature's popping eyeballs, the glistening liquid surface exploding away in a shower. The creature screamed and fell back.

But now the massive bearlike one began pushing in, its curved, saw-edged blades slashing into the breech, ripping the wood of the heavy door away in splinters. Megan aimed and fired again. The beast jerked, snarling in pain, but continued to slash at the door. She fired once more, the bullet tearing through one of the broad paws, sending the blade it held spinning away. This time the beast retreated.

But the skeletal warrior instantly replaced it, slipping its lank, wasted body through the opening, thrusting into the shadowed interior of the little room with its spear. The barbed point glimmered brightly with a silver fire in the darkness. The crimson lights of the being's eyes shone like twin flares.

Megan fired point-blank into its decayed face, the bullet cracking through the dried flesh and bone of its forehead. Its head jerked back on the scrawny neck, but the being only gave

2 6 9

a death-rattle laugh and thrust its spear toward the muzzle flash. The spear thudded into the table top inches below Megan's face, the force of the blow knocking table and girl backward.

As she tumbled to the floor, the table overturned upon her legs. Colin dove forward, swinging out the iron spit to clang the spear aside. Then he slammed the spit down on the being's forearm with all his power. There was a sharp, dry pop as the bone snapped in two. The arm withdrew, pulling back the spear.

Colin stood ready, spit lifted to fend off a new assault. Behind him Megan recovered, lifting the table off her legs and sitting up behind it again, gun pointing to the door.

But there was no new attack.

For long moments they waited tensely, eyes fixed on the long, ragged gap of light showing through the ruptured door, waiting for a new monstrous shadow to appear there.

"What happened?" Colin finally asked, lowering the spit and turning to Megan.

"The door's too narrow for them to come at us more than one at a time," she said, standing up. "They're at a disadvantage here."

"You know," he said, moving around the table to her, "if somebody'd told me last week that I'd be in Ireland, holed up in a closet with a girl from my dreams, my coat inside out, fighting off a bunch of I-don't-know-whats with a piece of iron from a fireplace . . . I just might not have believed it."

She looked at him in a curious way. "Have I told you yet that you're a very odd person?"

"Thanks. So now what?"

She shook her head. "I really don't know."

"What do you think they're doing?"

She shrugged. "Regrouping, I suppose."

They stood listening intently. It was very quiet, the only sound within the pantry the soft sobbing of Jenny, still huddled in the corner. From beyond the door there came the faint sounds of shufflings, growlings, and snortings, mingled with a low undertone of muttered speech.

"What's that?" he asked Megan. "You're the one with the military training."

"Could be a conference of war. Maybe they're trying to decide how to dig us out most easily."

"Unless they just board us up and leave us here," he said.

"How many of them did you count?" she asked.

"I saw five or six. Hard to tell. But I don't think the whole dirty dozen were at the party."

She drew the magazine from the butt of the automatic and checked it.

"I've only four rounds left," she told him, slipping it back into the gun.

"Wanna rush em, Clint?" he asked.

"You pick the strangest times for joking," she said, moving into the corner to kneel at Jenny's side.

"Joking's a nervous reaction to being scared to death," he told her. "You probably wouldn't know about that."

Megan ignored the gibe, putting a soothing hand on the woman's shaking shoulder, speaking gently:

"Jenny, get hold of yourself now. Please, we need your help. Tell me, is there any way out of here?"

With an effort the woman controlled her sobbing, looking up to Megan with streaming eyes.

"No . . . no ma'am," she gasped out. "Just the door."

"All right, Jenny," Megan told her. "It'll be all right." She patted the woman again soothingly, then rose and moved back to Colin.

They were very close in the darkness. She lifted her eyes to his. The light from the kitchen revealed the concern in them, although her voice stayed level as she spoke softly to him.

"It seems as if we're trapped. There's nothing to do but wait."

"Oh, I don't know," he said, putting a hand on each of her shoulders. "If we're doomed here, you wouldn't consider a last-minute fling?"

"Colin . . ." she began in protest.

"That was no joke," he said, pulling her toward him.

She didn't resist, leaning forward, lifting her head as he moved his lips toward hers.

A sharp tapping began to sound in the room.

Startled, they both turned toward the sound. It had come from the back wall of the pantry.

"What the hell?" said Colin, moving to the wall. He put his ear to it, shifting it up, down, and sideways, and finally stopping. "It's from right here," he said, putting a hand to a spot two feet above the floor.

The tapping became louder. The wall plaster shivered at the spot.

"Look out," she warned, and he pulled back as the sharp tip of a metal object poked through the wall's surface.

"Something's coming in," Colin said as the tip withdrew, only to sink through again, making the hole wider.

"What's back there?" he asked Jenny, who was sitting upright now, staring in wide-eyed horror at this new threat.

"It . . . it's the stables," she gasped out.

The metal object came through the hole again, jerking sideways this time, cracking through the lath. It withdrew, and then the crooked end of a crowbar poked through and pulled back, ripping a ragged gap in the lath.

Megan leveled the gun.

"Shall I?"

"No," he told her. "Wait till there's something to shoot at. Don't waste the bullet."

They waited. Outside the door, the rumble of talk and odd noises continued, as if the creatures were arguing over a plan of attack. Inside, a section of lath was pulled back through the growing gap. Colin stood beside it, back against the wall, spit lifted to strike downward. Megan crouched before it, gun ready in her hand.

The work stopped and both young people tensed. Hands appeared, not monstrous but human, grabbing at the loose pieces of lath, pulling them back, making a rough hole two feet across. Something showed in the hole, moving forward into view. The light through the broken door struck a silver glow from it.

Megan lifted the gun in both hands to aim.

The top of a head came through the hole. The glow came from its wealth of silver-white hair.

She began to squeeze the trigger.

"No!" Colin said quickly. "Don't!"

She eased pressure on the trigger just as a man's big, strong-featured face came into view beneath the hair. It poked into the room, grey eyes scanning cautiously. Then its wide mouth lifted in a most amiable smile as he saw them.

"Ah, I've gone right," the man said in a pleased way. "Well, then, can I be of any service to you?"

"The healer?" she gasped.

He lifted a thick eyebrow in surprise. "So you do remember me, my girl? I'm most gratified."

"No. That just popped into my head." She was a little confused. "I don't know you. I'm certain."

"He's the one I told you about," Colin supplied. "In my dream he called himself Gilla Decair."

"Ah, so you've met me there now, have you?" the man said. "Well, that's very fine. That means the awakening has proceeded well."

"About time you showed up again," Colin said in a disgruntled way.

"A most expedient time, I would say. Now shall we see about getting you out of there?"

"How?" asked Megan.

"Through here, if you'll help me. The stable's beyond. Its door is unguarded. So come on. Quick!"

Megan and Colin knelt down on either side of the hole.

"Just pull the lath out," he instructed. "Quiet now. Don't want to rouse them."

"Do you know what they're doing?" Colin asked as they fell to the work.

"They're all deeply occupied by a dispute. Seems the creatures, true to form, don't wish to incur more damage. That Brigadier character is giving a . . . I believe it's called a 'pep talk'?"

"He told me he's that druid named . . . Dubhdaleithe?"

"Yes, I thought he must be," the man said, carefully cracking back a large segment of plaster. "The name translates to Dudley in a modern form. As your own MacMathghamhain becomes simply McMahon. Both paternal descendants, obviously."

Colin stopped and looked at him in surprise. "Great. You knew that? Why didn't you warn me?"

"I thought I told you why I couldn't interfere," the man said testily. "Be grateful I'm doing what I am."

"Could we argue later?" asked Megan. "I don't think we have much time."

They went on with the work, soon opening the space to a four-foot square.

"Okay," said Colin. "Let's get Jenny through."

The woman was nearly incapacitated with fear.

"Jenny, we've got to move," Megan told her urgently. "Come on."

With Colin's help she shifted Jenny to the hole. Megan started to hand her through, the woman moving sluggishly, the one called Gilla helping from the other side.

There came a shuffling noise from the kitchen. Then a rattling sound came from just outside the door.

"Oh, oh," said Gilla. "They're coming!"

"Help her through," Colin told Megan. "I'll hold them."

"The gun?" she asked, holding it up to him.

"Keep it for a last resort. I've got this."

He waved the spit, then stood and moved resolutely toward the door. As he passed the shelves, his eye fell on a black iron skillet and he took it up in his other hand. Reaching the door, he struck a heroic pose before it, skillet and spit raised in defense.

"I think I'm more ready to cook than fight," he joked, throwing a game smile back toward Megan.

"Look out!" she warned.

He looked around as the flaring spear-point of the mummylike warrior shot through the broken door at him. He caught the weapon with a swing of his spit, pushing it aside, then swung out with the skillet, smashing it across the creature's face. The being staggered back, its bony jaw knocked askew.

The creature with the slug's head leaped at once into the same spot. Its ruptured eye bled a shining black mucus down its neck, but it ignored this in its fury to come at Colin.

It slashed downward with its sword. Colin raised the skillet in defense. The blade's impact slammed the skillet away. Colin winced and let go, the skillet sailing off to crash into the shelves.

The American then thrust out with the spit. Just as before, his weapon pierced the shell of the creature's chest. The iron sank deep into the oozing stuff beneath. And just as before, his weapon stuck there. The creature twisted and pulled away, yanking the spit from Colin's hand.

Now weaponless, he stepped back.

The bear with its remaining saw-edged, spinning blade came into the doorway again, two slashes of its weapon tearing away the door's splintered remains. It started toward Colin. But there was a bright flare of light and an explosion, and the beast staggered backward.

Colin looked around to see Megan alone now at the hole, smoking gun pointed toward the door.

"Quick!" she said. "Go through. I'll cover!"

He moved to the hole, dropped down and crawled through. She crawled through backward after him.

More creatures were coming into the doorway. She aimed and methodically squeezed off the last shots. There were grunts and squeals and they fell back in a tangle.

She came through the hole, rising to her feet beside Colin. Gilla was just throwing open the doors of the house's stable section. Moonlight flooded in. It revealed two open stalls and two magnificent long-limbed horses with glowing black coats, already saddled and bridled.

"I took the liberty of saddling them," Gilla said. In the pale light it could be seen that he wore a long tweed overcoat and muffler. One hand gripped his silver-headed stick.

He took the reins of one horse, pulling himself easily up into its saddle. "Best put poor Jenny up with me."

They lifted up the woman, now barely conscious, to sit before him.

Megan at once climbed onto the other horse.

"Hey!" Colin cried in protest.

"I was an amateur jumper from ages eight to nineteen years," she told him, settling herself into the saddle. "How about you?"

"Why didn't I guess?" he said resignedly. "Okay."

He climbed up behind her, gripping her about the waist.

"Least there's one compensation," he said.

"Not so tight," she warned, urging the horse forward after the silver-haired man's.

"Duck," she warned as they went through the low door, and then she at once put the horse into a gallop.

Ahead of them, Gilla had already done the same.

A dark figure came around the corner of the building, moving to block their escape. But Gilla swung his stick out, knocking the thing back as they rode by. In a moment they were away into the countryside.

They galloped across the moonlit meadows. Colin glanced back to see an automobile leaving the manor house, its headlights cones of light scanning down the drive to the road below. Then a copse of trees cut off his view of the house and he turned his attention ahead.

They kept up a dangerous pace across the dark, uneven landscape. Gilla stayed ahead, guiding his horse skillfully across the treacherous ground.

"He's very good," Megan commented admiringly.

"I hate this," Colin said, bouncing along behind her. "I think I'm seasick."

"Just keep hanging on."

Ahead of them, Gilla's horse went over what seemed a low ridge and suddenly disappeared.

"Where'd he go?" said Colin.

Megan reined in, slowing the horse to a walk, looking ahead cautiously. She urged it over the ridge.

The horse walked down into a hollow place beyond the ridge. Faintly visible not far ahead was a mound of earth thickly covered with brush and trees. Gilla's horse stood beside it, and the man had dismounted to help Jenny down.

"What are you doing?" Colin asked sharply. "We should keep going!"

"Jenny needs to rest," Gilla replied, easing the woman down against the side of the mound. "Besides, we can't do that."

"The hell we can't. We can still get away if we keep going."

"You have to stay," the other man said firmly. "You still have to stop Cromm."

"He's right," said Megan, swinging her leg over the saddle and sliding to the ground. "We can't leave now."

"Hey, don't you people get it?" said a disbelieving Colin, staying on the horse. "There is nothing I can do! I can't destroy Cromm. All I did . . . I mean, all that other jerk did back then was to get everybody killed. It's all over."

"No, Colin," said Gilla. "That's not so. Look around you. Don't you know this place?"

He peered around him. The hollow was circular, enclosed by a low, curved wall of earth.

"Yeah. Yeah, I do know this place," Colin said, sliding down from the horse. "Its that old fort outside the town. I was here before. What do they call it?"

"A rath," said Gilla. "Aislinn's rath. I've brought you here on purpose. Look around. Look closely. Concentrate. Do you feel? Do you see? Think, Colin. Think. Remember . . . remember . . . remember . . ."

The voice became a soft blur, fading away. Colin turned slowly, looking around into the darkness.

Sounds arose there: metallic clashes, shouting, the screams of men, all growing louder. A red-gold glow appeared from somewhere.

There came a sudden impact against his back. His breath "whoomped" from him and he was lying down, staring upward at a terrible face . . .

27

The boar-headed creature sitting upon Colin's chest was wrenched away suddenly.

A powerful sword thrust laid open its shoulder. The arm that had the lethal blade went instantly useless, dropping to its side. The beast screamed in rage, turning toward the new attacker. It was Aislinn's father. He swung out again with a hard and well-aimed thrust that struck the thick, muscled neck, hacking deep. The head jerked sideways, half severed, but the creature still charged at Flann. Coolly, the chieftain swung his sword back in another heavy blow, this time taking off the massive head.

The body toppled sideways, crashing down. Colin levered himself up, staring at the felled beast in amazement as both its head and its still thrashing body began to glow with a white-green light. The light quickly engulfed both parts, then burst into a thousand emerald sparks that flickered up and away like a cluster of fireflies dispelled by a gust of wind. No sign of the creature was left behind.

Colin scrambled to his feet, moving to Flann's side as the chieftain scooped up the young warrior's sword and handed it to him. Then the two men advanced upon the slug-faced creature and its slothlike companion.

Neither beast waited for their coming. They retreated to the wall and dove over the side.

Surprised, Colin looked around. All about the fortress the monsters of Cromm were retreating. Cromm's warriors were already in full flight, leaving a score of dead behind and carrying away twice as many wounded.

"They're beaten!" said Colin.

"They're never that," said the chieftain grimly. "Come. Let's help our own."

They sat about the fire in the main hall of the fortress, tending their wounds and evaluating the fight's outcome.

"Not bad," Flann was saying, honing away a nick in the blade of his sword. "We lost only three warriors."

Colin looked around. A dozen others lay moaning on pallets about the room. The silver-haired Gilla Decair was seeing to them, aided by Aislinn and her little brother Seanan. The healer used ointments and powders that he took from a voluminous leather pouch.

"I don't understand why they quit," said Colin. "I thought surely we were beaten."

"We nearly were, but our resistance lasted just a bit longer than their endurance," said Flann.

Gilla finished binding the wounds of the last hurt warrior and came over to them.

"My ointments and herbs will heal most of their wounds in a few days' time," he said. "They'll all fight again."

"But for how long?" asked Flann's elder son Seadna. "The warriors of Cromm are four times our number, and they have the creatures' help. They will wear us down."

"Maybe," said Flann. "But we should still be pleased at winning today. If the tales are true, not since Tighernmas himself defied Bloody Cromm has the monster been angry enough to unleash so much of his power. The High-King and three fourths of his people died that time. We have survived. The power of our God surely is strong in us."

"Still, we should have been stronger," Seadna complained, casting a bitter look at Colin. "If MacMathghamhain hadn't . . ."

"I think he had great courage to face Cromm," Seanan said sharply, moving toward his older brother. "More courage than the warriors of our clan. And he saved your life once too, if you'll recall."

"Is it a coward you're calling me, boy?" Seadna said in anger, rising to face Seanan. "I'll . . ."

"Wait!" said Flann, rising and stepping between his sons. "No warrior of this *dun* is a coward for not having faced so great a power as Cromm before," he told Seanan. Then, to Seadna, he added, "But though Colin might have acted in haste, he was not wrong. We can't be faulting him for saving those babes."

The brothers, both looking chastened by this, moved apart.

"Still, I'm sorry," Colin now put in contritely. "If I'd known what I'd be bringing upon your clan. Upon Aislinn . . ."

"You mustn't think of that," she said, moving to him. "I could never have wanted you to turn away from Magh Slecht and leave those children to be butchered."

"They've only been saved until the next sacrifice," said Seadna. "And what after that? With us wiped out, there'll be no one to spread God's word and free the people from the hold of Cromm. His power may not be broken for generations more . . . or never!"

"But you may have some time," put in the healer.

"How so?" asked Flann.

"Well, you see, my knowledge of him is perhaps just a bit wider than yours," Gilla said with a little smile, sitting down by the chieftain. "Oh, there's no doubt that he is powerful, but I understand some of the magic behind that power. Now, how many of Cromm's disciples do you normally see abroad at once?"

"Seldom more than one or two," Flann replied. "Rarely three."

"That's right. And when they are used, their purpose is more to frighten Cromm's subjects into obedience than to use force. I believe that's because Cromm expends tremendous energy to bring those creatures to life, and even more when they have to fight."

"Of course," said Colin. "And afterward they must go back to their stones and be recharged!"

The healer's eyes whipped around to Colin at this statement, widening in surprise.

"*Recharged?*" said Flann, looking curiously at the young warrior. "And just what does that strange word mean?"

"I . . . I'm not sure," Colin said, frowning. "It just seemed the word to use."

"I think I understand the lad's meaning," Gilla quickly put in. "And he is right. After each use, they must return to the stones. It's there, within them, that the creatures regenerate and repower. The greater the expenditure, the more disciples involved, the longer this regeneration takes. After Tighernmas was destroyed, it was a full two seasons before Cromm recovered his total power."

"How is it you know that?" asked Flann.

"Oh, my people have tales about it," Gilla said vaguely. "But what it means for you is that it will likely be many days before Cromm can send the full force of his beings against you again."

"Don't these creatures ever weary of suffering for the good of their master?" Colin wondered.

"They've no choice so long as Cromm chooses to send them out," Gilla said. "They're his slaves, their lives dependent upon him, on the blood he drinks. And no matter how damaged, the things still cannot die. He only restores them and sends them out again."

"Then in a way I pity them as I pity all the slaves of Cromm," said Colin.

"Pity those cruel and monstrous things?" Gilla said in surprise.

"Yes. They've a right to decide their own fates, just as we do."

"They decided that, lad, before the start of time, when they chose to follow Bloody Cromm."

"Accepting that the creatures might be much weakened now," the chieftain asked, "just how long will they remain so?"

Gilla nodded toward Colin. "Our young friend here may not have destroyed Cromm, but he certainly interfered with the Beltainne ceremony. You see, Cromm gets strength for himself and his creatures from the blood fed him at those rituals. Now Cromm has missed being fed, and he must have been drained of a great deal of energy by this battle as well. I'd say he could likely remain weakened until a new ritual, and that's not until Midsummer Night, many days from now."

"Then maybe we could strike at him!" said Seadna.

"No," said Flann. "He still controls the minds of Dun Mauran's warriors, and they have us besieged. Within our fortress we can withstand their greater numbers. Outside we'd be most disadvantaged. Perhaps we could fight through such odds, but it would be at a high cost."

"And if you did manage to reach Magh Slecht," added Gilla, "within the circle of stones, Cromm still has immense power to defend himself. His ability to dominate mortal minds would be so strong there that even this new faith might not be enough to shield you."

"That can't be true," said Seadna proudly. "God has freed our minds, and no power is strong enough to enslave them again."

"Maybe," said Gilla. "But Tighernmas thought himself free of Cromm too. Twenty centuries ago he challenged Cromm on Magh Slecht. Many thousands of his people died."

"All right, Healer. I understand," Seadna grudgingly admitted. "But what else can be done? Should we just sit here until Cromm's agents are restored to their full power and come to finish us?"

"You could leave," suggested Gilla. "Some of you might die, but the women and children could be saved. I'd help you see to that."

"You already know my answer," said Flann. "We'll not leave here. We've sworn it. Running would be no salvation to us."

"If we'd only had the time to turn more of the people to us," Seadna said in frustration, returning to that ruined plan again. "Now, besieged here, we'll never have a chance."

"No. Not alone," said Colin, suddenly animated. "But maybe it's time you quit trying to fight this battle all alone."

"What do you mean?" asked Flann.

"That you know someone who can free everyone enslaved by Cromm in a single stroke. One speech to them would do it. Cromm would lose his subjects. They would join you. Maybe then he could be destroyed."

"I understand," said Aislinn. "You're speaking of Patrick."

"Ah, that is madness!" Seadna told him. "You mean to bring Patrick here? We can't be endangering that holy man for our good."

"Why not?" asked Colin. "It's what he came to Ireland for:

to bring you light, to destroy the evil magic. If he has such power as you told me, he's in no danger from the likes of Cromm."

"That isn't the whole reason for not seeking Patrick's help," said Flann. "This is *our* fight. *Our* need. *Our* penance to be done."

"And for your need you'd let innocent babes die?" Colin fired back. "You'd sacrifice your lives? Tell me, Chieftain: if you don't act in some way, what will happen?"

"Very likely we will all be killed," Flann answered.

"For nothing," said Colin. "And the evil will continue, maybe for years. Do you think this holy man of yours would condone that for his safety? This man who faced the *ard*-druids of Tara? And do you think his god would look in kindness on your act of pride?"

"But, to bring Patrick to save us . . ." the chieftain began.

"*Not* to save you," Colin said with force. "To destroy Cromm!"

"Colin is right, Father," put in Aislinn. "Don't be so stubborn. If we do nothing but die here, our act becomes a selfish one. We have tried to destroy Cromm ourselves, but we've failed. We must accept that. Now the important thing is to see the sacrifices stopped and everyone freed from Cromm's slavery."

"I say the lad has an excellent idea," said Gilla. "If this Patrick has the powers you say, he may be your only chance of winning now . . . and of surviving too." He looked challengingly at Flann. "Unless you prefer the idiocy of dying a noble and completely useless death."

"All right, Healer," Flann growled, shooting him a look. "I think the point has been fully made."

"But it means we must find him and bring him back before Midsummer Day," said Aislinn.

"We can withstand their siege for that much time," said Flann. "At least so long as Cromm's disciples don't come against us in full force. We have the food and water stored by for such a case. But finding where the wandering Patrick has gone will not be easy or quick."

"Still, we couldn't spare many warriors for such a quest," said Seadna.

"One or two at most," Flann agreed. "And it's great danger they'd be in. Laimainech's warriors would soon discover the signs of those who'd left and surely set a strong force to hunting them."

"But it has to be done," said Seadna, drawing himself up. "I'll go."

"No," said Colin. "I should be the one to go."

"You?" said Seadna. "You're not even one of us."

"But I am the one who put you all in jeopardy. I have to be the one who brings you help. Call it my own penance if you want."

"I think he's right," said the healer. "He has an amazingly strong and independent mind. I don't believe it can be touched by Cromm. He's a fine warrior as well. I'd say he could very well have the best chance of surviving. Besides that, I mean to go along with him."

"You?" said Colin in surprise.

"Don't you worry about me, lad," he replied. "I can keep up with you well enough."

"That may be. But what can you do to help, old man?" Colin asked skeptically.

"I have a few small tricks that may speed your way and give you safety," was the modest reply.

"If the healer goes, you surely will have a chance," the chieftain declared, seemingly satisfied.

"Well, all right then," Colin agreed, but with doubt still in his tone. "But just how is it that we'll go? If Cromm's fighting men have a ring all about the rath . . ."

"For that we've already prepared a way," the chieftain said with a smile. "When night comes, you and the healer just be ready."

Hands lifted a large, flat slab of slate from the floor of the meeting hall. Beneath was revealed a square hole into the earth. It was dark in the meeting hall now, and the firelight revealed only the top of the hole and the end of a ladder in it, leaving its depths an unfathomable blackness.

"A souterrain," Flann said. "It takes us out at the bank of the stream, beyond the circle of Cromm's warriors."

The chieftain stood by the hole with Gilla and Colin. Around them Ailbe, Aislinn, and other inhabitants of the rath were gathered.

Gilla handed the chieftain a bulging leather bag.

"These medicines should keep you all well," he told Flann. "I've shown Aislinn how to mix and use them to heal wounds."

"I thank you for that, Healer," Flann said. "You've been a good friend to us."

"I'm only sorry I couldn't have done more."

"Just see that Colin succeeds. That'll be enough."

Flann moved to the fire, taking up a torch and lighting it from the flames. While he did this, Aislinn went to Colin. She took off the ornament that had hung on a leather thong about her neck. It was of silver, formed in the simple, gracefully curving fish symbol of her new faith.

"I know you don't believe," she said to him, "but will you still take this? With my prayers for you, it may keep you safe."

"I will," he said, bending forward.

She slipped the thong over his head, laid the glinting symbol gently against his chest. Then she hugged him, pulling herself tightly against him. He hugged her warmly in return, her father looking on with one eyebrow raised and a faint smile of approval on his lips.

She pulled back suddenly and turned away from Colin, firelight glinting on the tears welling in her eyes. Colin opened his mouth to speak, stepping toward her; but little Ailbe moved up into his way, face set in courageous lines.

"If you really mean to go foolishly risking your life again," Ailbe said stoutly, "then I'm going with you too."

"You're a loyal comrade, Ailbe," Colin told him. "But you can see we'll not be able to take a chariot. You'll stay here."

The little driver shook his head. "I don't know if you've done me a good turn or a bad."

He went to Colin, also putting arms about him in a great hug.

"Good fortune go with you, Master," he said feelingly. "And be coming back soon so we can finally go home."

"I'll do what I can," Colin promised. "But, if I don't come back . . ."

"That you had better do," the little man admonished him, "or your father will surely have my head. And remember, we still owe him a bull."

"Time to go," said the chieftain, moving back to the hole. He lifted the lit torch and started down the ladder. Gilla followed.

Colin looked around him for a last time. Aislinn turned, and he saw the shining streak of a tear upon her cheek.

"I . . ." he began, but then stopped, clearly at a loss. "Goodbye," he finished lamely, moving to the ladder.

She took a step forward. A determined light flared in her bright eyes.

"You will come back, Colin MacMathghamhain," she told him with fierce resolve. "I'll not abide anything else."

"I'll always come back to you," he answered her with equal certainty. Then he followed Gilla down the ladder and vanished from her sight.

When he reached the bottom of the hole, the chieftain and the healer were awaiting him. Flann's torch revealed a low and narrow tunnel running away into the darkness. The walls and ceiling were flat slabs of slate, their smooth surfaces softly reflecting the red glow of the flames.

Flann led the way. The low roof of the souterrain caused them to bend forward as they walked. They walked this way for some distance, the ladder vanishing behind them, and nothing visible in either direction but the short span of tunnel lit by the chieftain's torch.

Then a glinting speck showed ahead. Others appeared around it. Flann stopped, and Colin and Gilla peered past him. They were at the tunnel's far mouth, looking out from a hillside across a meadow and stream. Above it the stars showed in a clear night sky.

"You should be well beyond the circle of Cromm's men," Flann told them softly. "But go carefully. And may the power of God go with you."

"And if there truly is such a power," Gilla returned, "whether it be that of your new god or of the Old Ones, then may it protect you until we return."

Both Gilla and Colin gripped hands with the chieftain. Then they left the tunnel, stealing away into the night.

They splashed cautiously through the shallow waters of the stream and climbed the far bank. As they reached the top, Colin paused to cast a final look back at the ringfort. It was barely visible on its hill, a darker mound in the surrounding blackness, the curved top of its palisade dimly lit by the bonfires in its yard. Scores of other fires were spread around it in a wider curve, the red-gold cones of light marking the lines of the besieging warriors.

He turned back to see that Gilla had stopped too and was now facing him. The healer's eyes were gazing searchingly into his.

"What's wrong?" Colin asked.

The man didn't answer.

28

OCTOBER 30, 10:53 P.M.

"What's wrong?" Colin asked again, more insistently.

This time Gilla responded.

"Colin? Are you awake now?"

"Awake?" he said. "What do you mean? I . . ."

Then his gaze took in what lay beyond the man's shoulder. He looked at the curved mound and outer ring of the ancient fort, their shapes faintly visible in the night. Jenny sat huddled against the side of the mound. Nearby, the two horses grazed on tufts of dried grass.

Colin stared at these things for a surprised moment, then

glanced around to see the face of Megan who stood close beside him, peering up at him with an anxious expression. He blinked and shook his head.

"Colin?" Megan said. "Are you all right?"

"Meg!" he said, gripping her arm. "Was I here?"

"Here?" she repeated in confusion. "What do you mean?"

"I mean, have I been here the whole time? Did you see me? I didn't go anyplace, did I? Disappear?"

"No," she said, giving him a most curious look. "You were right here. You just went into a sort of . . . trance for a few moments. As you did in the mound."

"I just . . ." He shook his head. "I don't know. The damn things are so real now. Almost more real than this. It's like I'm really going there."

"Is it?" she said musingly. "And I thought you were so adamant that you weren't him."

"Okay, so I'm seeing things from inside his head," he said. "But that doesn't make us the same guy. I'm just a passenger. It's like being on a roller coaster that somebody strapped you into when you were asleep." He sighed and looked around him. "But I guess that ride's not much different from this one." He shook his head again, adding wearily, "Cheez, I hate this."

"But where were you this time?" she asked. "What was happening? You told me that last time you were killed."

"Nearly. But your father . . . her father . . . pulled me out. We actually chased the Monster Squad off . . . for a while anyway." He gestured around him. "Right here. I can still see it like it just happened."

"That's part of the Awakening," put in Gilla. "I hoped bringing you here would help it along. So you're through the battle, are you? Well, the effect *should* be growing stronger now, I'd think. You're getting nearer to the end."

"The end!" said Colin irritably. "You've got me playing parrot to you again. What end?"

Gilla shook his head. "I can't tell you. You know that."

"Yeah. Yeah. Great. Wonderful. I thought you said you were going to help me? What kind of help are you?"

"Besides saving you once or twice, you mean?" Gilla said

dryly. "I've likely been much more help than I ought to have been. I've been keeping an eye on you since you first landed in Ireland." He lifted his arms. "Do you like my disguise? Oh, and there's a hat!" He pulled a tweed hat from his coat pocket and put it on, then wrapped his long scarf around his lower face.

"I ran into you at that place by the ocean!" said Colin. "When I met Meg!"

"That's right, my boy. But for me you wouldn't have met Miss Conroy and followed her to Ballymauran."

"For you?" said Megan. "How?"

"Let's just say that I 'misdirected' both of you to your meeting by the sea. I hoped that Colin's seeing you might trigger more of his Awakening."

"How could you manage something like that?" she asked disbelievingly.

"It's really not so difficult with Ireland's roads," he said. "And I've a few tricks."

"Mr. Decair is sort of a magician," Colin supplied. "With a couple thousand years of experience, I guess."

"What? Not like the Brigadier?" she said.

"Oh . . . the Brigadier," Jenny wailed suddenly, and began to cry. "Oh, my God. We're all going to be killed."

"Easy, Jenny," Megan said, going to the woman. She knelt and put a comforting arm about her shoulders.

"My husband. My poor husband," the woman went on brokenly. "I'm so sorry. I didn't mean for this. But my poor husband, and the others. All taken by that thing. Their minds . . . taken."

"It's all right, Jenny," said Colin, moving to her. "There wasn't anything you could do."

"I wanted to warn you before," she sobbed, "but I was afraid. When it first came . . . I felt it trying to crawl into my mind. But I fought it. I've been a good Christian woman all my life. I prayed and prayed, and I kept it out. Still I pretended. I didn't know what would happen if it knew I was still free. I was so afraid."

"Hey, I don't blame you," Colin said with sympathy.

She looked up to him. "When you came, I wanted to warn you . . . but I couldn't. I just couldn't."

"We understand, Jenny," Megan said. "Fear can be a very powerful weapon."

"I was alone," she went on. "I didn't know who to trust, where to go. It's taken over almost the whole village. I don't know how far beyond."

"That's okay," Colin told her. "It doesn't matter anymore. We got away. We got the horses. They can't stop us. Jenny, you can ride again now, so we can just climb back on our ponies and gallop away from here—far, far away—to some nice town with electric lights and TV sets and bars, and we'll tell the police, the reporters, the goddamn army to go take care of this. Then we can sit down, have a nice drink, and watch the pictures of it on the eleven o'clock news."

"I'm afraid you really can't do that," Gilla said flatly.

"Oh yeah?" Colin said, turning to him. "Why not?"

"I've told you before," the man said patiently. "It won't help. It's likely no one will believe you. And, if they do, that bloody thing will never brook interference now. Only *you* have the ability to defy its control, and the means to defeat it. That means is still buried in your mind, in your memories. I know it!"

"Oh, you know it?" Colin said sarcastically.

"Yes, I know it. As I know that tonight, when the influence of the power of light is weakest, Cromm will become a force that can begin to reach out over the entire mortal world, with no limitation except the pitifully few minds left that are strong enough to fight."

"Colin, he's right," said Megan, leaving Jenny and moving back to him. "Even if we can reach another place, we'll not do any good. We wouldn't know who to trust. Anyone who we might get to help would only become more slaves or more sacrifices. You're the only chance of destroying it in time."

"If you believe all this," Colin added.

"I believe it," she said with conviction.

"*You* believe it? Are you the same one who was trying to get me into a strait jacket over lunch?"

"I know what I've seen since then. And I know what I feel. I believe it's true, and I believe your dreams are too. You can do it."

"Yeah?" he returned irritably. "Well, I think you're over-looking the fact that I don't *want* to do it anymore. I'm tired, dirty, sore, and really depressed. Lady—I have had it."

"I don't think that you have any other choice," she fired back.

"Sure I do. I only came here because that pack of Exterminators were out trying to kill me. But they don't care about me anymore. You heard Dudley: they think I'm harmless. I can get on a plane and fly away from this."

"And let Cromm do as he wants?" she asked.

He shrugged. "Hey, just another cult in a world full of them."

"A cult that sacrifices children, that enslaves minds, that kills anyone who defies it, that's killed your own friend."

"Look, I'm sorry Harry's dead. But I didn't do it. It's not my fault. And getting myself killed too isn't going to help anyone. Listen, Dudley had me pegged right. I'm just a scared little guy who only wants to stay alive."

"You don't really mean that."

"You're not listening! Believe me, there is nothing I can do!"

"The other Colin would never have said that."

"I'm glad you're so sure. But, once and for all, I'm not him! Hey, *you're* more a hero than I am. You've sure got the guts and the résumé for it. Hell, you and Gilla have been saving my hide from the first."

She glared at him for a moment, then shook her head. Her voice took on an angry and frustrated tone.

"I believe you," she snapped. "I thought I saw something, felt something—I thought that you had *him* somewhere inside. But I was wrong. You really *don't* care about anything."

"What's wrong with that?" he said defensively. "Look at that guy you think is so goddamn great. He cared. He got himself involved—playing Luke Skywalker, saving the girl with one hand and the universe with the other. He was so damn sure. And he ended up putting everybody's life on the line.

Well, that's what happens when you get yourself involved. That's why I stay out."

"And that's why Cromm will win," she said.

Her fierce gaze met his. He stared at her, scowling; then he grimaced in disgust.

"Crap. Crap, crap, crap!" he swore to the sky, fists clenched, feet stamping the ground. "This really is not fair! Christ, now I have the fate of the goddamn world on my head."

The anger faded and he sagged defeatedly, looking back toward her.

"All right," he said in a tone of grudging acquiescence. "All right, what should we do?"

"You mean you'll stay?" she said with dawning elation.

"I said 'all right,' didn't I?" he told her in a surly way. "Don't make a big thing out of it. Just help me figure out what I'm supposed to do."

"It seems that's up to you," she said. "The answer must still be somewhere in your head. Locked in your dreams."

"It'd be a lot easier if our pal here would tell me what he knows," Colin grumbled, turning toward Gilla. "This bit about it being too dangerous . . ."

The silver-haired man was gone.

Colin looked all around within the ringfort. There was no sign of the man.

"Oh good," he said bitterly. "Wonderful! The guy did a walk on me again."

"So, it's all up to you," she said practically. "There's no time to be wasted over him. We've got to look carefully at your new memories. What's happened in them now?"

"Well, your hero has decided to go off and get some guy to help. That Christian guy they talked about. You remember my telling you? He gave a sermon that broke the spell that was on them."

"Patrick?"

"That's the one. You think he's important to us?"

"Let me see that book you've been reading all day."

He pulled it from the pocket of his battered coat and handed it to her.

"And my torch."

He handed that over too. "But it doesn't work," he reminded her.

She crouched down in a sheltered spot between the mound and a fallen log. She shook the flashlight and clicked the switch. It went on.

He shrugged. "Sure. That figured."

With the thin beam masked by her hand, a trickle of light showed through her fingers onto the book. She leafed slowly through the index. He crouched to peer over her shoulder. She found a reference and flipped forward through the book before stopping at a page.

"Here," she said. "Listen to this:

" 'One section of an ancient poem relating to Magh Slecht says, "Since the rule of Eremon, the noble man of grace, there was worshiping of stones until the coming of good Patrick of Macha." This relates to the tradition that, at the approach of the all-conquering St. Patrick, the "demon" fled from his golden image, which thereupon sank forward in the earth in homage to the power that had come to supercede it.' "

"*St.* Patrick?" said Colin in surprise. "The one we have parties for?"

"I'm sure that's all *you'd* know about him," she said scathingly. "But, yes, that one."

"So, I . . . he did it?" Colin said. "He brought Patrick back and the guy knocked Rocky out?"

"Do you see what it means?" she said excitedly. "The answer must be Christianity. The power of God. The belief in something that strong. Jenny has it. It protected her."

"Yeah, and it protected you . . . that is, Aislinn . . . and her whole family. Maybe you're right. Dudley—I mean the druid guy back then—said that they were afraid of it."

"It must be. But now, it's become weaker. Remember what the Brigadier said tonight? It's lost the power to keep the evil away."

Colin nodded toward a now resting Jenny. "Not completely."

"That's true. And Dudley also said something about not being able to reach the minds of a priest and his monks."

"Bonny!" said Colin. "Sure. He must mean Father Bonaventure and the guys at his monastery. We can still trust them."

"And get their help."

"Help?"

"To destroy the thing."

"What do you mean? Like in *The Exorcist?*" he said skeptically. "You think Bonny can come and raise a cross and make old Stone-Face turn to dust?"

"I'm not certain. It may be that he can. Anyway, it's our best chance. We have to reach him. Talk to him."

"How far is that monastery, do you think?" he asked her.

"Three miles from here, along the road north of the town."

"Can we use the horses?"

"The countryside between is very treacherous at night. It would be dangerous. Especially with Jenny."

"Yeah, and they're probably out searching for us by now. Hell. I suppose it'd be safer to walk it."

"But we can't take Jenny," she told him. "The woman's drained. Look, I'll go. You can stay here with her."

"You'll go?" he said. "Not a chance. I'm going."

"But I know the way."

"I can find it. I've been there. And I'm sure not staying behind with that woman. What if she gets hysterical? What if she needs medical help?"

"I don't know," said Megan, eying him doubtfully. "Are you certain about this? If I get the priest, your part will be ended, just as you said you wanted. Why are you suddenly so willing to risk yourself?"

"It's *my* dream, remember?" he pointed out. "Maybe it's important that I go after the priest, just like I . . . he . . . did before. Maybe there's something else we don't know yet; some other memory that hasn't come back yet. Do you want to risk screwing that up? No, this is still *my* movie, kiddo, and I'm going to have to play the whole tape out."

"Well, maybe you are right," she said, but still with some misgiving. "And you promise you'll go right to Bonaventure?"

"Absolutely," he vowed, crossing his heart.

"You'll not leave me out of it either," she said. "Whatever happens, you'll likely still need help. Once you've reached the Father, you must come back for me."

"Just what I was planning. He's got a car. We'll shoot right back and pick you and Jenny up."

"All right then," she agreed. "I suppose that's best."

"Great," he said. "Then I'd better get going." He patted himself. "Let's see . . . no gun, no nifty spit, no tire iron. Right. That means I'm totally unarmed. Oh well." He eyed her. "How about a kiss for luck?"

"Now you are joking," she told him brusquely.

"Hey, *she* gave *him* one!"

"She apparently liked him."

"Oh, come on," he cajoled. "You like me just a little bit, don't you?"

"I don't feel anything for you," she said coldly.

"No. Just for him. But you said you thought part of him was in here. You could kiss that part." He pointed to one side of his lips.

"Don't be a fool," she said.

He suddenly took hold of her shoulders, pulled her to him, and kissed her hard. She tried to pull away, but then surrendered to the kiss, lifting her arms to grip his, prolonging the moment.

Finally they pulled apart, both breathless and somewhat flushed. She looked a little bewildered, he triumphant.

"See?" he declared. "You felt something."

Her expression hardened.

"Feel this," she fired back, swinging up her hand to deliver a stinging slap that jerked his head around.

"Ow!" he cried. "Thanks a lot. Look at the risk I'm taking!"

"To save yourself," she snapped.

"Yeah? Well, she's a better kisser than you are anyway. You got her looks, but not her lips."

"You are wasting time," she said testily.

"Okay. Okay. I'm going," he said, lifting his hands defensively.

He walked to the outer ring of the old fort, climbing onto the mound of earth. There he stopped to look back.

"Say, if I'm not back here in a couple of hours, you'd better not wait. Get out of here to someplace safe."

"Of course I'll wait!" she said. "Don't be absurd. I can't get away with Jenny, at least until dawn. And I'm certainly not going to run off and leave you to deal with this alone." She raised a finger to point at him, with a stern, warning tone coming into her voice as she added: "But Colin McMahon, you had better come back to me. I'll not stand for anything else!"

He gave a surprised laugh at that. "Close. But the tone could have been warmer."

"What?" she said, nonplussed by his odd return.

"Never mind. Just trust me." He grinned. "Would I *do* anything else?"

And he was off, into the darkness.

He found his way across the meadow to the road and started along it, heading toward the town. It was very dark, the moon having gone down. The stars were intensely bright in the black sky. He could see the road only dimly as a narrow cut between the high-reaching trees on either side.

He moved cautiously at first, looking constantly around. But as nothing showed, he gained more confidence, striding along with greater speed.

Until a brilliant spot of light suddenly flared into being, directly ahead. He looked into its glare in wide-eyed surprise . . .

29

He stared at the reflected orb of the rising sun, glaring from the lake's surface as a shimmering spot of fire.

But the reflection was shattered into glinting fragments as the leather water-bag was lowered beneath the lake's surface. The mouth of the bag burbled noisily as water was scooped into it, and then the swollen bag was lifted, dripping.

Colin rose upright and stood holding the water-filled bag, gazing down at the lake as the roiled surface calmed, the wavery reflections steadied, the clear water smoothed to reveal the sharp reflection of a face.

His face.

He gasped, staring at it as if shocked.

"What's wrong, lad?" said Gilla, and the healer's face came into view, reflected in the water beside Colin's.

"It's me!" the young man said in a strange way.

"And who else would you be expecting?" the other asked, smiling.

The young man turned to the healer. "I . . . I don't quite know," he said in some bewilderment. "For an odd moment, I was surprised to be looking at myself. As if I expected to see someone else . . . or . . . I don't know."

Gilla looked at the frowning young face, then down at the image.

"Well, it is you, my lad," he said with certainty. "And there's no question of it at all." He looked back to Colin and nodded. "Yes. The very same."

He took the water-bag from Colin and moved away. The warrior looked down again at his image. "The same," he muttered to himself. Then he shook himself as if to cast off his odd feelings and turned to follow Gilla.

"Where did you spring from just now?" the young warrior asked as they climbed the low lakeside hill where they had made camp. "You were nowhere to be seen when I awoke this morning.

"Ah, well, I had a bit of an errand to go on. I was fetching this!"

And as they came onto the crest of the hill he pointed ahead of him with a little flourish of pride.

A chariot and horses now sat beside the burned-out remains of their campfire.

"A chariot," Colin said in astonishment.

He walked around it, examining it with an expression of growing awe. It was a most finely wrought chariot. The edges, rails, and bulwarks were ornately fitted in bronze and silver metalwork, the long chariot-pole tipped with the shining gold image of a ram's head. The large, bronze-rimmed wheels were brightly painted, their hubs inlaid with intricate enameling.

The horses of the chariot's team were broad-chested, powerfully muscled animals with glowing white coats and flowing manes. They tossed their heads and pranced with energy. Their bits and harness mounts were also of bright bronze with glowing enamelwork, and great plumes of blue and white fluttered over the animals' heads.

"A most grand chariot and team they are!" Colin pronounced. Then he looked curiously to the healer. "And just how was it you happened to come by them?"

"Oh, from some friends," Gilla said vaguely, waving his silver-tipped rod around him. "They live nearby . . . somewhere."

"I don't see any settlements about the lake," Colin said, peering out around the shores.

"They're in the hills," Gilla told him. "But never mind that. We now have our means to travel." He gestured toward the bulging leather bags piled within the vehicle. "And we've plenty of food as well. I hate traveling on foot. And hunting our food?" He shuddered at the idea.

"Well, you have proven your worth already," Colin said brightly, buckling on his sword. "This will surely make our quest a swifter one." He took up his shield, grabbed a handhold of the chariot, and hopped in beside Gilla.

"I'm afraid it could still take us years to find this one wandering man of yours, if we have to search all Ireland for him," Gilla pointed out. "We don't even know where to begin."

Colin was examining a rack within the chariot that held a dozen spears with sleek, barbed heads of black iron. But at the healer's words, he reacted suddenly.

"Macha!" he said with force, his gaze jerking up toward the northeast.

"What?"

Colin looked around to the healer with an expression that was frowning, intense, but touched with puzzlement also.

"I said 'Macha.' I've a feeling that he is there."

"In Ulster? Why would you think so?"

"I . . . I don't know that. It's most strange, but when you said we didn't know where to find this wandering man, the words 'Patrick of Macha' came into my mind. It was as if I heard them being said. By a woman's voice, soft and very distant, but speaking them clearly in my ear."

"Well?" said the other, eying him curiously. "Perhaps you have a bit of special talent of your own."

"I don't know, Gilla," Colin said with more doubt. "It's a wild chance. If we're wrong . . ."

"No, it's more than a chance," Gilla told him. "I feel it. And, besides, one place is as good as another to us. So I say, Macha it is."

"All right then. But how do we go? Before my journey to Connacht I knew nothing of Ireland but the wild coast of Helvick Head."

"I've done a bit more traveling," Gilla replied in a modest way. "For Ulster I say we skirt Lough Derg to the north, then head northeast."

"I'm in your hands, Gilla."

"A very good place to be," the healer said. He lifted the reins. "Very well, my fine boys," he told the team, "let's be off."

The horses obeyed at once, pulling the chariot around, heading off at a trot along the lake's shoreline.

They rode in silence for some time. But Colin's gaze shifted often from the way ahead to the healer, his expression thoughtful. Finally he spoke.

"Just who are you really, Gilla? The powers you have. Your healing skills. Finding this chariot. They're more than simple magic. Tell me the truth now. If we're to work as comrades, I must know."

Gilla didn't reply at once. He stared ahead of him, clearly considering. Finally he nodded.

"All right. I suppose there's little need for hiding it. You'd know me as one of the Others."

Colin gave a sharp laugh, looking around to him. "What? You? Of the *Tuatha de Danann?*"

"You find that hard to believe?" the healer said in an offended tone.

"No offense to you, but shouldn't you be a cloudlike, shining being? Not a . . . a . . ." He hesitated.

"Not a worn and wrinkled old man?" the other finished. "Sorry to disappoint you, but the *de Dananns* are men, quite like yourself for the most part. They were even mortal once, too, before old Danu gave them powers and the food that stops their aging."

"Oh, I know the childhood tales. I've just never had any belief in them."

"As you didn't believe in monsters and great *sheoguey* beasts?" Gilla returned with a little smile.

Colin smiled in return. "All right. Maybe it really *is* one of Them that you are. But why are you here?"

"I thought that was clear by now. I'm trying to help those people."

"Why? Cromm's one of you, isn't he? One of the gods?"

"Careful, boy," Gilla said sharply. "You're near to insult. No, he is *not* one of us. First of all, we've never claimed to be gods of any kind. Secondly, we don't know when or how he came to Ireland. We loathe him and his blood sacrifices of innocents."

"Then couldn't you use your powers to destroy him?"

"I'm not certain even our combined magic could do that. But we'd never use it. He's never bothered us. It's only man he's plagued. And we, of course, don't help man."

"I don't understand," said Colin.

"It stands to reason, lad. We lived quite peacefully in Ireland before your mortals challenged us. You defeated us in battle, took our lands, forced us to retreat to our Hidden Places. You can't expect that we'd be eager to help you. Some of us are hostile. Most are indifferent. But there are a few who are sympathetic. I'm one of them."

"And that's why you've tried to help?"

"As much as I could. But it's a bit dangerous for me. You see, if my fellows believe I'm aiding you too much, well, there'd be a great uproar. I might even be exiled, lose my own powers. So I'm bound by rules, supposedly limited to little more than a mortal sorcerer's tricks: giving you advice, healing a few wounds, and the like."

Colin pointed to the man's silver-headed stick. "What about that?"

Gilla grinned. "I'm afraid I've gone somewhat beyond bounds in using that. But no more of me. All our thoughts now must center on finding this Patrick fellow. And let's pray to Danu that his magic's even more powerful than Aislinn's people say."

"Why?" asked Colin.

"Because if it's not, there'll be nothing else that can save them."

"You mean that you can't . . ." Colin began. But he cut off suddenly as a light flared before his eyes.

"What's that?" he said in astonishment.

"Where?" Gilla asked, looking around.

"Can't you see it?" Colin cried, pointing ahead to it. "There!"

30

OCTOBER 30, 11:38 P.M.

It was a car's headlights that had swept suddenly into view, catching him, and he was frozen for an instant like a startled rabbit. But then, as the roar of the engine grew louder, he came back to life, diving over the low stone wall into the brush.

The vehicle swept around the bend to the spot where he had stood, sliding to a stop with a screech of brakes. Doors opened and slammed.

Colin ducked farther down as the beam of a flashlight switched through the half-bared branches above him.

"See anything?" said a voice.

"Naw. Nothin' at all," another voice responded.

"I think it was a deer, maybe," said a third voice.

"Or a *pooka,* indeed, to vanish so quickly?" the first shot back. "If you really saw anything at all, Jamie."

"I was certain I did," came the peevish reply.

Colin lifted himself up cautiously to peer over the wall. Five yards away a battered old van was visible. Matthew the barman sat behind its wheel. Two other men stood in the road on either side of it, swinging their torches about them. One of the men held a large revolver in his other hand.

"Ah, it's nothing," said Matthew. "They'd be far beyond this point by now. Come on, you two. We'll go out the east road to Knockgawan crossroads."

The two climbed back into the car and it roared away. Colin watched as its tail lights dwindled into the distance. He was squinting after the tiny red points of light when a hand dropped onto his shoulder.

A "whoof!" of surprise was expelled from Colin as he whirled around and swung out with his fist.

A rod swept in and blocked the move, pushing the arm away.

"Easy, Colin," said a familiar and still unruffled voice. "It's only me."

He peered at the shadowy figure in hat and muffler, noting the glint of the rod's silver bird-head.

"Gilla?"

"I thought you might need a bit more help, so I followed."

"Well, don't do that again!" Colin said in an angry voice. "I've got enough bad guys jumping out at me from nowhere. Hell, they don't have to kill me. Sooner or later I'm going to have a heart attack!"

"Sorry," Gilla said, but with a little smile. "I quite understand."

"I suppose I should have expected you to show," said Colin. *"He* came along. Or . . . you did." He shook his head in exasperation. "God, it's a pain keeping it straight."

"I did?" said Gilla. "Have you had another memory then?"

"Yeah. They're coming faster now."

"So the intensity of the dreams is increasing. That's good. Very good."

"Maybe. But I wish they'd give me some warning. That one almost got me run over!"

"It'll likely take very little to trigger your recollections from here on. Where are you now . . . or I should say 'then'?"

"You just helped me out again." Colin shook his head. "Seems like somebody's doing that a lot for both of us . . . I mean, both of me. Anyway, we were on the way to get Patrick. You found me this chariot, and . . ." He paused, looking to the silver-haired man. "That is me, isn't it? I mean, that's really my own life, back there?"

"An incarnation. Yes. Most people have them. They just have no recollection of the details. Your own memory was revived by Cromm's awakening."

Colin shook his head. "I still don't feel like him. But what about you? I mean, you're no new life. No new body. You're the same guy, aren't you? You're one of *Them.*"

"Oh, that's right," said Gilla, nodding in understanding. "I did tell you what I was. Yes, I'm afraid this is the same old body, somewhat the worst for fifteen centuries of wear."

"You don't look any different," Colin told him.

"I thank you for that," the man said, giving a little bow. "But I've gained a few newer scars to add to that one on my forearm."

"So, why'd you disappear again back there?"

"To avoid awkward discussion," Gilla replied. "I sensed you'd be pressing me to reveal the past events. But it's more crucial than ever at this point to let them come by themselves."

"Why show up now?"

"Because I 'overheard' that you mean to go right through the town. That could be a bit touch-and-go."

"Look, I do want you to tell me more about all this. About both of me. About what we're doing."

"I'm sure you do, but don't you think we should be getting on?" The older man looked around him into the darkness. "Even standing still for very long might be dangerous tonight."

"Right," Colin agreed.

"And I suggest we stay off of the road."

Colin nodded. They began to make their way along through the fields behind the rock wall.

"I must admit I was rather surprised that you decided to do this," Gilla commented. "It's very courageous of you. Very . . . ah . . ."

"Unlike my regular self?" Colin finished. "Well, don't get your hopes up. I'm not doing this 'cause I think the Father can help. But he's got a car, and that can get us a long way from here by tomorrow night."

"Ah! So you're still contemplating flight?"

"I don't see any other way. No matter what she thinks, I don't have the stuff for this. Maybe *he* did. Maybe I even thought *I* did for a while. But not any more. And Bonny's sure not going to beat Our Gang . . ." he said, glancing sideways at Gilla and then adding, ". . . is he?"

"He . . ." the man began; then he stopped, giving a little laugh. "Sorry, Colin, but you won't trick me that way. I really, honestly can't say whether the priest might help you. The past doesn't tell me, and even I can't see the future."

"Yeah, well *I* can guess the future, and it doesn't include wiping out these guys with the Lord's Prayer!"

"Why didn't you tell her that?"

"Hey, I got a free kiss out of it, didn't I?"

Gilla shook his head. "Your lack of belief is amazing."

"I kept Tinker Bell alive by 'believing' when I was five years old. That was in a cartoon."

"So you mean that there are no fairies? No magic? No monstrous and *sheoguey* beasts?"

Colin looked around to see the older man's grin.

"I can't believe I walked into that one again," he said disgustedly. "Can't you come up with something new in fifteen hundred years? Okay, okay! So maybe anything *is* possible. That doesn't mean it's going to work."

They moved on farther, staying parallel to the winding lane. Only once were they forced to duck into cover as another car cruised by.

Finally, the road widened ahead. The sound of motors and

the soft murmur of voices became audible. The two moved to the wall, peering cautiously out through the screening brush.

They had reached the upper end of the village. They were looking out on the spot where three roads joined and formed a circle about a tiny mound where a tall stone high-cross rose up. Its polished marble surface glowed in the headlights of several cars that had pulled in about it, making it stand out sharply, starkly in the night.

In and around the cars a dozen men were milling, talking, gesturing in various directions out into the darkness. Light glinted ominously on rifles and shotguns that a few of them carried.

"Who are that bunch?" Colin whispered to Gilla.

"The weakest-minded, the most afraid, sometimes the most greedy," the other replied. "It's only mortals like those who Cromm can dominate most completely when they're outside his ring. He depends on them as he does his creatures to do his bidding and to control the rest."

"Weak-minded, afraid, greedy . . ." Colin repeated.

"Yes," Gilla said grimly. "And after tonight he'll be able to reach such people in the millions."

"I've heard the scenario before, thanks," Colin told him. "Come on. Let's get . . ."

"Wait," said Gilla, putting a hand on his arm.

Another vehicle had appeared, drawing up beside the cross. It was the battered van. And as the hidden pair watched, Matthew and his two companions got out, joining the rest.

There was an increase in the muttering. Matthew, clutching a double-barreled shotgun, moved through the others to the base of the high-cross, stopping there and standing rigidly, staring out across the gathering.

The muttering ceased. The door of one of the other vehicles opened. A figure emerged, moving into the lights.

It was Dudley.

He walked to the high-cross, stepping up onto its base to raise himself above the others. He stood for a moment, glaring around, a commanding figure highlighted against the cross.

"Did anyone find anything?" he called out.

"We searched the roads for ten miles out," one man replied. "No signs of them."

"Then never mind them now," Dudley ordered. "We needn't waste any more time with it. They're harmless anyway. Come light, if they're still here, the Ialtag and the Tarbh-Faol will hunt them down."

"And what is it we're to do?" another man asked. His voice was a slow and lifeless monotone.

"For you the task is to see that our lord is brought to his full power. The day has come. We must begin the Gathering Time. All should be collected at the pub by dusk. Everyone must be brought."

"They're those who'll struggle," Matthew put in.

"They must be gathered first," said Dudley. "You all know who they are. As the day passes toward the time of Darkness and our Master's power grows, most of them will succumb to his control. For those that do not, there'll be another way for them to feed his strength."

"And Mary?" asked a man.

"Mary most certainly," Dudley replied. "It's the firstborn whose strength Cromm needs the most. And you all know that's for your greatest good."

"She'll likely not be willing," the same man said.

"Love of the babe causes that," Dudley told him. "But even she will serve our Master in the end. Remember, all of you: it is for the will of Cromm."

"The will of Cromm," the men chorused in reply.

"Then begin the Gathering," he commanded. "Tonight Cromm's power will become supreme."

"Tonight?" whispered Colin. He looked at his watch. "Jeez, it's past midnight. It's Halloween day."

"Yes, and only some five hours until sunrise," added Gilla.

Dudley had now stepped down from the high-cross and was striding to his car. The group was swiftly breaking up, some men climbing into cars and driving off, others walking down into the village. Dudley watched them depart, then got into his own car and drove away.

"All right, let's go on," Gilla said. "But go carefully."

They moved cautiously around the buildings of the town. As they crept from spot to spot, they saw the men going into shops and cottages, bringing others out.

"They're really rounding up the whole village!" Colin said.

"It's now Samhain," said Gilla. "Every hour that passes makes Cromm the stronger. He'll be calling them to him just before nightfall. They're doing this Gathering of theirs little differently from fifteen hundred years ago. Or five thousand."

As the two stole around one cottage they paused in the shadows to watch a young woman being pushed out. She clutched a bundled infant tightly in her arms. Two men held her elbows, and a third man followed, carrying a rifle. The faces of the men were grimly set.

"No . . . Peter, why are you doing this?" the woman said, casting anguished glances back to the following man.

"We must do it, Mary," the man intoned in a flat, emotionless way. "It's for our lives. It's for all our lives."

Colin started to move out of the shadows after them. Gilla pulled him back.

"We can't let them do that," the young man said.

"I'm afraid we have to," said Gilla. "Our getting caught won't stop them. Only destroying Cromm will do that. Hurry now."

Colin watched in frustration as the woman and her captors moved off along the street. "Damn!" he said angrily. Then he turned and followed the older man away.

They went on through town, avoiding the others of the gathering party, finally achieving the safety of the countryside beyond the last buildings. Once more they moved through meadows just beyond the brush and the wall that screened them from the road.

"What still really hacks me off about all this is that your 'Others' won't get any more involved," Colin said after they had picked their way along for some time.

"So, you're finally taking up the discussion we began so long ago?" replied a bemused Gilla. "I suspected you'd do that eventually. But the accusation seems a strange one coming from *this*

Colin. *You* wouldn't be involved if you had a choice, would you?"

"Well . . . I . . . ah . . ." Colin stammered, stymied by this argument.

"The feelings of the *de Dananns* haven't changed, over all these years," Gilla went on. "Our resentment toward your people may be stronger, if anything. Once we were a proud race, respected by mortals. Now they've degenerated us to nothing more than a poor joke. Little people in green hats and pointed shoes. Banshees frightening children in the dark." He snorted indignantly. "Most insulting. You should be overjoyed that they've let me come to you at all."

"I get it," Colin said. "I just wish you could cheat a little bit."

"I've done a great deal of that already. But I don't dare cheat when it comes to your dreams. The answer is still there. You have to discover it."

"But you were back there. You saw it. You know!"

"Not all of it. There were things I didn't see, didn't hear, couldn't be a part of. I don't know what might work. I'd be guessing. But the secret is somewhere in your head. Careful now, here's the turning for the abbey."

They moved off the road and up the drive. The tower of the abbey came into sight. They left the drive and made their way on through the trees. Lighted windows came into view ahead.

"There it is," said Gilla, and they stopped to examine the building.

"Do you think they'll be here to 'gather' Bonny and his monks?" Colin asked.

"If they truly fear the Christians, they may not dare," Gilla replied. "But if there's any chance they might, it only means we must act all the more quickly. Still, let's not be rash. Stay here a moment, I'll just run a quick rekky to be certain no one nasty's creeping about."

He left Colin, slipping away through the shrubbery. The young man watched him go, then turned his attention back to the abbey. The great pile of a building thrust up into the night, a dark mass, its castelated walls and turrets showing raggedly against the lighter sky.

But as Colin looked at it, the stone of the building seemed to be growing lighter. And the structure's form began to alter, shrinking, turning, lines growing simpler, sharper, until . . .

31

. . . he was looking at a strange but simple building in the process of being built.

Many scores of men labored at its construction. Around it, on the slopes of its low hill, other men tended sprouting crops.

"Is that a *Tech Meadcartha* they're building?" Colin asked Gilla. "I've never seen the like in Ireland."

It was a most peculiar structure, a stark contrast to the country's typical round houses. Heavy timbers formed a sharp-cornered rectangular shape with flat walls and a high-peaked gable at either end. Long timber rafters ran from end to end, projecting out beyond the gables. Some men were at work neatly thatching the roof. Others were filling the spaces between wall timbers with woven sticks, carefully smoothing over this wattle with a thick, plasterlike daub.

"I'd say that building is more than a meeting hall," commented Gilla. He stood beside the young warrior in the chariot, the reins in his hands.

"And there are no defensive ditches, no earthen rings, no palisades," Colin went on in astonishment.

"It's clearly not meant as a rath or *dun*," Gilla replied. "Perhaps they think they have something else to defend them."

"It looks so alone, so alien here," Colin said musingly. "Like some creature of a place far from Ireland, something that's . . . invaded us."

He gave a sudden little shudder as if a chill wind had brushed him, and looked around to Gilla.

"Gilla," he said in a voice touched with alarm, "I hadn't

thought of it before, but things are going to be changed now, aren't they? I mean . . . for all of us? For Ireland?"

"It may be that some things will change here," Gilla told him in a reflective way, "but that's come often before, and I'm certain that it'll come again. Yet, for all the changes, there's always something in the spirit of this place that seems eternal."

"Do you mean, like love?" Colin asked.

Gilla turned to give Colin an odd little smile. "Yes, lad. Very much like that." He lifted the reins, his manner turning practical again. "But, come on now. Let's find this wondrous man of yours."

He shook the reins and the team moved forward, pulling the chariot up the slope of the low hill. Just before they reached the building under construction, Gilla pulled up the team and turned to Colin.

"I say we try inside," he suggested.

Gilla drew the chariot close up beside the high-peaked front wall. The two climbed down and went in on foot, passing under the projecting rafters of the gable and through a flat-headed doorway whose sides narrowed toward the top.

The half-enclosed interior of the structure was a large, single room, featureless except for a massive, smooth-topped rectangle of dressed stone sitting near the wall of the far end.

"What is this place?" Colin asked.

"Perhaps it is an assembly building for the worshipers of their god," Gilla guessed.

"And what's that large, flat stone at the other end?" the warrior asked, pointing.

"It looks to be an altar."

"An altar," Colin repeated meaningfully, looking toward Gilla. "A place for sacrifice?"

Gilla's response was an unknowing shrug.

Just before the altar they stopped by a group of men. They were all of a large, weathered, work-hardened type, dressed alike in simple laborers' garb of tunic and trousers. They were painstakingly smoothing the ground, spreading a thick layer of sand, and laying flat slabs of grey-black slate tightly together to form a stone floor for the building.

Colin noted that one of the men wrestling the stones into place was quite elderly. As he began to lift a large slab of the slate, the young warrior moved to his side.

"Here . . . let me help . . ." Colin offered.

"It's my own labor, young man," the other replied. With what seemed little effort, he raised the stone and fitted it into its prepared spot. Then he straightened and turned to Colin. "I thank you anyway," he said graciously.

Colin nodded in reply, then looked around him. "Could you tell us where we might find this one called Patrick?" he asked. "We've come a long way, and we've not much time."

"You've just spoken to him," the other said.

"What?" Colin looked again at the man before him in surprise.

He was clearly a man of a great number of years, perhaps sixty or even more. His hair was a thinning, grey-white fringe about his high-domed head. His long, large-featured face had been deeply lined by the years and weathered to a deep red-brown like ancient wood. The body was amazingly still free of the signs of age; it was large-boned, lean and sinewy, with long, powerful hands that had done much laboring. Bright hazel eyes watched Colin inquisitively. A little smile tugged at the corners of the wide mouth.

"I'm sorry," an abashed Colin told him, "I thought you would be a most powerful man. Like a great wizard, or an *ard-druid*."

"I am only Patrick," the man said in a humble way, "a servant of God.

"But for you to labor here . . ."

"Labor in the name of our good Lord is not demeaning but glorifying," he answered simply; then he asked more briskly, "But what about yourselves now? You said that you have little time. Just why is that?"

"Because," said Colin grimly, "in a few days more, many scores of innocent people may die."

Patrick looked deeply into the young man's anxious gaze, then nodded.

"Come with me," he said.

CROMM

The ladle was dropped into the stew-pot, stirred, then lifted up filled with steaming broth.

The man called Patrick tipped the liquid into a wooden bowl and set it down on the plank table-top before Colin. Across from the warrior, Gilla was already sipping tentatively at his own bowl.

"Go ahead," Patrick urged. "It's a good, hearty soup. There's little meat for us, but many fine vegetables."

"Yes, indeed!" Gilla pronounced, taking a deeper pull at his bowl. "Excellent."

Colin lifted his bowl, tasted the soup, and then began to eat with a like enthusiasm. He looked around curiously as he ate.

They were now in a small, round-walled, thatched house of the common Irish style. The place was very stark, devoid of decorations and of any but the most basic furniture: some plank tables, a few stools, crude pallet beds, and a wooden chest. A tiny, fragrant, but quite smoky fire of poorly dried peat struggled to stay alive in the central hearth.

"I have to say I'm surprised to find you living here," Colin said honestly. "I expected to find a man of your great powers living more . . . well, more . . ."

"Grandly?" the man finished. "Like a chieftain or an *ard-druid*? I understand your thinking so, young man. But in our belief it's not possessions that mark a man's worth; it's what he feels. This world is not important. Only the next is."

"The next?" Colin repeated, clearly not understanding. He exchanged another look with Gilla. The healer only lifted an eyebrow and shook his head fractionally.

Patrick filled a bowl with stew for himself, moved to the table, and sat down with his guests.

"Now," he said, looking to Colin, "tell me more about this Cromm. These creatures of the demon, have you actually seen them?"

"I have, Bishop. I've fought them more than once. They're as real as ourselves. No trickery."

Patrick shook his head. "It's a most amazing tale."

"Too amazing to believe?"

"In Ireland there are few things too amazing to believe.

When I was a young man, first come to Ireland, I heard a tale of something such as this. I thought it was a tale of something that had vanished long ago. I had hoped Ireland had given up things of such great cruelty."

"Not in that part of Ireland," Colin assured him. "It's stayed alive out there, in Connacht."

"On the farthest, most untouched, most savage edge of the world," said Patrick musingly. "Of course."

"Cromm is still a very powerful force amongst the clans in that place," Colin added. "In exchange for their worship, he seems to have made them both rich and invincible."

"And the people fighting this Cromm," said Patrick, "you say they are Christians?"

Colin nodded. "They heard your speech at the Tailteen Fair. It was your words there that moved them to you."

"I am grateful to know that the spirit which God's seen fit to pass through me has broken the hold of this thing."

"But only on this one clan. And they need help. You must go there."

"Into Connacht?" said Patrick, eagerness brightening his eyes. "To face this Cromm?" Then the light faded. "Ah, but no. I'm afraid that is impossible. There is so much to do here, and such vital work. The church to build, laws to be set down, people organized, clergy ordained. Perhaps if I could send some of my priests . . ."

"No," said Colin forcefully. "We don't know if those men would have the power to break Cromm's spell. We know you do! You have to come. Anyone else you sent might just be killed."

"The power of God works through all men ordained to be his priests," said Patrick. "Surely they would be able to fight this pagan thing."

Colin leaned across the table to the bishop, his voice growing more intense: "Good Patrick, listen, there can't be any creature, any druid magic, any force of evil you've yet seen that can match this one. It's an ancient being, a god of mists and darkness."

"There is only one God," Patrick pointed out.

"Whatever you call it," Colin said. "It is still a terrible power. It lives on blood—human blood. Uncountable thousands have been sacrificed to it: innocent men and women, and many helpless babes."

"We live in a land where great violence is a part of life every day," Patrick returned. "Countless people are dying everywhere. You can't expect that I can stop all of it at once."

"But these people are different," Colin said desperately. "They didn't mean for you to be involved. They meant to do it all themselves. And they might well have. It was myself who stirred Cromm to throw his full wrath against them. Now they'll be destroyed unless you come."

"I understand your feelings, my son," Patrick reasoned. "But to just leave here, leave my work to come with you . . ."

Colin pulled at the thong around his neck, drawing the fish symbol out of his tunic. "Do you see this?" he said with force. "A girl named Aislinn gave it to me before I left. She believes in you and in your power to free her people from evil. She will most gladly die for you . . . for *you*, Patrick. She'll die because of the words *you* spoke to her. Can you let that happen? Or will you do as you did with Tara's high-druids: dispel this darkness and bring back the light?"

Patrick lifted the silver ornament upon his wide and calloused palm. He looked at the symbol of the fish, its fragile, graceful curve of silver a bit twisted now from recent hard wear. He lifted his gaze to the young man's face, meeting his hope-filled eyes.

His own eyes flared with new, fierce light. He rose and went to the cottage wall, lifting a long staff from its pegs. He stared intently at the staff, at the large, hook-shaped end of it that was formed of shining silver. Then he looked to Colin.

"Very well, young man," he said with determination. "I will go with you."

The chariot rolled across the swelling green hills, away from the hilltop and its rising church.

The healer Gilla was at the vehicle's reins, apparently intent on the way ahead. But his inquisitive gaze slid sideways often as he silently took in the conversation of the two men behind him.

"So you don't believe in the power of fighting men," Colin was saying to Patrick.

"I believe in men," Patrick returned, "and in their power to make Ireland great, but by the strength of their spirit, not their arms. Why should the people of Ireland be condemned always to fighting one another, or carrying their bloody ways to other shores?"

"The warrior is an honorable man," said Colin defensively. "He's a man of courage."

"I've no doubt of that. But isn't it better that he use his courage in another way: to live at peace, to build new things with his hands and let his sword be eaten away by rust? Instead of death and suffering, couldn't he carry instead the words of Christ to his neighbors here and in other lands?"

Colin considered this for a moment; then he shook his head.

"It's strange ideas you put into my head, Patrick of the gentle way," he said. "Too much for a simple warrior like myself to understand. I don't know what changes you'll bring to us. And to be saying the truth to you, right now I've little concern with them. I'm asking you your feelings because of what I know about Cromm. What I'm thinking is: if you don't believe in warriors, if you are against using weapons or violence, how will you best a thing so terrible?"

"The power of god will give me strength to strike down this pagan abomination," Patrick assured him, lifting the staff he held in one hand up toward the sky.

Colin looked curiously at the object as it shone in the sunlight. Its end—a long, gracefully curving hook of hammered silver—formed a crook much like that of a shepherd's staff. Where it connected to the long wooden haft, there was a rounded silver knob on which a sweepingly stylized bird with outstretched wings was embossed.

"What is this peculiar rod that you carry?" he asked.

"It is called a crozier," explained Patrick as he lowered it, "the symbol of my station in the church and of the power God has seen fit to place in me."

"And that bird?" Colin pointed at the embossed image.

"A dove. The symbol of the Holy Spirit, one of the three persons of our Trinity."

"I thought you believed there was only one god," said Colin.

"We do. He is both three and one at once."

"Oh," said Colin.

He looked around to Gilla. The healer both shrugged and shook his head to signal his own lack of understanding.

"This crozier was given me by the Pope himself when he consecrated me for this mission," Patrick went on, his voice touched with a note of pride unusual for him. "It was many years I sought to win a place here, and many years I was disappointed, so this sign of my finally being chosen out by God is a most important one. But the crozier also has a special meaning to me in its being so like the shepherd's crook I carried all those years on the lonely hillsides. Then I served a pagan chief as slave, following his flocks. Now I serve Our Lord as a servant, leading men to Him."

Colin looked over at the rod with the glinting bird's head of silver that lay beside Gilla; then he looked back at Patrick's staff.

"Does it have magic?" he asked Patrick.

"There is no magic in my faith," the bishop answered. "There's only our belief in God. Magic is a force used by dark powers of pagan mind and evil intent. It is only the will of God that works through me."

Colin looked at him, at the face lifted to the sky, its expression so intense.

"So you mean to face Cromm with no warriors, no weapons, no magic," the young man said. "It's a great faith indeed that you must have in your God."

"As all should have," Patrick said. "And once the foul pagan beliefs that enslave people's minds are banished and the violence brought to an end, we can build a world where men don't need to fear and even the weakest can know peace."

"I understand what you're seeking," said Colin, "but it seems a hard task. The will to change, as you describe it, is neither in the nature of men or the spirit of Ireland."

"If it is there, as I believe, then all men have a chance of being free. If it is not, then dark and bloody idols like your Cromm will always rule mankind."

Colin shook his head. "I still believe it'll take a force like none ever known in Ireland to break the spell."

"That is exactly why I will face the demon myself," Patrick told him, "and before it is too late. So, Gilla," he said, turning to the driver, "make your best speed. That fine team of yours must make many days of travel into few if we're to arrive in time."

"We'll do it," Gilla assured him and snapped the reins, sending the team galloping ahead.

The chariot bounded forward across the countryside, and Colin, tossing and swaying violently with the movement, took a tighter grip on his handhold.

32

OCTOBER 31, 2:03 A.M.

"Steady, lad," said Gilla, grabbing him around the shoulders. "You looked like you were going to fall."

"What?" Colin McMahon looked blurrily at the healer in his coat and muffler and tweed hat; then he shook his head to clear it. "Oh . . . no. I'm okay. I was just riding in a chariot."

"Chariot?" Gilla said, for a moment nonplussed. Then, "Oh. I understand. You know, I'd almost forgotten about those things. It's one means of transportation I certainly don't miss. But tell me, just where were you this time?"

"Heading back toward Aislinn's rath with Patrick in tow."

"Ah. Well, that I *do* remember well. He was a most interesting fellow."

"Not much like I'd expected a saint to be."

"They're men too," Gilla said, "just as ourselves."

"I think he must have been something more than that, because I guess he's really going to take care of the Blood Drinker for us."

Gilla said nothing, his expression neutral.

"So that *is* it, right, Gilla?" Colin prodded. "The priest really must be the key? Christianity can beat this thing?"

"What do you think?" Gilla countered.

"Damn it, I don't know," Colin said with irritation. "You're driving me crazy."

"Look here, Colin," the older man said in a deliberate way, "I honestly don't know what to tell you. Any opinion I gave you would be only that . . . right or wrong. It could very well lead you astray, confuse your own memories, even destroy them. If you've a feeling that this is the right course, then follow it out. That's all that you can do."

"Yeah. Right. Well, if it doesn't work, there's always Bonaventure's car."

"Keep that thought if it helps comfort you. I skirted the entire house. The way is clear. No one's about the abbey. We can go up."

Colin looked at his watch. "Cheez, it's already after two. We'd better move it then."

They crossed the yard and the parking area to the front door. Colin rang the bell.

It was some moments before the door was answered by the balding, elderly little monk Colin had seen at the abbey the evening before. He peered out with sleep-filled eyes at the two visitors.

"We're sorry," said Colin, "but we've got to see Father Bonaventure. It's . . ." He paused, shaking his head. "God, I never thought I'd have to say this . . . but it's life and death."

The little man's eyes widened. He stepped back and waved them in.

They stepped through a vestibule into a large, wood-paneled hall, poorly lit by a single floor lamp. Its glow cast looming and fantastic shadows of the surrounding furniture far up on the high walls.

"Wait here," the man said in a hoarse voice that echoed in the hall. Then he shuffled away into the darkness.

"He's not very lively," Colin remarked.

"If you'd awakened me this time of night, I wouldn't be either," said Gilla. "End of the world or not."

"Look, what should I tell Bonny about this?" asked Colin. "If he's like Meg, it's going to be tough to convince him that what's happened isn't just some kind of fairy tale. I mean, hearing that his buddy the Brigadier is really a fifteen-hundred-year-old druid?"

"It's my feeling that you have to tell him everything. Keep it as simple as you can, of course, or we'll be all night about it. If he is meant to help you, I think that he will understand."

"Oh, yeah?" Colin said disbelievingly. "Well, if he does, he should be a saint himself. Look, couldn't you do him a little trick with the magic wand or . . ."

Gilla opened his mouth to reply. Colin raised a hand to stop him.

"Never mind," he said. "I know: it's against the rules."

They heard a shuffling from the far end of the hall and the little monk reappeared from the shadows. He signaled them toward him and they crossed the hall, passing through a doorway and along a dark corridor to stop before a massive pair of doors. The monk opened these, ushering them past and into the octagon-shaped library.

This huge room was choked in shadows. But here they were shifting ones created by the light of flames from a hearty wood fire crackling in the central fireplace.

Bonaventure stood before its hearth dressed in his familiar long black cassock. He turned to them as they came in.

"Father," said Colin, "sorry we had to get you up so late. But we are in big trouble."

Bonaventure put out a hand toward Colin as the young man approached. Though it was late, he looked wide awake. He smiled in greeting.

"You're not going to believe this," Colin said, putting out his own hand as he moved toward the priest, "but you may be our only chance to save the world from . . ."

"Colin," said Gilla sharply, "wait! The eyes!"

"What?" said Colin, his gaze fixing on the eyes of Bonaventure.

But they were not the priest's eyes. They were gleaming yellow-green and slitted, like a reptile's.

"Get back, Colin!" Gilla warned.

Colin's startled gaze dropped to the priest's fingertips, only inches from touching his own, as they stretched in an instant into taloned claws. Bonaventure's smiling face suddenly distended forward as if a giant fist was being rammed through a rubber mask. Then the face burst outward, tearing down the middle, peeling back as an enormous head ripped free and thrust its slavering jaws out to snap at him.

Colin jumped back and stumbled, falling to one knee.

Gilla moved forward, lifting his rod. As he did, the monk charged upon him from behind. He wheeled around to see the little man also transforming, the monk's form shredding away, the body swelling up and out into that of the boar-headed creature, and the single blade that formed one hand flicking into view with the swiftness of a switch-blade knife.

Gilla swung the rod up in defense as the curved blade swept in. The metal claw caught it in the center of the wooden shaft, yanking it from his hand. The rod clattered away across the floor.

By the fire, the form of Bonaventure had now completely vanished, replaced by the muscled reptilian creature that Colin had first met in a tavern brawl. The thing took a stride forward and swung a paw down at Colin's head.

He rolled sideways under it, slamming up hard against the stones of the hearth. The creature turned, stooping forward, its jaws opening. The rows of pointed teeth glinted redly in the firelight. Colin lifted himself partially up and desperately reached over the hearth into the fireplace. He managed to grip the end of a log. Its other end was ablaze. He swung it up and around against the creature's head, striking it on one eye.

The creature bellowed and swung out with a forepaw as it jerked its head around, knocking the brand from Colin's hand. The burning wood sailed across the room to land against the base of a hanging tapestry. Colin climbed to his feet and backed away, looking around for help.

There was none. Over by the doors, Gilla was locked in a

struggle with the Torc, using one hand to keep the metal claw away while he kneed the being repeatedly in the groin. The only effect of this was to bring the beast's wide, drooping mouth up in a smile.

"Oh, you like that, do you?" Gilla said, and jerked his head suddenly forward, slamming his forehead into the thing's wide, soft nose.

It grunted and fell back, tears coming into its eyes. Gilla broke away and ran for his stick.

By the fireplace, Colin's opponent was coming on again. He didn't wait for it, leading it on a little hide-and-seek around the central pier of the room. Sparks from the burning log were at the same time catching hold in the frayed bottom of the tapestry. Flames began to eat their way upward through the dried and dusty cloth.

Gilla reached his silver-tipped rod and grabbed it up. The hardwood haft was cut nearly through, and the stick folded back limply upon itself. Still, when he straightened it and swung around toward the boar-headed creature, fear came into its streaming eyes and it backed away.

But the Torc retreated only a few steps before realizing that no singeing blue light was shooting from the rod. It then stopped, grinning again.

"Oh, oh," said Gilla.

Colin came around the central pier of the library once more, the reptilian creature in hot pursuit and closing fast. The fire was climbing up through the whole tapestry now, its glare throwing giant, wavering shadows of the combatants against the other walls. Smoke was beginning to fill the room.

Coughing from a lungful of smoke, the young American looked back at his pursuer. That was a mistake. He tripped on a crumpled rug, stumbled and pitched forward, crashing against a table. The being closed in.

Colin recovered and moved around the table. The creature slammed the furniture from its path with the sweep of a foreleg and came after him. He looked desperately about for a weapon, his eyes falling on the blazing tapestry.

He ran to it, braving the heat to grab an unburned section of the cloth. He turned and boldly charged toward his adversary, sweeping the tapestry around and over it. Then, with a great yank, he pulled the tapestry free of its hangers.

The huge sheet of flaming cloth fluttered down upon the creature, covering it. It bellowed in rage and began to thrash wildly to throw the tapestry off.

Colin's move brought the startled boar-head wheeling around to look. Gilla wasted no time in snatching a large and solid high-cross replica of bronze from a nearby table, and swinging it hard against the side of the Torc's head. The beast staggered away and fell, thudding to the floor.

Colin ran to Gilla. Behind him, the reptilian monster was screeching in pain, its frantic efforts to battle free of the flaming tapestry only winding the cloth more tightly around its body. In moments the creature was totally enveloped by the fire, and burning fragments were being spread everywhere, igniting other tapestries, books, furniture, and rugs.

The two men ran to the doors and pulled them open. The room was turning swiftly to a whirling maelstrom of fire as they went out, slamming the doors behind them. They headed up the corridor to the front hall at a run.

"Brilliant move," commented Gilla as they went.

"Not mine. I saw it in an Errol Flynn movie."

Behind there was a frantic crashing. The doors flew open and the Torc charged out, starting after them. But by now Gilla and Colin were entering the hall.

They headed for the front door but pulled up as something moved from the shadowed vestibule into view. It was the skeletal warrior, spear up and ready, eyes a bright crimson glow.

"Not Brom Bones again," groaned Colin.

It started forward.

"Blast it with the wand!" Colin said.

Gilla held out the damaged cane that he had folded in half in one hand. "Sorry."

Behind them the boar-headed beast was just coming into view from the corridor, smoke rolling after it.

"Upstairs!" said Gilla, and they ran for the open stairs leading up the room's back wall.

They were halfway up before the creatures converged at the bottom and started up after them. As Colin passed a niche in the wall, he grabbed its marble statue of a man clutching a huge club, and yanked it forward. The statue toppled from the niche onto the stairs behind him, somersaulting down onto the two below. It knocked them backward, sending them crashing into a tangle at the bottom.

While the creatures struggled to rise again, the two men gained the top of the stairs. They ran down a corridor, trying the doors they passed. The first three were locked.

A loud clattering behind them announced that their pursuers were on the way up again. Gilla pushed Colin on to a fourth door. It opened and they went through. They found themselves in a windowless room so dark its features were indiscernible. Gilla sniffed at the air.

"Smoke," he said. "Where is the light switch?"

He began to feel along the wall.

There was a sound of cracking wood from beyond the door and along the corridor.

"They're breaking into the rooms," said Colin. "We've got to block the door."

He stepped forward, hands out, cautiously feeling his way ahead. Then he tripped, pitching forward, falling to the floor with a soft thud.

"Ow! Damn!" he said. "I tripped on some damn . . ."

Gilla flipped a switch. A ceiling light flashed on. Colin found himself looking into the glazed and staring eyes of a dead face.

"God!" said Colin. He pulled back, lifting himself off of the body he'd fallen upon. It was the balding little monk. His throat was slashed, his blood making a wide, half-coagulated pool beneath his head. Beside him lay the bodies of Bonaventure and another man, their throats cut as well. All three wore pajamas and robes.

"Now we know what happened to them," said Gilla flatly.

The stunned Colin looked up to him.

"How can you be so calm?" he asked.

Another crashing sound came from the corridor. It was closer this time.

"There's no time for anything else," Gilla answered. "Come on."

He crossed the floor of the room, now revealed as a small study. He opened a door on its far side, looking through.

"A bedroom," he announced. "As I hoped."

He went in, Colin behind. It was a good-sized bedroom, its furnishings visible in the faint light through large windows in one wall.

"Look!" said Gilla, pointing toward a floor vent. Smoke was boiling up through it, already drifting in grey-white streamers about the room. "It'll be spreading through the whole abbey in minutes."

"I thought this place was stone."

"Not ceiling and inner walls and furniture," Gilla rapped out, crossing to a window. "Old and dry as sticks. Go like a tinder box."

He threw up the sash on the window, and pointed outside. "Jump!" he said.

Colin stuck his head through. It was a fifteen-foot drop to the ground.

"Again?" he said.

There was a sound of more crashing from the room beyond.

"Oh well," Colin said resignedly, climbing across the sill.

"Try to hit a bush," Gilla advised as the younger man lowered himself by his arms.

"Thanks," said Colin. He dangled for a moment, then let go, landing upright in an open space and then falling backward to strike the ground hard with his seat.

Gilla dropped down lightly beside him.

"You a gymnast too?" Colin asked curtly as he got to his feet.

Together they ran away from the house, crossing the open yard and diving into the cover of the first shrubs. They peered cautiously back toward the abbey. Red flames were already visible behind the windows of some of the downstairs rooms.

"That was the statue of St. Jude you dropped upon them," Gilla commented as they watched. "The Patron of Lost Causes, I believe. Most appropriate."

"I thought you didn't know anything about Christianity?" Colin said.

"In fifteen hundred years of having it about, one picks up a few things."

"Poor Bonaventure," said Colin bitterly. "Somebody else I've managed to get killed in this."

"It was Cromm who did this, not you," Gilla said. "And he'd most likely have died in any case. But he was a good man."

"I wish I could do last rites for him," said Colin.

"That is something I haven't learned to do," said Gilla. "But he has the honor of a chieftain's funeral at least." He suddenly pointed. "Look, there they go."

The figures of the Torc and the skeletal warrior had appeared from the front door. They ran away into the night, leaving a thick tongue of smoke rolling out of the abbey behind them.

"Wonder where Godzilla Junior is," said Colin.

"Hopefully still in there."

The main floor was well involved by now, the central portion about the library an inferno of swirling flame.

"We should move away from here," said Gilla.

There was no reply.

"Colin?" said Gilla, looking around at the younger man.

But Colin was staring ahead, his gaze fixed upward on the rising column of grey smoke and flickering sparks.

33

The smoke was a dark grey coil against the bright daylight sky.

Gilla saw it first, pulling up the chariot to point ahead. "Look there!"

"It's from beyond the next hill," said Patrick.

"But that's where Aislinn's rath lies," Colin said in alarm. "Gilla, hurry!"

The chariot rolled forward behind the galloping team, racing up the last hillside and across. The rath of the Mulconrys clan came into view ahead.

It had been devastated.

The gates stood gaping open. Gilla steered the chariot over the foss and through into the yard, bringing it to a sliding stop. The main hall and the stables were now little more than smoking piles of ash. Bodies were scattered everywhere, and the sudden entrance of the vehicle caused a host of feeding crows to flap up together, cawing in alarm.

The three jumped from the chariot, looking about in shock. "Aislinn," said Colin, and began immediately to examine the bodies nearby. Gilla knelt beside the body of an elderly man with a sword clutched in his hands and a spear through his chest.

"From the condition of the slain, this happened within the past two days," the healer declared. "Look carefully. There may be some alive."

The three separated, moving out to scour different sections of the yard.

Gilla made the next discovery, raising a hand and calling the others to him.

They looked down at the body of Seadna, elder son of the Chieftain Flann. His body had been pierced completely through with a wound whose edges were blackened, as if the weapon had burned with scorching heat.

"The Craimhneach did that," said Gilla. "That spear of his is charged with a strange power."

"Craimhneach?" repeated Patrick.

"A savage warrior who looks like one long dead," the healer explained. "One of the disciples of Cromm."

"Walking dead," said Patrick in revulsion, lifting his eyes to scan the yard, "and such butchery. If Cromm is the source of such monstrous things, he must be a great evil indeed."

"Keep looking," Colin said curtly.

They went on with the search, Patrick looking through the remaining buildings, Colin and Gilla carefully scouring the yard, moving in opposite directions around the burned main hall. The two met behind it, Colin rising from a last body and looking around him in frustration.

"No sign of Aislinn, or her father, or her brother Seanan," he said. "Could they have survived?"

"They could be here," said Gilla.

He had been poking carefully through the still-smoldering remains of the hall. Beneath a charred heap of roof timbers, he had come across something else.

Colin moved up beside him, sending up clouds of fine grey-white ash as he moved through the ruins. He looked down at a tangled pile of human remains, wasted by the intense heat until little more than blackened skeletons were left.

"By Danu, Gilla," Colin said in horror. "Could she be there?"

"From the sizes, I'd say these were women and children," Gilla said. "Likely they came here as a last refuge and were caught in the fire."

He gently moved some debris aside and knelt down, peering at a charred hand, its bony fingertips seemingly caught in a crack of what had been the floor. He brushed aside more ash.

"See here," he said grimly. "This is the slate that covers the souterrain. They were trying to get out. The stone must have been too heavy."

"Bloody Raven!" Colin swore, turning away. "It can't be her, Gilla. Aislinn can't be one of those . . . those awful things."

"Colin!" came the voice of Patrick. "Gilla! Come quickly. I've found someone!"

He was calling from the door of one of the houses. The two men rushed across the yard to him.

They went into the dimness. A figure lay propped against one wall. One of its hands gripped a heavy stick of wood, the other was around a dead raven's wrung neck. The man's face was blackened by soot. His hands seemed badly burned, the skin red, blistered, cracked. A great streak of red-black blood marked his tunic across the stomach.

But he was alive. His breath came in slow, irregular pants.

He opened his eyes as the men came in, his gaze falling on Colin. A smile lifted his wide mouth, making him recognizable.

"Ailbe!" said Colin, kneeling by the little driver.

"So, you did come back alive," said Ailbe, gasping out the words. "Your father won't have to be taking my hide off after all."

"Ailbe, how are you?" Colin asked as Gilla knelt down on the driver's other side.

"Not so bad," the man forced out in short breaths. "Got a bit of a wound. Lay out there for a day and night. Fire kept away the crows 'til today. Then they came after me. I took care of them."

"I see," said Colin, prying the dead bird from Ailbe's hand.

"Finally crawled in here to get away. Needed to rest."

Gilla gingerly, gently lifted the torn tunic and looked at the wound. It went deep, slicing across the whole abdomen, exposing the slashed tangle of his insides. Gilla and Colin looked at it for a moment, and then their eyes lifted to meet. Gilla shook his head infinitesimally. He recovered the wound and patted the little man's shoulder soothingly.

"You'll be better soon. Rest a moment while I get my things."

He rose and moved to a table, emptying his bag on its top. Colin rose too, moving up close to him.

"What did you mean?" he asked in a hushed but emphatic voice. "Can't Ailbe be saved?"

"Even my skills aren't enough for that," the healer told him somberly. "It's too deep, and it's been left too long."

Colin turned to Patrick who had been watching silently.

"And what about you, holy Patrick? Can your god's power help?"

"I'm sorry," the bishop said. "I've neither a physician's nor a sorcerer's skills."

"Then what good are you?" Colin said bitterly.

"I can pray for his soul."

"He is a charioteer," Colin said, "son of a proud family of charioteers. He needs no other comforts." He looked back to the little man, tears in his eyes.

"Ailbe . . ." he said, voice thick with sorrow, "my friend . . ."

Gilla put a hand on Colin's shoulder. "I can make him more comfortable. Ease his pain."

"Do it, then," said Colin.

They went back, warrior and healer kneeling again at either side of Ailbe. Colin forced back his sorrow, putting on a stolid face. He watched as Gilla rubbed salve on Ailbe's burned hands, sprinkled powders on the stomach wound and dressed it with a cloth compress, then lifted Ailbe's head to help him drink a golden potion from a vial.

"Ah," said Ailbe, "like fine mead that is." He pulled himself a little more upright. He seemed stronger, his breathing growing easier, his pain-knotted face relaxing. "I feel better now. It's fine work you do, healer."

"Ailbe," said Colin, "what happened to Aislinn?"

"Captured she was, along with Flann and her brother and the rest that weren't killed. That druid ordered them taken alive. Seemed to want her especially."

"How did you escape?" Gilla asked.

"Ah, well they thought I was dead. Put up quite a fight before that, so I did. And I tried to save the ones trapped in the burning hall." He raised his blistered hands and shook his head regretfully. "You can see I failed in that. Then this pig-headed thing slashed my belly open and I was done."

"How did it happen?" Colin asked. "Was Cromm back to his full strength sooner than we'd thought?"

"No. It was trickery. One day the warriors around us were in great commotion. Then a chariot came through them heading for the rath. Two men were in it. One looked like you, Colin. The other was like him." He nodded to Gilla. "There was a whole host chasing you, getting close. Flann ordered the gates opened to you, and the chariot barely made it inside. Aislinn came out to greet you. But when she came close, she began to scream. You . . . it wasn't you . . . it was one of them. A head grew upward out of yours . . . long arms . . . a great, scaled thing. And the other was changing to a warrior more skeleton than man, with a blazing spear."

"Was Aislinn hurt?"

"No. She fell back as they charged. Her brother leaped forward and saved her, but at the cost of his own life. We all tried to fight then, but there was no chance. The two kept the gates open. Others poured in. There was . . . no chance."

He stopped suddenly, grimacing in pain. "Oh! Healer, your medicines do sting a bit while they're working, don't they?"

Gilla exchanged a quick, meaningful glance with Colin, then put a hand lightly on the driver's brow.

"It's all right, Ailbe. You've only wearied yourself too much with the talk. Just rest easy."

"I will that," the little man agreed. "I am feeling very weary, but there's a comfort spreading through me too, like a warm sea rising about me. It's not bad."

Colin put a hand on the driver's arm.

"You're a good friend, Ailbe," he said earnestly. "None could be more loyal or more courageous. My father and your own will know of it."

"Just tell me one thing, Colin," Ailbe said in a fading voice, "can we be getting our bull and going home now?"

"Yes, Ailbe," Colin said. "We can go home."

Ailbe smiled, but then his body relaxed, chest sinking down as his last breath was expelled. Gilla leaned forward and closed the staring eyes.

He rose and moved away to stand beside Patrick, but Colin sat unmoving, looking down at his dead friend.

Colin carried the body of Ailbe into one of the remaining huts. Gilla followed, carrying an armload of wood. The young warrior laid his driver down with the other dead who were already inside. Then he and Gilla stacked wood around and over them.

"That should be sufficient," Gilla declared, examining the makeshift funeral pyre.

They went outside where Patrick stood, awaiting them.

"Such martyred people should have a fitting burial," the bishop said.

"It would take us too long," Colin told him, walking to a small fire in the yard.

"And I'm afraid the scavengers won't wait," said Gilla, glancing up to the black ravens circling in great numbers overhead.

"Very well," Patrick said resignedly. "How long is it until the others will die?"

"The day after tomorrow, at the moment of sunset, the ritual will begin," said Gilla. "Likely they're beginning their Gathering now. Clans will come from some distance about."

"Do you still mean to face them?" Colin asked, taking up a flaming brand from the fire.

"My need to do so is even greater now," Patrick told him. "But I have to wait until they've gathered. Then I can challenge Cromm before them all, free them, and destroy this foul thing before it destroys more innocent lives."

Colin went to the hut, thrusting the flaming torch into the thatched roof in several spots, lighting it. He tossed the brand through the hut door and stepped back. In moments the building was well ablaze.

Patrick knelt, grasping his crozier in both hands. He bent his head forward and spoke out in a powerful but supplicating voice:

"The sorrow of death compassed me, and the perils of hell have found me. Tribulation and sorrow have overwhelmed me, and I called on the name of the Lord. O Lord, deliver my soul. The Lord is merciful and righteous and our God is full of compassion. I humbled myself and he delivered me. Eternal rest grant unto them, and let perpetual light shine on them."

He lifted his eyes to the burning hut. The round building was engulfed in fire now. The dried thatch of its roof sent crackling flames leaping far up into the sky.

34

The interior of the abbey was a maelstrom, its lower part filled with fire, flames licking upward through the other floors, smoke gushing from its gothic towers in thick streams.

Colin McMahon stared at the blazing structure, then turned around to Gilla.

"Gilla . . . they destroyed it!"

"Yes, it's all going to burn, I'm afraid."

"No . . . I mean the ringfort," he said, grabbing the older man's arm. "Aislinn's ringfort. They . . ." He stopped, a new realization widening his eyes. "Oh, my God!"

"What?" said Gilla.

"They knew I'd come here," Colin told him. "Don't you see? They know what I did back then, just like you do. They must have guessed I'd try to see the priest. That means they could have guessed that I'd go back to the old ringfort too! Quick, we've got to get back!"

He turned and started away through the shrubbery, headed toward the road.

"You can't just go crashing off across the countryside," Gilla said, going after him. "You don't even know the best way."

"Then show me," Colin demanded. "We've got to get back. We could already be too late . . . again."

They crossed the encircling ridge and dropped down into the shadows within the ancient ringfort. Colin looked around searchingly. A faint greyness was seeping up into the eastern sky and there was enough light to reveal the features of the sheltered area.

It was empty.

He moved around it frantically, climbing the inner mound to search through its covering of trees and brush.

No one was there. Megan was gone, Jenny was gone, and the

horses were gone too. But in the soft earth and fallen leaves of the old rath, there were signs of many footprints.

"It looks like she put a struggle," said Colin, looking at the torn-up ground and overlapping prints.

"There are no signs of blood," said Gilla, eyes scanning the ground slowly. And when Colin looked around at him in shock, he added: "Well, that *is* a good sign. She wasn't hurt."

"You mean she wasn't sawed open, or bitten, or clawed by one of those damned things," Colin said angrily. "No. They're going to save her blood for that vampire. Damn!" he cursed, stamping around, slamming a fist hard into a palm. "Damn. Damn. Damn. Damn. Damn!"

"Don't be so harsh with yourself," Gilla said in a calming way. He fished in a pocket of his tweed overcoat, pulling forth a length of twine. "This isn't your fault."

"No? I'm the one who left her here to go off on that worthless little quest. I should have known that they'd think about this place."

"No, you should not have," said Gilla, sitting down by the mound and carefully straightening his damaged stick. "There was no reason for you to realize that they might follow the same impulses that brought you back here."

"Wait a minute," said Colin, swinging around to him. "What about you?"

"Hum?" said Gilla, bending forward and beginning to wrap the twine around the split in the rod.

"*I* didn't come back here. *You* brought me here. Why didn't it occur to you that it'd be dangerous? Or did it?"

"I'm sorry," Gilla said vaguely, "I don't follow you." He seemed fully absorbed in his painstaking binding of the broken rod.

Colin stalked closer to him, his voice taking on a hard, accusing tone:

"Were you so goddamn hot to get me into another dream that you weren't worried about that?"

"Certainly not," the healer said in his unruffled way, not even looking up. "And if I was, it was only to give you more help."

"Put that thing down and talk to me," Colin demanded, striding up right before him.

"This 'thing' has saved your life more than once," Gilla replied, continuing his work.

An angered Colin knocked the stick from Gilla's hands and grabbed the man's coat lapels, dragging him upright.

"You knew this would happen, didn't you?" Colin grated. "You knew they'd take her now, just like then?"

"That's absurd," Gilla said indignantly. "Let go of me."

Colin hung on. "Was it supposed to be some kind of new jolt to my memory? Playing out the same thing again?"

"I assure you I had no idea," Gilla said, growing angry too. "I don't know how the past affects the present any more than you do. I'm trying to help you, and you're being a fool!"

"Bull crap. You've led me like a guide dog leading a blind man through a mine field. I've had it with the tiptoeing. Tell me what's going on."

"I can't. And let me go." The older man grabbed Colin's hands, yanking them away.

Colin swung a punch. Gilla ducked it and then countered by grabbing Colin's arm. The younger man dove forward, and the two locked together in a clinch. They struggled, swayed, and went down, rolling back and forth, crackling over the carpet of dead leaves.

A shadow passed over them.

They pulled apart, looking upward in surprise. The sky was now a rapidly lightening blue. A form with large, outspread wings and needlelike beak soared through it, swooping low over the rath. The Ialtag.

"Ah, we're both fools!" said Gilla vehemently. "The dawn's come on us while we were fighting. Now we've been seen."

"It'll tell the rest where we are," said Colin. "We can't get away from it on foot."

"Thank you for the obvious," said Gilla.

"Forget the sarcasm," said Colin. "Do something! Blast the sucker down!"

"I can't. The rod is broken, remember?" The healer picked it up from the leaves. The broken half swung limply down, string dangling from it. "If you had let me finish . . ."

"Try it anyway!"

Gilla shrugged and nodded. He straightened the rod, holding it at the broken spot. He thrust it upward, pointing its silver tip at the creature swooping overhead. Nothing happened.

"Do you see?" he said, lowering it. "Until it's properly mended it's useless."

But the creature seemed not to know that. Seeing Gilla brandishing the stick, it gave a caw of alarm and wheeled around.

"The damn thing's going to get away," said Colin in despair. "There must be some other magic you can use."

"It would take more power than I have to mend this rod in time."

"Gilla, please! Do anything you can!"

"It's going to create a problem."

"There's no choice! Whatever it takes—do it!"

"All right," the healer said resignedly.

He took the stick at both ends, holding it up. He closed his eyes, and spoke in a tone of fervent appeal:

"Hear me, good Danu. Please hear me! I must have the power."

He began suddenly to vibrate. A blue-white glow appeared, seeming to emanate from his heart, swiftly forming a bright dome of light across his chest. Then it divided, streaming out along his quaking arms as if it were a liquid, reaching his hands, flowing onto the rod from both ends, running together, meeting at the cut. An intense spot of light flared there, like the point of a welder's torch against the steel. Colin looked away as it rose in an instant to blinding intensity, then faded.

He looked again to see the cut gone, the damage miraculously healed as if it had never been.

"Now for you," said Gilla, lifting the rod to point toward the rapidly departing creature.

The silver tip blazed with light and a familiar jet of lightninglike energy spouted from it, darting upward.

The jet's tip struck against the Ialtag's underbelly, bursting there in a dazzling blossom of azure light. The creature jerked violently, its head snapping upward, body going rigid as the crackling tendrils of energy played over it. Then, as the web of light died, it went limp, wings flopping back loosely as it began to fall. Like a stricken fighter plane it spun downward, out of control, trailing a plume of smoke as it crashed to the earth.

The two men left the rath, running out across the meadows to the Ialtag. Its wings were shattered, twisted, their leathery membranes ripped to tatters. But the tough creature was still very much alive, and just as vicious, struggling to untangle itself and rise, craning its head around to snap at them as they approached.

"Shall we finish it?" asked Gilla, pointing the rod at its head.

"No. It'll only regenerate then. Better if we can leave it alive and see that it can't get back to home base. Can we find something to tie it?"

"I've some rope," Gilla said, producing a coil from inside his coat.

Colin managed to pin the thing's head by planting one foot on the leathery neck, another on the long bill. Gilla moved in and swiftly, skillfully, thoroughly bound the creature's wings against its sides. Then he tied its feet, looping the cord back to muzzle its beak.

They released it and stepped back from it to inspect their work. The creature hissed and struggled fiercely, but to no avail.

"At least we can go where we want without being spotted from the air," Colin said. "Come on, let's dump it over there."

They carried it to a thick copse of trees nearby and stowed it well inside. For good measure they covered the being with fallen branches and a blanket of dead leaves. The pile shook from the Ialtag's continued struggles, but to any but the most careful searcher, the creature was well hidden.

"Okay. So, we're free to move," said Colin, looking to Gilla. "But what about it? I mean, what do we do? Poor Bonaventure's no good to us. One more little tip from fantasyland that turns out useless. Christianity sure didn't save him. No secret there we can use against Rocky and his friends."

"We don't know that yet," Gilla told him emphatically.

"Bonaventure couldn't help us, but there must be something else that can. You've got to go back again. You're so very near the end. You've got to finish it."

"Another waste of time," Colin said. "Meg convinced me to play out that last clue and all it did was get her caught. So now they've got her and Jenny someplace, waiting for cocktail hour . . ." He consulted his watch, "We've got about ten hours, and there's nobody left to help."

"Even if you went in there with an army, Miss Conroy would likely not survive," Gilla reasoned. "So, do you have any other choice but to search your memory for some weapon you can use?"

"Okay then, let's say that you're right. We can't sit around here waiting for another little piece of the Titanic to just pop up to the surface on its own. I mean, I don't know what'll trigger another dream, or how long it'll take."

"You're right," Gilla agreed. "You have to bring it on. It's dangerous, but it's something you must risk now."

"Bring it on? How?"

"You feel his mind. I think that he felt yours somehow as well. Not as intensely, but still, at times, your thoughts were one. You have to touch those thoughts, find him within you. Awaken him and join with him."

"I can't do that," said Colin. "I don't feel him. I can't become him. There's too much time between. Too many lives. We're different guys."

"You're not," Gilla countered with force. "You can't believe that or you've no chance at all."

He fished inside his coat, pulled out a pocket mirror and handed it to Colin. "Use this. Look at it . . . at yourself . . . at him. Concentrate, Colin. Concentrate. Find yourself."

Colin stared into the mirror, into his own eyes. He stared fixedly into them, face tensing with his concentration.

"Come on, buddy," he murmured, "where are you? You've been taking over my brain whenever you wanted. Where are you when I need you? Come on. Come out of there."

Then, as he stared, the reflected face suddenly grew larger. It seemed to rush upward from the mirror as he at the same time fell downward into it, the two heads meeting in between—not colliding but melting together, blending, turning, forming into one.

35

Colin realized that he was looking at the cloaked figures of the Bishop Patrick and Gilla Decair, moving ahead of him through a darkened wood.

"Hey, I made it!" he said in elation.

The English words were only an alien gibberish to the other two men. They stopped and turned to him with startled looks.

"What did you say?" asked Gilla.

The young warrior shook his head. "I don't know," he said in his own tongue, sounding bewildered. "Suddenly it just came into my head, and my lips seemed to speak it out unbidden."

"A strange voice, speaking a strange tongue," said Patrick thoughtfully. "Some would say another spirit had possessed you."

"Lad, you've had little rest these past days," said Gilla, looking closely at him in the darkness. "Are you certain you're all right?"

"Yes, yes, I'm fine," Colin assured him impatiently. "Now let's go on. We've no time for any talk."

"I agree," said Gilla, "but try to hold back from any more outbursts, if you can. We're nearly to Magh Slecht."

They moved cautiously onward through the trees, and the healer's words quickly proved true. It was only a few strides more before they reached the last screen of trees about the plain.

They stopped there, peering out toward the ring of stones. As before, a thick, boiling mass of fog formed a canopy just above the statues' heads. The crimson glow of the bonfires lit the fog and filled the interior of the ring, radiating out in widening spokes across the surrounding plain. The sound of drums was a heavy, rhythmic throbbing, so intense it seemed to shake the ground.

"The ritual's well along," said Gilla. "Not long now until the blood rite begins."

"Patrick, listen to me," Colin said imploringly, "you can't do this alone. Without the protection of Flann's warriors, you'll not survive in that ring long enough to act."

"God will grant me time," Patrick said with assurance.

"I'm glad of your faith in that. But at least let us go too. Between my sword and Gilla's rod . . ."

"No, Colin," said Gilla. "I can't go into that place again. I've already angered my people. They've discovered how far I've gone in helping you. I can hear them calling me back."

"Calling?"

"It's only a keening wind in the tree tops to you. But to me it's angry cries of outrage and harsh threats. My task is finished anyway. I've brought you here. You know why I can't use my power against Cromm. It's for mortals to fight that last battle alone."

The drums stopped suddenly. A great silence fell over the plain.

"They'll begin the blood rite now," said Colin. "We have to go. Please, Gilla . . ."

"I'm sorry, Colin," he said, stepping back. "I can only pray to Danu that the good Patrick's god will save you. Goodbye. Likely we'll never meet again."

"But Patrick can't do it alone."

"He seems to think he can," said Gilla, nodding past the young warrior.

Colin turned to see the bishop striding away, crozier uplifted before him.

"Gilla . . ." Colin said, turning back.

But the healer had vanished.

Colin wheeled, looking all around. There was no sign of the silver-haired man. Patrick had meanwhile walked halfway to the ring of stones, striding up openly within one of the wedge-shaped spokes of crimson light. The young warrior had no choice but to hurry after him.

He came up close behind the bishop just as Patrick reached the stones.

CROMM

They both paused there, peering through into the ring. Beyond the stones they could see the druid Dubhdaleithe in his feather robe and headdress already at the altar.

The druid raised his glinting sword before the obscene, leering statue of Black Cromm. He began to intone a prayer to the gold-bedecked image.

Patrick started forward.

"Be careful," Colin warned. "There's an unseen barrier between the stones."

Patrick lifted the crozier before him, marching through. Colin followed, spear and shield ready. There was no hindrance.

They came unnoticed to the edge of the crowd gathered tightly around Cromm. But as Patrick advanced boldly into it, with Colin close behind, people turned in astonishment, and then pulled quickly away, faces registering fear at the sudden intrusion of this old man and the single warrior.

At the altar the white-robed druid, his sword lifted, was continuing his prayer to Cromm. Beside him, beneath the gloating gaze of the black idol, the surviving members of the Mulconrys clan were grouped, watched by the chieftain Laimainech and a score of warriors who were naked but fully armed.

The captives, wearing their own clothes, stood huddled together. Most were downcast, sagging in defeat and misery. But the chieftain Flann and his son Seanan stood proudly, gazing fearlessly into the faces of their enemies. And Aislinn comforted a woman large with child while casting a defiant look around her at the crowd.

Then, as the crowd began to move back and the mutterings of its disturbance spread, the attention of those by the altar— captors and prisoners alike—was drawn to the approaching men. The intervening crowd thinned quickly, clearing an avenue to the center of the ring, and the eyes of Aislinn's family fell upon the two striding toward them.

"Colin," said Aislinn, new hope lighting her face.

"And Patrick," said Flann. "Bless the Lord. He's come."

"Patrick?" said the druid, his eyes—with a hint of fear in them—fixing on the man.

Warrior and bishop stopped a dozen paces from Cromm. The people all around them had pulled well back from the pair, crowding close to the encircling statues.

Colin looked warily about at them. Patrick stepped forward, raising his staff in a gesture that encompassed all around him.

"People of Ireland," the bishop called out, his strong, clear voice echoing among the stones. "I am Patrick, a simple man the Lord God has sent among you to preach the Gospel."

His gaze swept the people encircling him, meeting their bewildered, amazed, and frightened eyes as they huddled back from this strange invader.

"I mean to destroy the idol you have been forced to worship," he went on, "to drive out the demons and evil spirits which have enslaved you, to bring you from the darkness of sin into the light of faith and good works.

"By the will of Our Lord and the power he gives me, I will guide your souls from the gates of hell to the gates of the kingdom of heaven."

The people were clearly affected by his words. Their dazed expressions began giving way to ones of fascination, their looks of fear transforming to looks of frail but growing hope. But the white-feathered druid, looking past Patrick and seeing only Colin with him, grew bolder. He laughed derisively.

"You come alone into the heart of Cromm's power?" he said. "How foolish are you, and your 'god'? None are so strong as we are. We will destroy you."

"These are not your people, but souls that should be free," Patrick answered him. He lifted his crozier, voice ringing out over the crowd:

"Do not be held thrall to this creature by your fears of violent death, or poverty, or affliction, or the coming of some calamity. I fear none of those things because of the promise of heaven. Cast yourselves into the hands of Almighty God, for He rules everything. And, as the prophet has said, 'Cast thy cares upon the Lord, and He Himself will sustain them.'"

He lifted the staff higher, the crimson light flaring from its silver crook.

"The blessing of God upon you all, men of Erin and sons,

women, daughters! The blessing of Light, Glory, and Freedom come to you as I pray."

A power seemed to emanate from him as he spoke these words: a soft radiance that shone out about him, spreading over the gathering. At its touch the heavy clouds above appeared to dissipate, the harsh red glare of the fires to dwindle. A strange, soft, lilting sound as of distant singing filled the air.

The faces of those gathered around Patrick were washed clean of their last traces of fear. They glowed now with a gentle light of peace and serenity.

"Kill that man, Laimainech," the druid commanded his chieftain.

"No. Not this time," the chieftain told him. "I feel the truth that this holy man has brought. It has driven out the lies Cromm has put into our minds. We have been forced into great evil to serve you. But no more."

"Then you'll die with him," Dubhdaleithe said as a rumbling in the earth began, and the stone of Cromm grew luminescent with its own green light. He stepped forward, lifting his sword to point at the bishop.

"So, Patrick, you think that you have broken Cromm's power by turning his subjects from him. But you will not stop these."

The emerald light flared up within each of the encircling statues. The glow of each spread outward as it brightened, flooding into the spaces between the stones, joining and filling them up, forming a solid wall of green light that pulsed with the rhythmic, low, growling sound that rose out of the earth.

At the same time, the gold-adorned statue of Cromm sent up a geyser of emerald light that mushroomed above, spreading to form a roof for the glowing walls, enclosing the circle of stones completely, trapping all within.

The twelve graven images of the disciples blazed brighter, turning translucent as if they had been transmuted from rough stone into a green-hued crystal, lighted from within. In the depths of the stones, vague shadows became visible, swelling, stretching, growing clearer. They moved outward from the idols, passing through the shimmering surfaces which seemed to have lost their solidity.

Now the forms became clearly discernible. There were the monstrous servants of the Bloody Cromm that were emerging from their stone prisons.

In moments, the Ialtag itself was sitting perched atop its graven likeness, leathery wings furled around it. And before each of the eleven other statues stood its own creature, whole, powerful, and menacing.

"I have no fear of these demons," Patrick said in a steady voice, gazing around at them. "The power of God protects me from their evil. With His help, they will now be banished forever from this world."

"Destroy Patrick!" the druid commanded them. "Quickly!"

Together they started forward, pushing through the cringing, terror-stricken people to close in around Patrick.

Patrick raised his crozier toward Cromm.

"In the name of Our Lord, Jesus Christ, I call on you . . ."

"His staff!" cried the druid. "Stop him!"

The Ialtag spread its wings and shot suddenly forward off of its stone, swooping down in an instant upon the bishop.

Colin jumped forward to ward off the attack, but too late. One claw of the being clutched the crozier's top, yanking it up.

Patrick was jerked from his feet and fell forward, releasing the staff. Desperately, Colin threw his spear upward. The point struck the creature's belly, sinking deep. It cawed in pain, letting the staff drop; then it banked away sharply, crashing into the head of one of the stones. Stunned by the impact, it toppled down to land in a crumpled heap upon the ground.

Colin moved to the fallen bishop.

"I'm all right," Patrick said, taking Colin's arm and climbing to his feet.

But the other creatures were now entering the cleared space about the two. The young warrior drew his sword, moving up before the bishop defensively.

"You people," he shouted to the cowering mass, "you're free now. Stay free! Don't let these creatures win. Fight them!"

It was the chieftain Laimainech who moved first. Shouting a

battle cry, he charged forward, striking out at the skeletal Craimhneach. It wheeled, forced to defend itself against the furious onslaught. Laimainech's warriors followed him, engaging others of the creatures. Then, with a roar of unleashed rage, the rest of the crowd—men, women, and children, naked and unarmed—swarmed in to the attack.

In a moment the disciples of Cromm were embroiled in a wild melée, struggling under the weight of their attackers' numbers. Colin and Patrick were left untouched in the cleared center of the struggle, as if they stood in the calm eye of a violent whirlwind.

"My crozier," Patrick said, pointing. "I have to stop this!"

The bishop's staff was now being trampled under the feet of a heaving mass of people beating, tearing, and crawling upon the lizardlike creature as it turned, snarling, whipping its tail around and striking out with its talons, trying to seize the attackers in its jaws.

Colin charged at once into the press.

By the altar, meanwhile, the druid watched in disbelief as his creatures were mobbed by the unleashed crowd. Free of Cromm's control for the first time, the people were taking revenge for centuries of debasement and fear, their rage giving them the strength and the courage to battle savagely. And though the creatures wreaked great carnage on them, the people's attack only grew more determined.

"They are weakening," Dubhdaleithe said to himself, looking at the frantically struggling creatures. "Blood!" he said. "Cromm must have blood!"

He moved to the prisoners, taking hold of Aislinn. But her father stepped in, seizing the druid's sword arm, pulling him away from the girl. The two men locked together in a desperate struggle.

By now, Colin had reached the lizardlike creature. It stood with one massive foot planted atop the crozier as it fought off its adversaries. Colin pushed in, swinging a sword blow at its head in an attempt to drive it back. It ducked away, swept a valiant but unarmed attacker aside with a move of one muscled arm, and then snapped out at Colin. The warrior went under the creature's jaws, lunging forward to slam his sword into its stomach. The blade went in all the way to the hilt, and the creature reared back, squealing in pain. Its foot came off the crozier.

Colin yanked his blade free and grabbed up the staff with his shield hand. He stayed crouched, sword up defensively as the beast stepped forward again, looming over him.

But the chieftain Laimainech came to his rescue, attacking the creature from the side, scoring its thick hide deeply with a hard cut. The creature swung around to him and Colin rose up, moving back to Patrick.

By the altar, Dubhdaleithe still struggled with the chieftain Flann. Flann's face was drawn taut in determination as he used his greater weight and muscle against the more slender druid, forcing his head back with an arm against his neck. The druid's face was flushed a deep red from the pressure, his breath rasping in his throat. He struggled vainly to break the chieftain's hold.

"Cromm, give me strength!" he grated through clenched teeth.

The glowing statue above him throbbed brighter. The roaring sound increased. The druid seemed suddenly empowered. Snarling in triumph, he yanked free of Flann with a quick move, shoving the surprised chieftain away. Dubhdaleithe's sword shot out, the point driving into Flann's throat. He staggered back, falling into his son's arms, with his lifeblood pulsing from the wound. Aislinn cried out in her shock.

Colin was putting the staff back into Patrick's hands when he heard the cry. He turned to see Aislinn as the druid grabbed her, dragging the struggling girl to him. The young warrior started toward her.

Aislinn saw him coming, but then her eyes went to something behind him.

"No!" she called out desperately. "No Colin, not me. Save Patrick!"

Colin turned again. The slothlike Ladhrach had broken free of the melée and had attacked the bishop. The tough and vigorous man was fighting strenuously to escape, but the beast had one clawed hand around the crook of his staff, while the other hand moved ever closer to his face as he fought to hold it away.

For several heartbeats the young man stood paralyzed by indecision, his face drawn in agony and his head swinging from Aislinn to Patrick.

Then, giving vent to an anguished cry, he moved.

The sloth's hand was drawing closer in, the keen-tipped, poisoned claws nearly touching the bishop's face. The other hand pulled at the crozier, drawing it from Patrick's weakening grip.

A sword swept down, taking off the clawed hand that gripped the staff. Screaming in pain, the creature turned from Patrick to its new attacker. It was Colin. His sword flashed out again, the keen blade taking off the Ladhrach's other hand.

The now helpless creature turned and staggered away, only to be quickly overwhelmed and dragged down by the crowd.

"Thank you," Patrick told the warrior.

But Colin's attention had already returned to Aislinn. The druid had managed to drag her to the altar. Now he released her and shoved her back, and she fell against the stone. In the glaring green light of the idol behind them, the two were silhouettes, sharply outlined. They seemed to move in nightmarish slow motion as Colin started toward them.

Aislinn recovered, trying to stand. The druid stepped forward, swinging a hand out to cuff her back down. She was spun around and fell, her upper body upon the stone.

"Aislinn!" Colin shouted.

Cromm moved. His withered thighs seemed to stir, his massive head to lift. The leering smile of the tiny mouth grew wider in pleasure.

The druid rolled Aislinn fully onto the stone. He lifted his sword. Colin was now only strides away. But the savage bull-wolf leaped into his path, snarling in challenge. He charged upon it, striking out furiously with his sword as it dove to the attack.

Behind him Patrick lifted his crozier, pointing the silver crook toward Cromm.

"May the power of God fall upon this abomination," he called out. "Banish it forever from His sight."

A silver light shone out from the crozier, growing to a bright sphere that enveloped Patrick. The statue shuddered, its own green light flickering.

The druid gave a shrill cry of agony and stepped back, the sword dropping to his side. His body began to spasm uncontrollably. He seemed to shrivel, his limbs growing thinner, the flesh of his face melting away from beneath the skin as if his vitality was being sucked from him.

The light about the bishop grew brighter, swelling out until it formed a silver globe larger than the idol. The battle about it stopped, both the creatures and the people held enthralled by the dazzling sight.

Within the sphere, the shimmering form of Patrick could be glimpsed, the staff upheld in his two hands. His voice came out clearly from within the light, resounding with great power about the ring of stones:

"Let God's light drive out the darkness from this place. Let God's bright spirit shine out over this plain. May God's strength cast down this foul idol and hurl its demon into the deepest bowels of the earth, back down into the Hell from which it came."

The statue shook violently, as if from a great tremor of the earth beneath it. Cracks appeared, running upward through the idol from its base. Gold ornaments fell from its wasted limbs.

The druid too was caught in a destructive throe. The paroxysm held him quivering while his body wasted away. The arms shrank to bony sticks. The face withered to a flesh-covered skull, like the hundreds of severed heads hung in the trees about the plain, save that the still-living, glistening eyes bulged from their black sockets.

The girl sat up on the altar, staring in horror at the grotesque thing the druid had become. Only feet away, Colin took advantage of the distraction to ram his sword deep into the Tarbh-Faol's back. It twisted, yanking the weapon from Colin's grip. He then swung out with his shield, slamming the creature from his way, and went on, reaching the altar's base.

Above them Cromm was crumbling, cracks running through the smooth dome of its vast head, stone fragments raining down.

Colin moved toward Aislinn. She stood, turning, arms reaching out to him.

In a last, malicious expenditure of his final strength, the wasted druid lurched forward, thrusting out his sword. Colin saw the movement, throwing up his shield to deflect the blow.

He was too late. The slender blade went into the girl's side and she stumbled, sagging forward as Colin reached her and caught her in his arms.

The statue gave a final, massive heave that seemed to tear it from the earth. It rocked, then toppled, falling upon the druid. He looked up to see it descending upon him and cried out in terror. His cry was cut off abruptly as the huge idol crashed to the earth, crushing the shriveled remains of Dubhdaleithe beneath it.

The emerald glow within the other stones was extinguished instantly, like a blown-out flame. In the same instant each of the creatures of Bloody Cromm was caught in a swelling chrysalis of green light that flared up brilliantly. Then all of them burst at once into myriad sparks spewing upward from the circle in a single column, spreading out high in the night sky, and dying there.

The silver glow about Patrick faded away as well, and he lowered his crozier to look around. The ring had been suddenly left in a vast quiet and darkness, the only light coming from the flickering remains of the bonfires, the only sounds the moaning of the scores of wounded.

But these moans were quickly drowned out by another sound: the exultant cheer of the triumphant crowd as they moved in to surround Patrick.

Patrick lifted a hand to bless the thankful, jubilant people milling about him.

Colin paid no heed to this. He had eased Aislinn gently down beside the altar and now knelt, one arm about her shoulders, a hand pressed to her wound.

She looked up to him, eyes bright, mouth lifted in a smile.

"We've beaten him," she said.

"Yes," he said. "You've won your redemption."

"My only sorrow is that we'll not be coming to heaven's gate together," she told him.

"I've no interest in some other life," he told her with a great intensity. "I want you here, in this one! Aislinn, you have to stay with me!"

"My love," she said, lifting her arms to encircle him as he bent down, hugging her close.

Patrick moved forward through the crowd, finally reaching the altar and the fallen idol. Here he found young Seanan, cradling his dead father's head upon his lap. And close to him sat Colin, holding the body of Aislinn in his arms.

Young Seanan and the chieftain Laimainech strode sorrowfully out through the gates of the devastated rath of Seanan's clan.

The two crossed the foss and joined a group of warriors waiting there with their chariots. Behind them, in the yard of the fortress, they had left two figures: Colin MacMathghamhain and the bishop, Patrick.

The pair stood looking at the two just-completed graves, piled with rock and marked by square ogham stones. Colin listened there while Patrick finished a prayer.

"Eternal rest give unto them, O Lord, and let perpetual light shine upon them. Amen."

He turned to Colin whose eyes were fixed upon the smaller of the graves, his face set in grim lines that made him seem much aged.

"They are at peace now, Colin," Patrick said soothingly.

"They didn't have to die," Colin told him. "It was myself that killed them."

The bishop put a comforting hand upon Colin's shoulder. "That's not true, my son. Think of all those you saved."

"It wasn't worth it," Colin said bitterly. "It wasn't worth it to lose her."

"And you saved the boy," Patrick said. "Laimainech said he will take him as his foster son. He promises to look after Seanan as his own."

The young warrior made no reply, his despairing gaze still fixed on Aislinn's grave.

"Colin, please listen," the bishop implored. "What you've done has saved those people. You must believe that. But it may be that one day you will have to act again."

This brought the young man's gaze up to the bishop's earnest face.

"Again? What do you mean?"

"God's power drove away the demons. But they may not be destroyed. Faith can defeat evil, but never end it. One day, if wills grow weak, if calamities befall, if God is forgotten here, Cromm may return."

"You mean there was all this death, all this devastation, and still that monster wasn't destroyed?"

"I don't know," Patrick said frankly. "But I do know that only you have a will that Cromm cannot control. I believe that's why God sent you here. I believe that's why he means for you to stay. I feel it in my heart. I must return to my people. Laimainech's warriors are waiting to take me back now. Someday—soon, I hope—we'll come back into this land and we'll ordain priests, build churches, and truly make this a place where our Lord dwells. Until then, I ask you to watch over these people."

"But I'm not one of you," Colin told him. "I don't believe."

"In your heart you must," Patrick assured him. "This is something that you must do. And as a sign of it, I give you this." He held out his crozier to Colin. "I pass into your hands my own symbol of faith in God and God's power to hold back the darkness."

Colin made no move to take it. "I don't want that. I told you I don't believe—not in your god or in anything. I thought I believed in being a great warrior; I was a fool. I should never have involved myself in this, forced myself into this, only to see so many die."

"The people have freedom now. You may be their only hope of keeping it. Please, take this." Patrick stuck the crozier's pointed tip into the ground and left it standing next to Colin.

"Think of what I say: for their sakes, for mine, find it in your heart to stay."

He turned and went off, crossing to the chariots. He climbed into one behind Laimainech and Seanan and looked back. Colin still stood there looking after him, a lone figure in the empty yard, the staff beside him.

"Is he coming?" Seanan asked.

"No," said Patrick. "I think he wishes to be left here alone. He has a decision he must make. If he's the man I believe he is, he'll make the right one . . . in time."

Colin watched as the chieftain gave the signal to his warriors. The chariots turned, rolling away from the ringfort. He looked around him at the yard, at the graves, at the burned remains of the houses. His eyes went to the crozier, its silver crook glinting in the sun.

"Not me, Patrick," he said, pulling the staff from the ground. "Never me again."

He walked into the ashes of the *teac.* Kneeling down, he lifted the square of slate over the souterrain. He removed his cloak, carefully wrapping the crozier in its folds. Then he lowered it into the hole and moved the slab back, sealing it within.

He rose and strode away, out of the fortress and down the slope, heading to the south, back toward his own home.

He didn't look back.

36

OCTOBER 31, 6:52 A.M.

"She's dead!" Colin said, throwing down the pocket mirror and turning upon the silver-haired man. "Gilla, she died!"

"So, you've finally reached the end," Gilla said. "Good!"

"Good? Goddammit Gilla, she died. She died! And you, you son-of-a-bitch, you could have saved her."

"You don't know that," the other said defensively.

"Well, you sure could have been some help, instead of just saving yourself!"

Gilla was clearly stung by that.

"Do you really think that's fair?" he shot back. "After the times I risked myself for you, kept you alive, helped you find the way? After all that, can you really say to me that you don't believe I would have helped you if I could have?"

He turned from Colin, stalking away, shaking his head angrily.

"Do you think that for these fifteen hundred years I haven't considered what I might have done then?" he said. He swung back to Colin, and the young man could see the pain in his eyes. "*You!* You had no memory of it from life to life. But *I've* lived with it every single day of all those centuries."

"Is that why you came back? To work off the guilt?"

"That may be part of it," he agreed, fixing Colin with a forthright, earnest gaze. "But, more importantly, I came back because I had thought of you as a friend and I knew that you'd have no chance alone."

Colin looked searchingly into the man's eyes for a long moment, and then he nodded.

"I'm sorry, Gilla," he said. "I guess I'm looking for excuses to blame anyone but me. Her dying wasn't your fault. It was mine . . . I mean his. No, I guess I really do mean *mine.* I nosed in where I shouldn't have been. My dumb hero act put them all on the line. My choice got her killed. I could have saved her."

"And let Cromm live?" said Gilla.

"Cromm lived anyway," Colin told him. "Don't you get it? Patrick didn't wipe him out. He just scared him away!"

"Maybe. But he still defeated Cromm. He drove the bloody thing underground for fifteen hundred years. How did he do that? What was his secret?"

"Secret?" Colin said uncertainly. "I . . . I don't know."

"There must be something," Gilla said urgently. "Think. You were the only one who spoke to Patrick. You were the only one left. He must have told you something. There must have been something to make Cromm so afraid of you. Think!"

An image came into Colin's mind: a long staff with a gleaming silver crook.

"The crozier," he said. "He used it on Cromm. Something came through it. The power of God or something. He gave it to me."

"The crozier. So he did give it to you? But you didn't take it away with you. It vanished from history. What happened to it?"

"I didn't want anything more to do with it," Colin said. "I hid it." He looked across the meadow to the old ringfort. "I hid it there."

"Where?"

"In that tunnel, under that flat stone."

"The souterrain!" Gilla exclaimed, leaping up and rushing toward the fort.

Colin rose and followed the healer. But Gilla, for his apparent age, quickly outdistanced the younger man. When Colin crossed the ridge into the hollow, he found Gilla already on the central mound. He was moving around on the flattened top, swinging the rod before him, its silver-shod tip close to the ground.

Then Gilla dropped down, drawing away earth with his hands, finally revealing a flat slab. Colin watched as he worked his fingers into a crack, pulling it up.

The tunnel mouth beneath it was revealed. Thick cobwebs were stretched across the space, half blocking it. But the silver-haired man didn't hesitate, swinging his body in to knock the webs aside, then dangling by his hands and dropping into the darkness below.

Colin looked down to see Gilla feeling around himself through shadows and more cobwebs. Then Gilla gave a cry of discovery.

"I've got it!" he said, lifting a long object in one hand, stretching the other up to Colin. "Pull me up."

Colin leaned down and hauled the other man out. Gilla climbed over the edge, clutching the object carefully. Once out of the hole he sat down immediately, laying the object on the ground with a great gentleness.

CROMM

It was clearly the crozier that the past Colin had hidden away so many years before. The shape of the long staff and the crook were unmistakable, though they were covered by the rotted remains of the old cloak that still clung to them.

"Come on, Gilla," Colin said. "After so long, all these centuries, there can't be anything left of it."

Gilla's reply was to begin pulling at the cloth. It came away in pieces, shredding to dusty tatters. He worked swiftly but carefully to strip it all away. Then he and Colin sat staring at what had been revealed.

Though the shrouding cloth had decayed nearly away, the staff of Patrick appeared still untouched by time, its polished wood shaft as smooth and whole, its gleaming silver crook as untarnished as the day that the other Colin had laid it in its hiding place.

"Perfect," said Gilla, and gently lifted it from the pile of rags. The sun caught the crook, making it glint cleanly, sharply, with a pure white radiance.

"So that's it," Colin said, staring at the crozier in amazement. But then he began to laugh—a soft chuckling at first, but quickly rising to a long, loud, donkey-braying guffaw that made Gilla look to him in alarm.

"Colin? What's wrong with you?"

"Hey, don't you get the joke?" Colin gasped out through his laughter. "This thing . . . this stick is what it was all about! Your big secret, Gilla! You spent all that time, all that trouble waltzing me through my dreams, looking for this. The great weapon that was going to beat the Devil. And it was all for nothing. Don't you think that's a riot?"

He went off into another gale of laughter, but the humor of the situation seemed lost on Gilla.

"I'm afraid I don't understand you," he said, nonplussed. "It *was* a weapon for Patrick. It *did* help to defeat Cromm."

"Did it?" Colin asked, managing to regain his sobriety with an effort. "Think again, Gilla. That thing's no good to me. I don't have God doing miracles for me."

"What are you saying?"

"That it wasn't this staff that did the job on Cromm, pal, it was him. Patrick. I mean, he was a saint, wasn't he? And I'm just a poor, dumb loser who got into it by accident, no matter what he thought about 'God's Will.' Besides, even if that thing had some kind of power, and I had the Holy juice to use it, I don't think it'd be much good."

"Why not?"

"Because Cromm was a losing proposition back then, his power fading fast. Patrick was sort of a last straw. It could be that that blood-sucker even *let* the old guy win. The Brig told us the overgrown fetus was smart. Hell, he's got a big enough head to be. Well, maybe he saw what was going to happen anyway. So, instead of fighting it, he just gave up. What's that old line? 'He who fights and runs away . . .'?"

" '. . . lives to fight another day'?" Gilla finished. "Perhaps. He knew he wouldn't die, just sleep away, waiting for the beliefs that had defeated him to fade."

"Yeah. He had nothing but time and human nature on his side. Dudley was sure right about that. So he just went on vacation, waiting for the right time to come home again. And Patrick knew that. He knew Cromm would come back again someday. That's why he left me this."

He took the crozier from Gilla, looked at it, then met the older man's eyes searchingly.

"Now, tell me the truth, Gilla," he said somberly. "Do you really believe that Our Boy—who's ready to tap into the biggest vein of power he's ever had in a very few hours—is going to shiver and drop dead if I shake this at him?"

Gilla stared at him, then at the simple staff and its silver hook. He opened his mouth as if to protest, but then the protest died. For the first time the silver-haired man looked defeated, weary, old.

"I'm afraid you're right," he said, sighing resignedly. "I was so, so certain there had to be something. But I was wrong. Then that's it, isn't it? You were right all along. Nothing from your past has helped. The only thing left after all is to run, to save yourself. Run far and hope he can't find you."

"Wrong," said Colin, putting down the crozier and getting

to his feet. "The only thing left is to go face that mother down."

"What?" the older man said in surprise, looking up to him.

"Maybe I haven't got some miracle to stop Cromm, but I sure can't leave *her* with him. Not to die again."

"I don't understand," said Gilla, rising as well. "I thought surely you'd give up now."

"I'm giving up being jerked around by everyone else," Colin replied. "Look, I've been nothing but a big Kermit the Frog through this whole thing. Everybody's had their hand up my back: you, Cromm and the Boys, Megan, Patrick, even that other Colin! You made me do all the hopping. Well, guess what —looks like you were all wrong. So, for once in my life, *I'm* going to call the shots. This time I'm doing things my way!"

"Your way? But you've just said there's no weapon to stop Cromm. What can you do?"

"I may not have gotten a secret, but I sure as hell learned a lot from those little flashbacks. I don't know exactly what Cromm is, but he's no demon, and he doesn't work by magic. He's some kind of living thing who has the mental power to take over minds. He needs those minds to get stronger, right?"

"Yes," Gilla agreed. "It would seem that every mind that is turned to him allows him to widen his sphere of control."

"But first he needs blood to give him the power," Colin went on, "and to let him pump some life into those goons of his. Without the minds and the blood, he's only a beat-up lump of rock. So he can't have them. Simple as that!"

"Simple," repeated Gilla, eying him doubtfully. "And just how will you accomplish it?"

"I'm going to cut that sucker off from his sources," Colin said determinedly. "Mr. Vampire is going to go cold turkey, and we've got about nine hours left to make him do it."

Colin and Gilla peered out around the fence of the peat yard, into the main street of Ballymauran. Across from them was the village pub. The street was lined on both sides with vehicles.

As Colin and Gilla watched, another car drove in, parking down the street. What looked to be a family—a man, a woman, two small girls, and a teenage boy—got out and walked up to the pub. Their gazes were fixed ahead, their faces expressionless. They walked in a stiff, mechanical way.

"How many do you count now?" whispered Colin as the group entered the pub.

"Seventy-two," said Gilla. "There can't be any more left in the town."

"Could still be some coming in from the countryside."

"But you can't wait too much longer," Gilla told him. He glanced up to the sky and the lowering sun, then pulled a heavy pocketwatch from inside his overcoat, consulting it. "Sunset is at exactly 4:58 P.M. today."

"Is that a wild guess?" asked Colin.

"You get quite proficient at judging the sun's movements after a few centuries of observation," the other replied.

Colin looked at his own watch. "3:54."

"Yes. They'll be starting up to Cromm very soon."

A man came around the side of the tavern and walked past its front. He carried a double-barreled shotgun and looked about him searchingly.

"They're still being cautious," Gilla said.

"I'm going to have to take care of that guy first," Colin said. "I'll need his gun."

"Of course," Gilla said. "That, at least, should be quite easy. You go up the street, cross over unobserved, slip up behind the pub. When I get his attention, you can deal with him. Here . . ." he fished inside the coat, pulling out a leather-bound blackjack and handing it to Colin, ". . . you'll need this."

Colin looked from it to him. "Got a machine gun in that coat?"

Gilla smiled. "Sorry. Never had a use for firearms. Nasty things."

"Well, give me a couple of minutes to get set," Colin said, and slipped away.

He got safely across the street, making his way cautiously up behind the pub. He watched the guard pass by and then followed him around the building. As the man rounded a corner, he stopped abruptly, looking startled. Gilla had appeared suddenly before him.

"Hello," the silver-haired man said affably, giving him a broad smile. "I was wondering if you'd like to hand that gun to me."

The man began to lift the shotgun toward him.

"I thought so," said Gilla. "Colin?"

Colin stepped out and swung the cosh. The man's head was jerked back by the blow and he toppled forward. Gilla caught him, eased him down, handed his weapon to the young American.

"Now what?" Gilla asked, producing more rope from a pocket and proficiently binding the unconscious man.

"Now I go inside."

"To face them all?"

"That's right. Are you with me?"

"Do you really know what you're doing?"

"I've got a sketch," Colin told him. "I'm inking in details as I go along."

Gilla laughed. "All right then, warrior. Go in the front. I'll find a way in from the rear."

The crowd that all but filled the pub glanced up briefly, incuriously as Colin walked in; then they looked again as they realized he was not one of them.

A man at a table near the door stood up, reaching for a large revolver on the table top. Colin moved quickly, swinging the shotgun butt out to strike his forehead, slamming the man back.

Behind the bar, the ruddy-faced Matthew began to raise his arms. A shotgun's barrels lifted into view. Colin was faster, lifting his own weapon to point at the man's head.

"I'll kill you if you move another inch!" he said simply, the twin barrels rock-steady on their target.

Matthew stopped moving.

"Put the gun on the bar," Colin ordered.

Matthew did so. As he did, a scuffle erupted at the rear of the pub. All eyes turned to see Gilla yanking a pump shotgun from the hands of another man and shoving him away.

Their invasion had taken seconds, and the crowd seemed stunned by its suddenness. Most of them stared around dazedly.

"What is it you're doing?" Matthew demanded.

"Saving your lives," Colin said brusquely, picking up the revolver to slip into his coat pocket. "Gilla, see any more guns?"

"No. But what will we do with this lot now?"

"This place has a basement, doesn't it?"

"A cellar? Yes. For keeping the wines and the kegs."

"Big enough for them all?"

"With a bit of squeezing."

"Find the door," Colin ordered.

"But you can't put us down there," said Matthew, aghast. "We have to go to Cromm!"

Gilla had already found a door and opened it to reveal a stairway leading down.

"No," Colin said to Matthew, "you have to get locked up. Now, all of you, move it." He gestured with the shotgun. "Head for the stairs."

They went, for the most part, like cattle, letting Colin and Gilla herd them through the doorway.

One man protested as he went by, his face white with fear: "Cromm will destroy us! You'll bring death on all of us!"

"Hey, I'm doing you a favor," Colin said. "Keep moving."

The woman named Mary went by him, clutching her baby. Colin stopped her, looking into her face. The eyes were staring blankly, and the face was stone. He looked to Gilla.

"Looks like the Monster Mind has gotten to her, too," he said.

"We must assume all of them are affected," said Gilla. "The Samhain forces are becoming very strong now."

Colin let her go on, following the others down the stairs into the cellar. Matthew went last, stopping inside the door and turning to them, his expression pleading.

"Why are you doing this? Cromm means to help us. To protect us. He'll bring us health and strength and prosperity."

"He'll suck all your damn blood and eat your brains," Colin

shot back, prodding him in his soft stomach with the gun barrels. "Now shut up and move. You can thank me later!"

Reluctantly the man stepped back. Colin swung the door closed. It was of thick wood, but without a lock.

"Now, how to keep them in there?" said Colin. He examined heavy metal staples set in the door and the jamb. "If we had a padlock for these . . ."

"Like this, perhaps?" asked Gilla, drawing a large, old-fashioned padlock from an outer pocket of his coat.

"Who did you get that coat from—Captain Kangaroo?" Colin asked, taking the lock.

"I'm afraid I've never met the gentleman," Gilla replied. "Is he Australian?"

"Never mind," Colin said, slipping the padlock through the staples and snapping it closed. "Grab that gun on the bar and come on."

Gilla picked up Matthew's shotgun and followed Colin outside.

"We have to move fast now," Colin said as he strode rapidly up the street away from the pub. "That basement probably won't hold 'em long. And if the Big Brain picks up vibes that they're in trouble, he could send somebody here to break them out. I've got to be inside the mound before that."

"So where are we going now?" Gilla asked.

"Megan's. Her place has what I need."

Colin poured gasoline from the Land Rover's petrol can into an empty wine bottle. Most of the liquid burbled down the outside, but enough got through the narrow neck to fill it.

He set down the can and stuffed a strip of cloth into the neck. He set the finished Molotov cocktail aside as Gilla came out of Megan's house, brandishing another empty bottle and a set of keys.

"I found her vehicle's keys," he said, "and another bottle. But only one, I'm afraid."

"Two's about all I can handle," said Colin, taking the bottle and proceeding to fill it with gasoline too.

"Can you tell me more of what you intend?" the silver-haired man asked, watching the procedure with interest.

"We've cut the Big C off from the villagers," Colin explained as he worked, "but he's still got the Boys. I'm hoping that their strength is really down now. Like you told me after the time they attacked the rath: they've got to recharge after a lot of activity. Well they've had plenty of *that* these last couple days, and no chance for a rejuvenation session with the Boss. They must be in pretty weakened condition by now."

"Cromm's own resources must be very low as well," added Gilla, "at least until the full coming of Samhain. But he'll still be very dangerous within his own ring."

"I'm just praying that if I hit 'em fast . . . well, maybe I'll at least have a chance to get *her* away."

He finished filling the second bottle and stuffed in a cloth. He took both Molotovs, slipping one into each big outer pocket of his trenchcoat.

"I hate having to wear this thing," he said, "but I don't have anywhere else to carry these." He shook his head. "Wish I had a lighter."

"How about this?" asked Gilla, holding out a silver-colored object to him.

He took it. "A Zippo? Where did you get this?"

"In the nineteen-forties, I believe. I tried smoking for around two hundred years. I decided it's bad for the health."

Colin tested it once to be sure it lit, then slipped it into his pocket with one of the bottles. He went to a little table outside Megan's door where the weapons they had captured were laid out. He checked the pump shotgun, levering out the shells.

"Can you use that?" asked Gilla.

"I went duck-hunting. Once." He counted the shells. "Five," he said, and fed them back into the gun's magazine.

He put the gun back on the table and looked over the other weapons. The revolver was heavy and of large caliber. All six chambers were full. He nodded and thrust the weapon into his belt.

Finally he looked over the other shotguns. One of them was old but looked serviceable, and was fitted with a leather shoul-

der-sling. He picked it up, along with the pump shotgun, turning to Gilla.

"Well, how do I look?"

Gilla examined him critically. Colin presented quite a rough-
and-ready sight, bristling with weapons, his face stubbled, hair
disheveled, coat ripped and filthy, trousers torn.

"Very formidable," the silver-haired man said, "if a bit un-
kempt."

"Thanks," said Colin. He walked to Megan's Land Rover
and opened the driver's door, sliding the two shotguns onto the
front seat.

He turned to Gilla. "Got the keys?"

The silver-haired man handed them to him.

"I have something else," Gilla added. "Wait."

He moved away, returning in a moment with a familiar staff
whose silver crook glistened redly in the evening sun. He held
it out to Colin.

"Take this."

"I told you, it won't help."

"You can't know that. Please, Colin. Patrick felt it might
help you. There are powers beyond what you understand. All
this must have at least taught you that by now. There had to be
a reason for all those dreams."

Colin looked into the man's earnest, pleading face, and then
nodded. "All right, Gilla. For him, and for you, I'll take the
thing, if I can figure how to carry it with no hands."

He slipped it onto the Rover's seat with the guns, then
looked back to Gilla again.

"You're not coming, are you," Colin stated as a fact.

"I can't," Gilla said flatly, "and you know why. When I
repaired the rod, I envoked Danu's power. She knows, and
likely they all know now how much I've done. I'm afraid any
more wouldn't be tolerated."

"So Cromm's still the mortals' problem."

"I'm sorry," Gilla said in a helpless way.

"Yeah. So am I," Colin said. He climbed in behind the Rover's wheel. "But look," he added as he slipped the key into the
ignition, "you made a big deal of telling me once that, immor-

tal or not, you were still men too. Well, if Cromm wins, men are going to lose." He turned his head to squarely meet the other's gaze. "Maybe you should decide which side you're really on."

He looked down at his watch. "4:45. Showtime." He started the Rover, gave the older man a jaunty little wave. "Goodbye, Gilla. See you in the fairy tales."

He gunned the Rover forward, wheeled it around and roared away, directly up the hillside toward the mound. Gilla looked after him, anguish showing in his eyes.

37

OCTOBER 31, 4:48 P.M.

A swelling sun was nearing the end of its slide toward the horizon as the Land Rover roared up the hillside toward the mound.

Colin was within a hundred yards of it when the skeletal warrior called the Craimhneach emerged from the passageway. The creature stopped when it saw the vehicle speeding toward it. Then it lifted its spear.

Colin's foot shoved the accelerator to the floor. He aimed the Rover directly at the being. The creature stood its ground, casting the spear as the vehicle came into range. The spearhead, flaring with its strange energy, crashed through the car's grill, and there was an explosion within the engine compartment. The hood was blown open, releasing a ball of smoke and flames. The windshield shattered. Colin opened his door and rolled out as the Rover's momentum carried it on to strike the Craimhneach squarely, pick it up, carry it back, and slam it into one of the broad stones at the tunnel's mouth, crushing the being between unyielding rock and crumpling metal.

Colin got quickly to his feet, running to the Rover. With the engine knocked out, the vehicle began to roll back, releasing the skeletal warrior who then toppled to the ground. Colin leaned in through the open door and yanked up the handbrake lever, stopping the car. He stepped forward, looking past the still-smoking engine compartment to the fallen Craimhneach.

The impact had reduced the creature to a pile of shattered bones, with little but the sinews and the tattered remains of dried flesh still connecting its broken joints.

"Like a turkey carcass two weeks after Thanksgiving," Colin said with grim satisfaction. "Soup time for you, pal."

He grabbed up the two shotguns, slinging the double-barreled one over a shoulder. His eye fell on the crozier of Patrick and he stared at it, hesitating.

"Oh, what the hell," he said. He took it up and shoved the staff down through the back of his overcoat belt, leaving the crook sticking up past his shoulder. Then, levering a round into the pump shotgun's chamber, he moved past the Rover toward the tunnel entrance.

But as he reached the opening, something clutched his leg.

He wheeled around in surprise, shotgun ready. Horribly, the disjointed mass of the skeletal being was still moving, hands dragging it forward, jumbled bones stringing out behind. One still-intact arm had managed to lift up, the hand grasping feebly at Colin's pants as he went by.

Colin looked down into the cracked and now jawless skull, into the cavernous eye sockets where a red light of hatred still flickered. Shaking his head in amazement, the young man knocked the hand from his leg and ground it into the hard earth with his foot. The bones of the hand crackled as it splintered apart.

"That's for Seadna!" Colin said, leaving the helplessly writhing pile of ruins and striding on into the mound.

Halfway along the stone-walled passage, something loomed up ahead. It was the bearlike creature, its massive form nearly filling the passageway. One of its paws seemed still incapacitated by Megan's earlier shot, but a saw-toothed blade glinted in its undamaged paw.

From ten feet away Colin lifted his shotgun to fire into the creature's chest. The sound was nearly deafening in the narrow space, echoing away along the passage. The full impact of the heavy blast from so close rocked the beast backward, stopping it. Colin stepped closer, pumped a new round into the shotgun, aimed carefully, and fired again. This time the shot tore through the beast's good paw, sending the blade spinning away.

Colin cocked the gun again, moving forward. The thing retreated before him, whimpering in pain. He followed on its heels, passing through into the main chamber of the mound.

The vast domed space was fully lit by the scores of floodlights. It was ready for the crowd of worshipers who should now have been entering. Colin gazed around him at the nightmare scene.

Beside the altar that was set before Black Cromm stood Dudley, dressed in the feathered robe and headdress trappings of his ancestor, and holding a slender, glinting sword. Beside him sat Jenny, bound hand and foot, her eyes bulging with terror. Upon the altar Megan lay outstretched, tied hands and feet to the corners, struggling mightily but unable to move.

Around the ring, the remaining creatures stood before their own statues. Several of these last disciples of Cromm were indeed a most battered sight by now: the Ladhrach with its long muzzle half blown away, the slug-headed creature with its shell cracked open and one shattered eye still weeping down its side, the Torc with the skull of its boar's head dented by Gilla's blow. The lizardlike being was there as well, still alive, still moving, though the abbey fire had reduced it to a charred and twisted mass, its body half eaten by the flames. Its yellow-green eyes blazed from the blackened lump that was a head, and its rows of pointed teeth were fully exposed in its now fleshless jaws.

With the Craimhneach, the Ialtag, and the bearlike creature having already been put out of the action, only five of the dozen beings remained whole.

All eyes there went to Colin as he moved between two idols into the ring. Megan lifted her head from the stone with an effort, calling out to him.

"Colin! No, Colin! Get away!"

He kept on toward the altar, striding purposefully, his face set in grim, determined lines.

The boar-headed Torc was the first to act, charging on him with its sword hand sweeping out.

He swung the gun up and fired into its knee. It staggered and went down.

"That was for Harry," Colin said, savagely pumping in a new round, firing again to shatter its other knee. "And that was for Ailbe."

From his other side the being of weasel head and wiry body trilled a battle cry and leaped at him, two swords swinging out in a dazzling whirl of light. Colin cocked the gun and swung it around in a single swift motion, firing into the creature's chest, sending it stumbling back.

The pump shotgun was empty. He dropped it, pulling a Molotov and the Zippo from a pocket. The other creatures were moving in on him as he thumbed the lighter to get a flame. He lit the bottle's wick and hurled the bomb at the head of the looming, mantis-like creature that had now crawled close.

The bottle shattered against the hard shell of its head, the instantly flaming gasoline running down the neck, body, and forelimbs. The bristly hair of the creature sizzled up as it burned. Flames enveloped the head. Its body convulsed by pain, it gave a piercing shriek and began to dance frantically, waving its burning limbs.

Colin wasted no time, quickly lighting the second Molotov. Its target was the massive squidlike being that oozed toward him on gelatinous tentacles, leaving a trail of slime. The bottle smashed on the ground before it, the flaming gasoline sweeping under it. The thing was caught, its tentacles contracting and coiling back. The clear mucus it secreted sputtered and bubbled, frying like egg white, turning opaque as the creature thrashed violently in an attempt to crawl off the burning spot.

The other creatures now hesitated, clearly intimidated by the bombs' awful effects, waiting for another. Colin yanked the shotgun from his back and went on, taking advantage of their pause to advance more than halfway to the altar.

"Kill him!" Dudley screamed. "Cowards! You cowards! Kill him!"

The Ladhrach responded first, moving in from the right. One shot from the double-barrel tore through its shoulder, spinning it around. Colin kept walking. The bull-wolf charged in from the left. Colin swung as the creature leaped, firing again, the full blast of the second barrel catching it square in the chest, sending it tumbling backward.

Colin dropped the emptied shotgun as he continued walking steadily forward, and yanked the pistol from his belt. The slug-headed creature moved, not very eagerly, into his path. It raised its flaring sword. Colin fired, and one shot went through the hole in its shell-like chest, sinking into the pulpy flesh. It jerked, lifting a hand to cover the vulnerable spot. A second shot went into the pulsing mouth, tearing out through the soft cheek just below the undamaged eye. The creature shied away this time, lifting its other arm before its face in defense of its remaining sight.

Colin was only yards from the altar. Dudley took a step toward it and the bound Megan. Colin stopped, pointing the gun at him.

"No closer to her, or you're next," Colin grated.

"Don't be foolish," Dudley told him. "You've lost already. You're too late. In moments the sun will touch the horizon. Its last rays will sweep up the tunnel to strike Cromm. Then its power will fade and his power will return."

"Not without blood it won't," Colin said.

"Oh, he will have blood," Dudley assured him. "First hers, and then yours. Nothing will please him more. You can't win. You've only four shots left, and even if you kill me that cannot stop them."

Colin glanced around him. The last six of Cromm's beings were moving in. Two of the others lay motionless in the still-flaming pools of gas, the foul smoke of their burning now eddying beneath the dome. Two others were too crippled to attack. The remaining six, though each still dangerous, were badly battered, moving sluggishly, clearly not eager to continue this brutal fight.

Colin's guess seemed to have proven true. So long in the

struggle, so long without an infusion of regenerative power from Cromm, the strength of the beings had ebbed.

"Wait!" Colin called to them. "Listen to me, all of you: look at yourselves. Do you see the wounds? Do you feel the pain? How long have you had to live with that?"

They stopped, exchanging looks, strangely affected by his words. Colin glanced behind him. The last rays of the sun were already shooting up the tunnel. He looked around him at the creatures again. His voice came steadily, strongly, convincingly:

"How many centuries have you been slaves? For what? Eternal life? How about eternal pain? I know you're not cowards like this bastard says. I know better than anyone. You've fought hard for five thousand years. Do you want it to go on for another five thousand? You can end it right now. *You* can make the choice to be free. And you can finally rest."

"No! Kill him!" Dudley shouted desperately. "Cromm must live!"

The beings looked from him to Colin to each other. They waited. None of them moved.

"Looks like just you and me, Dudley," Colin said.

The sun's last rays along the tunnel began fading. As the warm red-gold of its light died away, a green light appeared within the stone of Cromm, pulsing brighter. And from the earth there rose a throbbing sound, matching the light's rhythm, swelling in volume.

Dudley lifted his sword and started for the altar.

Colin fired into his chest, knocking him back against the base of Cromm. The man looked startled as his eyes dropped to see the spot of red blossoming on his chest.

"That was for Aislinn," Colin said.

Dudley's gaze rose to Colin. Then the man snarled in rage and charged at him.

"This is for Flann," Colin said, firing again.

Dudley jerked but continued to come on. Colin stood his ground, emptying the last two bullets into the man. Their impact stopped him, staggered him back. His sword arm dropped. He stood stiffly a moment, staring at Colin, eyes glazing.

"And those were for all the rest, you son-of-a-bitch," Colin spat out.

Dudley toppled backward, crashing to the ground. Colin stepped closer to look down at him.

"Stay dead this time," he said, and stooped to pull the sword from the clutching hand.

The statue was glowing rapidly brighter as the last light faded away outside. Colin moved quickly to Jenny, sawing through her bonds with the keen edge of Dudley's sword.

"Can you walk?" he asked her as he helped her to her feet.

"Yes. Yes!" she gasped out. "I think I can."

"Get out of here then. Quick!"

Her terror galvanized her. She didn't hesitate, starting away across the ground while looking fearfully around her at the creatures who stood immobile, watching her as she passed through.

Colin went to the altar, cutting Megan loose, helping her off the stone.

"Follow Jenny," he said, taking an elbow to guide her away from the altar and out across the ground.

He and she were halfway to the passageway when Jenny entered it, scampering out to safety. Here Colin released Megan's arm.

"Keep going," he told her and turned back toward the statue.

"Wait!" she said, turning back as well. "What about you?"

"Never mind," he said, striding on. "Just get out before these guys change their minds!"

She caught him, grabbing his arm to make him stop.

"What are you going to do?" she demanded.

"I never thought I'd get this far," he said. "But I have, and I'm going to finish the job this time. I think I know how to do it now."

"You said that before," she reminded him.

"Thanks for the confidence," he said, slipping an arm around her and hustling her back a few steps more, "but I can't leave it this way. He's still alive. It's still Samhain. If the people from town get up here, he could still win the whole sweepstakes. You just get away from here fast."

"You don't think I'm leaving you!" She pulled loose, stopping again, facing him squarely with her hands on her hips.

"Hey, if you noticed, I went to a little trouble to rescue you," he said in exasperation. "Now get out! Whatever else happens, I'm not getting you killed again."

"Again?"

"Please, just keep moving," he pleaded.

"No chance of that. I know how much help you need."

"Damn, you're stubborn. What can you do?"

"Likely as much as you," she shot back. "You've only got that sword."

"It's enough if I can get that snail out of his shell."

"Out?" she said in surprise. "Can you do that?"

"I sure hope so."

"Then you'd best be getting at it," she told him in a determined way, "because I'm not leaving."

He sighed in frustration. Then, resignedly, he turned to the luminous idol, lifting his voice to call out:

"Okay, Dracula, it's your move now. It's night, and you must really be dying for a little drink. But you've got nobody left to help you. If you want blood this time, you're going to have to come out here and get it for yourself!"

At once the stone idol began to grow translucent. It was only moments before a form could be seen moving inside, its vague shadow growing swiftly clearer.

"Are you certain this is a good idea?" she asked, a faint tremor in her voice betraying her nervousness.

"I think it's the only way," Colin said. "Even Patrick couldn't finish him as long as he could hide inside that stone."

The stone's surface grew wavery, becoming an insubstantial wall of light. And then, out of the glow, a thing emerged. Cromm himself crawled forth into the ring.

The living creature was more repulsive than its stone image. Like a half-developed fetus of immense size, its naked body was covered with a white, damp, wrinkled skin that was so thin the inner organs and blood vessels were faintly visible. The face was infantlike, tiny beneath the wide forehead and the enormous swell of hairless skull. The browless eyes, set wide apart, were bulging orbs of an intense, glowing emerald color.

The hunched, wizened body, though larger than a man's, was far too weak to uphold the huge head on the narrow shoulders. Cromm was forced to crawl along slowly, agonizingly on its stubby, frail limbs, carefully balancing its badly wobbling head.

"No wonder it stayed in the rock," Colin said. "It's almost helpless."

"More pitiful than monstrous," Megan said. "Look. There's its cord."

From the swell of Cromm's belly came a twisted cable, clearly an umbilical cord, trailing back to link Cromm to the statue's base.

The being worked its laborious way across the dozen feet of ground to the altar. It propped its withered body against the stone. With an effort it lifted its massive head, resting the pointed chin upon the stone. The head was like an enormous egg balanced on end there, teetering slightly, the green eyes fixing on them. The expression on the tiny face was strangely benign, innocent, the bow of mouth curving upward in a little smile.

"All right, Humpty Dumpty . . . me and you," Colin said, stepping forward.

"What are you going to do?" said Megan.

"Cut that baby's cord," Colin said shortly. "So at least stay in back of me."

He strode closer, Megan following.

"Be careful," she told him.

"Come on," he said. "That thing can't even . . ."

Cromm's eyes widened. At once the idol attached to the being began to grow dimmer and the cord more radiant, light pulsing outward along it as if Cromm were drawing energy to itself. The eyes were suddenly ablaze with emerald light.

At the same time a mist-like green haze appeared around Colin, enveloping him. It seemed to take a physical hold upon him, and he drew up stiffly, body tensing, struggling to pull back.

His effort was useless. Inexorably he was dragged toward the altar, fighting all the way, but staggering forward step after step.

"Colin!" cried Megan, moving toward him, hands out to help.

"Stay back from it!" he managed to gasp out. "You'll just get caught too!"

He reached the altar's base. His body jerked forward, shins striking the lower edge, and he fell onto the stone. He tried to push himself up, but the force within the mist was clearly too strong. He was shoved down against the stone, then rolled onto his back.

Megan looked about desperately for help. The creatures were still motionless, watching the struggle intently, apparently content to await the outcome that would decide their fates.

A more intense haze of light now formed around the sword in Colin's hand. The weapon began to move upward, the glinting, razor-honed edge inching toward Colin's throat. He fought it, his face drawn tight, arm vibrating from the strain. But the sword still moved.

Megan's gaze fell on the twisted, pulsing cable that ran back into the stone.

"The cord!" she muttered.

With Cromm's attention fixed on Colin, she was able to run around to it, grabbing up a coil. On the altar, the sword was nearly touching Colin's neck. Megan doubled the umbilical over, savagely twisting it into a tight knot. The flow of light from the statue was instantly cut off.

The creature jerked as if it had been stabbed. The massive head swiveled around with surprising speed. The haze about Colin faded, and the young man released the sword, rolling sideways off the stone, landing on the ground stunned, breathless, shaking, but still conscious.

Megan had saved Colin, but before she could move, the dreadful gaze reached her. Instantly she was enveloped by the emerald haze, thrown back to slam against the feet of the idol, pressed there as if pinned by a great weight. Her hands released the cable, and the pulsing flow of light resumed, growing in intensity.

The sword lay on the altar. It still glowed within its own chrysalis of light. Now that glow brightened. The weapon slowly lifted from the stone, hung suspended, then sailed across toward Megan, the keen point aiming for her chest.

A bolt of blue-white light burst against the back of Cromm's head. The being spasmed violently as the tendrils of energy crackled across its skull. The sword flying toward Megan went askew, missing her to clang sideways against the stone, the force shattering the blade. The broken pieces clattered to the ground. The haze around Megan faded and she slipped down, her body going limp.

The blue lights dancing over Cromm flickered out. The great head turned again, bringing its emerald gaze around to this new threat. Colin grabbed the edge of the altar, hauling himself up to look around it.

An imposing figure with silver-white hair was striding forward from the passageway.

"Gilla!" breathed Colin.

The healer passed through the waiting creatures. They cowered back as he lifted the rod to point its silver tip. Another bolt shot out.

This time a haze of shimmering green rose around Cromm himself. The bolt of light struck the haze, bursting there, dispersing over its surface without reaching the being inside.

Gilla Decair moved forward, firing again. The effect was the same. But he kept advancing, firing bolt after bolt.

Colin used the cover of this strange duel to crawl slowly, painfully around the distracted creature to Megan. She lay motionless, eyes closed. He lifted her gently, held her in his arms. Her breathing was coming slowly, shallowly.

Meantime, Gilla had moved closer, closer, until he was only strides from Cromm. Still the bolts of energy were wasted, crackling away harmlessly against the misty green shield.

Gilla took another step. Suddenly Cromm's gaze flared brighter. A new, more brilliant haze of green light enveloped the silver-haired man. This time it grew stronger, intensifying with the rhythm of the power coursing to Cromm. At the same time, the stone idol grew steadily darker as its store of vital energy was siphoned away, running out the umbilical to the creature.

Colin's gaze lifted from Megan to see the healer trapped in the shining mist.

"No!" he cried. "No! You can't do that!"

His gaze searched frantically around him. It fell on the shattered sword.

"Damn!" he cursed. He laid Megan back down and managed to climb to his feet. He started a painful shuffling toward Cromm, empty-handed but moving with determination; his face was hard, and cold anger was in his eyes.

The haze about Gilla had now all but hidden him. The light seemed to be consuming him, burning him up. Emerald flames danced across his body, filled his eyes, flickered in his hair. His rod blazed with the green fire. He stood rigid, shuddering, mouth opened in a soundless scream.

Cromm's mouth twisted upward in a grotesque smile of malevolent satisfaction.

Colin was only feet behind the occupied Cromm now. He lifted his empty hands, ready to leap unarmed upon the thing. But then a clear, white light flared in the corner of his eye. He turned his head to see Patrick's crozier in his belt, the silver-crooked end of it brightly aglow.

He grabbed the crook, hauling out the crozier. Its graceful silver curve was brilliantly luminous, like a winter's full moon, surrounded by a hazy aura of milky light.

Colin stared at it in amazement for a moment, and then he smiled. He stepped up behind the being and lifted the blazing crozier in both hands over the vast head, its tip inches above the skull.

"This one's for the world, Cromm," he said, ramming the point down.

The staff pierced through the top of the domed skull. The result was as if a balloon had been punctured, the massive head rupturing, exploding outward in a blast of light and energy that flung Colin back. He was slammed against the stones, plastered there as the tidal wave of emerald power surged over him, around him, finally spreading out and dying away.

The last streamers of the energy faded. Colin sank down against the base of a statue that was reduced once more to nothing but rough, dark stone. In the ring before the altar, the now freed creatures of Bloody Cromm sagged, their own life forces instantaneously drained, and toppled to the earth.

Groaning, Colin dragged himself over to Megan.

"Meg . . ." he said in agony, touching her face.

She stirred, lifted her head, opened her eyes.

"I knew that you'd need my help," she said.

"You're alive!" he said in elation. "Thank the good God."

"What happened?"

"We beat him." He lifted her with an effort, groaning. "Oh, my aching body. I think all my bones are broken."

They managed to get up, holding together for support. They moved forward, looking across the ring, over the bodies of the creatures and then down at the awful remains of Cromm.

"No more resurrections for the old boy this time," said Colin. "The power is finally gone. *All* gone."

The crozier of St. Patrick seemed to be gone as well. In the small pile of blackened remnants that had been Cromm there was no sign at all of the staff or its silver crook.

"The staff's disappeared!" said Colin, eyes searching through the debris. "It must have finally finished the job it was meant to do. Like me."

"Colin, I thought I saw Gilla," Megan said.

"Yeah. He came this time. I guess he finally made his own penance."

"But, where is he?"

They both looked around again. There was no sign of the man.

"He was right over there," said Colin.

Together they hobbled to the spot where Gilla had last stood. Only a scorched patch on the earth was left to mark it . . . and one thing more.

Colin leaned down to pick up a stick, its wood charred black, its silver tip and bird-shaped head melted to formless lumps.

38

Megan sat beside Colin as he drove his rented Vauxhall slowly up the main street of Ballymauran. The village was quiet, sleeping in a clear, bright autumn morning.

"It's hard to believe it even happened," she remarked, gazing out at the shops and cottages as they passed.

"Like a dream?" he said, looking to her and smiling.

"Like a nightmare," she answered, not smiling in return.

He sobered. "Sorry. That really wasn't funny. I wish it *had* all been a dream. But I'm through with those things now. Let somebody else sort out the fairy tales from the facts."

"I don't think it will be easy," she said.

"Why? How much of our story do you figure they believed?"

"Well, they certainly had plenty of physical remains to corroborate it, as well as the testimony of Jenny and the entire town. I don't think they wanted to believe. But they really hadn't very much other choice."

"They sure had enough people in on the thing. God! I must've talked to a million policemen, politicians, scientists, even priests. You'd think that bunch could figure something out."

"If they really wanted to. But perhaps they feel more comfortable otherwise. I know the type." This time she smiled at him. "I've been one, haven't I? Likely they'll rationalize it away somehow, just as I did."

They reached the upper end of town, passing the stone high-cross there and heading out into the countryside.

"I guess I'm sort of surprised they let me go," he said.

"I've a feeling they felt that letting you go without further ado was preferable to having it all become public."

"They did make me agree not to spread the thing around if they'd 'overlook' my part in it."

"That's for the best," she said. "We'd only both be branded lunatics."

"But we're the only ones who know it all."

"Ourselves . . . and Gilla," she corrected.

"And Gilla," he repeated somberly. "Yeah."

They came around a bend, and a broad meadow came into view. Not far out in it was a low ridge encircling a small grove of trees. He pulled the car up.

"What are you doing?" she asked.

"I just wanted another look at this place before I go," he said.

They walked out across the meadow, crossing over the old ringfort's outer ridge and dropping down into the hollow with its central mound.

"You know, there's one thing I didn't tell them about," he said as he climbed onto the mound.

"Gilla," she said. "And neither did I."

"Funny, but they didn't really ask. It's like they didn't know about him, or care. Just as well. They'd *really* never have believed that 'Others' bit."

"Nobody did know about him but ourselves . . . and Cromm," Megan said, following Colin up onto the mound. He was standing beside the still-open entrance of the souterrain.

"I also managed to keep something they don't know about," Colin said.

From inside his trenchcoat he pulled Gilla's damaged rod.

"I didn't think I should take this home with me. I wanted to leave it here, in someplace safe. This seemed like the right spot."

He took off the trusty but well-battered trenchcoat and laid it on the ground. Gently he laid the rod upon it and then carefully wrapped the rod within the folds of the coat.

"I was going to keep the coat for a souvenir," he explained as he worked, "but it feels better to do this with it instead."

He picked up the folded coat, held it out over the hole and dropped it in.

"There," he said, locating the slab that had covered the hole for centuries and sliding it back into place. "So in case anybody comes looking for it . . ." He raised his eyes to her. "I mean, he'd think to look here, if he's . . ." He trailed off, unable to finish the thought.

She put a hand on his shoulder. "I understand."

He got to his feet and the two stood there a moment, silently, looking at the stone. Then Colin turned to her.

"I've got a feeling they won't be wanting me to hurry back to Ireland," he said.

"Very likely not," she agreed.

"Too bad. Except for the extracurricular activities, I was getting to like it here. With you. You . . . wouldn't consider going back with me? Just for a visit, of course. Separate rooms and everything."

"I'm sorry. I've still my work here."

"Oh, yeah," he said. "How could I forget. The Great Commitment. No time for any frivolity."

He looked around him. "You know, a lot happened here . . . some of it twice." He stared fixedly at the ringfort, his face tensing for a moment in concentration. Then he relaxed.

"No feelings?" she said. "No dreams?"

"Just testing. In a way I guess I'll miss them. First time I ever really had some kind of purpose in my life."

"I almost envy you the chance of having had them." She looked around her. "I don't suppose I'll ever experience the me . . . or the part of me . . . that actually lived here once."

"And you . . . she . . . was buried here." He pointed across to the other side of the ringfort. "Somewhere over there, I think."

"Strange," she said musingly, gazing at the spot. "Even now, I don't feel anything of her."

"Too bad," he said with real regret. He looked at his watch. "Well, we'd better get on," he added, his voice taking on a brisk, businesslike tone. "Don't want to miss the plane. I've got lots to do back home."

"Do you?"

"Yeah. There're a few things to straighten out with the police. And the holiday season's coming up. Got a business to keep going by myself now. So, come on."

He took a few steps toward the outer ring, then stopped and turned back. She still stood in the same spot.

"What's the matter?" he asked.

"I think that I'll stay," she said.

"But—I thought you were going to see me off."

"It might be awkward, mightn't it?" she said. "Much better, much cleaner to say our goodbyes here . . . now."

"And very practical, as usual," he told her. Then he shrugged. "But I guess you're right. Well, can I take you back to town?"

"It's a fine day. I can walk. I'd prefer it."

"I suppose that's it then," he said awkwardly. He put out a hand. "See you in some other life, maybe?"

She stepped forward and kissed him firmly, warmly on the lips, then stepped back.

"For luck," she said.

"Was that for me or him?" he asked her in surprise.

"For both of you. I think it's one man now. Goodbye to you, Colin McMahon. Don't lose him again."

He nodded. Then, at a loss for anything else to say, he lifted a hand in farewell and turned away, walking out of the ringfort.

He turned back one final time as he crossed the outer ring. She still stood there on the inner mound, watching him, the fall breeze tugging her long mackintosh and teasing her thick flow of red-gold hair.

The office of River City Graphics had been restored, its damaged furniture replaced and white walls repainted. No sign of what had happened there remained.

Colin sat alone in it, hunched over his easel, diligently at work.

The door opened and the bearded Tom came in.

"Col!" he greeted him breezily. "How are you doing? Haven't seen much of you since you got back!"

"Just been getting some designs done, Tom," Colin said, continuing to draw. "This one's three weeks overdue."

The other man came around the easel to look. Laid out across the paper was the name "Olaffsen's Pizza" emblazoned by a bold, sweeping design.

"Nice," Tom commented, "but it's after five. And you're still at it?"

"Hey, there's a lot of stuff to do," Colin said seriously. "Got the business to run, Harry's family to support . . ."

"I get it," Tom said quickly. He shook his head. "Too bad about Harry. You know, I don't think I got the whole story there. Did the police ever figure who it was?"

"I never saw anything in the papers," Colin answered vaguely.

"Some kind of cult, huh?" Tom said. "That was my guess. Some wackos dressed up, thinking they were monsters?"

"Maybe something like that."

"Sure it was. I *knew* that thing in the tavern was a phony." He laughed. "Sure had *you* fooled though, didn't they? But what were they after you for?"

"They thought I was somebody else," Colin replied.

"Oh yeah? Who?"

Colin looked up from the drawing with an odd little smile. *"Me,* as it turned out."

"Huh?" said a puzzled Tom. "I'm not sure I follow . . ."

"Tom, sorry, but it's getting late," Colin said, rising from the easel. "I really need to have this logo done today." He began to usher Tom toward the door.

"But I figured you'd want to go out," Tom said. "There's a new Irish place. A pub. Should be right up your alley."

"Some other time," Colin said, opening the door. "I'm kind of off Irish stuff right now."

"Okay," Tom said resignedly, going out. "Don't work too hard then. Oh, and Happy Thanksgiving, since you missed Halloween."

"Not completely," Colin told him, lifting a hand in farewell and closing the door.

He returned to the easel and his work, finally glancing up to see the wall clock reading 7:45.

"Enough," he said, and put his work away.

He came out onto the street of the old market area and

paused to slip on a new trenchcoat before starting his walk home.

It had grown rather cold, and the trees were bare except for a few stubbornly clinging leaves. The shops around him showed Thanksgiving decorations, and some places already sported Christmas lights.

The streets were nearly empty; the people behind the windows of restaurants and bars looked cozy in the light and warmth and companionship. He passed the chrome diner, already closed for the night. Then he crossed the street and rounded the corner onto his own block.

His building with the Mexican restaurant was visible ahead. But his gaze went from it to another place farther along the street. A long neon sign proclaimed "The Dubliner" in green letters, with a large shamrock symbol and an arrow pointing down.

He paused, examining it. Then he walked toward it, stopping to look down the stairway that led to the basement-level door.

He hesitated there, looking from the door to the sign and then to his apartment building and back.

"What the hell," he said, and went down.

The interior was a long, narrow room with a bar on one hand and tables on the other. The crowd was mixed—young couples mostly, with a few men of what might well have been Irish ancestry lining the bar. The smoke was fairly thick, the talk loud and jovial. The atmosphere was soft, warm, amiable, like an old sweater worn on a chill day.

He found a spot at the bar and sat looking around him, waiting for a bartender to approach.

Something plumped down on the bar beside him.

He glanced over to see a familiar-looking bundle there: his much-battered trenchcoat. He stared at it in astonishment.

"You wouldn't want to forget an old friend like this," said a voice.

His eyes lifted to a craggy-featured, silver-haired man who grinned across the bar at him.

"Gilla?"

"Barman Gilla now. This is my own place." He looked around him with a proprietary air. "Like it?"

"Gilla, you're alive?"

"Did you doubt it?"

"But—what are you doing here?"

"Well, you see, I'm rather on the outs back home right now. They didn't like my last little bit of help."

"What did they do? Did they take away your powers?"

"Let's just say I'm living strictly in the mortal world for now. I must say, I prefer it. It had gotten rather dull back there." He poured Colin a shot glass of Irish whiskey and filled another for himself.

"But it sure as hell was interesting for a little while," said Colin, raising his glass.

"That it was," the man agreed. They touched glasses and drank.

"I'd like to go back," Colin said wistfully. "I know what I need to do here, but I feel like something's . . . I don't know . . . missing."

"Still you do have something that you didn't have before," Gilla told him. "You found out that there are often things you *have* to do . . . not look away from, but do . . . yourself. And I found it out as well." He laughed. "You know, perhaps there was a secret to be discovered after all. Something that, in the end, even Cromm couldn't fight. Something in the human heart."

"Like love?" Colin said with a little smile.

The older man nodded. "Aye, my boy. Just like that. Oh, and by the way, I didn't come alone." He lifted a hand and pointed toward the back.

She was sitting by herself at a table there, red hair glowing softly in the subdued light. Smiling, she watched him move toward her from the bar.

"What are you doing here?" he asked as he reached her.

"It seems that I've begun having these dreams," she said. "There's someone in them that I think you know very well."

"Is there?" he said, sitting down beside her. "Tell me all about them. I've got lots of time."

Gilla watched them, grinning. One of his hands slipped from the bar to rest on an object lying on a shelf below.

It was a slender rod of polished wood, a silver tip at one end, the stylized silver head of a long-necked bird at the other.

And, as he touched the rod, the silver head and tip glowed softly with a curious blue-white light.

NOTES

The legend of Cromm—his many centuries of bloody reign and his destruction by Patrick—does exist. Some authorities feel that a belief in Cromm persists to this day in the form of a mythic *Crom Dubh,* or "Black Crom," whose festival occurs on the first Sunday in August (what the ancient Celtic peoples called *Lughnasa,* a feast to celebrate a bountiful harvest).

The legend of Cromm, however, is extremely fragmentary, most of the details apparently having been lost or suppressed by religious writers and patriotic Irishmen over the centuries. For this reason, the nature of Cromm, the workings of his rituals, and the exact manner of his destruction are of my own surmising.

In addition, although the statues of Cromm and his disciples did once stand on Magh Slecht in County Cavan, I have altered the name and exact location of the modern village near the site, allowing me to fictionalize the inhabitants without giving offense.

Here follows a list of some of the Celtic words that readers might appreciate some help in pronouncing (I know *I* would):

Ailbe	*ale-bee*	Ladhrach	*lar-ak*
Aislinn	*ace-lin*	Laimainech	*lame-nek*
Craimhneach	*kraym-nock*	Seadna	*sid-ney*
Cromm Cruaich	*krom kru-ayke*	Seanan	*sin-an*

Eanna   *an-na*   Tarbh-Faol   *tar-fol*
Ialtag   *ile-tag*   Torc   *tork*

The following words might also benefit from a bit of definition:

Bobd Dezrg   *(bov derg)* a hero of the race of "Others," Son of the Dagda and later a king of his people.

Calends of Iulius—Latin date   Calends = first day of the month. Iulius = the month of July.

Cavan   a modern-day county of Ireland, it was part of the ancient province of Connacht in western Ireland.

Connacht   an ancient province of Ireland. It was once ruled by the famous and ruthless Queen Meave.

Cuculain   *(koo-koo-lin)* the hero of the Ulster Branch cycle of ancient Irish mythology.

Danu   the queen of the Tuatha de Danann. She is said to reside on Tir-na-nog, a mythical isle in the Atlantic Ocean.

Dagda   another of the great heroes of the Tuatha de Danann. He figures as a major character in many old Irish myths.

Dinnsenchus   *(djin-sen-kus)* ancient Gaelic tracts in which famous places are enumerated, together with the legends relating to them.

Dubhdaleithe   *(dud-a-lee)* an ancient Irish name meaning "the black man of the two sides (halves)." It has become simply "Dudley" in modern times.

Dun   a fortified hilltop or mound, usually the seat of an Irish chieftain or king.

Faitcha   *(fait-ka)* the central yard of a Celtic ringfort or dun.

Finn McCool   originally Finn MacCumhal. A hero of the Ossian cycle of ancient Irish mythology.

Fleadh   *(flee-ah)* simply means "fair" in Gaelic.

Gilla Decair   *(gilla dek-air)* Gilla = servant. Decaire = hard. This was a pseudonym occasionally assumed by Manannan MacLir, a rather peculiar member of the Others, when he entered the mortal world on several adventures.

Helvick Head   a promontory of land thrusting into the sea from Munster, on the south coast of Ireland.

NOTES

Laoghaire *(lou-a-ree)* a high-king of Ireland in historical times, he is said to have challenged Patrick and then given the saint permission to preach in Ireland, thus beginning the downfall of the Celtic civilization there.

Lough Derg *(lok derg)* Lough = lake. It marks part of the border between Galway, Clare, and Offaly Counties in western Ireland.

Macha (Maha) refers to Emain Macha, once the seat of the kings of Ulster, Ireland's northernmost province (now in Northern Ireland). It was here that Saint Patrick established his seat in Ireland.

MacMathghamhain *(mak-may-han)* translates as "son of the bear." In modern times it has been simplified to McMahon.

Magh Slecht *(moy slekt)* Magh = plain. Slecht = adoration. The spot where Cromm's subjects came to prostrate themselves and offer sacrifice.

Morrigan another Celtic goddess, a battle goddess also called the Bloody Raven. She would assume a raven's shape to fly over battlefields and feed on the dead.

Munster an ancient province of Ireland located to the extreme south of the country.

Newgrange a neolithic (Stone Age) burial tomb. It is a large and quite striking archeological feature and a fascinating tourist site, located no more than an hour's drive northwest of Dublin.

O'Mulconrys the "O" in Gaelic means "of the family of." Mulconrys in modern times has been simplified to "Conroy."

Oghams squared-off pillars of stone used by the Celts to record their curious writing—an alphabet system composed of slashes cut in the corners of the stone. Oghams served to mark graves and the locations of other important geographical spots.

Samhain the most important of several Celtic festivals, it marked the day when the Otherworld became visible to mankind, and all the forces of the supernatural world were let go upon the natural world. A time of great mortal danger and spiritual vulnerability, it was celebrated on the night preceding November 1. We continue to pay homage to this ancient festival with our modern Halloween observance. There can be no doubt that in ancient times sacrifices were made on this day to appease the more hostile Otherworld forces.

Sheoguey *(sho-gee)* literally meaning haunted, or having supernatural ties.

Sidhe *(shee)* a supernatural race also known as the Tuatha de Danann. Their name derives from the names of their hidden palaces (called Sids), and thus means "People of the Sids." In more recent times, this noble race has been degenerated by man to such familiar caricatures as the leprechaun and the banshee (ban = woman, shee = sidhe).

Souterrain an underground tunnel dug outward from a Celtic fortress to serve as an escape route in times of danger. At one time the small passages were thought to be those of the "faerie folk" who lived in the old forts.

Tailteen Fair a great fair held upon Tailteen Hill, near Tara. It was here that Patrick is said to have given his first great sermon in Ireland, converting thousands.

Tara fully, Tara an Rie, or Tara of the Kings, the famous seat of the high-kings of Ireland.

Teac Meadhcarta *(tyech mi-cuar-ta)* Teac = house. Meadhcarta = central or major. It was a name for the main hall, the meeting house of the Celtic raths and *duns*.

Tighernmas an Irish king said to have reigned some twenty-five hundred years before Christ. He was called a "culture-king," bringing much of civilization to the Irish people. But his challenge of Cromm's power brought his death, along with those of three fourths of his people.

Tuatha de Danann *(too-a-ha de don-en)* literally "Children of the Goddess Danu." This once mortal people were among Ireland's oldest settlers. Given magical powers and immortality by Danu, they are said to live on in Ireland in hidden underground palaces called "Sids." Thence derives their alternative name "Sidhe." The more superstitious Irishman refers to them as "the Others" to avoid giving offense.

BOOK MARK

The text of this book was set in the typeface Bembo by Berryville Graphics, Berryville, Virginia.

It was printed on 50 lb. Glatfelter, an acid-free paper, and bound by Berryville Graphics, Berryville, Virginia.

Designed by Ann Gold